THE GEORGIA REGIONAL
LIBRARY FOR THE BLIND
AND PHYSICALLY
HANDICAPPED IS A FREE
SERVICE FOR INDIVIDUALS
UNABLE TO READ
STANDARD PRINT.

ASK AT OUR CIRCULATION
DESK HOW TO REGISTER
FOR THIS SERVICE, AS WELL
AS OTHER SERVICES
OFFERED BY THIS LIBRARY.

Wildcat Wine

Wildcat Wine

Claire Matturro

LARGE PRINT

This large print edition published in 2005 by
RB Large Print
A division of Recorded Books
A Haights Cross Communications Company
270 Skipjack Road
Prince Frederick, MD 20678

Published by arrangement with HarperCollins Publishers, Inc.

This book is a work of fiction. Names, characters, places, and incidents
either are products of the author's imagination or are used fictitiously. Any
resemblance to actual events or locales or persons, living or dead, is
entirely coincidental.

Publisher's Cataloging In Publication Data
(Prepared by Donohue Group, Inc.)

Matturro, Claire Hamner, 1954-
    Wildcat wine / Claire Matturro.

    p. (large print) ; cm.

    ISBN: 1-4193-5138-9

1. Women lawyers—Fiction. 2. Lawyers—Crimes against—Fiction. 3. Large
type books. 4. Sarasota (Fla.)—Fiction. 5. Mystery fiction. 6. Legal stories.
I. Title.

PS3613.A87 W55 2005b
813/.54

Printed in the United States of America

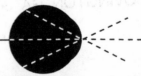

**This Large Print Book carries the
Seal of Approval of N.A.V.H.**

TO
JOHN THOMAS HAMNER

ACKNOWLEDGMENTS

Thank you to the vintners at Rosa Fiorelli Winery in east Manatee County for their tour, their samples, and for the time they took to share their knowledge about muscadine grapes, making wine, sulfites, and growing grapes in the Florida climate.

Mike Lehner and Bill Matturro provided their language skills in translating English to Spanish. I appreciate their help.

Debra Smietanski, CPA, board-certified estate planner and Tampa lawyer extraordinaire, I thank you for answering my questions about personal representatives, estates, and all things numerical.

My husband, Bill, also a lawyer, kept me straight on the patent process and the difficulties of bringing a new product to market, read all seven drafts, and provided a calm, well-reasoned sounding board for my ideas. Thank you, Bill.

As before, my brother, Lieutenant William D. Hamner of the Selma, Alabama, police department, was an endless source of information on forensics and weapons. Brother Bill, thanks again.

These fine folks were all very helpful and generous

with their knowledge and skills. Any mistakes are of my own making, not theirs.

No acknowledgment is complete without thanking Carolyn Marino, Jennifer Civiletto, and all the wonderful people at HarperCollins for their professionalism, their talents, and their time.

PROLOGUE

I wasn't at all sure I had a real life anymore.

Here it was, a perfectly fine Friday night, and instead of being out having fun, I was about the last person inside the Smith, O'Leary, and Stanley law firm.

Reviewing paper. Looking through stacks and stacks of paper for just the right words in all of the words in all of the paper in all of the files for something that might save my butt—I mean, that is, technically, my client's butt.

Sometimes being a lawyer sucks.

Nursing a cup of lukewarm green tea and a bad attitude, I riffled through my files, seeking inspiration. I sighed, rubbed my eyes, and read on.

My office windows were open, so I could breathe real oxygen, not the stale refrigerated air of the law firm. The humidity of a Sarasota night drifted in, dispersing a subtle scent of orange blossoms, car fumes, and fishy low tide throughout my office. The classic spring bouquet on the Gulf Coast of Florida.

But I had barely settled into rereading my client's

deposition when my door banged open, and critically overchilled air rushed in. I had my mouth prepared to say something rude to whoever dared intrude when I saw Jackson Winchester Smith, the firm's founding and controlling partner, my mentor, the living, breathing reincarnation of Stonewall Jackson, standing there in my doorway, big as a mad grizzly.

"You got everything under control here? Cases all right?"

"Yes, thank you. Everything is under control."

That was a whopper, but I held my eyes steady on Jackson and nothing in my body language gave me away.

"Good, good."

I waited during the pause for the real reason for Jackson's visit.

"Man bought a Hummer and now he's demanding a bonus to pay it off."

Okay, nothing to do with me and I had work to do. I blinked twice, hoping that would make Jackson go away.

"That son of a bitch. A Hummer. A yellow one, color of a legal pad. Piss ugly."

"Who got a Hummer?" Not that I really cared, but if I ignored him, Jackson would just get louder.

"Kenneth Mallory."

Well, of course, the only partner in the firm vapid and pretentious enough to pay twice the average salary of the secretaries at the firm for a large, yellow box with wheels and an ad campaign that appealed equally to the insecure and the show-off.

Having hexed my first year at the firm, Kenneth was the one partner I studiously avoided and hoped, frankly, that he would one day drop into the Gulf of Mexico and get eaten by an octopus, or run over by a backhoe, or implode from too much inherent dishonesty in one lifetime, and leave the rest of us to the honorable task of defending hapless doctors, hospitals, and lawyers sued by their disgruntled clients.

"Kenneth is demanding that the executive committee vote him a midyear bonus, then follow up with a larger Christmas bonus."

"Just say no," I said. "It worked for Nancy Reagan."

"He's our top biller, you know." Jackson paused to glare at me, as if I should be the partner in the firm who billed the most hours. "Son of a bitch's threatening to pull out of the firm and take his clients if we don't give him a bigger cut of the pie."

"I'm sure you'll figure out how to handle him," I said, and dusted off my pert smile and fluffed my hair. So, okay, where Jackson was concerned, Gloria Steinem I was not.

"He's got that damn sailboat and that mansion out in the sticks and now that Hummer. So we're supposed to vote him a special-performance bonus at the midyear meeting to pay for all that or he takes his clients and starts his own firm."

What I wanted to say was, let the bastard leave the firm. We all hate him, he has a profligate lifestyle and rubs our noses in it, and buying a Hummer at least proved that. But I suddenly focused on the finances. If Kenneth went and took his clients, all the income he brought into the firm—and that was a lot—went with him. This wasn't a matter of Jackson's control, it was a matter of money.

At a fundamental level, I understood that the trick was to get rid of Kenneth and keep his clients. So, okay, how hard could that be?

"Let's start a rumor he's on drugs," I said, inspired by the fact that one of our partners was currently detoxing in a swanky rehab center in L.A. "Maybe tell his clients he's shipping out to a rehab program. I can call his biggest clients, say I'm his partner, and explain that we are transferring his files to . . . me." Then I could be the top biller.

Jackson glowered at me and I was quick to see my error. I'm only a junior partner, and we don't get such plums.

"Transferring Kenneth's files to you, and, eh, Fred, and some, a few, to me," I corrected.

Jackson nodded. He reached into his pocket and pulled out a lemon and then reached into his other pocket and brought out a pocket knife, and he cut a wedge out of the lemon and ate the pulp, down to the rind. "Want a slice?"

"No, thank you."

While Jackson ate his lemon, I pondered the

4

Kenneth problem. Maybe we *could* actually send Kenneth to a detox center. How hard was it to Baker Act somebody? I'd put one of the law clerks into looking at what it took to involuntarily commit someone under that act.

"You might have something there." Jackson's voice vibrated off my walls. Then he stroked his beard and pitched the lemon rind into the bottom of my potted peace lily. He saluted me and said, "Could've used a good trench fighter like you in 'Nam. You think on that plan some more, bring me the pros and cons, the mechanics." And he slammed my door on the way out.

Mierda. He thought of me as a trench fighter. Hardly the image I had in mind.

A trench fighter in a black slip with equally black, lacy bikini panties, and Jackson in a gray uniform with gold-braid trim, wearing a broad-brimmed hat with a plume, and . . .

Needless to say, I didn't get very far in delving into my vats of paper and verbiage, though I did perfect the fantasy.

CHAPTER 1

It's hard being Lillian Belle Rosemary Cleary.

And if I didn't know that already, Bonita, my legal secretary supreme and secondary therapist, kept reminding me.

"*Carita*," she said, shaking her head and handing me the pink highlighter at my hyperventilated request so that I could mark another obscure legal point I needed to memorize for my upcoming appellate argument. "You make this so much more difficult than it needs to be."

So spank me, I'm a lawyer, and complicating things at a high hourly rate is my specialty.

I ignored Bonita's implied protest and recited a choice quote I had just underlined in pink, and Bonita typed it into my laptop for future reference. We were both sitting on my shiny terrazzo floor on pure-cotton yoga mats. I was only on the seventh legal opinion of questionable value for my argument, busily color-coding impressive language from jurists I hoped to twist to the benefit of my client, a charlatan to be sure, but not without his charm and definitely with the liability policy that would pay me.

Thinking of how much work I still had to do made me gulp air and jump up to wash my hands and face.

"I wouldn't be you," Bonita said, sighing as I plopped down again beside her. This from a widow with five accident-prone children.

While I reached for the yellow highligher, Benicio, Bonita's teenage son who insisted that we call him Benny, pounded his size-twelve boots into the kitchen, where in one gulp he consumed about three dollars' worth of my GMO-free, hormone-free, fat-free organic milk—slogan: "Our Cows Aren't on Drugs." He was cutting my grass, apparently at about a square foot per quart of milk, and relentlessly bitching that I didn't have any real peanut butter.

"This soy peanut butter sucks," he said, eating a spoonful straight from the jar. "Positively sucks," Benny reiterated, as if somehow I had managed to miss his point.

"Please don't talk like that to Lilly," Bonita said, her voice low and sweet.

"But this soy stuff is so gross."

Before we finessed the soy peanut butter debate further, Bearess, my one-hundred-pound rottweiler that I inherited from a dingbat mass-murderer wanna-be, lifted her head and growled at the front door.

"Doorbell," I said, stifling the urge to jump up and scream that everybody had to get out and leave me alone with my hearing transcripts, my depositions, my photocopied legal opinions, and my multicolored highlighters.

"I didn't hear a doorbell," Benny said.

Bearess growled again and rose from her organic cedar-chip dog bed, which she drags around the house to follow the rotating patches of sunlight through the windows and which cost me not much less than tuition at my first community college on my seven-year quest for a law degree. The dog advanced on the front door, even as the bell rang.

"Told you," I said, pulling myself away from the thousands of sheets of paper that I would boil down into a convincing appellate argument to save my client, a pet psychic/alien-abductee counselor.

Edgy with visions of having a judge in a black robe smite me from behind the appellate bench, I opened the door without peeking, as it was the middle of a bright afternoon and having a large celebrity rottweiler vastly reduced the fear of home invasions. Besides, this was Southgate, a Sarasota neighborhood with safe, middle-class streets. I lived on Tulip Street and one didn't have home invasions on Tulip Street.

"Lilly Belle, my old sweetheart," bellowed a long-haired man in cutoffs, standing barefoot in my doorway. He was built like a middleweight boxer with big, big hands and a face that looked like he had spent about a hundred years in the bright subtropical sunshine. His T-shirt was a crudely painted white dove flitting among red opium poppies—my brother Delvon's handiwork.

"Farmer Dave," I said, and Bearess stopped growling and stuck her big black-and-tan mug in between us until Dave petted her. Then I let him hug me, biting back my twenty questions and sniffing him, primeval and patchouli.

"Why aren't you at my apple orchard?" I gave in to the primary question. Dave was the caretaker of my 180-acre heavily mortgaged apple orchard in north Georgia, as well as my mad-hatter brother Delvon's best friend.

"'On the road again,'" he sang out in a decent mimic of Willie Nelson's theme song. Willie is Farmer Dave's secondary god, next to illegalities of the nonviolent persuasion. Willie worship marginally explained the two pigtails Farmer Dave's head sprouted and the long, wayward gray beard.

"You left my orchard for a road trip?" I snapped, imagining rats burrowing through my house and barn and the trees withering from neglect, never to bear fruit again, while Dave went on a frolic.

"Ah, Delvon's up there, now that he's done saving your life and the GBI put him out of business. He's taking care of things. Gave me a chance to get out of Georgia for a while."

Dave grabbed me again, kissed me on the cheek, and was heading for my mouth when the phone rang. As I moved toward it, I pointed to Bonita and said, "Bonita, meet Dave Baggwell. Dave, meet Bonita Hernández de Vasquez. And this is Benicio, her son, my alleged yardman."

"Benny," Benicio corrected, glowering at me as I grabbed up the phone.

"You can't leave that mile-long truck out there," screeched my neighbor, the hall monitor of the universe. "I'll call the police. It's a violation of clause two of the neighborhood covenants."

"Move to a condo, you blue-haired Nazi," I screeched back. I hung up the phone with a clunk.

While Bonita and Dave eyed each other cautiously, I looked out the front window. It was a pretty big truck for a U-Haul. The phone started ringing again, no doubt Mrs. Covenant Nazi next door. "What's in the truck?"

"Wine," Dave answered. "Cases of pure, organic, muscadine Florida wine. Sells for about twenty bucks a bottle."

"Muscadine wine? From Florida?" I'd grown up eating muscadine grapes off the wild vines back home in the red hills of southwest Georgia, where we called them scuppernongs. But I wasn't aware of any commercial Florida muscadine wineries.

"Man, there's vineyards popping up all over Florida. Got one in east Sarasota, near Myakka River State Park. It's like a new thing, this Florida wine industry, with muscadine grapes. Can't grow them pinot noir and such grapes here, they can't take all this heat and humidity. Ain't tough like us," Dave puffed, all but pounding on his chest. "This organic stuff beats the cake. Want to try a bottle?"

Well, certainly, I thought, wine ranking up there

10

with coffee on my list of essential liquids. But not when I needed to be preparing for my appellate argument. "Sure, but I can't drink it now. I've got to work."

"Sweetheart, it's Saturday."

Yeah, I should have stayed at the office, I thought, listening to the unanswered phone ringing and wondering how much trouble Dave was going to be. "I still have to work," I said.

"Tonight then, we'll drink a bottle," he said, and winked. "My old lady's husband's back, so I need to crash here."

Bonita tsked-tsked, but we ignored her.

"Hey, I can stay the night, can't I?"

"Where'd you get the wine?" Being a lawyer, I'm trained to never actually answer a direct question unless, possibly, it is asked by a judge in a particularly belligerent mood.

"Long story, Lilly Belle."

Oh, frigging great, I thought, knowing what that meant. At least the phone stopped ringing.

"Benny," he said, and turned to Benicio. "Hey, man. I know something about you."

"Yeah?" Benny studied Dave with far less suspicious eyes than I noted his mother was using.

"Yeah. Lilly Belle here," he said, pointing at me as if Benny might have forgotten who I was, "she sent me that paper you wrote on the jaguarundi cats in Myakka. I've been driving rock-hoppers out of Lakeland, then I got this, ah, special deal

11

on that wine, but before I truck off to sell it, I'd sure like to see if I can't track me a jaguarundi."

Benny looked at me. "You sent him my paper?" He couldn't hide his pleasure, though in a too-late attempt to show indignation he squinted his eyes after they had popped open in what looked like pride.

"It was a great paper," Bonita said. "He got an A."

Farmer Dave turned to Bonita, tall, perfectly groomed Bonita, with her chocolate-colored hair smoothed back into a silver barrette. As I watched, Dave took her in more fully, and he smiled, big and full mouthed, making me wonder if he hadn't gotten his teeth capped. "Bonita, yeah, we've talked on the phone, at Lilly's office." Grin, grin from Dave, his pelvis jutting out in a Mick Jaggar imitation. "Your son's a great writer. Fruit don't fall far from the tree."

Sure, okay, Bonita's a looker, but flattering her son wasn't going to make her flirt back with a man who had two pigtails and a married girlfriend, no matter how pearly his teeth.

"What's all this got to do with Benny's jaguarundi paper?" I asked. Benny had written a paper for school about the elusive South American wildcats long rumored to be living, in scarce numbers, in Florida, and he had collected enough of the old Florida-cracker accounts to make a convincing case that the long-tailed cats prowled around at Myakka, the cypress-swamp state park in the eastern part of

12

the county. Rich travelers from the 1920s had brought the cats back from South America, planning to domesticate them. When that didn't work, the cats were either turned loose or escaped into the wild lands in the area and reproduced.

"Man, that paper convinced me those cats are out there. Hey, man, I'm a real good tracker. Why don't I leave the truck here and borrow Lilly Belle's car and go check it out? Then tomorrow, at the crack of day, I gotta go, get to Gainesville and sell me some cases of wine there. Them college kids suck up that organic wine. After that, up to Atlanta. Got a bunch of health food stores and fancy-ass wine stores in that town." He grinned again at Bonita, then turned to me.

"Hey, Lilly Belle, why don't you come with me, like old times, you and me in the woods." He winked, implying exactly the kind of thing I'd rather Bonita never suspected.

"I can't. Not today. I'm getting ready for an oral argument."

"What's that?"

"It's an appellate argument."

"Yeah, oh, sure, like all those high-priced boys did before the Supreme Court so we'd know who our president was gonna be."

"Precisely. I have twenty minutes to convince a three-judge panel in the appellate court in Lakeland to affirm the summary judgment I won at the trial level for my client, who is a counselor, and one of his patients claimed that his, er, his . . . therapy fell below the applicable standard of care." Yeah, the woman who was suing my guy thought she'd been abducted by space aliens, oh, and get this, had the nerve to accuse my client of malpractice, just because he thought for an hourly fee rivaling my own that he could reduce her lingering emotional trauma. This would, no doubt, play good in the rarified air of the appellate court.

"You always were one to plan everything down to a gnat's eyebrows, but what's so hard about a twenty-minute speech you gotta spend all day working on it?"

"Because, while I'm trying to argue my client's position, the judges can, and do, interrupt with questions. They can ask me anything about the case and I absolutely have to know the answers, no matter how obscure the question, and then I have to twist my answers to support the summary judgment I won at the trial level. See, a summary judgment is when the trial judge rules on a case before it goes to the jury, because the facts are not really in dispute and the law is clear, and in my case—"

"Whoa, Lilly Belle. Stop. TMI, babe."

"'TMI'?" Bonita asked.

"Too much info. Way too much," Dave said.

"Hey, bud, you made me listen to your entire monologue on how the combustion engine works in an average car, which took hours, days even, and—"

"Belle, I didn't want you helpless, broke down

on the side of the road, or taken advantage of by some mechanic thinking girls don't know spit about cars. But, sweetheart, when do you think I might need to know what a summary judgment is?"

"Okay, but you asked. And no, I can't go with you to Myakka. I'm busy. I already told you I'm working. I work for a living. I have clients. I can't run off with you at the drop of a hat just because you show up from out of nowhere."

"Whoa. Got it, Belle. Got it, okay." Dave turned to Benicio. "Hey, Benny, you want to come with me to Myakka, see if we can track us a jaguarundi?"

"Cool," Benny said before Bonita could object. "We can take my Ford Ranger. It's a 1992, but it's only got 170,000 miles on it."

"You got a Ford with 170,000 miles, and it still runs? You a mechanic or a mojo?" Then Dave eyed Benny closer. "You can't be no sixteen."

"Almost, and I got a learner's permit, but I've been driving since I was twelve. Lilly taught me. She got me that truck too."

Yep, and Bonita was still working on forgiving me for both facts.

"Let's go then, son."

Bonita put a hand on Benny's shoulder. "*No conoces tu aquel hombre.*"

"Yeah, but *I* know him, known him all my life," I said, overlooking for the moment how much trouble I'd gotten in with Dave when I was fifteen. "He's cool." That Dave was cool was true, but largely irrelevant from a mother's point of view.

15

Bonita gave me the same look she'd given me when I bought Benny the truck.

"I'll take care of him, have him back by night," Dave said.

As Benny reached for his jacket and his keys, Bonita reached for him. "Do not drink or smoke anything."

"While your momma finishes the don't dos, I'll get my gear and bring it in," Dave said. "No sense letting it bake in that truck." A minute later, Dave dropped a worn-out backpack on the floor and handed me a ring of keys. "Hang on to these, will you? I'm always losing 'em. And here's the truck key. Don't lose that, you hear?" And he handed me a single key on a U-Haul plastic key ring.

I followed Dave and Benny to the door. "Did you get your teeth fixed?"

"Yeah, looks great, huh? Delvon and me had some loose cash after—"

I cut my eyes to Benny.

"Ah, after our, er, last harvest, *apple* harvest." Grin, grin at me. "Hey, sweetheart, I'll take good care of your boy here."

As Dave and Benny drove off, Benny steady at the wheel, Bonita fingered the gold cross on the chain around her neck and moved her lips in prayer. "I should not have let him go, but he is so, so . . . *obsessed.*" Bonita stopped and looked at me as if obsessive behavior was contagious. "He is so intense about seeing a jaguarundi."

The phone rang, and this time I answered it.

"I've called the police on that truck. You've got to move it, now."

"Got that nursing-home application filled out yet?" I snapped, and hung up. Mrs. Covenant Nazi had reported me to the police a number of times before. Imagine how it improved my mood to come home after ten hours at the Smith, O'Leary, Stanley whipping post to find that a member of the city police force had pulled up my okra plants after the Nazi next door told them I was growing marijuana. I still had a pending damages claim.

"He'll be all right," I said to Bonita, and washed my hands and poured coffee for Bonita and me, then went back to the den where the floor was covered by perfectly organized piles of stuff we still had to do.

Well, okay, maybe I'm not the Mother Teresa of godmothers, but honest, I wouldn't have let Benny go if I'd had any idea that they would find a dead body and a suitcase of money in the outreaches of Myakka.

CHAPTER 2

There's just something about setting aside a day for the peaceful, quiet preparation of an appellate argument that signals the lesser cosmic gods to rain down phones and doorbells.

Every ten minutes, the phone rang. I timed it. Covenant Nazi, I figured. The phone would ring six times, stop, and then start again in ten minutes. When this started, I had stomped to the phone, snatched it up and plunged it down with a bang, and cursed it, thus inviting Bearess's protective nature. Now when the phone rang, Bearess barked at it.

"Want me to answer it?" Bonita asked, then sighed low down and deep.

"Better idea," I said, and snapped the phone line out of the wall. The now-silent phone puzzled Bearess, who continued to sit by it and growl even though it didn't ring.

Somewhere in there was the perfect analogy to practicing law, but I didn't have time to work out the pieces just now.

You can unplug a phone, but not a front door.

After highlighting twelve pages of my summary-judgment hearing transcript, the doorbell rang again. Bearess was so intent on growling at the not-ringing phone, she hadn't issued her early-warning bark.

I figured it for the Nazi Next Door and went to answer it, my irritation crowning. Wrenching the door open, I perfected a leave-me-the-hell-alone stare.

Instead of my neighbor, my client stood there. The very man responsible for my having to spend a beautiful May afternoon inside with small hills of paper and a secretary who kept sighing and rubbing her gold cross.

My client. A dyed-hair, salon-tanned man wearing a long, bright-yellow silk Nehru jacket over white pants. Gandhi Singh thrust a bouquet of gladioli at me. "You are going to have troubles," he said, and walked in before I invited him.

"Gandhi," I said, "how'd you find out where I live?" My phone and address were unlisted, and I never gave clients either. And Covenant Nazi's imprudent calling habits illustrated the folly of having let a few neighbors know my number.

"I'm a psychic," he said. "You forget?"

What he was, was a fraud. At least that was my assessment. The blackness of his hair was too perfectly consistent to be natural, his perpetual tan had an undertone of orange, suggestive of a cheaper brand of those self-tanning lotions, and even his eyes were brown because of colored contacts. But he was my client, and at least he wasn't boring.

"Mr. Singh," Bonita said, rising from her yoga mat with grace and offering her hand. "Good day to you. May I offer you a drink? Coffee?"

"No, thank you." Gandhi Singh walked through my living room and into the kitchen, opened a cabinet where I had a crystal vase that had been my aunt's, got it out, filled it with water, and put the glads in it.

Gandhi turned back to me. "I've come to warn you, but I haven't got a clear picture of the danger yet. It will come. I wouldn't have come over to your home, but I've been trying to call. First someone slammed down the phone and then it rang, and rang. I got worried."

Well, isn't that sweet, I thought, eyeing the glads and wondering how he knew where the vase was.

What I said was, "I'm busy, getting ready for your oral argument. The phone is off the hook because the Nazi next store keeps calling."

"You have a Nazi next door?"

But before I could answer him, Gandhi said, "I had a Holocaust victim for a patient once. He survived a concentration camp. Very troubled man."

Well, no doubt. But I didn't say anything because I didn't want to encourage conversation. I wanted Gandhi to leave.

"He was very old. He died before I could get him to release his hatred of the Nazis through forgiveness."

"The woman next door to Lilly is not a Nazi," Bonita offered. "They just had a misunderstanding over some okra. *Curandero,* you should work with Lilly on forgiveness."

Bonita considered Gandhi a *curandero,* a healer, while I thought his chosen profession was ripping off gullible people, usually middle-aged rich women from Longboat Key who thought they could talk to their dead husbands and their live cats through Gandhi. His most recent specialty was counseling women who thought they had been kidnapped by Martians and had lingering emotional problems as a result. Oddly, there was quite a pod of such women on the Key, a barrier island off Sarasota's coast that attracted the rich carpetbaggers who were taking over the state.

"You are busy, yes? I will leave. Our appellate argument is Tuesday, and I will see you that morning. Do take care."

"You are not going with me to that argument," I sputtered, a point I'd been making repeatedly since the notice for the argument had come in the mail. Clients rarely go with lawyers to oral arguments, and if they do, they invariably add nothing but another level of stress.

Gandhi stepped to the door and opened it. "You said you would leave by six-thirty, so I will see you a few minutes before."

Quickly, I calculated. The drive to the appeals court in Lakeland could take anywhere from one hour to two depending on the vagaries of back-road

Florida travel. I needed to be at the courthouse to sign in by eight-thirty, and I'm never late. But getting there too early is not a good idea, as years of the collective anxiety had created a kind of freak-out miasma that could make even the normally calm Bonita nuts.

Okay, I thought, I will leave by six A.M., an extra few minutes of pacing the sacred halls of justice being the lesser projected evil than having my client tagging along in a yellow Nehru jacket and fake tan.

Gandhi stood in my doorway, looking out. "That truck. I think it has something to do with your troubles. You should get rid of it."

Well, Mrs. Covenant Nazi next door would agree with that.

After Gandhi left, I made another pot of coffee, wondering as I did if I should buy a bigger French press, and Bonita and I were sipping and snipping and working, and the sun was beginning to set in the west when the doorbell rang again.

"Did you put an open-house notice in the paper, or what?" I said, snapping at Bonita as if she was personally responsible for the repetitive invasions of my planned preparation time.

Bearess trotted to the door with me. A very big man stood there, his brow furrowed. He was dressed in a black T-shirt with "These Colors Don't Run" on top of an American flag and the Kmart house brand of jeans, worn over Frye boots. His T-shirt emphasized the gallons of beer he had drunk in his life. In other words, he was the generic male of my hometown in Georgia. Bearess was trying to dance away from my grip on her collar, and barking and doing a fiend-dog routine. I took a quick look to make sure this man wasn't holding a weapon, and his worn hands told me that in any crisis he would have the right tools and know just what to do.

"I'm Waylon," he said.

Well, of course you are, I thought, and tightened my restraining hand on Bearess. In a fair fight, Waylon might be able to put a hurt on her.

"That dog bite?" he asked.

"Yes." In truth, I'd never known Bearess to bite anyone, but she seemed ready to learn a new trick.

"Well, no need of that. You jes' calm it down. Dave sent me to pick up that truck there."

After I patted Bearess and whispered her into a wary calmness, I asked Waylon how he knew Dave.

"Dave and me drove them rock-hoppers out of Lakeland," Waylon said. "Till we up and quit. Now we both work at a vineyard, out in east county. Cool gig, working in a vineyard."

"How'd you know Dave was going to be here?"

"He told me. Look, Dave and me work together, awright? He said he was coming by here, even got me your address 'cause it ain't in the book." Waylon pulled out a page torn from a phone book with my name and address scribbled on it in Farmer Dave's distinctive handwriting. "In case I needed to pick up the wine, which I do, 'cause he called, and—"

"Yeah, okay." It didn't make a whole bunch of

sense, but Farmer Dave operated in a different sphere from most of us, and at least Waylon knew him well enough to have a sample of his handwriting. So, more or less satisfied, and wanting Waylon and the truck of wine to leave, I said, "Cool. Take it. But Dave said I could have a couple cases of the wine."

Okay, so, spank me. Dave had only offered me a bottle, but Dave was off in a cypress swamp turning my secretary's son either into a delinquent or an ace tracker and couldn't challenge my version.

"Yeah, sounds good," Waylon said, and held out his hand. "Key?"

I gave Waylon the key Dave had left with me and Bonita and I followed him out to the truck, then each of us carried a case of organic muscadine wine back inside my house. Then we went back outside to watch Waylon depart.

A white pickup, which I assumed Waylon had driven up in, was parked in my driveway. Inside its cab, a woman wearing a red scarf hippie style over her dark hair watched, and then started the truck and followed Waylon as he drove off.

Bonita and I went back inside. A muscle in the back of my neck twitched when I saw Dave's dirty backpack dumped on my clean floor. Touching as little of it as possible, I picked up the backpack, took it to the bathroom where I got a clean towel, and then carried the pack to my second bedroom and put the towel on the futon, then the pack on the towel.

But little snoop bells of curiosity went off. I peeled back the cover flap and perused the contents. Most of it was pretty ordinary stuff, though there seemed to be an extraordinary amount of dental-cleaning paraphernalia, plus the usual stash of sativa, aka pot, which I smelled appreciatively and otherwise left alone. The thing that gave me pause was the gun at the bottom of the pack, carefully wrapped in a soft chamois cloth. A cardboard box of bullets, labeled "158-grain roundnoses," was stuffed under the gun. The box looked old when I pulled it out and opened it. Yeah, bullets, huh? As I was putting the roundnoses back in Dave's pack, I saw that someone had scribbled JEB on the side of the box.

I picked up the gun, which looked like a perfectly ordinary .38, and saw that someone had scratched JEB on the side of the handle. There were oily smudges on the gun, which I polished off with the cloth, admiring the practical appeal of the sturdy little gun. I checked the cylinder and saw that the gun was not loaded. After pretending to shoot out my own window, I was putting the weapon away when Bonita stuck her head in the room.

Whatever she was going to ask me, she didn't, opting instead for, "Is that a gun?"

I bit back the obvious sarcasm, as I've learned over the years that Bonita never thinks I'm as clever as I do. "It's a classic. Not loaded. Want to see it?" I offered the gun to her.

Bonita took the pistol gingerly. Then she held it

with more assurance and pointed it at the same window I had. She shuddered. "Dave wouldn't have a gun with him, not with Benny, would he?"

"No," I said, though not having a personal clue as to the truth of that. Winging it, a trial lawyer's specialty, I added, "This is just . . . for . . . long road trips and stuff. You don't need a gun to go hiking in Myakka State Park. Plus, it's illegal." Oh, yeah, like that would stop Dave.

Bonita handed the gun to me, and I put it in the backpack while she fingered her cross and watched me. I guessed from her expression that she was regretting her decision to let Benny go off with Dave.

"It will be all right," I said, hoping fervently that it would be.

"*Si Dios quiere.*"

Shutting the door on the gun and the backpack, we headed back toward the kitchen.

I didn't know which bothered me more, the thought of a potentially unarmed Dave in the cypress swamp with Benny, or the thought that he might have another gun on him.

CHAPTER 3

Henry Platt, liability-insurance claims adjuster mediocre and malleable guardian of most of my malpractice expense accounts and legal fees, and still my friend despite the fact that I had briefly thought he had killed one of my clients last year, persisted in his courtship of Bonita.

Neither Bonita nor her children had made up their minds about the chubby, pink-faced man with the soft hands and the scared-bunny expression, though Bonita was definitely more inclined toward him than her children were. But there he was in a navy blue suit in his brand-new spruce green Sienna van, loaded down with four of Bonita's five kids, ready to pick up Bonita and take her and her kids to six o'clock Mass.

But first, we all had to stop everything, though I was the only one actually trying to accomplish anything anymore, and clean up Armando's bloody arm.

"How did you cut it?" Bonita asked, pulling one of my crisp, clean linen towels from the kitchen drawer, and then pulling her son's arm over my sink.

Well, that was going to take some Clorox to

clean up, I thought, watching blood flow into my sink and into my formerly fine linen towel.

"On a CD case," Henry explained. "Is it deep? Does he need stitches?"

Bonita peered at the cut. I peered at the mess in my sink and thought, A CD case? "How do you cut yourself on that?"

"It stuck, and he was . . . ah, he was . . . prying it open," Henry bleated, then blushed, and I suspected a cover-up. Bonita's children were not warming to the thought of Henry as a permanent figure in their lives, and though he kept plugging away at winning their affections, there were multiple acts of sabotage from the kids. I envisioned Armando trying to rip the upholstery in Henry's new van with the jagged edge of something sharp. But whatever the real story, Henry would keep it between him and Armando, and I hoped Armando would appreciate that.

"No stitches," Bonita said, and gathered Armando in her arms, looked him in the eyes, and smiled. "Just a big Band-Aid and we can still make Mass." Armando struggled like a wild coyote to escape her arms.

"Hey, Armando," I finally said, once he was free of his mom. "What's happening?"

"Nothing," he said, and shifted his stance to morose-early-teen mode. Javy, Armando's twin brother, who looks and acts nothing like him, took a good look at his arm. "Cool," he said, after examining the wound.

"Hey, Javy," I said. "What's happening?"

"*Tia* Lilly, I ran second in a track meet at the district," he said, and beamed.

"Good for you. That's great," I said, noticing the glower Armando directed first at Javy and then at me. Of course, Bonita had already told me Javy won second place, but it was still cool news. Javy was a thin, wiry boy with a runner's body and sharp features, while Armando had flat cheeks and a flat nose and a squat wrestler's body.

After studying the contrast between the twins, I turned to the other two kids. "Hey, Carmen, hey, Felipe. You guys cool?"

Carmen, the only girl and just six, hugged me and promptly launched into a story in half Spanish, half English that I couldn't quite follow, but seemed to have a winged horse at its center. Felipe, named for his father, tried to get a few words in, and I just patted his head. At ten, he was still young enough to let me do this.

While her youngest child entertained me, Bonita, who kept a virtual first-aid kit in her purse, got the requisite Band-Aid and fixed up Armando. Then, in a whisk and a wink, they were all out of my house.

Silence. Blessed silence.

Now I could really get some work done.

Bearess pranced over to the still-unplugged phone and started barking.

★　　★　　★

29

I had Cloroxed down my kitchen and bathroom and wiped down the front door and perfected the order of the piles of paper on my floor and ground more coffee beans by the time Bearess turned from barking at the phone and barked at the door.

I opened it before the bell rang and there was Benny, apparently safe, though appearances can certainly lie. He wouldn't look me in the eye.

Uh-oh, I thought, watching as he walked inside, not even trying his casual-cool saunter or banter on me.

"What's wrong?" I asked, but my own voice was drowned out by Farmer Dave.

"Where's my wine?" he shouted at me, getting entirely too much in my face.

"Waylon came and got it. He said you sent him for it."

"Waylon? Huh? Must be a change of plan. Hard work, transporting that wine. Must be, eh, a . . . change in the market."

Farmer Dave did not specialize in plans, honest or dishonest, and he certainly didn't specialize in honest labor on the open market, and I'd had to ride roughshod over him as my caretaker not to do something illegal at my orchard and get my 180 acres stolen by the federal government under its generous confiscation statutes. But I decided to pass on quizzing him on any deep, hidden meaning because I was worried about Benny, who had disappeared into my bathroom.

"I'll just have to go after Waylon, see what I can

see," Dave said. "Hey, man, Ben, you wanna come? Drive me over to Waylon's house in that fine Ford truck of yours?"

"No, I don't think Benny should go with you." Firm, I said it, firm.

"Okay, Lilly Belle, then you'll have to drive me over to Waylon's. He took my truck, you know."

Oh. I didn't want to get caught driving Dave around on a mission to find his wine. I wanted to continue to memorize legal nuances. And Benny was already out of the bathroom and nodding his head up and down like an eager bubblehead.

Still, a tired caution light in my brain tried to flag me down. "Maybe you should stay with me," I said to Benny. "Just let Dave borrow your truck."

Yeah, right. Like any fifteen-year-old boy would let his first truck out of his sight so he could hang inside waiting for his momma to come back from Mass if instead he could drive a long-haired felon on a quest to find the mysterious Waylon and the probably stolen wine.

"Naw, he's a good kid, let 'im drive me." Dave smiled at Benny.

"No violence," I said, reducing my concerns to the primary one.

"Hey, I'm a radical pacifist," Dave said, and grinned at me. But then he frowned and asked, "Belle, where's my backpack?"

"Guest room." I pointed down the hallway.

When Dave came out, he had the backpack slung over his arm. Okay, I thought, that meant he was armed again with the sturdy little .38. But how much trouble could they get in over wine? I naively thought. Besides, I was enormously tired and still had to do, during the evening, all the work I hadn't done during the day. I didn't have the time to chauffeur Dave around, and if Benny loaned Dave his truck there was a fair chance he'd never get it back.

So I gave in, but repeated Bonita's instructions to Benny not to drink or smoke anything.

They were out the door before I thought to add, don't call the police from Waylon's house, use a pay phone, and don't give your name.

CHAPTER 4

T he criminal-justice system functions wholly outside my sphere of expertise and operates with its own mysteries and tricks and tactics, about which I know very little. Though I am a defense attorney, I am strictly a civil attorney.

Like the federal income tax system, the criminal-justice system is not something I intended to mess with. You got a tax problem, I told my clients, get a tax attorney or a CPA. You get busted for DWI or bank robbery, get a criminal-defense attorney. You get sued for malpractice by a client, and you have money or good liability insurance, *then* you come to me.

So it was later that night, when I learned Waylon and Dave were in jail and needed to get out, I knew I wasn't the one to help. This news came to me with a bang and a thud at my door. While Bearess snuffled beside me, I peered out my peephole and saw what appeared to be the same woman in the red scarf who had driven off behind Waylon. Having made a career of reading jurors' and judges' faces, I saw she was not a happy woman.

But counting on Bearess to protect me if she turned out to be a contemporary Charles Manson girl, I cracked the door.

"You Lilly Cleary, the lawyer?"

"Yes, though I much prefer that people make appointments through my secretary during business hours."

"Look," she said, "Dave and Waylon are in the county jail for stealing a truckload of wine and they need you to go down and bail them out. Right now. Use this for bail. Here." With that, Unhappy Hippie Girl thrust a brown paper bag at me. I took the bag, and when I looked inside, she turned and skittered off down my driveway.

The bag, an ordinary, though crumpled, grocery store bag from Winn-Dixie, was full of money. Cash. Bills. Green paper.

I riffled through the bag to see if there was anything else in it, and when I saw that the entire bag was full of money, I looked up after Hippie Girl and shouted, "Hey, wait a minute."

She got in a pickup, slammed the door, and drove off.

Well, now what?

For starters, I took the sack of money and went back inside and shut and locked the door.

Then I thought about Farmer Dave's impressive list of old felony warrants. Oh, *mierda*, I said, and wondered if there was some kind of statute of limitations on old warrants.

I didn't have a clue as to how to get people out

34

of jail. There's something about a bond, a bailsman, and maybe a hearing, and you have a right to remain silent, and that's about the sum total of what I knew about criminal justice in any kind of practical sense. In other words, even with my law degree and my closetful of tailored gray suits, I knew what the average television viewer knew.

In short, I needed a criminal-defense attorney. Mentally, I ran down the list of the ones I knew from the Sarasota Bar Association functions, and then remembered how my now very much ex-boyfriend Sam Santuri, a homicide detective and seriously humorless man, had ranted when this Philip Cohen guy had shredded him on a cross-examination. Cohen had gotten a decidedly guilty man off scot-free, at least according to Sam. That was the attorney for Dave, I thought, dragging out my phone book. Naturally there was no home listing for Cohen, and no emergency, after-hours number. I yanked out my Sarasota Bar Association yearbook, took a quick look at Cohen's photo, assessed him in the grainy mug shot as a standard-looking attorney in glasses and dark suit, noted his law degree was from Notre Dame and his under-graduate degree was from UCLA, and threw down the yearbook in disgust at its lack of a home number.

On a mission now, and not giving a rat's ass that it was getting pretty late to be calling people on a Saturday night, I punched in the number for Jackson Smith, alias Stonewall. Aside from being my mentor and the object of my fantasies, Jackson is also Mr. Bar Association and knows just about everything anybody needs to know. If he ever sold his list of secret phone numbers, the peace and privacy of most of the professional denizens of the greater Sarasota Bay area would be shot to hell and back.

Jackson answered the phone with a snarl. After my necessary apology for calling this late, and calling period, I asked if he had Philip Cohen's home number.

"Did you get arrested?" he shouted.

"No," I snapped, making sure I was emphatically indignant-sounding. "It's for a—" Okay, just how did I describe Farmer Dave to my mentor, the man who kept trying to mold me into a sophisticated trial lawyer? What was Dave to me? Friend? Employee? First love? The man who took Delvon and me in when we came back from a frolic in Florida as teenagers and found our mother had sold our bedroom furniture and clothes? Dave was all of those things. As well as a long-haired career criminal.

"—acquaintance of my brother." I chose the safe and the neutral.

"Not that crazy brother, one who thinks he's John the Baptist?" This, from a man who thought he was the reincarnation of Stonewall Jackson, struck me as just a tad sanctimonious.

"No, not Delvon. This is Dan's friend. Dan's the normal one." Of course Dan might have nodded at Dave if they'd passed close enough to each other, but it was Delvon and Dave who were fully bonded blood brothers. However, Jackson disapproved of Delvon.

"Cohen, huh? Yeah, he's good. Wait a minute," Jackson bellowed, and I heard the phone go clunk against something. A moment later, he came back on the line and repeated a number.

"Unlisted," he thundered. "Don't tell him you got it from me."

"Deal," I said, "and thanks," and then I hung up without saying good-bye and punched in the numbers Jackson had recited.

A woman answered, sounding peeved.

"May I please speak with Mr. Cohen?" I asked, making myself sound as professional and polite as I could.

"Call his office on Monday," she said, and hung up.

I called right back.

This time a man answered. "How'd you get this number?"

Despite his bad phone manners, I assumed this was Cohen. The anger in his voice suggested that a direct answer was the quickest way for me to get to my real point. But I wasn't ratting out Jackson for giving me Cohen's private number, and, besides, I was still mad at Sam for dumping me with scant explanation. So I told Cohen that Detective Sam Santuri had given me his home number and hoped it was remotely possible that Sam could have had it.

In the pause that followed, I braced for a hang-up.

"Who are you and why would Sam give you my private number?"

"Sam investigated the murder of one of my clients recently." A doctor killed by a toxic marijuana cigarette. "We became . . . friends. I'm a partner at Smith, O'Leary, and Stanley, and—"

"That'd make you Lilly Cleary, then."

I was immediately flattered.

"I know you," he said, the tone suddenly flirtatious. "Black hair worn like Lauren Bacall, you always wear gray suits, and you pummeled that Miami attorney in that brain-damaged infant case last year."

Pearl gray, I corrected to myself, and sometimes midnight blue suits.

"Yes," I said, notching my voice down to low and sexy. "Jackson Smith tells me you are absolutely brilliant. The best criminal-defense attorney anywhere." Well, okay, that was close enough to what Stonewall had said for lawyer-to-lawyer communications.

"Any chance this could wait until Monday?" The flirt was over.

"If it could have waited until Monday, I would have waited until Monday. But a friend of mine and one of his buddies got arrested. I'm not sure yet exactly what the charges are, but I suspect they've been arrested for stealing a truck full of organic wine and I need to get them out of jail tonight."

"And just how am I supposed to do that?"

"If I knew, I wouldn't be calling you." Yes, the flirt was definitely over.

"A truckload of stolen wine? That's probably a first- or second-degree felony. You think I just go down there, sign some papers, post the bail, and they walk?"

Well, I had hoped it was something like that, but his tone suggested otherwise, so I took a wild guess, and said, "No, of course, I know it's not that simple, but, please, could you just meet me at the jail and speak to Dave? His name is Dave Asa Baggwell."

I could hear the woman in the background. The sound became muffled, and I suspected Cohen had put his hand over the phone. In a couple of seconds, he came back on, and said, "I'll meet you there in half an hour. Bring a checkbook."

He hung up before I could ask if he minded cash in a sack.

For a few minutes, I pondered the proper attire to wear to jail, then opted for basic black jeans and a dainty, white peasant blouse. I did a light makeup, fluffed out my half a yard of black hair, and was slipping on my kicky little red sling backs and considering whether White Linen was a good perfume for jail when my phone rang.

When I picked it up, Bonita spoke before I could say hello. "Benicio needs to see you. He is very upset, and he won't tell me a thing. But it must be about that . . . that man with the pigtails."

39

Oh, yes, please, cosmic forces, I needed something else to go wrong tonight. I mean, it wasn't midnight yet, I could probably fit in at least two or three more crises before it was technically Sunday.

But this was Benny. After all, he had gone off with Farmer Dave not once but twice with my blessings, so I had doubled the odds that something would happen, and I told Bonita to put him on the phone.

"He's locked in his room. You need to come over here."

"I'll be right there."

Before I left, I grabbed up the grocery bag full of cash, fully expecting to use the bills to either pay to get Dave out of jail or to put down a retainer on Philip's services. Then I sped off to Benny.

Bonita lived six streets over, in another vintage Southgate house built in the late sixties in a developed orange grove. The basic concrete block, Florida ranch. I was in her driveway before the radio even played a song. Yak, yak, yak, even WMNF, the alt station for cool people, is way too much yak. My car is too old for a CD player, and the cassette player bit the dust years ago, and for the $500 or so it would take to replace it, I'd opted for the radio and humming.

The porch light was on, and Bonita opened the door before I knocked. Pausing only to say "Don't worry," I headed straight to Benny's bedroom.

Benny was curled up on his bed, wearing head-phones, and the only light was from inside the closet. I turned on the overhead light, and he flinched.

"Benny, what's wrong?"

He turned up the volume on his Walkman so loud I could hear the sound of some dreadful rap crap escaping from the headphones.

"Look, Benny, I'm supposed to be at the county jail right now getting Dave out, and I'm sorry you're upset, but you need to tell me what is going on, right now and real quick."

Bonita is always telling me children need firm limits, and though I'd yet to see her actually use any, I thought I'd give it a whirl.

"I've never seen a dead man before," he said, jolting me. I had figured this was Catholic guilt over smoking a cigarette, marijuana at the worst, not a corpse scenario.

"You saw a dead body?"

"In that swamp. With Dave. He'd been snakebit. A couple of times, maybe more. It was so . . . so gross. I thought I'd puke."

"How'd you find it?"

"We were looking for jaguarundi tracks, and just stumbled on it."

Yeah, that would about be Farmer Dave's karma.

"And that's not all," Benny said, with a faint hint of a sniffle sound. "There was a suitcase and it was full of money. Cash money. Lots of it."

"Where's the money now?" Okay, I know, I know, but I'm a civil litigator and we're trained to follow the money. Plus, I had a sudden suspicion about the cash in the grocery sack.

"Dave took the suitcase and told me to keep my mouth shut. He kept telling me that accidents happen, with the snake, you know, and I shouldn't go off in the woods by myself, and not to call the police. But I wanted to call the police. About the body."

"Then what? I mean, was this before you came back to my house? Or after?"

"He had the suitcase with the money in my pickup when we got to your house. And he was going to, you know, leave me, but then his wine truck was gone. So we had to ask you where the wine was, and then we went to look for Waylon."

"What happened after you and Dave left, looking for Waylon?"

"We went to his house, Waylon's, I mean, and they got into some kinda talk, and they seemed upset, and told me to wait in the kitchen, and there was a phone in the kitchen."

Benny stopped talking and studied his big feet as if the answers to the mysteries of life were engraved there in gold.

"Benny, did you call the police on the body? From Waylon's kitchen phone?"

"Dave said not to. Dave said it wasn't a good idea to call the police."

Sure, I thought, that would be Farmer Dave's point of view. But Benny was Bonita's son, raised right on the fear of God and a blind trust in the

American justice system. Not a fifty-year-old man with pigtails and a list of felony warrants dating back to Woodstock.

"But I called the police and told them about the body. I mean, aren't you supposed to call 911 when you find a body?"

Yes, in a big, general sense, but maybe not when you're in the kitchen of a house where a man you like is obviously up to something if not illegal, at least strange. "Best to call from a pay phone, and don't give a name," I said, hoping Bonita wasn't listening at the door.

"A whole bunch of cops came, and an ambulance—I guess I got confused on the phone call, or something, about where the dead body was— and the cops were from the sheriff's, I think, and Dave heard them coming and told me to shut up about the money and then him and Waylon flushed a bunch of stuff down the toilet, and Dave ran off into the woods, but this one deputy caught him, and then a bunch of deputies arrested him and Waylon 'cause of the wine."

How did they know it was stolen? I wondered, but asked, "Where was the money?"

"Still in my truck. They had sirens and all when they came down the road, so we had a few minutes before they got to us and Dave made me promise to take the suitcase full of money back to a woman he knew and he gave me directions to her house and told me to tell her to give half the money to you to get them out of jail."

Benny hesitated.

"Is that all?" I mean, that was enough, but something in the way he stopped talking and took up the religious study of his feet again suggested he might be hiding something. "You need to tell me everything that happened, I mean, if I'm going to help you."

Pause. Sniffle noise. Eyes up, eyes down.

"Benny?"

"Yeah, sure, that's what happened. All of it."

"No, it isn't. I can tell when you're lying. You aren't any good at it at all."

"Dave told me to take half the money and keep it for myself. That woman divided it up and put it in grocery sacks."

Whew. Quite the night for an altar-boy type. One afternoon and evening with Farmer Dave and Waylon had potentially wiped out fifteen years of Bonita's scrupulous churchgoing child rearing.

"Listen, Benny, don't beat yourself up over this, and don't tell your mother. Okay, let me go see Dave at the jail, and then you and me, we'll talk more, and sort this out."

"What do I do with the sack of money?"

"Hide it," I said, "and don't tell anybody, not even your mom, about this." So okay, as a godmother, I sucked. That's why I have a large dog and no children. And technically, I am not Benny's official godmother, that honor goes to his aunt, Gracie of the order of the ex-nun, but I'm the one he's been running to since we first met ten years

44

ago, and I think of myself as his stepgodmother. Find a Hallmark card for that.

"Especially, don't tell your mom," I reiterated.

Benny nodded.

"Benny, I have got to go. I'm sorry."

I didn't feel good about leaving him, but then I hadn't felt good about anything since Farmer Dave had rung my doorbell.

I didn't know that, comparatively speaking, the night was still young.

CHAPTER 5

J ails are creepy, okay.

Seriously creepy on a Saturday night.

And this one smelled bad. The place was manic with too many people—screaming women, crying men, stoic law-enforcement types of diverse size and make. A small, dark man was throwing up in a trash can in the corner.

Too late I realized I should have sprayed myself down with Lysol, not White Linen perfume. I tried not to inhale or touch anything. Pulling my arms in as close to my body as I could, I inched through the crowd and toward what I assumed was the front desk.

A serious meat-eater type with dirty glasses didn't even look up at me when I cleared my throat.

"I'm looking for Philip Cohen, a lawyer, and I'm a lawyer too, and we are supposed to visit our client, a man named David Baggwell, that's with two *g*s, and I—"

"Room on the left. Down that way." Beef Eater then looked over me to the man behind me breathing car-exhaust fumes onto my dainty white

46

blouse, which I figured I would have to boil in Clorox before I could wear it again.

I walked down the hallway and, using the tail of my shirt as a protective sheath so I wouldn't have to actually touch it, I opened the door. Two men, seated at what was little more than a card table, were drinking out of white plastic cups and a bottle of wine was on the table. I recognized the label— they were drinking some of Farmer Dave's wine.

"Lillian," a well-dressed man wearing glasses said, and stood up and offered his hand. "I'm Philip Cohen."

Though I would rather not have touched anything that had been touching things in the jail, I took his hand. We traded firm handshakes, and I looked through his glasses into large, black eyes, and read nothing there. His black hair needed either a good cut or a dab of gel, but was glossy and thick. In a taller man, his face and hair would have made him handsome. But he was a good two, maybe three inches shorter than me, which made him about average since I'm six feet and was wearing one-inch heels. Compact body, probably trim under an immaculately cut gray jacket. Unless I missed my guess, his white shirt was starched and hand pressed.

"May I present T. R. Johnson, Tired Johnson, that is," Cohen said, "an investigator with the Sarasota County Sheriff's Department. Investigator Johnson, may I present Lillian Cleary, attorney."

47

The other man stood up and walked around the card table and offered me his hand.

While his hand dangled there, I studied him with the feeling that I knew him. Investigator Tired Johnson studied me right back and then I saw his eyes pop open with a surprised recognition, and he sucked in his cheeks.

That did the trick. Twenty pounds lighter, this man and I had met in a screaming fit in my own backyard.

"How in the hell could you not know the difference between okra and marijuana?" I blurted out.

"Ma'am, I did, I knew that was just okra, but that lady next door was raising such a complete ruckus, and she wouldn't take my word for it, so I thought the best thing to do was just take the plants in and have them officially ID'd for her."

"You couldn't have taken a couple of cuttings? You had to rip them up, roots and all?"

"Like I told you, she was having a fit. You wouldn't believe her."

Yes, actually, I would believe my neighbor Covenant Nazi and her capacity to pitch a conniption. But that didn't excuse this man's mistake. I mean, come on, he was a hefty boy, and he carried a gun. What? He couldn't stand up to a skinny old woman?

"What, may I inquire, are you two talking about?" Philip asked.

"Okra," Tired and I answered in concert.

48

"Why?"

"It's a long story," Tired answered. "Look," he said, turning to me, "I'm sorry."

"Would you like some wine, Lillian? I'm sure I can procure another cup," Philip offered.

Oh, yeah, right, like I'm drinking stolen wine out of a jailhouse plastic cup that's been touched by who knows who. "No, thank you."

"Officer T. R. Johnson is the arresting investigator on your . . . your friend Dave's case, and he just happened to be here, so I asked him to wait until after I saw Dave, and his friend Waylon."

"So you've seen them. Are they all right? Is Dave okay?"

"They are both fine."

"Can I see Dave?"

"That would be unnecessary now, and perhaps difficult. Tired and I have been discussing the matter."

"I want to see Dave."

"Ma'am, he's all right," Officer Tired said. "He didn't get hurt or anything during the arrest. He did run like hell, but just his luck one of our deputies—we call him Sprint—was on duty and he wrestled him down."

"I want to see Dave."

Philip leaned in toward me, put his hand on my arm, and said in a crooner's voice, "I assure you that Dave is fine. I've seen him. To go through the procedures for a second lawyer to visit him would sorely tax the Saturday-night jailer, and I

49

am sure you can comprehend why I attempt to stay on positive terms with him."

Philip's hand lay on my arm like a caress, sending off a warmth that made me overlook the possible jail germs migrating up my arm.

I nodded, muted by his touch and his Dean Martin voice.

As Philip removed his hand from my arm, and blood circulated in my brain again, Tired, or T.R., said, "We've been, you know, talking over the situation."

Talking, and drinking Dave's wine, I noted. "What's the T.R. stand for?"

"Tired Rufus."

"That's got to be a—" I wanted to say joke, but these country boys can be sensitive about their names, their mommas, and their dogs, so I finished with "—nickname. Tired, I mean."

"No, ma'am, it's on my birth certificate. Tired Rufus Johnson."

Well, there was probably a story there, but I didn't intend to know Tired long enough to learn it, and so I just nodded. I never did shake his hand.

"Well, I've got to go. I'm still on duty," he said, continuing to stand rooted to the space in front of me. But then he reached back to his plastic cup and swallowed the last of the wine. "You take care now," he said toward both of us, nodded his head, and ducked out the door.

"He is a decent man, a proficient officer. You should not be rude to him."

"Why are you drinking Dave's wine? And where is it, the truck of wine, I mean, and when can you get Dave out of jail?"

Philip smiled at me, a long, slow, sensual type of smile. A smile that changed things. His lips were full, and wide.

"Perhaps you would be more comfortable discussing this somewhere else?"

Yeah, after about two or three hot showers to wash off the jailhouse scud. I nodded, numbed by his smile and his voice.

"If we go to my office, I'd have to disarm the security system. What about your office? Or, my house?"

I nodded, frozen to the dirty floor.

Philip stopped smiling. "You understand, it will be twenty-four hours before Dave's first appearance. He will be informed of the charges against him and his rights in a more formal setting, though I assure you he is aware of both after our discussion. At that first appearance, the terms of Dave's pretrial release will be discussed, and the reasonable conditions for such release determined by the judge. As Dave is not a resident, I suspect the assistant state attorney will ask for some kind of bond even though the crime is nonviolent, though a second-degree felony. What works against Dave, besides the lack of community ties, is his past history."

Philip paused and I tried to erase the uh-oh look that no doubt flitted across my features at the mention of Dave's past history.

51

"As you apparently know, there is a problem with an outstanding warrant from Georgia on Dave for bulldozing a motocross track into ruin. It came up on the NCIC."

Just the one warrant? I thought, relieved and momentarily attributing the other alleged warrants to Dave's exaggeration.

"If, as I suspect, Dave is detained after his first appearance until the officials can work out whether they will extradite him, the state attorney's office has thirty days to file its information, that is, its formal charges, but I doubt we will proceed that far."

Philip paused, took off his glasses with one hand, and with his other hand, put his fingertips to his eyelids as if to rub them, but didn't. Then, dropping his hands from his face, he studied me as I studied him. He kept his glasses off, and let me have a full, deep look into his eyes, wide open, guileless, honest, and soulful. A good, theatrical gesture, widely used by attorneys. Even knowing that Philip was deliberately playing me like a juror, or a pickup in a bar, I was soaked right up into all that liquid darkness of his eyes.

"We'll go to my house and discuss this further." Philip put his hand on my arm and guided me toward the door and down the hallway and out into the fresh air of the spring night. The lingering warmth of Philip's touch on my arm made me tingle. I wasn't at all sure I cared where the damn truck of wine was.

CHAPTER 6

All I remembered about criminal law 101 from law school was that our professor kept talking about *scienter* the first day. I confused this with sphincter, and given the professor's fascination with it, pegged him right off for a pervert until I actually read my assignment, out of a book that had cost me a fourth of my life's savings, and learned that *scienter* was a fancy Latin word for criminal intent. Or guilty knowledge.

So, along with that right-to-silence thing, I did know that one had to possess *scienter* to be convicted of a crime.

That's what I was thinking about, oh, and about Philip's black eyes and his very long fingers, as I dutifully drove behind his car toward his house on the bay. I had my window down and in the night air caught the saltwater and fish smell of the Gulf of Mexico. Philip drove an Infinity, a black one, but not new, so as I followed in my cobalt blue Honda with its 194,000 miles on it, I gave him brownie points for not driving an SUV or something right off the showroom floor.

When I parked behind Philip in a long, circular

driveway, he was quick to open my door and offer his hand as I crawled out of my Honda. I looked up at the sky as if I could actually see stars with all the light pollution, and then looked square into the black eyes of Philip Cohen, pursed my lips for the perfect, witty comment, and said, "So?"

"So?" he said back, smiling with those sensual lips. He let go of my hand, which I noted he had held longer than strictly necessary to guide me from my car, and ran his freed hand through his hair as if I had, perhaps, failed to notice that he had a full head of it. It was as black as mine, though he was letting his gray show through and I wasn't.

"So. Can you get him out on bail?"

"Probably." He stopped smiling and popped open the trunk of his car, then lifted out a case of wine. I could see there was another case still in the trunk.

"So. Is that Dave's wine?"

"Dave's? Waylon's? A vintner named Earl Stallings? It depends upon whom you ask."

I followed Philip into his kitchen, where he put the case of wine down, and then put his middle finger on the inside of my arm, right below where the sleeve of my dainty, white blouse ended. "Shall we share a bottle?"

"So," I repeated, feeling my chin bob up and down.

I talk for a living. I talk for a hobby. I talk to think. I talk to live. And this man smiles at me, and then puts one finger on one tiny spot of my exposed skin and *so* is the best I can do.

I hoped the woman on the phone wasn't his wife.

"Perhaps you'd like to freshen up?" Philip then directed me to the guest bath.

The bathroom looked brand new and wholly unused. But still I had to wash the bar of soap under hot water until my hands turned red and a third of the bar of soap was down the drain, then I had to wash my hands after handling the previously unwashed soap, then I had to wash the soap and my hands again, all the way up to my elbows, and then I scalded them off, and then started over so I could wash my face, washing off not only the jail's floating air germs but my light coating of makeup.

Then I snooped. Nothing of interest in the bathroom cabinet, no good prescription drugs or even any worthy OTC stuff. The closet held towels. The shower and tub were clean and the soap in the dish was still in its wrapper, and I wished I had noticed that before I used the unwrapped soap by the sink, which might have been used by who knows who for who knows what.

There being nothing else to snoop into, I drifted back to the kitchen, taking in as much as I could of the lay of the land.

In the kitchen, as Philip poured the wine, I looked about me some more. Okay, his car wasn't too Big Lawyer Ostentatious, but the house gave me pause. It was exactly the kind of big, pink, fake-Spanish stucco monster house on the bay that rankled me, exemplifying what the carpetbaggers and scally-wags had done to Sarasota. Built on dredged-up sand, big enough to sleep my entire high school graduation class, and totally too well decorated, Philip's home was like a house version of a Cadillac SUV. Totally overpriced, wholly unnecessary, and pretentious enough to spit up supper over.

Still, there was his smile. I sipped the wine. It was good. But my tongue couldn't say so.

"Remind me to give you a case of this wine before you leave," Philip said. "Shall we sit in the den?"

"So," I said, and nodded, and followed him into a room with walls a shade of purplish maroon that only a professional decorator or a person on good hallucinogens could have chosen, and I told myself that if I didn't speak a sensible sentence without the word *so* in the next five minutes, I was going to cut my hair into spikes and dye it maroon for penance.

I sat where he pointed, on a simple beige couch. Real leather. Sitting, I sniffed the air for the woman who had answered the phone. Philip said something I didn't catch, intent as I was at detecting other female presences.

"Business first," he said, and smiled that smile again, and my toes curled in my kicky little shoes.

I nodded.

"First, I will need a check for my services, just to start us off. Dave assured me you would pay me from funds he has entrusted to you."

His pause, I thought, signified it was my turn to talk. Funds Dave had entrusted me with? That must be the sack of money in the backseat of my Honda.

"So," I said, and stopped long enough to bite the inside of my mouth. "I've got some cash in the car that Dave left with me. How much do you want?"

Tactless, even for me.

"I don't take cash. There are ethical issues, IRS problems, money-laundering allegation potentials. Criminal-defense attorneys need to be careful about the funds they accept in payment. Perhaps you've read about the government's prosecution of Miami criminal-defense attorneys for accepting cash from their clients when the cash was from drug deals? The law precludes an attorney from accepting payment from a client where the money is raised from an illegal source, and cash in today's culture of plastic suggests dirty business."

"So," I nodded. Nice speech. Only an edge of indignation. And yes, thank you, I didn't live in a potato and I had read about the persecution of the criminal-defense attorneys in Miami by a federal government that didn't have enough to do they had to pick on lawyers too.

"So," I summed up.

"No cash. I'd suggest you count the money and put it in a safe somewhere, probably in your firm's office. You have a safe there, don't you?"

I nodded.

Philip reached into his jacket's inside pocket and

pulled out a folded sheet of paper. "My standard contract. The initial fee is at the bottom. Dave has already signed it."

"So. Okay. I'll write a check."

"I can recommend any one of a half dozen decent bondsmen. I even know a few who will accept your cash without asking questions. I'll need one, maybe two business days to clear up the Georgia warrant. Barring undue complications, we should have your friend out by Tuesday."

Oh, *mierda*, I thought. Tuesday I was supposed to be in Lakeland with that frigging appellate argument. Caught up in the drama of Dave and the smile of Philip, I had forgotten. Either I needed to go home right now and prepare, or go home and sleep.

"I thought you might like to go over your friend's case," Philip said. "What we talked about, Dave and I. The apparent owner of the wine is a vintner named Earl Stallings who lives in east Sarasota, near Myakka River State Park. He has a showroom, a winery, and a vineyard out there. Tired Johnson also presented me with a detailed narrative. Mr. Stallings reported the theft of the wine mid-afternoon, soon after he returned home and discovered that his warehouse was practically empty. Assuming Dave did take it without permission, a truckload of stolen wine I calculate to be a second-degree felony. However, there are other charges. Besides grand theft, Dave is charged with several violations of chapter 812, fleeing a police officer to

58

avoid arrest, third-degree burglary of an unoccupied structure, criminal mischief, and farm theft."

Farm theft? There's a special category for that?

"Given the facts as I know them to be now, a good defense doesn't immediately present itself, so we should consider negotiating a reasonable plea bargain if, as Dave suggested, Mr. Stallings doesn't agree to drop the charges after recovering his wine. What Dave has suggested is—"

I interrupted. There was no need to go over Farmer Dave's case in detail because my plan was that as soon as he was physically free, he was skipping out on bail and going west or north or anywhere but in my backyard, and I had about ten more volumes of transcripts to commit to color-coded memory, plus a zillion cases that Angela, my associate who was busy gestating a baby in her womb, had studiously compiled for me in her own color-coded way, and Bonita won't work on Sundays no matter how I threaten or cajole, and I should be drinking coffee not wine, even if it is organic, and so I blurted out, "I've got to go. I'll write a check right now. Get Dave out as soon as possible."

There, I said three whole sentences in a minute without once saying the word *so*.

CHAPTER 7

I still had the damn Winn-Dixie sack full of money with me when I drove into my own driveway. I also had a lighter checking-account balance and another case of Mr. Stallings's very fine wine, both products of my last ten minutes with Philip, my putative new boyfriend. But it was the sack of money that occupied my tired brain at the moment. Philip's first idea—that I count it and lock it in the Smith, O'Leary, and Stanley safe—didn't really appeal to me now, as it was the wee hours and all I wanted to do was shower about four times and crash in my own bed. I decided just to stash the money in the kitchen cupboard as if the sack was full of groceries.

My purse lurched off my arm as I grabbed the paper sack and crawled out of my Honda, and as I bent to pick it up, I heard Bearess, behind my front door, set up a howl. Oh, good, that'll cause a few Covenant Nazi phone calls, I thought as I picked up my purse and took a couple of steps toward the door. The key lime tree, which had proved to be an impressively aggressive grower, cast part of the walkway to the door in total darkness; I stepped into that circle of pitch-black and was struggling for my keys when I heard an odd cracking noise and then felt a jolt of pain in my head.

I stumbled down, and a dark shadow snatched the Winn-Dixie sack, and I yelled, and the black shape ran off.

Shutting my eyes seemed appealing to me at that moment, so I did. When I opened them again, Bearess was howling like a vampire dog at the full moon of Armageddon, and Covenant Nazi had my head in her lap, stroking my forehead and murmuring that "it will be all right."

"Let me up," I said, intent upon opening the door and letting Bearess out before she exploded with pent-up doggy anxiety.

"I've called the police and an ambulance," the now surprisingly gentle voice of Covenant Nazi said. "Just lie still." Her fingers on my forehead were feathery. Her lap was soft. She smelled like the same Avon stuff my grandmother used to wear. I might have fallen asleep in this soft, sweet-smelling lap except for the increasingly shrill noise that my dog was making as she clawed at the other side of my door.

Okay, I get it. The Rapture happened, I got zapped as a near miss, Nazi Lady was transformed into an angel of mercy, and Bearess was now the eight-horned Beast from Revelations. Or was it ten horns and eight heads? I'd have to ask Delvon, my Pentecostal, dope-growing, mad-hatter brother, how many horns and heads the Beast had. He knew these things.

Then I forgot to wonder how many horns the beast had because my head throbbed like a son of a bitch, but I half sat up and looked around me. I was a little swimmy headed. My purse strap was still twisted about my shoulder and the purse itself lay by my side, but I couldn't see or feel the grocery sack of money.

"Where's my sack?" I asked, lying back down and reaching my hands out as far as I could and feeling in the grass, even as I heard the sound of approaching sirens. Oh, great, if anybody on the entire street of Tulip had managed to sleep through the Hound from Hell, the sirens should wake them up.

"Oh, sweetie, don't worry about your groceries."

I wasn't worried about groceries, I was worried about the uncounted cash from gosh-knows-what source that a time-warp hippie had thrust into my caretaking to use to get Dave out of jail. But explaining this to my neighbor didn't seem like a good idea.

A flash of bright red lights flew up my driveway, and as I wiggled my fingers and toes and decided I didn't need an ambulance, I wondered if I had to pay for it since I didn't call it and was it too late to send it back?

But then, as the paramedic leaned over me, I closed my eyes again. If an ambulance took me to the hospital and I got admitted, then surely I could postpone that damned appellate argument in the case of the alien-nut lady versus the fake Indian man.

As it turned out, I didn't get admitted to the hospital. I didn't even get an X ray, CAT scan, or MRI. I waited exactly three hours and twenty minutes to have a woman doctor, who, I might add, should maybe ease up on the carbs or at least wear control-top hose, spend about two minutes and proclaim me okay.

Okay? Somebody had hit me on the head. Hard. How could I be okay? Didn't I at least get an MRI?

"You don't need an MRI," she said, and blabbered words until I translated that my health insurer had denied the request.

"Ice the bump. Take some aspirin," the broad-butted doctor said without sympathy.

Not a productive doctor visit by my standards. And that three-hour wait didn't improve my mood. Nor had the entertainment options done much to appease me while I waited for my two minutes with the doc. During the first part of the wait, a police officer had grilled me on what happened.

"I dropped my purse, a dark shadow stole my groceries, and this woman called the police," I said, pointing at my new best friend, Covenant Nazi, who had insisted on riding with me in the ambulance to the ER. She had patted my hand the whole way.

When the police officer gave me a look of disgust at my succinct, but from my view, totally accurate summary of events, my new best friend said, "What happened, Mr. Officer, was that a man, probably one of the homeless you people don't seem very effective at controlling, hid behind her key lime tree, which I've been telling her and telling her to trim, and he knocked her down and stole her groceries, though why anyone would go grocery shopping at the Winn-Dixie at that hour of the night is beyond me, but you know these young professional women."

I sighed.

Then my neighbor launched into a twenty-minute story about a cat, and I couldn't tell whether it was her cat, or someone else's cat, or what, and didn't much care, but the reason, so she claimed, she saw all this, the key lime tree and the homeless man, that is, was she was outside because of this cat.

Yeah, right. She was peeking out the window spying on me.

For purposes of his paperwork, the cop asked me the approximate value of my groceries.

"Thirty dollars," I lied.

Explaining about the money would be digging the hole deeper, so I didn't. But who could have known about the money and waited for me? Hippie Woman, maybe, but why give me the money and then steal it back? Was it a homeless person thinking he was getting a sack of food?

I was still pondering the who and the how when I was released by Dr. Big Butt, and I ambled out into the bright lights and sour smell of the ER waiting room to find my neighbor sipping a cup of coffee with someone in a white uniform. "Your grandmother is so sweet," this person said as she left.

"How are we going to get home?" my new grandmother asked.

I sighed. I didn't suppose the ambulance would take us home, and the cop had long since heard enough about the cat and left, so I looked around for a cabdriver type.

Though I was the wounded one, I had to look outside for a cab while Grandmom finished her coffee. Typical Sarasota, all the traffic and crime of a big city with few of the conveniences like all-night cab service. Then I had to use my last quarters to call all the cabs in the yellow pages, only to find out that at 4:25 A.M., no one was going to get out of bed to drive me the six blocks to my house.

"I'm in the ER. I'm hurt and I've got a ninety-year-old woman with me, I can't walk home at night," I shouted at the phone.

"I'm only seventy-seven," Grandmom said, "and it isn't night, it's morning."

I slammed down the phone, and glowered at my neighbor.

"Why don't you call that Mexican who's always coming over? That one who wears that yellow dress over his pants."

At first I thought she meant Benny, but the yellow dress sounded like Gandhi Singh.

"He's not Mexican," I said.

He's not even Indian, I thought. Gandhi was a bummed-up surfer, a natural blond, with an Internet degree in counseling and a mediocre hair-dye job. But given a choice between waking up Gandhi or waiting in the ER until the cab-drivers woke up, I opted to bother Gandhi. After I panhandled some more quarters, I punched in Gandhi's number on the pay phone, made a mental note to disinfect myself from the ER phone and the ER as soon as I got home, and spilled a condensed version of the problem to Gandhi. Once I reassured him I was fine, he said he'd be right there.

When he arrived a half hour later, he waved some smoldering dried flowers over me—sage, to burn off the evil spirits of the night, he explained—then handed the sage to a hunched man in a chair, said a blessing over the man, and told my new grandmom that her aura indicated a new person would soon enter her life, perhaps a child.

Okay, so he looked like a fool and talked like a fortune cookie, but Gandhi had gotten out of bed at dawn to drive me and a previously unknown seventy-seven-year-old woman six blocks. I had to appreciate a guy like that.

CHAPTER 8

When the collective cosmic forces are so obviously against one taking a chosen path, it is better just to give up that chosen path and go, as they say, with the flow.

Or at least that's one of the theories of life that Farmer Dave had taught me in my formative years, when I was a teenager living with him and my brother in a house in the woods in a place where neither UPS nor the U.S. mail would go, but as it turned out, the state police would.

Go with the flow, I thought.

And the flow of cosmic forces having thus far decreed that I was not to spend the weekend in quiet preparation for my upcoming appellate argument, I rose midmorning on Sunday and said the hell with it.

I was woozy from fatigue and the lump on my head, and I chewed some chocolate-covered roasted coffee beans—I mean, really, why do people need amphetamines when you can chew chocolate-coated pure caffeine?—while I brewed my organic, shade-grown, fair-trade coffee in my nonplastic French press and formulated plan B.

After all, I still had Monday to work on my oral argument.

Today, once I was coherent, I was going to drive out to Earl Stallings's winery, meet the man, utterly charm the man, and convince him to drop the charges against Dave. Wasn't that one of Philip's plans? I mean, if Earl got his wine back, why wouldn't he drop the charges? I marshaled my arguments—all that time testifying in depositions and at trial, having Philip making him look like a fool, et cetera.

Surely, if I took care of Earl, Philip could deal with the little matter of the outstanding warrant for trashing out Delvon's neighbors' motocross track. I mean, come on, there's real crime out there: Was Georgia really going to extradite Dave for plowing down fake hills that the boys used to race their motorcycles on?

As I drank my coffee, I rubbed the back of my head and made a note to have Bonita send Gandhi and my new grandmom some fruit or something by way of thanks for their help last night. After Gandhi had driven us home from the ER, I had finally tumbled into my own house, to find a totally hysterical Bearess, and after walking her, calming her, petting her, cleaning up the indiscretions she'd left in her doggy frenzy, and then taking my anti-jail-germ shower, soaking in the tub to ease my sore muscles, and then showering off the tub residue, there was sunlight before I actually got to crash out in my own bed. Naturally I had just hit the dream stage when the phone rang and it was Grandmom, aka Covenant Nazi, wanting to know how I was doing.

"I was sleeping."

"Well, you shouldn't do that, you might have a concussion, and you are not supposed to sleep when you have a concussion."

"That's why the ER doctor told me to go home and get some sleep?"

"Well, that young woman was so busy, she wasn't paying you enough attention. Would you like for me to bring you over some breakfast? I have some nice bran muffins. With raisins."

As tempting as that was, I declined because I doubted she cooked organically and I didn't know what her cleanliness standards were, and also, frankly, I wondered if I didn't like my new grandmom better wearing her World Hall Monitor personality.

Having dodged breakfast with Grandmom, I crashed out once more, was dancing at the edge of some decent REM sleep, and, damn, the phone rang again.

"Hey, babe, guess who I'm in a hot tub with?"

"Wrong number." I clunked down the phone.

Bearess snuffled around my bed, and I was debating whether I should take her out or make her wait while I napped some more when the phone rang again.

"Lilly, babe. It's Ashton. Babe, don't hang up."

I gurgled. Ashton Stanley was the third of the

three named partners at Smith, O'Leary, and Stanley. He was my law partner, my friend in a loony, not-centered sort of way, but definitely not my mentor.

"So, guess who I'm in a hot tub with."

"Ashton, it's too early for games."

"Hey, you want to know what time it is out here?"

Out here would be California, Los Angeles, to be specific, where Ashton had gone last month to check into one of those swanky drug rehabilitation centers that catered to movie stars and rich people (slogan: Detox Among the Stars). After his girlfriend had tried to kill me last year, and then jumped off the Sunshine Skyway Bridge in a flash of bare skin and midnight blue panties, Ashton, never a totem pole of sanity or sobriety to begin with, did quite the nosedive. Finally, Jackson and I had done a two-person intervention and forced Ashton to admit that for a man of his age, his chemical recreational habits weren't cute anymore. Hence, he had taken a leave of absence, creating a manic power struggle as the other partners scrambled for his lucrative files and clients and, not incidentally, taking a lot of the fun out of my life and Smith, O'Leary, and Stanley.

I missed the maniac.

But my head hurt, I was exhausted, and I didn't care who he was in a hot tub with, or what time it was in L.A., so I said, "I don't care, I was asleep."

"You can't tell anyone, she's famous," Ashton said, and I heard a girlish squeal in the background.

"But I'll give you a hint. You've seen her on television. Not this season, but, I don't know, couple, few years back."

The shortest way out of this was obviously to play along. "Okay, who are you in the hot tub with?"

I heard a splash, a louder girlish squeal, Ashton's own squeal, not unlike I imagined an elk's rutting song, and there was a bigger splash and the phone went dead.

Oh, well.

Whether I wanted it to or not, my day had begun. I accepted the cosmic message that sleep wasn't in my particular cards, and I got up, waited on my one-hundred-pound dog, swallowed my aspirin and ate my coco-coffee beans and drank my pot of coffee, and decided that on the off-chance I might want a stomach lining in my old age, I should eat some food to soften the blow of the coffee. So I ate some granola. Then I called Benny to see how he was doing. In that teenage I'm-too-cool-to-worry tone he was perfecting, he assured me he was doing just fine. I doubted this, and suggested I go over later that afternoon and we'd talk. While I didn't hear the sound of happy feet dancing in glee, he more or less agreed.

Still worrying about Benny, I showered. By the time I finished showering, washing my hair again, and contemplating what one wore to a winery to convince a man to drop charges for felony theft, it was early afternoon. Dressed in a short jeans skirt and a cropped knit blouse and another pair

71

of kicky sandals, I drove out to the winery. Fortunately, the wine labels gave an address on a road I recognized, and the sun was bright, the sky cloudless, and the air warm and damp as I peeled out of my driveway and headed east.

And practically stopped, hitting the traffic pockets on Clark Road.

By the time I got to the winery, which advertised on its label that it was open seven days a week, my gel-sleeked hair was a wiry, fuzzy halo in the humidity and I seriously craved iced tea.

Pulling into a long, dirt road, I followed the signs to the "Gift and Wine Shoppe" and parked. Why on earth were there other people here? Why weren't they at the beach? It was spring, it was Sunday, it was prime skin-cancer and jellyfish-sting time.

Inside, I saw a thin man, with wire-framed glasses and a high forehead, very high, actually, and a blond ponytail. He was chatting with two women who had big heads of permed hair teased into ridiculous ball fluffs that looked like wet poodles on crystal meth.

The squatter of the two women was asking what a muscadine was as I sashayed up to join them. The man looked at me, tentatively, I thought, so I smiled brightly and he nodded. His brow was permanently furrowed, but his eyes were bright blue, and his chin was strong and clean. A nice-looking man, a man who looked smart, dressed in his khakis and a white polo and brown loafers. William Hurt, twenty pounds underweight, I thought. I smiled so persistently at him, he finally smiled back.

"What's a muscadine?" the squat woman whined through her nose again, as her buddy turned to glare at me.

"It is a particular kind of grape . . ."

Uh-huh, I thought. Now how do I get this man alone and find out if he is Earl Stallings and then convince him to let old Dave and Waylon go their way in peace? I ran a finger slowly along the scooped neckline of my knit shirt, and, for icing on the Look-at-Me, Look-at-Me cake, I made a ponytail of my thick hair with my hand, lifting it high in the air as if cooling off my neck, and then I let it fall in a slow cascade. Works every time. Maybe-Earl watched me, smiled, and paused in his monologue.

"You'se gonna tell us about that grape, now, or what?" Poodle Head asked.

Pulling his eyes from me, our host said, "The muscadine grape is actually a Florida native."

That was certainly more than these ladies, or 99 percent of the Sarasota population, could claim, I thought, and made myself look fascinated by Maybe-Earl's recitation of the wonders of our native grape.

By the time he had finished his muscadine monologue, the permed hairs were noticeably bored. I raised my hand, and smiled again.

"Yes," the man who might be Earl said.

"Excuse me," I said, "but I was wondering if you could explain about why your wine is organic?"

I know all about organic myself, but I pegged my nonnative companions as the sorts who would walk off in boredom or disgust as Maybe-Earl launched into a second monologue about farming organically. Damn them, the ladies held their place as our teacher preached the dangers of strip farming and the lost topsoil and the horrors of pesticides— cancer, dead birds, dead good bugs, disruption of the balance of nature, reproductive abnormalities among humans and reptiles, et cetera, et cetera. Rachel Carson would have been proud.

As Maybe-Earl talked, I began to appreciate his voice, a deep, clear voice with the softening trace of a southern accent, with perfect grammar and well-chosen words. Definitely a smart man. The more I looked at him, the more he seemed to me to be one of those New Age nerd hippies who either make money in software or go to jail for starting meth labs.

But Poodle Heads hung in there, not listening, exactly, but holding their ground.

"What about the sulfite-free sign you've got up there," I asked, figuring a similar lecture on sulfites would surely drive the two women away.

"Sulfites occur naturally, to some degree, in wines, but the problem is that sulfites are added during the wine-making process as both a disinfectant and a preservative. Sulfites are controversial, that is, whether they are innately unhealthy or not, but it's an accepted fact that many people are allergic to them. There's a well-supported theory that the infamous wine headache is actually a reaction to the added sulfites."

I nodded and smiled.

"To get an organic label, a wine must be made without sulfites. But to make a large amount of wine without sulfites is tricky. Everything has to be perfect. The least miscalculation and you've got a barrel of moldy wine."

"That's disgusting," squat Poodle Head said.

"Ah," our environmentally sound vintner added, "but I don't have that problem because I've perfected the system. There are neither sulfites nor mold in my wine. My system is labor intensive and that drives up the cost. But it also increases the quality, the taste, and the healthfulness of my wine."

"Let's try some and see," the lesser-squat woman said.

Oh, great. If they started drinking free wine, I'd never get them to leave me and this smart, Maybe-Earl man alone.

Remembering the flirty-girl tip to always ask a man questions about stuff he wants to talk about, I asked if muscadine grapes gave the wine any distinctive qualities.

Smiling now in earnest, he explained that the native muscadine grapes are distinctive because of their 2-phenylethanol content. One of the ladies harrumphed, but he ignored her, and asked me if I knew what that was.

Yeah, sure, it's a long, boring word. But I leaned toward Maybe-Earl. "No. Please explain."

Earl, if this was Earl, was warming up to me and he was pleased to explain. "It's the substance that also gives roses their characteristic fragrance."

I made a little gasp of appreciation.

Outside, there was a sound of engine, a gust of diesel smell, and the slamming of doors, and I stretched my neck until I could see out the window and saw a whole damn busload of old people getting off. Didn't the snowbirds go home in the spring anymore?

They toddled in. Maybe-Earl went to greet them, and it became quickly obvious that this was an arranged tour. He invited me and the two Poodle Heads to join them. A tour I didn't need; privacy with the real Earl I needed, so I thanked him, but declined.

As I declined, I offered my hand. "Lilly," I said. "I've so enjoyed this. Count on me coming back."

"Earl Stallings," he said, "please do."

"Actually," I said, not wanting to give up now that I knew this was the famous Earl the Vintner, "but, with your permission"—big smile and little pause—"I think I'll just wander around a bit on my own, until you have a few minutes for me. I'd sure like to talk to you."

"That would be fine," Earl said. "Look around and I'll get this tour started in the shop, and then I'll step outside and speak with you."

We smiled so hard at each other my jaws ached, and Poodle Heads clucked their tongues together as if Earl and I were consummating our little flirts right there.

I went outside to amble around in the fresh air and wait until Earl had the tour group infatuated with his many different items for sale. Tired of watching the old folks nodding their heads at Earl through the plate-glass window, I cruised through the lot, toward the vineyard, until a big barnlike structure caught my eye. Someone had made a border of red bricks and planted a hedge of gardenias and hibiscus along the side of the barn. I huffed over toward it and poked my head right in through the big door. Nobody was home.

The barn was cool and dim, with light coming in the windows. Buckets, rakes, a little tractor, and this and thats of what I took to be the usual accouterments of farming were scattered about. I read the labels on some sacks of rock phosphate and then wandered over to a table under a window with two big, bulky things on it under a tarp.

Since nobody was about, and Earl did say, more or less, I could explore on my own, I pulled the tarp off. Under it, two strange-looking *Star Wars*-type models, or toys, or something mechanical and mostly metal sat on the table. They were similar, and they were each about four or five feet high, little models that appeared to be workable, with little, metal, robot-type arms on the sides of miniature motors in a center frame. They appeared complex, but with no obvious purpose.

Weird. What, Earl made *Star Wars* models for

recreation when he wasn't making sulfite-free wine?

Behind me, the barn door opened and I turned and saw a small, dark man with the look of mixed Spanish and Indian blood. "You no supposed to be here," he said.

"Oh, no, it's all right. I'm a friend of Earl and he said it was okay."

"No. *¡Fuera de aqui!* Get." The short, dark man pulled his features into a vaguely menacing look.

Well, all right. Be that way.

"Can do," I said. Jogging through the barn toward the exit, I shoved past the little man and walked out.

Behind me, the little man slammed the barn door.

Not totally frustrated yet, but close, I went back around to the front door of the Gift and Wine Shoppe and went in. Earl was explaining to the tour group what a muscadine was.

Earl raised his eyebrows at me, and I smiled as a bent man screeched a question into Earl's face. Then Earl poured little wine samples for the tour group, and slipped over to me while they slurped down his fine, organic wine.

"Lilly," he said, smiled, and pushed his glasses up on his nose.

"Earl."

Okay, we knew who we were. Now how did I launch into my mission? "I'm actually here on business, of a sort."

"You'd like to buy in bulk?"

"No. Thank you. But I would like to buy a case. I'm a lawyer, and I'm here on behalf of Dave Baggwell, and his friend Waylon, er, Waylon." I realized I didn't know Waylon's last name.

Earl nodded, and I thought he looked disappointed in me. "You want me to forget prosecuting them over the wine, that is, if I get it back?"

"Oh, yes, that would be so much better for everybody. Oh, and better for you especially. You really don't want to get tied up in testifying and wasting all that time going to court. Do you have any idea how much time it takes, and how irritating it is, to be sucked into the criminal-justice system, even as the"—technically, *victim* was the word here, but that wasn't the connotation I wanted, so I paused and waited for the blue god of wordsmithing to descend with just the right phrase—"eh, witness, and if you drop the charges, I will personally see that you are reimbursed for any losses. Plus, of course, the wine will be returned."

"Yeah. That other lawyer, Philip Cohen, has already spoken with me too."

Oh, good for Philip, I thought, early worm and all that. Of course, not having spent the night in the ER, he could get up earlier.

"And we can count on your cooperation?" Beam, beam, beam toward Earl.

"I will tell you what I told him. I will think about it. I'll call him and let him know what I've decided. But Dave and Waylon were employees of mine, and I can't tolerate theft by employees."

"Oh, I think it was more of a"—A what exactly, a bad joke? An extremely bad idea? A typical Dave money-for-nothing adventure?—"a frolic. They're not career criminals, or anything. I don't think they will bother you again."

"No, one way or the other, I'm sure they won't. And like I said, I will think about dropping the charges. But I have other things on my mind now, more important things."

"Earl, thank you. I know you will do the right thing." I offered my hand, and to my pleasant surprise, he took it. "You do have a wonderful place here, and I would like to buy a case of your wine."

"You don't have to. I can't be bribed that easily."

"I really like your wine, it's not bribery."

He nodded, and I bought a case of his wine, and I tried during the transaction to get us back to the smile, smile, flirt, flirt stage, but he wasn't going back there, so I took my wine and left him to his old-people tour.

In light of future events, I should have stayed longer and asked more questions. Or gone back after the tour was over. But, after all, I'd had a pretty rough Saturday and, unlike Gandhi, I didn't have the gift of seeing beyond the moment, and was nearly nauseous with exhaustion and thirst. So I went home, drank iced tea, washed up, and then Bearess and I went over to Bonita's and picked up Benny.

Benny was in no mood to talk. He was in no mood to do anything. If there was anything more to his Saturday adventures with Farmer Dave, he wasn't telling me about it, bent as he was on a course of action that involved staring at his feet and mumbling incoherent not-sweet nothings. We hung out on the track at the middle school and watched Bearess run around in circles while Benny refused to talk to me. Finally Bearess laid her big head on Benny's legs and slobbered until she caught her breath.

I took it as a bad sign that Benny did not pet Bearess as she draped herself over him.

CHAPTER 9

Monday morning I awoke early with a sense of panic pounding my chest and watering my eyes.

Most lawyers, the litigators at least, wake up on Monday mornings with exactly that same feeling.

Having lost the weekend, and with a looming appellate argument on Tuesday morning, I was left with a frantic sense of having run out of time. I hustled myself to the office as quick as a little bunny on steroids, and I hoped my hands would stop sweating as the day wore on.

Inside Smith, O'Leary, and Stanley, I marched past Bonita, sitting prim and pretty at her desk in her little cubbyhole office outside my big office, and I hissed, "Don't let anyone, not anybody, past my door."

I slammed my way into my office with its scenic view of the parking lot and cranked open the window for a touch of real air and threw my briefcase on my desk.

When I turned around twice, like a cat selecting a nap spot, I saw that Bonita had already made my coffee, so I poured a cup and smelled it and began to formulate a plan of preparation that didn't involve stolen organic wine or boys from my past.

But first I called Earl and got no answer. Then I called Philip, and after working my way through his receptionist and then his secretary, I demanded a direct line, which Philip gave me.

"Do you charge a set fee for phone calls, or bill according to the actual time spent on the phone?" This would determine how much flirty, polite stuff I said.

"I bill the actual time," Philip said.

"Dave still in jail?"

"Yes."

"Earl drop the charges?"

"No, not yet."

"Okay, 'bye." I hung up the phone, jotted down two minutes so I could check Philip for honest billing, and picked up my cup of coffee.

Before I had finished my first cup, my office door burst open with a blast of the chilly, artificial office air and I shivered.

My associate, Angela, huge with child, teetered on her feet with the misbalance caused by a gestating baby on her petite frame.

Poor Angela. Pregnancy had not made her glow. She had three inches of orange roots showing in her curly auburn bob and not a speck of Maybelline on her pale eyes.

"Brock, every six weeks, rain or shine or baby," I said, pointing at her hair as if she had barged in for beauty advice. Brock was our hairdresser and my primary therapist and I'd introduced Angela to him when I had decided that instead of being my overworked, mousy-faced, orange-haired associate, Angela should be an overworked world-class beauty. That makeover had also facilitated her theft of my own boyfriend Newly Moneta, who was now her husband and the father of the baby brewing inside her. Her world-class beauty, in pint size, had lasted only until she blew up with unnamed Baby Moneta and stopped using her makeup and having Brock color her hair.

Angela shook a handful of paper at me.

"Brock, once every six weeks, Angela, and Maybelline on the lashes and L'Oréal on the lips," I repeated in case being pregnant made her deaf.

"Chemicals," she said. "Baby."

Since becoming huge with child, Angela was too tired and frazzled to waste time on extraneous words. Though she still communicated what was necessary, her terseness was not a great trait in a lawyer, lawyers being paid to talk, that is, and I was a little afraid to send her to hearings these days.

As I mused on Angela's immediate future, she advanced upon me and practically smashed my face with her handful of paper. Pregnancy had also, I noted, and not for the first time, made her unusually aggressive. This was a good trait in a lawyer, although not necessarily when directed at me, but I let it go and took the papers.

They were copies of a memo to the law clerks, requesting legal research on the issue of whether a plaintiff's fraud in calculating the amount of damages in a wrongful-death claim could be used to vacate the whole judgment.

Oh, yawn.

"This doesn't have anything to do with us. You're not a law clerk and it's not my case." I thrust the papers back at Angela.

Angela took the papers only to rustle them under my nose and shove them back into my hand.

Okay, okay, okay. I looked past the first paragraph in the memo. I didn't see my name in it, or Angela's, for that matter, so I scanned again for the gist. A request for legal research on recouping a judgment in a wrongful-death case. Something about fraudulently claiming the decedent had more children than he actually did to jack up the amount of the ultimate judgment.

When I looked up from the memo, Angela nodded her head emphatically.

Okay, a whole sentence from her would be helpful. But I took a whirl at interpretation.

"You found this in the library?"

Nod, nod.

I looked down at the memo again. Dated today, and fresh from the desk of Kenneth U. Mallory. Nothing of Kenneth's was anything I wanted anything to do with, especially not right now, the morning of the last day on earth I had to complete the preparation for my oral argument.

But I wasn't going to cross that look on Angela's face, and so I said, "Kenneth is doing research, on fraud and recoupment? Right? Relief from judgment, right? And this is important to you and me, why?"

Angela turned and pointed to the wall beyond which Bonita was allegedly busily protecting me by keeping people like Angela out of my office.

No bells went off.

Angela again punched at the paper in my hand.

I continued scanning down the paragraphs of Kenneth's request for legal research. Then I saw it: the words *widow* and *dependents* and *five*.

Bonita was a widow with five dependents, and Newly had won her a sizable wrongful-death judgment in a product-liability case when a bottling machine at the local orange-juice processing plant had eaten Bonita's husband alive. His workers' compensation benefits had been wholly insignificant, as, of course, they always are, but the product-liability award in the wrongful-death case was not.

That Kenneth was looking into this didn't smell right. Spearheading research aimed at trying to take back the judgment from Bonita and her five kids seemed evil even for Kenneth. Especially since she worked for the same law firm where he was a partner. And especially since he had not represented the bottling company in the initial wrongful-death suit.

What the hell?

"This is wrong," Angela said, and punched the paper in my hand with her finger. "Stop him."

Oh, good, I thought, a whole sentence. Plus, a command.

"Would you like to sit down?" I asked.

But Angela had already turned away and was lurching back out my door, which Bonita, rising from her chair, tiptoed over to close behind her.

Kenneth Mallory. *Mierda.*

Why on earth would Kenneth take a case against one of our own people?

Then a bigger question occurred to me: Why, in a city with an average of one attorney per ten people, would the bottling company hire Kenneth to go after a secretary from his own law firm?

That suggested to me that Kenneth was the instigator in luring the bottling company to him as a client and convincing them to sue Bonita for fraud and relief from judgment.

Of course, lawyers in a competitive society were not above recruiting their own clients. When done with finesse, this was called rainmaking. When done with sleeze, it was called ambulance chasing.

Okay, odd as this was, I was going to have to do something. It was one thing that Kenneth was bugging the crap out of Jackson to make the firm pay for his stupid Hummer, but Jackson was a big boy and could fight back, fair and unfair. But for Kenneth to be inducing the bottling company to go after Bonita was unconscionable.

Bonita was my secretary, and my friend, and the rock upon which I daily hurled my obsessions and petty complaints and half-baked theories, and she never raised her voice at me, well, almost never, and I owed her, owed her big, and Kenneth was the slime left in the bottom of the trash Dumpster. I would, as Angela the Petite had said, find some way to stop him.

But not now. Now I had an appellate argument looming in the very near and scary future and a fifteen-year-old boy to worry about and a missing grocery sack of gosh-knows whose or how much money.

I leaned over my desk and punched a key on my laptop, which Bonita had already booted up and opened to WordPerfect, and I began a cursory first draft of my proposed appellate argument. Everything else was just going to have to wait.

CHAPTER 10

On my oral argument D day, I woke early, did a double dose of visualizations, a double dose of coffee just in case I wasn't jittery enough, threw up the coffee, redid the visualization, drank more coffee, and showered a second time because, air-conditioning or not, I was sweating like a pig.

At 5:30 A.M., Bearess started barking at the front door.

Dressed in my lucky oral-argument slip and in the middle of my warrior visualization, I tiptoed to the door to look out the peephole, under the general assumption that my new grandmom next door was spying on me or bringing me muffins, or that Bearess was hallucinating. Gandhi and some skinny woman with spiked white hair, and who was totally overcrystalized, stood there. Whoa, didn't she know those crystal things were so very eighties?

Too stunned not to, I let them in, but with the opening admonition that Gandhi was not going with me to Lakeland to the oral argument.

Gandhi introduced the skinny woman, who wore

crystal earrings, crystal necklaces one on top of the other, and a crystal charm bracelet, as Keisha.

Crystal Girl and I nodded at each other.

Keisha, Gandhi explained, was his girlfriend. And she had generously come to help me get centered by laying crystals on my meridians and manipulating my chakras and otherwise doing hokum-pocus stuff.

"Don't have the time," I snapped.

"I insist, and I'm the client," Gandhi said. "You are not well centered. Your aura is not right."

Glancing at the wall clock, I did a quick calculation, allowing for the possibility of another throw up and another shower, and said, "Ten minutes, but I'm billing you for this."

Keisha made me lie down, and she did whatever it was she did, including something with hot rocks, and Bearess kept whining as if somebody was blowing one of those whistles that only dogs hear. Then it was over. Keisha mercifully left, and Gandhi said he would drive us to the courthouse in Lakeland in his car as he didn't trust my car, and until then, he would wait outside, and by the way, I looked very nice in my slip.

In my anxiety, I had forgotten that I wasn't dressed.

That should have been a clue as to how my appellate argument was going to go.

CHAPTER 11

Driving the back roads from Sarasota to Lakeland was like taking the road through the Florida that used to be. In spots, that is. Small orange groves and tomato fields and pastures with long-horned cattle grazing among the palmetto scrubs, and little towns like Duette and Fort Lonesome, with tin-roofed cracker houses, and long, straight, worn-out roads traveled by people in old pickups who waved at you when you passed them. In the early spring, when the orange trees were blooming, I particularly loved this drive through the dense groves of Hardee County, where the orange-blossom perfume would permeate my car and cling to my hair for hours.

Some mornings I had driven through these blooming orange groves with the sun coming up behind the bright green trees and thought that God might be a Florida cracker who lived in an orange grove and ate fresh mullet and homegrown tomatoes.

But this morning, with Gandhi driving and me frantically reviewing my typed and indexed and color-coded notes, to my horror I saw that the

Hardee County grove I loved the most had been plowed down, and a "Coming Soon, Orange Blossom Plaza" sign stood in a field of mud and stumps where just two months ago thick green trees with rich orange fruit had been living. The sign had what looked to me like a big peach painted on it. Damn Yankee developers didn't even know a peach from an orange. That set me off on a verbal rant about mall warts and developers. Gandhi patted my leg.

About the time I stopped hyperventilating over the plowed-up oranges, we hit bone valley, the phosphate-rich region in central Florida, and I heard Gandhi gasp as he slowed his car to look.

"What is it?" he said, staring out the windows as a strange fog rolled in over the scarred, moonscape world of phosphate strip mining.

"Phosphate mines," I said. "Be careful, there are a lot of phosphate trucks hauling ass on these roads."

Even as I warned him, a rock-hopper loomed suddenly out of the fog in the plundered landscape, riding our bumper, honking, and then hurling past us, passing blind in the morning fog; there was a touch of the netherworld about it.

Shivering, I stopped looking at my notes and looked about me at the gray, gouged-out pathos of these holes, these ruined scrublands, desolate even before the miners were done, pockmarked with holes and studded with earthen dams full of radioactive phosphate-gypsum slime, slime that leached its poisons into the meager remaining groundwaters.

Yeah, definitely, God gave up on Florida and left.

Why not? He gave us paradise, complete with dolphins and manatees and palms and oranges, and plenty of water, a subtropical wonder of rich soil, sunlight, and rain, where you could plant a stick in the dirt and it would grow into a tree, and look what we had done to it. Pink condos, malls and strip malls, Disney and phosphate, tourists and people who came here to die. We'd messed it up so bad it wouldn't even rain anymore, the concrete earth and the high buildings having blocked the flow of the clouds and the moisture-heavy Gulf breezes and disturbed the natural processes that had once given us steady summer-afternoon showers.

Rather than stop building and paving and mining, the state just built desalinization plants so we could drink the Gulf of Mexico and then dump the waste brine back into the Gulf in an experiment to see how long it would take to kill the Gulf of Mexico.

Maybe when we were down to the last orange grove, Disney would buy it and charge admission. Maybe when we were down to the last fish and the last glass of water, the carpetbaggers would quit and leave.

Naturally, pondering these things, I was good and pissed off by the time we got to the courthouse in Lakeland. Better than coffee to keep one alert after only three hours of sleep.

After signing in, I milled around, tried to fake

out the other attorneys who were milling around and trying to fake me out. Then we went into the courtroom and waited.

The bailiff stood up just as I had finished explaining to Gandhi that the judges would not rule today, but would discuss the case post-oral argument. After reaching a decision, one of them would write a formal opinion of the court, which would be mailed to me. It could be anywhere from two weeks to two months, or longer, before I got a copy of the decision from the court.

Gandhi nodded and I reiterated that he was to sit still and under no circumstances say a word to anyone about anything. As my stomach lurched, the bailiff did her "May God save this honorable court," and I wiped my hands. When the case of the Nut Lady Alien Abductee versus the Fake Indian Guru was called, I proudly went and took my place at the counsel table, my face to the judges, my back to my client.

My opposing counsel, who had arrived without his client, and judging from his visible disarray, without having had his chakras manipulated, argued first, as he represented the party seeking the appeal. Hair awhirl and tie askew, Nut Lady's attorney stood behind the podium and began the time-honored plea, "May it please the court . . ."

Pen poised for jotting down any good rebuttal points his argument might inspire, I studiously listened. According to the man with the crooked tie, his client, the very nice and not at all wacky lady from Longboat Key, had in good faith hired my client, the evil and wholly inept defendant, to help her recover from the emotional trauma of having been kidnapped by space aliens.

The good lawyer in his disarrayed gray said this with a steady voice.

But my client, the lawyer continued, far from helping his client, had in fact made things worse through a series of unrecognized and unprofessional techniques involving past-life regressions, deep hypnosis, submersion therapy, crystal acupuncture, and drum circles, all of which had led this woman to ultimately believe, whether falsely or truly, that she herself was a space alien, left behind in another life and therefore homeless (though she lived in a mansion on the Gulf of Mexico), and now she was out all of that money, and was worse off than ever. And I, evil defense lawyer that I was, unfairly and sinfully and unethically and probably through other undiscovered skullduggery had convinced the very old and totally ignorant trial judge to grant Fake Indian Counselor a summary judgment, depriving Miss Not-a-Nut of her fair and constitutional day before a jury of her peers. Blah, blah, blah, blah.

Okay, standard plaintiff's-attorney stuff. Boiled down to let the lady have her crapshoot with a jury.

Not one of the three-judge panel asked him a single question.

Good, I thought, a cold bench. I can recite my speech, while looking earnest and pert, and go home, no worse for the wear.

This was pretty naive from a woman who had answered her front door in her slip at 5:30 A.M., and then ridden through the fog-and-phosphate netherworld with a man in a yellow dress over his khakis.

I moved forward slowly, projecting a confidence I didn't feel but had learned to fake nicely, and gliding behind the podium, I adjusted my notes, smiled at the bailiff to let her know to start the clock running on my twenty minutes, and I said, "May it please the court, I am Lillian Cleary, with the law firm of Smith, O'Leary, and—"

From behind me, I heard the sound of movement, and Gandhi said, "And Your Honors, I am Gandhi Singh."

Whirling around, I glared at him. "Please do not speak." I said this with my eyes glinted down and my lips stretched wide and thin, a look Jackson had taught me, one that says, "I *will* hurt you."

I turned back to the judges, transforming my face back to earnest and pert.

"I am here this morning," I began again, "on behalf of my client—"

"Is it true, Ms. Cleary," the presiding chief judge interrupted, "that your sole legal argument before the trial judge was that this case was just, let's see, what was your quote from the hearing, 'just plain silly.' I believe that's what the transcript revealed."

"Your Honor, as the record reflects, I filed an extensive memorandum of law with the trial judge before that hearing, in support of our position that there simply is no standard of care in this type of situation as a matter of law, and without a set medical protocol or an established standard to deviate from, there can be no deviation from the established standard of care, which is, as you know, the predicate for a malpractice lawsuit, and—"

From behind me, I heard movement, and Gandhi whispered to me, "Tell them about that Oregon doctor. He used practically the same techniques I did, and—"

I whipped around and said, "Be quiet, Mr. Singh." With my back to the panel of judges and my hands hidden from their sight, I made a fist and fake-punched the air at the height of Gandhi's stomach.

When I turned back to the three judges, the presiding chief judge glared over his glasses and asked, "Are you arguing that because there are no other therapists who provide this particular service, that is, helping people who believe they have been abducted by aliens, that the plaintiff has no cause of action because a jury cannot determine if malpractice occurred, as there is nothing to measure the defendant's actions against?"

Well, boiled down, yes, though he made it sound less attractive than I had in my brief. But I smelled a trap and was trying to sidestep it, when behind me, I heard movement, and Gandhi rose up again and said, "Your Honors, it is not true that there are no other counselors who provide assistance to those who have been kidnapped by aliens.

In Sarasota alone, there is at least one other, and in Oregon, there are—"

"Shut up, Gandhi," I hissed, whirling around to face him, and preparing to give full voice to a threat. This time my hand, still hidden from the judges, made like a pistol, one that I was firing at Gandhi's stomach.

"Is that so, Ms. Cleary?" the judge asked.

Whirling back around to the bench, I felt myself begin to redden.

"Is that so?" the judge repeated.

Yes, but I didn't want to admit to a fact that would hurt my argument, a fact that my opposing counsel had failed to establish at the trial level.

"Your Honor, the record does not reflect that information." Lawyer talk for appellate cover-up.

"But is it true? Do you know?"

"Your Honor, the record does not reflect that fact, and I am not allowed to testify before this court." Lawyer admission for yes.

"Very well, continue."

"May I testify?" Gandhi asked.

"No," I spun back toward him and shouted. "Sit down this minute. And do not say another word."

"One does not testify before an appellate court, young man," the presiding judge said. "Receiving testimony is a trial-court function. An appellate court reviews the record of the proceedings from the trial court to be certain no reversible error occurred."

Oh, as if I hadn't explained that to Gandhi about five thousand dollars' worth of times.

"But if you have a statement you would like to make," the judge continued, to my horror, "and opposing counsel has no objection, I will permit it."

Opposing counsel, no doubt enjoying the circus, jumped up and said, "No objection."

Gandhi began to walk up toward the podium.

"I object," I said.

"Lilly, it will be all right," Gandhi said, and smiled. He looked both ridiculous and oddly benign in his fake tan and yellow dress, and I wanted to kick him hard enough to make his face turn purple.

"This is all about my client's cat."

Okay, Gandhi was not a linear thinker, that I knew, but what did a cat have to do with it?

"We were making great strides toward understanding and forgiving when her cat disappeared. My other specialty is that I am a pet psychic, and after a long trance, I was able to channel this cat, who had been picked up by a neighbor. The cat was well fed, but he wanted to come home."

"Your Honor, I do object," I said, but without spirit. Everybody ignored me.

"When my client went to this neighbor, the one who had taken the cat, he naturally denied stealing the cat, and there was an altercation of sorts, and as a result, bad feelings. I believe the neighbor called the police. My client blames me for this, as the cat came home on its own the next day, but the neighbor is still angry."

"But she didn't sue you for . . . cat . . . ?" Even as intelligent a jurist as the presiding judge was, he couldn't figure out what the cat cause of action would be.

"Any count for fraud?" asked the judge on the left.

"No, Your Honor," I said, jumping in. I shoved Gandhi aside, and was fully hopeful of regaining the moment and making at least some valid point on Gandhi's behalf. "As I was saying, there being no established standard—"

The judge on the right asked, "Any reason we shouldn't remand and let the plaintiff amend her complaint to plead fraud?"

Oh, a hundred reasons, primarily that I might possibly lose a fraud lawsuit, but no reasons that were legally cognizable at this time popped into my head.

"I am not a fraud," Gandhi proclaimed.

"Isn't that a classic question of fact for the jury?" the judge on the left asked.

"Your Honor," I started, "there is nothing in the plaintiff's complaint even vaguely suggestive of a fraud count." Stamp, stamp went my one foot. "The plaintiff did not plead fraud in her complaint. This case is not about fraud."

"Isn't it?" The judge on the right was not giving up easily.

"Your twenty minutes are up," said the presiding judge.

I had been having so much fun, I hadn't noticed how the time had flown by.

"Your Honors, if I might just have a moment to finish addressing the questions raised about fraud?"

"No," the presiding judge said. "We have your appellate brief." Translation: Sit down and shut up.

"We'll take this under advisement, and we will let you know our decision." Having so spoken, the presiding judge nodded to the bailiff as if to say, "Next."

Mumbling, "Thank you," to the court, I sat down and decided then and there that I would fire Gandhi as a client if I didn't kill him first.

CHAPTER 12

In law school, they have this thing called moot court in which some of the students dress up like lawyers and pretend to make appellate arguments about lofty constitutional issues of the sort that 99 percent of us will not once encounter in our actual law practice. Law professors who have never in their lives made an actual court appearance pretend to teach these students how to properly present a persuasive legal argument in these dress-up mock arguments. The better students then do moot-court competitions all over the country to see who can do the best pretend arguments. Moot-court competition winners then get something impressive to put on their résumés, and get plush positions at the grand old law firms in the grand old cities, while the rest of us hump and grind and get the best jobs we can.

For law students who don't have the gumption to stand up and pretend to make mock arguments, but still want the ultimate plush jobs, law schools have something called law reviews, in which usually nerdy students rewrite law professors' multifaceted and obscenely footnoted articles. While working on law reviews, these students spend exorbitant amounts of time deciding such highly critical things as whether the period goes inside the parenthesis or outside the parenthesis.

The better law-review students from the better law schools are then hired to clerk for appellate judges, where they spend one to two years primarily summarizing huge vats of paper verbiage into smaller vats of paper verbiage so that the judges do not have to personally read the trial transcripts, briefs, and such things. The better of these lucky clerks are then offered jobs teaching at law schools. And people like me pay tuition to learn from them how to be lawyers, when in fact all these people primarily know how to do is punctuate, research, and summarize.

Thus, after three years of exhaustively dull and detailed theories taught by people who have no functional lawyering skills, and after having become impressively indebted due to the high cost of tuition and textbooks, the average law student graduates and doesn't know a single thing about how to actually practice law.

That leaves these students with two options: (1) the painful road of self-education, fraught with the embarrassment of learning almost exclusively from the process of screwing up; or (2) finding and learning from a mentor, an experienced attorney who rarely gives a rat's ass whether the period goes inside or outside the parenthesis, but knows exactly how to goad a witness on cross-examination into blowing up the opponent's whole case.

Given these options, I had been lucky my first year out of law school. After I spent a few months floundering in the cesspool of Kenneth's workers'-compensation defense work, Jackson Smith had adopted me. The fact that Jackson believed himself to be the physical reincarnation of Stonewall Jackson never bothered me in the least because I grew up in a family of crazy people. When Jackson, with his gray beard trimmed square to replicate his lemon-sucking, military-genius hero, stared at me eagle-eyed, like the portrait of his past-life persona that hung behind his desk, I didn't blanch at all. I listened. And while I listened, Jackson trained me to be a top-notch trial attorney.

Unfortunately, Jackson wasn't much of an appellate attorney himself, not having the patience for the nuances and intellectualism of that higher form of litigation. That is, he was a Rambo with Results in a jury trial, but a bull in a Palm Avenue antiques shoppe when it came to the appellate court. Thus, my training from him on conducting an appellate argument had been brief and embarrassing. When I was a first-year associate, one day without warning, Jackson picked me up by the scruff of my neck and hurled me into the deep end of the ocean, and when I clambered back to shore, he stroked his beard and nodded. I had done my first appellate argument with less than two hours of notice, but I had lived and I didn't quit and in Jackson's eyes, that was good enough.

All of which is to say that my woeful and embarrassing performance before the appellate court on Gandhi's behalf had some basis in my lack of appellate training, if not lack of preparation, but nonetheless I could hardly blame Jackson or my law school for failing to teach me how to strangle my own client in the middle of an oral argument without attracting undue attention from the panel of judges.

So naturally I blamed Gandhi.

After I had vented my spleen on him for at least a half hour under a shade tree in the parking lot of the appellate court, I informally resigned as his counsel, fired him as a client, threatened him with bodily harm if he ever came near me again, and yanked the keys from his hands and jumped in behind his Acura's driver's seat.

If he hadn't been quicker than me, I would have left him standing under the shade tree in the parking lot of the court. But even as I was backing up, he ran fast enough to hop into the passenger side of his car, which in my anger I had forgotten to lock against him.

He finally had sense enough to keep his mouth shut.

In no mood for the scenic back roads through the grimly harvested plains of bone-valley Florida, I picked up I-4 at the first chance and hurled our car west, toward Tampa. Unlike my own ancient Honda, Gandhi's car had a CD player, and after perusing his CD selections while driving ninety miles an hour in the perpetually heavy traffic, I picked out a Sheryl Crow CD, and tapped my fingers to "Run, Baby, Run" while negotiating the multicircled interchange onto I-75 south with the plan of being back in Sarasota in a jiffy so I could file a motion to withdraw as Gandhi's lawyer and kick him in his privates.

As I approached the Fruitville Road exit to Sarasota, I thought of Earl and Farmer Dave and, on a pure whim, decided to go down to the next exit, drive to the vineyard, and see personally if Earl had decided yet to drop the charges against Dave. If he hadn't, I was in just the right mood to sweet-talk him into changing his mind and freeing my man Dave.

That is, if Dave was still in jail, which he most assuredly was when I had called Philip Cohen Monday night to inquire. Philip reported that Earl had not yet dropped the charges and Dave's first court appearance had stalled out on the open question of extraditing him to Georgia. Wondering if there had been any changes this morning while Gandhi humiliated me in court, I grappled for my cell, punched in Philip's private number, and got a recording and an invitation to leave a message. "You better be getting Dave out of jail right now," I snapped, as if it were Philip's fault that Dave had trashed a motocross, stolen a truck of wine, and failed to outrun a deputy sheriff.

Earl's it was, I thought, tossing the cell in the

general vicinity of Gandhi's lap. Gandhi didn't ask where I was going when I passed our interstate exit for the next one, and then whipped his red Acura around a sharp bend and headed east with a vengeance. He had not said one word on the entire trip back.

The subdued Gandhi finally spoke as I took the turn into the vineyard too fast and spun off the pavement for a moment, sending up showers of gravel. "I don't think this is a good idea."

"Shut up," I said, neither sure nor particularly caring if he meant the side trip, my driving, or some cosmic concept beyond my immediate comprehension.

I slammed on the brakes in front of the Gift and Wine Shoppe, and stomped toward it. The door was locked and it took me a few seconds of raging before I realized there was a sign on the door that read: "In the vineyard, second road on left."

In the heat of the noon hour, I pulled off my jacket and even in my pissed-off mood, I smoothed it and folded it carefully over the seat as I got back into the car and drove down the second road on the left.

"This is definitely not a good idea," Gandhi repeated.

"Shut up," I repeated.

At the end of the dirt road, rows and rows of muscadine grapes grew on trellises of wood and wire. I got out of the car and walked toward the first row of muscadines. This early in the spring, their leaves were still a bright green, and no grapes yet bunched among the small leaves. The ground beneath the vines was clean, and at the base of each plant there was a circle of well-mulched dirt. I bent close enough to the mulch to inhale the pungent smell of mushroom compost. Short, well-tended grass grew where the grapes didn't.

Picturesque. I nodded approvingly, and stood back to study the grounds cared for by someone who obviously took pride in his vineyard.

The neat green rows began to calm me down.

Okay, I thought, looking out at the stakes with the grape tendrils crawling their way out into the bright sun on the arbor wires, so what if I lost the appeal, which certainly appeared likely. That just meant I would have to try the case. I'd get more money for trying the case, and I was entirely confident of my ability to win before a jury. Henry, being the generally docile claims adjuster that he was, wouldn't blame me for losing the appeal, not if I handled him just so.

"All right," I said, looking at Gandhi. "You can get out of the car."

He crawled out, tentatively, and together we began walking down a path toward a shed half hidden behind the vineyard.

Before we got to the shed, I saw a large and profoundly odd-looking machine. A square tractorlike thing, with metal tentacles, so tall as to appear top-heavy, big and ugly, with a white iris incongruously painted on its side. I was so intent on studying the top arch of the machine with its mechanical spider arms that I wasn't looking or listening to Gandhi until I heard him gasp and then hiccup.

The strangling noise he kept making between hiccups made me suddenly wish I had gotten around to taking that CPR course.

"Are you all right?" I asked, patting him on the back.

He shook his head emphatically. Taking a great gulp of air, he said, "I knew this wasn't a good idea."

I turned back to the machine and tried to follow Gandhi's eyes.

There, on the other side of the machine, extending at a most unnatural angle, was a leg with a foot on the end. And a large pool of dark maroon.

Leaving Gandhi to his hiccups, I ran around the machine.

There, crushed or mauled beneath it, was Earl Stallings. I did not want to look close enough to figure out the exact mechanics of the matter, but spun away from the body and thought for a moment I might faint. Dizzy gray fuzz enveloped me, like the phosphate fog from the netherworld. I teetered.

Gandhi, still hiccupping, came up behind me, and with both hands he covered my eyes and pulled my head into his chest, and he held me as if I were a sweet child, and he patted my back, and when his breathing began to normalize and I was past my near faint, I said, "We've got to call 911."

That the CPR course I never took wouldn't have done any good, we both knew.

CHAPTER 13

Though I had had a physician client murdered with a marijuana joint spiked with deadly oleander, I had never seen his body. In fact, I had never even seen a photograph of his dead body.

That was definitely the better approach, not seeing, I thought as I sat sideways in the opened door of Gandi's car with my head bent over my legs while waiting for my stomach to settle. Gandhi clucked and patted and tried to do calming things, but all I wanted to do was go home and shower and drink a belt of Absolut and go to bed and wake up in my next lifetime.

But in the distance, I heard the sound of sirens gaining on us.

Then sirens, noise, and official people exploded all around us, and I glanced up to see paramedics hovering over poor Earl, and then I shut my eyes and had a sudden insight into just how horrific Benny's experience of finding the dead man in the swamp really must have been for him.

Two uniformed deputy sheriffs descended upon Gandhi and me, and started asking basic questions, like who we were, and issuing standard orders, like show some ID, and don't go anywhere. One of them pulled Gandhi away from me, and on the car stereo Sheryl Crow's CD, going round the third or fourth time, hit "No one said it would be easy."

While a uniformed deputy watched me, I searched my purse for a stray Valium, found only Tums and Advil, and took both. With rising levels of agitation, I was digging in Gandhi's glove compartment looking for a stray Valium when I found a stray joint and shoved it back under his car manual. I hoped we weren't suspects and that my guard deputy either hadn't noticed or didn't care about the joint. Then new cars drove up. I pulled myself out of Gandhi's Acura, stood up, looked at the sun, blinked, and told myself to go forth and be useful.

Damned if Tired Johnson wasn't crawling out of an unmarked car, holding a baby. Looked about nine months or so. Alert, round red face. Tired looked haggard.

Calling out Tired's name, I started toward him, but the deputy who was guarding me put a hand out in front of me. "Give him a chance to look over the scene," the deputy said. "And whatever you do, don't ask him about that baby's momma."

"What the hell is he doing with a baby out here?"

The deputy shrugged. "Baby-sitting problems, probably. Hard being a single dad and raising a son. Just don't ask him—"

"Yeah, about the mom," I finished. Got it.

"Sets him right off," Mr. Deputy Chatty added.

Nodding, I looked around for Gandhi and spied him cornered between two uniformed deputies yammering away. I sent shut-up waves toward him, but for a psychic, he didn't get my message at all.

"Maybe you want to turn off the radio? You know, save the battery," Mr. Deputy Helpful said. "You're probably gonna be here a while."

Oh, great, an afternoon with Mr. Chatty Deputy, SO Investigator Tired and Son, Dead Earl, Mr. Motor-mouth Client, and no lunch.

I switched the CD off, picked up my cell, walked to the back of Gandhi's car, and hit Bonita's number. Mr. Deputy followed me, and made no particular effort to hide the fact that he was listening.

"Bonita," I said, "Gandhi is with me, and we're going to be late."

Before she was halfway through her questions, I cut her off and folded up the cell and tossed it into the car, and I studiously kept my back to Earl's mangled body.

Tired groused his way toward me. I could hear him coming with a running monologue of things he was most certainly unhappy about, his son's baby-sitter topping the list.

I looked at him. He was red faced and sweating. I looked at his son, and was struck immediately by the resemblance. "He looks just like you," I blurted out, taking in the child's round, red, sweaty face, and alert hazel eyes, and daffy whirls of dark-blond hair.

"Thank you," Tired said, though I had not necessarily meant it as a compliment. He thrust the baby toward me. "Want to hold him?"

No, I did not. Babies are sticky, and they can do the most disgusting things without the least prompting, and they invariably burst into tears if I so much as look twice at them.

"His name is Redfish," Tired said, still holding the baby out toward me when I didn't answer.

"Why on earth do you have that baby out here? There's a dead man over there, for heaven's sake, Tired."

I saw Mr. Deputy wave his hands behind Tired, and run his hand under his throat and then do a frantic time-out gesture with his hands. Okay, yeah, all right, I know, I'm not supposed to ask about the kid's mom, I thought, and looked over Tired's head toward the frantic hand motions of the deputy whose name I had never bothered to learn. I gave that deputy my best Hard Look.

Then I turned back to Tired, who was blowing the gnats off Redfish's face. "His real name is Joshua Rodney, but my daddy started calling him Redfish when he wasn't but a week old, and it kinda stuck."

"Look, Tired, I'm not, like, a child psychologist or anything, but by the time he's in, say, preschool, maybe you ought to call him Josh, and stop bringing him to see dead people."

"Ma'am, look, okay, I didn't have a choice. The baby-sitter called an hour ago and had to go home.

I didn't have time to get another one, so I took the day off, but then this came up."

The baby giggled and turned even redder.

"He's cute, ain't he?" Deputy Helpful piped in.

"Then you take him," I said.

"On duty," he said, and took two steps backward.

Yeah, on duty spying on me, I thought, and, wholly against my better judgment, I reached out and took the proffered baby.

"I got to talk to you about all this, ma'am, but first I got to, well, you know, look around and stuff. Looks like that grape harvester must've malfunctioned and knocked him off."

A grape harvester—so that's what that big, ugly tractorlike thing was. But I didn't have time to study on this new piece of information because as Tired walked off, young Redfish turned toward me, took inventory of the situation, inhaled, and let out a scream that even poor dead Earl must have shuddered at. Tired looked back at me and said, "He likes it if you sing to him."

Sing to him? Who exactly did Tired think I was?

Redfish continued to share his negative view of the state of affairs, as Gandhi began to trot toward us with his guard deputy closely behind, trying to intercept.

I sat down in the car, turned on Sheryl Crow again, and the kid screeched a whole other octave. Okay, the na-na song wasn't a lullaby. I cut off the CD and turned the radio on and flipped the dial until I heard music. Toby Keith was asking his high school crush what she thought of him now, and, damn, little Redfish shut right up and reached for the radio dial.

Gandhi was by the opened car door now and looked in. "You doing all right?"

Under the circumstances. I nodded. And I was doing way better than poor Earl.

Poor Earl. The man who was pursuing a criminal complaint against Farmer Dave. Not for a fraction of a portion of a second did I think Dave would kill a man over a felony-theft charge, but Tired and the local state attorney wouldn't know that about Dave. I felt a prickle of panic sweat start down my face. Picking up my cell, I punched in Philip's private line, and, when he answered, I asked, "Dave still in jail?"

"Yes. And I have a client with me now and can't talk."

"Fine. Don't bill for this call then." I hit the end call button as Redfish reached for the cell phone.

As Redfish began to trace sticky all over me, and throughout Gandhi's car, I sighed with no small measure of relief that at least Dave had the perfect alibi.

CHAPTER 14

By the time I finally arrived home and shucked off my clothes and stood under the hot, steady stream of my shower, I had to admit that Tired and I had come a long way together since the okra incident.

Which didn't mean I was taking his son to raise or anything. But I had to grudgingly admit that the man did seem to know what he was doing.

Something about the physics and the biology of the body had convinced Tired that poor Earl was dead because he had been climbing on the side of the grape harvester, possibly to fix something, when he had fallen, and somehow the grape harvester turned itself on, and had taken a run at picking poor Earl. These matters of physics and biology Tired had explained in far more detail than Gandhi or I wanted to know, or than I thought mentally helpful for the tender ears of Redfish.

But Tired had left entirely open the question of how or why the grape picker had turned itself on. Unless Earl had been stupid enough to have climbed the side of the machine while it was running and then to have fallen off in front of the wide, spidery arms of the harvester.

Didn't work for me, and I had tried to impress upon Tired that my limited acquaintance with Earl had convinced me that Earl was anything but stupid.

"Even a smart man can be careless," Tired had said, but he seemed open to my idea that Earl wouldn't be *that* careless.

While I had been pondering the question of who and why someone would want to push Earl off his grape picker and turn it on so it would maul him to death, Tired had suddenly become fascinated with the fact that I had a prior acquaintance with Earl. What was that all about and why was I here, and grill, grill, grill until I ended up with both a head-ache and heartburn despite the Advil and the Tums.

The upshot of our exchange was that Tired leaned toward the notion that Earl might have been assisted in his fatal fall and I renewed my thanks to heavenly forces that Dave possessed the ultimate alibi, what with being in jail and all.

Having replayed this while showering, I hoped to put it out of my mind. After my shower, I threw away the slip I had once considered lucky and on bare feet padded into my kitchen where Bearess was guarding the refrigerator and waiting patiently to consume her five dollars' worth of dye-free, organic dog food.

While she steadily crunched her little doggy nuggets, I poured a bowl of multigrain organic cereal and doused it with rice milk, and ate half

117

before I shoved it away with a faint wave of nausea. Dead Earl's mangled corpse was still playing across the screen of my mind, and I thought again of Benny, and went to the phone to check on him. Discovering a dead body at his young age had to be worse than my experience.

Nobody answered.

I called Philip's unlisted number, and when he answered, I asked, "Is Dave still in jail?"

"Not for long. Waylon is out."

I had more or less forgotten about Waylon, Dave's truck-driving buddy.

"Why isn't Dave out?"

"Mrs. Stallings, Earl's widow, dropped the charges against both of them. Waylon's going back to Lakeland. Dave's still in custody until the Georgia officials resolve that matter of the motocross warrant. But I've talked at length with the county attorney in Grady County, and he's not inclined to pursue it, so I believe Dave will be a liberated man by tomorrow."

The use of the term *widow* suggested Philip knew Earl was dead, but I wondered if he knew the details. "You know about Earl? I mean, what happened to him?"

"Of course."

"I found the body."

"Yes. Tired informed me. That must have been distressing."

Well, Tired and Philip were certainly chummy considering they were on opposite sides.

Philip and I paused, waiting for somebody to take the next step.

"Are you all right? Would you like to talk about it? I can come over, or we can meet someplace," Philip offered.

"Thank you, but I'm very tired and still have some things to do."

Yeah, like drink a bottle of poor dead Earl's good organic wine in his memory.

"I'll check in on you tomorrow then. Call me anytime."

Never, ever tell me to call anytime. I take things very literally.

The next morning I rose early to run wind sprints down at the middle school with the notion that exercise would blot out the image of poor dead Earl and my disastrous appellate argument, and would work off the calories from that extra wine.

Once home from running, I made coffee and called Benny. He was busy getting ready for school and assured me he was doing fine.

Though I pretended to take him at his word, I made a note to ask Bonita about him, and to take him out for ice cream soon.

Thus, modestly fortified for the day by coffee, wind sprints, and good deeds, I showered, dressed, made up, fluffed my hair, and snuck into Smith, O'Leary, and Stanley through the back door, where Angela and Bonita perched like carrion birds in Bonita's cubbyhole outside my office.

"I don't want to talk about it," I snapped, and slammed into my office.

Angela followed me right in. She thrust another handful of paper at me. I took it.

It was a draft of a relief-from-judgment pleading, which sought to recoup the judgment Newly had won for Bonita in her lawsuit against the company that had manufactured the machine that had sucked Bonita's husband in and spit him out in fragments.

"Where'd you get this?"

Angela didn't say a word.

"Bonita," I more or less shouted through the doorway between my office and her cubbyhole. "Where'd you get this?"

"Around."

Okay, so the Sisterhood of the Secretaries was probably at work here. Bonita was very popular among the legal secretaries, and Angela seemed to be an honorary member of the Sisterhood, and one of them had probably chanced upon the draft and taken it to Bonita.

Regardless of the source, something had to be done to stop this.

To relive any of that would be painful for Bonita, and devastating for her children.

"Read it," Angela commanded.

I glanced through it, skipping the boilerplate, and came, finally, to the gist of the complaint—that some of the children alleged to be the natural children of the deceased were not, and that Bonita knew this and had willfully defrauded the court to increase the value of the judgment, and on the basis of that fraud, all the sums paid should be recovered. The concept was simple enough—in a wrongful-death case involving a widow and surviving minor children, the widow brought suit in her own right, but also as the "best friend" of the minor children. Each minor child was due compensation for the loss of his or her father, including for emotional damages and the loss of support. In other words, five children meant five times the amount of money the company had to pay for manufacturing a defective product that had resulted in Felipe's death.

Or, from the bottling company's point of view, fewer children meant less money. And lying about the number of children meant fraud, and fraud meant the court could throw out the whole judgment.

"Have you read this?" I shouted through my office toward the space Bonita usually occupied.

Something that sounded like a muffled, unhappy yes came from Bonita, so low in tone I had to strain to hear.

"If you're going to talk to me about this, then get in my office," I said.

Within seconds, Bonita appeared, shut my door, and stood before me.

Knowing Bonita like I did, it never once occurred to me to question the accuracy of these claims that some of her children were not the children of her husband, Felipe. But I knew how court proceedings alleging that her husband was not the father of her children would hurt her. How the story would spread, transformed through repetition from allegation to accepted fact among the community. Although she was in this country legally, Bonita had never become a naturalized citizen, and that might hurt her credibility among a populace who would perceive her first and foremost as a Mexican.

You say Mexican immigrant and the immediate images of the wetback, the drug smuggler, the migrant, the shacks and the poor, the great unwashed spring to many minds, and the American prejudices being what they were, many assumed that poor meant criminal. No matter that Bonita and her husband, Felipe, with Benicio a toddler and Armando and Javy babes in arms, had come into this country legally some eleven years before. In fact, they had both been recruited. The orange-juice plant wanted Felipe, with his industrial-engineering degree from California Polytech. And the plant had made Bonita a good offer for a human-resources position, what with her bilingual skills and her communications degree from California Polytech. Though Felipe stayed with the orange-juice plant until it killed him, Bonita had left it almost immediately and ended up with me, where we had learned the practice of law together.

Despite all that, Bonita would still be a wetback to some people. Someone's illegal maid, at best.

But the damage to her reputation wrought by

Kenneth's fraud lawsuit would be nothing compared to the damage to her children. A protracted trial of the matter would force them all to relive the horror of the death of their father. Only their ex-nun aunt, Gracie, and Bonita's own steel spine had pulled her children through the first lawsuit.

Damn it.

Then I thought, Whoa, it's the age of DNA testing.

But even as relief tried to raise its hopeful little puppy head, I realized with renewed horror that there was no body to exhume; Felipe had been more or less pulverized. What remains had been scraped together had been cremated.

Damn, damn, damn.

Okay, there was a way out; there is always a way out.

"Let's see what he's got first, I mean, by evidence, or theory, or support," I said. "I'll go through his office tonight. If Kenneth did get hold of something, and then induced the company to go along with this, there must be a trace. I mean, like a PI report, or something. A memo in the file about a conference with the bottle manufacturer. Something. You don't start a suit like this without leaving a pretty broad trail."

Even Kenneth the slime drool wouldn't go into court without some kind of evidence.

I had to get into Kenneth's office, which, of course, he would lock at night.

My mind began to run over with thoughts of excuses, tricks, lies, subterfuges of a hundred myriad kinds, and plain old-fashioned breaking and entering. Some way to get into Kenneth's office when he was not there.

Bonita was either a mind reader or I was getting too easy to read.

"You don't need to steal keys or break in," she said, looking at me with a great sadness in her eyes.

"I do if I want to get into Kenneth's office."

"Henry can get you in."

"Henry?" I blurted it out in a tone I realized too late was probably rude. Henry, Bonita's more or less boyfriend, Henry the meek claims adjuster, Henry the man whose company had sold Gandhi the very liability-insurance policy that was paying my bill for defending him.

Henry, a master of breaking and entering? When had he learned that skill?

"His father was a locksmith. Henry worked for him during the summers in high school and college," Bonita said, answering the question I hadn't yet asked.

Well, that might come in handy, I thought, filing away that fact, along with the information on Henry I'd collected over the years—that he had a college degree in education with a minor in botany, but couldn't keep discipline among the teenagers in middle school, and had became an insurance salesman after only a few years of teaching. He had been promoted up the ranks of his company mostly because he had seniority and because he was a pretty nice guy.

And because he was head over heels in love with Bonita, my secretary, I could pretty much make Henry do anything I wanted him to do.

Bonita knew all this. Thus, the fact that she told me Henry knew how to pick locks let me know how far she'd go to find out just what Kenneth might have on her by way of evidence.

I looked at Bonita and worried. But I said, "Please tell Henry to meet me here tonight at ten. Everybody should be gone by then. And, Bonita and Angela, I don't want either of you here in case Henry and I get caught. We can talk ourselves out of this, but not you two." Translation: Partners were accorded a certain latitude that secretaries and young associates were not. And nobody at Smith, O'Leary, and Stanley would prosecute claims adjusters like Henry because they were the very people inside insurance companies who ladled out the cases upon which we as defense lawyers feasted.

But I wasn't planning on getting caught.

CHAPTER 15

Henry wore a suit and tie to meet me surreptitiously at night to break into my own law partner's office.

Such a gentleman, I thought as Henry began to tinker with a thin metal pick and the door to Kenneth's office. Standing behind him, I snuck in a quick report on Gandhi's oral argument, including the fact that the judges seemed to favor sending the case back for a jury trial, and possibly allowing the plaintiff to amend her complaint to allege fraud. I'd have to put this in writing, but wanted to soften Henry up first with a cursory verbal version.

"Yes, Gandhi told me the judges didn't, ah, like, ah, understand, ah, believe him. He explained that he gave, er, presented . . . made a bit of a presentation. He says that he is so glad I assigned the case to you. That you two are simpatico. And he's sorry he screwed up, er, I mean messed up . . . disrupted your oral argument. He said you were brilliant."

Overlooking for the moment the fact that Gandhi was communicating directly with Henry, a situation

I did not at all care for, I thought, Brilliant? In what universe? In that universe where Gandhi lived with his alien abductees and crystal girlfriend and psychic cats?

Too ashamed of my performance at the oral argument to emphasize Gandhi's compliment, but too savvy to deny it, I modified the subject. "So, Henry, why on earth did your company issue a liability policy to Gandhi in the first place? I mean, the man runs an ad in the Sunday paper that says, 'Have you been abducted by space aliens? Call this eight hundred number.' Didn't you see the potential risk?"

"That policy was issued, er, sold long after my promotion out of sales, so I don't really know. The man had a degree and a license from the state of Florida and no prior malpractice suits. Guess it looked okay."

Yeah, a suspect degree from an Internet school, and a license from what must surely be one of the laxest agencies in the state. But before I could pursue that, the tumblers clicked in the lock and Henry opened the door and bleated out, "Do you think that Bonita will ever get over her husband?"

No.

But I didn't want to discourage Henry, Henry with his chubby, ruddy face and Paul Newman eyes, his damp hands, and Henry with his newfound skills that I could use to my great advantage.

"Henry, Bonita is very fond of you. Give her time."

Oh, great, the Dear Abby of the claims-adjuster set.

"Here we go," Henry said, his face two shades redder as we walked into Kenneth's office.

After switching on the light, I booted up Kenneth's computer first thing, and while it was humming awake, I started to sneak about.

Being a literate sort, I honored the "Purloined Letter" concept and went to the most obvious place first, Kenneth's personal filing cabinet. I flipped through the tabs on the files looking for Bonita's name or that of the bottling manufacturer. Nada, nothing, not in any of the four drawers.

"Want me to look, er, search, I mean, access his files, and do a . . . on his computer, conduct a—"

"Yeah, Henry, do a descriptive word search of all his files on his hard drive, will you, while I keep looking."

I headed next to Kenneth's credenza, found his liquor stash and contemplated a generous sample of his Absolut, but then reminded myself to focus on the task at hand.

"Er, it's, ah, password protected," Henry muttered.

I stood up a minute, and tried to think—Kenneth's wife had left him, he had no children, he had no pets, so what might he use for a password?

He had that sailboat that Jackson liked to rant about. There on the desk where the rest of us had pictures of children or spouses, and where I had a photo of Benny hugging Bearess, was a photo of Kenneth's boat. I squinted at the tiny print on it—it looked like it spelled out *The Esquire*. Trust Kenneth for something pompous.

"Henry, try *esquire*. If that doesn't work, try esquire with numbers at the end, or the beginning or the middle."

"Got it," he said, with unusual assurance for him. I peered over his shoulder for a moment as he typed in "Esquire" and "1Esquire" and "Es1quire." Then I was grateful that he was doing that tedious task and not me, and went back to plundering the credenza.

Not two minutes later I found, stuffed in the recesses of the dark back corner, a Winn-Dixie grocery sack. That sack so surprised me, I jerked up and hit my head on the overhanging fern, cursed in surprise at hitting a hanging basket, and thought any number of simultaneous things, none of which made sense.

"Find something?" Henry asked.

"Ah, don't know yet. You?"

"Not yet."

I dug back to the paper sack, and pulled it out and looked into it. Sure enough, it was full of crumpled cash.

Henry had stopped typing various versions of the word *esquire*, and turned around and looked into the sack.

"Oh my Lord. What do you think that's about?"

Precisely.

"Nobody keeps cash around in a sack, not unless there's something . . . funny . . . about it," I said.

Henry nodded.

"I'm going to take this as . . . evidence. We can . . . maybe"—okay, *blackmail* was the word I started to say, but then wordsmithed it to something softer for Henry's sensibilities—"use it for leverage . . . you know, against Kenneth and whatever he's doing to Bonita."

I studied Henry to see how he might be taking this.

"Good idea."

Henry was so easy.

Finding that sack of money was weird. Scary weird. How on earth would Kenneth have known I would arrive at home alone on a dark night with a Winn-Dixie paper bag full of green cash money? Definitely a bit weird.

Also, a bit criminal. Let's see, he hit me, that's battery, he stole something, that's robbery. My heart leapt in joy at the thought of a pilloried Kenneth, mired in the criminal-justice system on the charges of robbing me.

But there was an obvious problem with ratting out Kenneth to the police: How did I explain that sack of money in the first place without tying Dave, Benny, and me to a dead man in the swamp? And though I was admittedly no criminal-law scholar, even I suspected there might be something illegal about finding a dead body with a sack of money, and keeping the money without mentioning it to anyone in Officialdom.

No, this was a private matter.

"Let me handle it," I said. "Trust me, okay, Henry, and don't, please, don't tell anyone about this sack of money. And don't tell Bonita. You know how she . . . you know the way she sighs when she's disappointed, don't you?"

Henry nodded, and I understood that he understood that Bonita might tolerate us breaking into Kenneth's office on her behalf, but she wouldn't want me stealing money from him, and that, to her and Henry, was exactly what my taking the money would look like.

"Okay." I smiled at Henry. "Deal."

"Bonita told . . . confided in me what that son of a bitch is doing to her. Claiming he's got this proof that Benny and Armando aren't Felipe's sons, threatening her with it. Trying to reopen that case, and get the money back. Over such a, such a . . . such a—"

"Spurious claim?" I offered.

"Wholly ridiculous accusation."

That too.

"You know, I'd love the chance to . . . to . . . to—"

Henry always did have trouble picking words, especially verbs. "Yeah. Me too," I agreed, knowing the gist if not the actual terminology.

"Let's do . . . something, let's . . ." Henry paused, his normally placid manner sliding out beneath this Henry version of anger. "Let's stop him."

"Yeah. Let's."

So, without formulating the details, Henry and

I became fellow conspirators in a vague, general plan to stop Kenneth from hurting Bonita.

We never did find anything to indicate what, if any, evidence Kenneth had that Benny or any other of her children were not the natural children of Felipe. We never did figure out Kenneth's password.

But I took the sack of money and Henry drove us to his office, where we counted the bills. After musing over the amount, he put it in a briefcase with a lock and shoved it into the bottom drawer of his desk.

As I drove home, I realized that there weren't many people I would trust with $15,000 in cash money. I guess I thought more of Henry than I'd given either of us credit for.

And then, later that night when I wasn't sleeping, I realized the particular way Henry had phrased his rant against Kenneth. That Kenneth was "threatening" Bonita. That wasn't how Bonita and Henry, both experienced in the ways of litigation, would have phrased a rant at an attorney who was merely doing the bidding of his client.

Henry hadn't said the bottling company was suing Bonita.

He had said Kenneth was threatening her.

That merited some attention.

The next morning, emboldened by years of smoldering contempt, plus evidence that Kenneth had knocked me out in my own front yard, I pushed into his office after only a tap-tap at his door. For some reason, his door wasn't being guarded by his secretary, a thirty-something blonde named Cristal who could have been a Victoria's Secret model, but actually seemed to be proficient, and not at all stupid, as her name, her hair, and her flaunted body would suggest to those who buy into blond jokes.

Kenneth, sitting behind his huge rosewood antique desk, glowered at me. Behind him, an oil painting of a monarch butterfly took up several feet of wall. "What do you want?"

I didn't bother to smile. The man wasn't stupid. "We need to talk. About Bonita. Why are you threatening her?"

His normally snide face was passive. He didn't respond by word or expression or gesture.

The phone rang.

"Get that for me. Cristal's out today. Girl vapors, I guess. She was out yesterday too."

"Get it yourself."

"Look, I can't answer my own phone. It doesn't look right. Just act like my secretary. That's not too hard for your backwater education, is it?"

I jerked up the phone. "Kenneth Mallory's office."

Blah, blah, blah on the other end. But the speaker did identify himself as a claims adjuster for one of Kenneth's insurance companies.

"No, I'm sorry, but Kenneth can't come to the

phone. He's just checked into a twenty-eight-day rehab center, you know, for people addicted to cocaine, and his files will be referred to—"

Kenneth jumped up from behind his desk and showed amazing speed in snatching at the phone, but I hung it up before he could wrench it out of my hands.

"You little bitch. Who was that?"

"Your mother."

"Like hell. Now who was it? You're going to call them back and explain—"

"Like hell."

We glared at each other. Then Kenneth punched in our receptionist's number and demanded to know who had just called him. Our receptionist called Kenneth "Pig Lawyer" behind his back, and judging from Kenneth's reaction, she wasn't forthcoming about who had called him.

Already very tired of Kenneth, I said, "Look, I know you're threatening Bonita, that you are planning to file an action against Bonita on behalf of the bottling company, to vacate the award in her husband's death. You deny that?"

"It's none of your business."

Overlooking this, I plowed on toward my ultimate goal. "You are going to convince the bottling company to drop this case against Bonita."

"Or what?"

"Or else I report you to the police for assaulting me and stealing that sack of money out of my front yard." I was, of course, ardently hoping he wouldn't realize I was possibly, probably, in no legal position to hurl that first stone.

Kenneth shoved past me to the credenza and yanked it open. In no time at all he saw that the money was gone.

He spun around at me like a whirling dervish of evil and said, "You bring that money back to me."

"As soon as you agree to talk the bottler out of its planned suit."

Of course, I saw right off the problems with this plan. Kenneth hadn't filed the complaint yet, and he could promise he wouldn't, but as soon as I gave the money back, he could file the complaint anyway, or the bottling company could just hire another lawyer and another private investigator and go right on. And, of course, if Kenneth did persist in the lawsuit, and even if I took the chance of getting Dave, Benny, and me in trouble by reporting Kenneth to the police, that sack of money would be gone and I'd look like an idiot with a bogus complaint, and Bonita would spend the next five years of her life in court proceedings.

I had to admit that as it stood right now, Kenneth had the better hand.

CHAPTER 16

That night, glad to see my truly suck-ass day nearing its natural end, I parked my car in my carport, walked out to the mailbox on the street, gathered in my daily quota of catalogs and bills, walked up the driveway to my front door, and stopped.

There was a dead fish lying across the stoop in front of my front door, and a rolled sheet of white paper was stuck in its dead-fish mouth. I stared at it. Behind my door, Bearess started barking.

At the barking, my new grandmom popped out of her house and cheerily shouted across her unnaturally green lawn, "Hello, dearie, how are you feeling?"

Grandmom walked on over to where I was still staring at the dead fish, wholly unsure of the proper course of action.

"Did you see who put this here?" I asked her.

"Why no, but isn't it a nice big bass. So glad it's a bass. I never did understand you locals, how you could eat those mullet."

I glared at her. What good was a neighborhood

spy if she missed the essentials, like who left a dead fish on my doorstep?

Grandmom bent over and studied the dead fish. "Looks pretty fresh. The eyes are clear, no fishy smell. We could have fried fish tonight. I'll make the coleslaw if you'll make the hush puppies."

"What?"

"Oh, I'll clean it, don't worry. I'm just not good at hush puppies. It's a southern thing."

"What?"

"Dinner?"

"I'm a vegetarian."

"Or we could bake it, a nice fish like that."

"I'm a vegetarian."

"Would you like to come over to my house? Or shall I come over here?"

"I'm a vegetarian," I shouted, to which Bearess responded with a howl of doggy frustration from behind my front door.

"Well, listen, dear, you better let that dog out. And see who sent that nice fish." Grandmom pointed at the note.

I pulled the note out of the dead fish's mouth.

"BUTT OUT" had been sprawled in large, childish letters in black highlighter.

Obviously Kenneth's handiwork, I thought, though the language was a bit crude for a man who liked to put on airs. I contemplated calling the police, calculating risk versus benefit, and keenly aware of the law of unintended consequences.

"Maybe garlic bread would be better than hush

puppies. But you know, whoever left you that fish really should have iced it." Grandmom picked up the bass and sniffed it. "It's fine, really. Dinner in an hour? You just come to my house. I don't have dog hair all over everything." Grandmom started off back to her house, carrying the fish.

"I don't have dog hair over things, and I'm a vegetarian," I shouted after her.

"I'm Methodist myself, but we're known for our tolerance of other religions," Grandmom said, and slipped into her own house.

I let Bearess out in the backyard before I punched in 911 and reported a dead fish and a sinister note, to a dispatcher who couldn't care less but transferred my call to a police officer who was so uninterested as to decline my polite invitation to come out and actually investigate. Apparently, you can't pick up fingerprints on a dead bass, even if your neighbor hasn't already skinned and filleted it.

CHAPTER 17

The next morning I conducted my new daily ritual and phoned Philip Cohen as soon as I woke up, which, given the bad dream about being beaten with dead fish, was 5:30 A.M. Yeah, sure, that's not generally regarded as a civilized time, but he *had* said I could call him at any time, and I was perilously behind in my law practice and knew this would be a long, busy day, and that I also had to do something about Kenneth and the money and the dead fish and Bonita, and maybe I should check on Benny too, and calling when I first woke up, predawn or not, seemed to be a very efficient use of my time.

Also, okay so spank me, I wanted to see if that woman answered Philip's phone again.

She didn't.

He was very glad to hear from me in the predawn hours, and once we got past that, I asked per my daily ritual if Dave was still in jail.

He was, but it looked good for his release sometime later this morning. Blah, blah, blah, and I cut Philip off before he billed for another five minutes. After I hung up, I fixed and drank a gallon of coffee and, with the idea of actually working on billable files today, I skipped an early-morning workout at the YMCA and managed to get to my office long before the morning rush hour.

Having managed to beat Bonita to work, which rarely happens, I looked at my calendar, took dull notice of the afternoon's scheduled deposition in a really very stupid car-motorcycle case—a drunk in a car hit a drunk on a motorcycle in the middle of a four-way-stop intersection, both traveling at higher rates of speed than they should have been, and the drunk on the cycle was suing the corner convenience store for putting up a spotlight that he claimed blinded him to the oncoming drunk in the car, and not, like, say, those seven beers and whiskey chasers. Angela should be handling these depos, as I had progressed in my career beyond car wrecks. But in her current state, I didn't wholly trust Angela to use enough words to do a proper examination.

Stumbling over Bonita's boxful of something that looked like Girl Scout cookies—was it that time of year already?—I pulled out the files to review. If I was going to do car-wreck depos all afternoon, I needed to be prepared by knowing every word in the pleadings and the interrogatories so I could get the deposed witnesses to admit to the facts in the light most favorable to my client, the man who owned the store with the spotlight. Trying to get my mind around the fact that I was defending a big, bright light, I trudged back to my desk with volumes of paper.

Having plunked the file on my desk, I had started grinding coffee beans when I heard a tap-tap-tap on my window and saw Gandhi motioning toward the back door. Against my better judgment I let him in.

Once he was standing inside my office, I spoke in official lawyer voice. "Gandhi, I appreciate that we will need to get together and work out a new defense if the appellate court sends your case back for a trial, which, as I've mentioned, is most likely to happen, but let's wait until that remand does, in fact, occur."

Translation: Leave.

"Keisha is breaking up with me."

Sigh. I wasn't his counselor, I wasn't his confidante, and though I was his lawyer, I had other cases to work on.

"She says I am not serious enough about things."

A man in a yellow Nehru jacket who channels lost cats and counsels space-alien kidnap victims. Not serious? Get real.

"She says I'm insincere."

Well, duh. The fake Indian routine and the dyed hair and fake tan might just possibly, maybe, perhaps, have suggested that notion to Keisha the crystal lady.

"But I love her and I want to marry her."

Nothing in my training or personal life qualified me to give advice on love relationships. But I thought I'd give it a whirl anyway.

"Okay, go to Brock, my hairdresser, and he can

get the dye out of your hair, stay out of the tanning salon, and don't even think about that fake-tan cream, pop out the brown contacts, get a normal T-shirt and a pair of jeans, and at least an antique diamond ring, possibly one with rubies or emeralds, and propose to her at sunset on Island Park."

Okay, the antique diamond ring with rubies and a proposal at sunset at Island Park were my fantasies, but I figured, hey, there's bound to be a core of universal appeal. "Oh," I added, "promise a lifetime of serious sincerity."

And leave my office so I might be able to do some legal work for which I am trained and for which I can bill.

"I will try this. Thank you." And he walked out, closing the door politely behind him.

But not ten minutes later, my phone rang. I snatched it up and grunted a sort of hello.

"Lilly?"

"Tired?"

"Yes, ma'am. I was hoping you could come down to the jailhouse."

Oh, yes, my favorite place to hang. "Why?"

"Dave is being released, but before he goes, I have some questions I want to ask him, and he says he won't talk until he sees you. Actually, I've got some questions for you too."

"Philip Cohen is Dave's attorney. Call him."

"I need to see you, ask you a few things, and Dave insists upon you being there when I question

142

him. About that man in the swamp. And Earl. I think, maybe, there's some connection."

"I'm sure I don't know a thing about that." And Dave better not know anything about any connection between dead swamp man and dead Earl.

"Lilly, just come to the jail, okay? The sooner you get here, the sooner Dave gets out."

For a man who couldn't stand up to a skinny old lady over some okra plants, Tired certainly managed to project the stern tone of a direct order from a law-enforcement official. One who might hold up Dave's release from jail if I didn't comply.

After I conveyed both my acquiescence and my general displeasure, we said good-bye, and I punched in Philip's private number, got the recording, left a terse message, picked up the Drunk vs. Bright Light file, and walked down the hallway to Angela's office. Since it had been her case to begin with, she probably knew more about it than me, so I dumped it on her desk and said, "See if you can use whole sentences." And I stomped out to my car.

At the front desk of the jail, a woman who could have set the lowest common denominator for bad hair was scratching a pen over paper, trying to make it write, and muttering, "Damn thing."

"Hi. I'm here to see Officer Tired Johnson."

The woman looked up, and suddenly beamed. "T.R. is here?" She smoothed back her drastically overprocessed hair and looked around, as if Tired was hiding in a corner.

"Yes, I'm supposed to meet him here."

"Business? Or pleasure?" Bleached-hair lady looked suddenly hostile.

"I assure you it's purely business. About an inmate, Dave Baggwell, two gs."

She smiled again, and I noticed that she actually had a rather sweet face. "I'll page him," she offered.

While she paged, I fished around in my purse till I found one of Brock's cards. Aside from being my hairdresser and primary therapist, Brock works wonders with makeovers.

"T.R. will be right here, in a minute." She radiated anticipation.

Twenty-something, sweet face, bad hair, mastery of the paging system if not the ballpoint pen. I wondered how she felt about Redfish.

"Do you like babies?"

The woman didn't even blink to signal that this might be an odd question from a perfect stranger. "Oh, I just love babies. I baby-sit for my cousins' kids all the time."

Perfect, more or less, I thought. "Look," I said, offering her Brock's card, "this man is a genius with hair. Especially color. With your, eh, peaches-and-cream complexion, you should be a strawberry blonde. That white-blond look is too"—what, too tacky to show yourself in public?—"old for you. Tell him Lilly sent you, and he'll work you in."

She took the card, and her expression indicated

some confusion as to whether she had been insulted and how she might respond. "Does this Brock do your hair?"

"Yes, he does," I said.

"Wow, your hair is like totally beautiful."

Yes it is, and I smiled, and thanked her, and then she smiled and thanked me, and I added good manners to the list of her assets. Definitely, I should mention her to Tired as a prospect.

Tired came bounding out of one of the hallways, holding a cup of coffee in one hand and sticking out the other for me. He didn't even acknowledge Miss Bleached Head, but I bet he would when Brock finished making her over.

After the preliminaries, Tired led me back to a small room that smelled very bad, and I sat down in the offered chair with great reluctance, and made a mental note to be sure to shower and change clothes as soon as I left here. "Where is Dave?"

"Oh, I'll bring him out soon."

"Is he all right?"

"Oh, he's fine, don't worry. Now, I've got some questions for you."

"I already told you I don't know anything."

"A young fellow named Benicio called in a dead man in the Myakka swamp last week. You know anything about that?"

"No. I mean, I know Benicio, Benny. He's my secretary's son."

"Yeah, I found that out. Thought that was kinda interesting."

"Why?"

"You don't know anything about him calling 911 on last Saturday night?"

"No."

Tired stared at me a long time. I didn't blink or let my eyes wander and I didn't wipe my hands or do anything to give myself away. But still, the lie bubbled there in the air between us.

"You know, the more you tell me about what you know, the better off we'll all be."

Let me be the judge of that, I thought, but said nothing.

"Okay, did you know that Benny was with Dave when he made the call?" Tired asked.

"I think I might have known that Benny and Dave had gone to Myakka together."

Tired sighed. "Look . . . oh, hell, all right, here's the deal."

Finally.

"That man in the swamp was a man named Mike Daniels. Ring any bells?"

"None. Honest."

"Michael Andrews Daniels, nickname of Mad."

"I never heard of him."

"He did some work for Earl Stallings, you know, the wine guy."

"Yeah, I know the wine guy."

"So how exactly do you know the wine guy?"

"We've been over this."

"So, go over it again."

"Here is the whole story, everything I know, and

once I tell you—again—I want to see Dave, you hear."

"All right."

"The night Dave was arrested, some woman came to my door and said Dave and Waylon were in jail and Dave wanted me to get them out. I called Philip Cohen, and you remember, we all met here. Philip explained to me that Earl Stallings was pressing charges for the theft of a warehouse full of organic wine. The next day, Sunday, I went to the winery to try and talk Earl into dropping the charges for the allegedly stolen wine. We met, we talked, and he said he'd think it over."

"So who was the woman who came to your door?"

"I don't know."

"What'd she look like?"

"Like 1969, a real hippie, dark hair."

From the expression on Tired's face, I gleaned that he probably knew who the woman was.

"So who was she?" I asked.

"Continue, please, ma'am, with your story about Earl."

"So Monday, Earl talked with Philip, but he didn't drop the charges. Tuesday I had to go to court in Lakeland, and I had my client with me, and—"

"That guy in the yellow thing over his pants?"

"Yes, Gandhi Singh."

"That's not his real name, is it?"

"You'd have to ask him."

147

"Okay, go on."

"So, I swung by the winery to see Earl, to see if I could persuade him to drop the charges. That's all. And Gandhi and I discovered his body, and called 911, and you came out, and that's the end of the story."

"Not hardly." Tired glared at me.

I remained silent.

"Ma'am, look at it from my point of view. There's a guy out in the swamp, snakebit to all hell and back, and he worked for Earl. This guy's car had been run off the road, and it looked like he had hopped out and run off into the swamp."

Uh-oh, that was news to me.

"Then Dave and Benny, both guys you know pretty well, find the body, and Benny calls it in a few hours later, and then Dave and Waylon get arrested. Okay, so then you get mugged in your own front lawn."

So how'd Tired know about that? That was a matter for the city police.

"Then, you see Earl, and two days later, you find Earl dead, and then somebody puts a dead fish on your front stoop and you call 911 again. Did I leave anything out?"

Well, a few things, but I continued to exercise my right to remain silent.

"So, something is going on and I want to know what." Tired glowered, and leaned over at me. "You seem to be slap dab in the middle of this. Now what is going on?"

Damned if I knew. I shook my head. "Honest, Tired, I don't know."

Despite my assurances that I didn't have a personal clue as to what sinister plans were at work, Tired persisted and we went another twenty rounds, and I got plain rude and demanded to see Dave.

Tired went somewhere and brought Dave back into the room. Dave looked healthy enough and nobody had cut his pigtails. After a full-toothed smile, Dave gave me a big bear hug.

"Hey, Lilly Belle, my old sweetheart." And he gave me another bear hug.

"How are you? You handling this all right?" I asked.

"Well, beats picking cotton, but not by much," he answered. "Tell you what though, I'm about give out."

Dave did look exceptionally worn out and while I considered chastising someone for failing to take better care of him, Tired insisted we all sit down. "Let me handle this," he said to me, and then Tired turned to Dave and asked, "Do you know a man named Mike Daniels?"

"Nope."

"Did you find a body in Myakka Park last Saturday night?"

Dave paused, looked over at me, which caused Tired to look over at me, and I thought we needed Philip Cohen here because I didn't know the general rules of criminal defense and had the feeling I hadn't done so well with Tired myself, and I dug my cell out of my purse and punched in Philip's number. When he answered, I snapped, "Why aren't you at the jail?"

Tired sighed.

Upon Philip's advice, I told Dave not to say anything at all until Philip was able to get to the jail.

"Look," Tired said, "if you're not going to be any more help than this, you might as well go."

Okay, I suspected Tired wanted me out of there on the off chance he could trick Dave into telling him something before Philip got there to tell Dave to shut up, but I trusted Dave to keep him mouth shut, he wasn't like Gandhi, all right? and I was desperate to change clothes and shower off the jail.

"Well, all right, be that way," I said, got up, clumped out of the jail, and shook my hands in the warm air and headed toward my car.

My parting words to Dave were, "Keep your mouth closed, and I will see you later."

CHAPTER 18

When I was in first grade, my grandmother, who lived in a brick house on a dirt road in the middle of Bug-Fest, Georgia, taught me to gut and skin a squirrel, how to pee in the woods without getting it on my feet, and everything my six-year-old head could hold on the subject of snakes.

The snake thing definitely proved useful when I crawled into my cobalt-blue Honda after sniping with Tired at the jail. Both windows were down, and the door wasn't locked, and I didn't remember leaving it that way, and swore that if my priceless collection of germ-killing Handi Wipes was gone, I was going to raise holy hell. But I wasn't going back to complain now. I was thinking about showering and my hand was poised in midair to stick the key in the ignition.

But then I saw it. Sprawled out on the floorboard of the passenger side was a snake.

A big snake.

And not just a big snake.

A big rattlesnake.

Even in my limited-caffeine stupor, I couldn't

mistake the rows of diamond-shaped brown markings outlined against the cream-colored scales. I was close enough to see the white oblique stripes on the side of the snake's face.

Sit still. Don't move. That much of the childhood lessons came back to me. My grandmother's voice floated down from the cosmic rays in perfect clarity. "Don't piss that snake off," she said, "and don't move."

The thing is, a snake doesn't see the way we do. It sees by sensing motion and vibration. Apparently I was lighter and more graceful than I might have believed, since I had slipped into the car without disturbing the snake into a coil or rattling mode.

If I didn't move or vibrate, that diamondback wouldn't know I was there.

So, how long could I sit perfectly still with my hand in midair?

The rest of my life was my immediate goal.

I had begun to sweat profusely when I saw, from the corner of my tearing eye (I was afraid to blink), Tired Johnson sauntering toward me with that cowboy gait that seemed so out of place in Sarasota, even for a county sheriff's investigator. I was too scared to wonder then what afterthought might have led him to the parking lot to catch me before I drove off.

As Tired began to lean into my opened window, I said, "Snake." I willed the word to come out of my very pores, and didn't move my lips. Later I wondered if I had a hidden talent for ventriloquy, but at the moment I was concentrating on not moving and not pissing off that snake.

"Don't move," Tired said.

Quicker than I could not blink, Tired whipped out a long-blade knife and threw it with his right hand, and at precisely the same time he yanked open my car door with his left hand, and I fell out in a thunk against his legs and landed bottom down in a pool of greasy car oil.

Tired snatched me up and dragged me bodily away from my Honda as if it were in flames and due to explode at any second.

"Stay put, ma'am," he said, and began to stalk back toward the Honda.

As I picked myself up from another puddle of grease, a crew of trusties from the county jail who were washing the patrol cars all came a running.

To my relief, but no doubt the great sorrow of the rattler, the snake had been neatly decapitated by Tired's knife throw. The trusties, arriving en masse at the scene of the execution, took great glee in tossing the poor headless thing around at each other as if it were still capable of biting one of them.

One of the trusties giggled as he wrapped the snake around his neck like a feather boa.

"You boys stop that," Tired said. The trusty just pranced off, on his tiptoes, adorned by a headless rattler, sashaying like a chorus girl, and I hoped I never went to jail.

One of the trusties knocked down the snake-dancing chorus girl and grabbed the snake. As I watched him examine the snake, I saw disgust on his lean, weathered face. When he threw the snake down, and the trusties began to drift off as if the show was over, I walked toward him, my curiosity up.

"Ma'am, ma'am, you better stay away from them. They're prisoners. Ma'am?"

No, duh? I thought the gray-white overalls were just some new kind of fashion statement, like a retro-disco leisure suit for the workingman crowd. I kept walking. The jail parking lot was more or less full of men with guns, and I couldn't imagine one of the inmates making any kind of move on me. Tired pattered after me, ma'aming me the whole way.

"What's wrong with the snake?" I asked the lean-faced man. He looked like one of the men out of the famous Depression photographs, with squinty, drained eyes in a sharp face.

"It's dead." He wiped his hands on his overalls, took a pointed look at my breasts, and then turned away as an armed guard approached.

"Of course, it's dead. Tired cut its head off," I said to the departing trusty.

` "That deputy man done cut the head off a dead snake then," the inmate said, and kept walking.

By then Tired was beside me. I bent down and touched the snake, then picked it up. Like hard rubber. Definitely dead. Definitely dead for longer than five minutes.

Somebody had put a dead snake in my Honda.

Which, on balance, beat putting a live one in the car, but in my mind, Tired was no less the hero.

"Now why would anybody do a thing like that?" Tired asked the humid air around us.

A dead snakebit man in a swamp. Poor smashed Earl under his grape harvester. A dead rattler in my car.

I guess Gandhi Singh's appellate argument hadn't been so bad after all.

CHAPTER 19

I couldn't get out of those clothes and into my shower quick enough, and while I was letting the hot steam work out my aggravation and flush off the jail germs, the phone rang. The machine kicked in, but over the flow of the hot water I couldn't hear the message.

When I played the machine, it turned out the message was from Philip. Checking on me, worried, dead-snake assault and all, and asking that I call him to let him know how I was doing. I penciled myself a note to challenge any bill for that call, as it was strictly personal.

Once dressed, I called Philip back, and asked where Dave was.

"I dropped him off at Waylon's duplex. It seemed that Waylon decided he did not like the wine business so much after all and he has returned to Lakeland. As his rent was paid until the end of the month, he bequeathed his duplex to Dave for the next two weeks."

Well, Waylon sure bailed out at the first sign of trouble, I thought.

"Dave did ask me to remind you that he would

need, what he referred to as his . . . I believe the phrase was, just how did he put it?"

"Spit it out, okay? What'd he want to remind me about?"

"His 'sack of personal assets,' that's the phrase, I believe."

Okay, I thought, Dave wants that grocery bag of money back. But not until I deducted from the cash what I had already paid Philip from my personal checking account.

Then Philip went back to the snake thing, and what did I think it meant, and was I really all right. Dadeda, dadeda about the snake thing, and I reassured him a hundred times that I was just fine, and finally he said, "Lilly, it is the beginning of the weekend. Might I have the pleasure of your company for dinner tonight?"

The pleasure of my company? Did this man live in the nineteenth century?

"Business or pleasure?" Translation: Was he going to bill for this?

"Absolutely pleasure."

Ahhh, that Dean Martin voice just radiated out of that phone and melted over me like warm lavender lotion.

Of course, it took me a few minutes after the phone call to remember that I needed to talk with Benny and find Dave, and that if I had a date with Philip, I would have to put off Benny and Dave until Saturday. So how much harm could there be in that? I blithely thought, and peered into my refrigerator for a light lunch before returning to work.

My mood lifted, especially for someone so recently assaulted with a dead rattler. By the time I finally returned to the salt mines at Smith, O'Leary, and Stanley, well past the noon hour, I was flushed with anticipation over a date with Philip Cohen, the crooner-voiced, sensuous-lipped man who had once rendered me practically mute simply by touching the skin of the inside of my arm and smiling at me.

This could be just the thing I needed.

I actually whistled when I sauntered in the back door at Smith, O'Leary, and Stanley. Whistled until I saw Kenneth glowering over Bonita, who was seated behind her desk in her cubbyhole outside my office.

The infernal Muzak, which is piped into every office and hallway and corridor as a fundamental part of our office manager's experiment to see how many of us she can drive stark, raving mad, must have drowned out my whistling. But then Kenneth looked up, saw me, and glared back at Bonita and said something in Spanish I couldn't catch over the sound of piped-in pseudo-music.

Kenneth turned from Bonita and started down the hallway without further acknowledging me.

"What was that about?" I asked.

For a moment, Bonita slumped at her desk, her normally perfect posture lost to the moment, and then she put her head down on her desk.

"Bonita? What's wrong?"

"That Kenneth," she said, and lifted her head, straightened her shoulders, and pointed at a clipped collection of paper on the top of her neat desk.

As Bonita put the iron back into her spine, I reached over and picked up the paper. A quick glance told me it was a refined version of the complaint for relief from judgment that Angela had shoved at me just days before.

"He told me . . . he told me that he could convince the company to file it, or not. Depending upon—" Bonita stopped.

"Depending upon what?"

Bonita continued to sit, and not speak, her face a filling-in-the-blank slate.

Okay, I thought, she doesn't want to make me feel bad that Kenneth's going after her to get back at me for stealing the money that he stole from me. "He's just bluffing, Bonita, he's just . . . trying to get back at me."

A flit of puzzlement crossed her face as I studied her, and then the blank slate was back.

But the puzzlement stopped me. Then logic interceded. Kenneth had started this nonsense before he knew I had taken the money from his credenza.

But not before he knew I had the money in the first place.

This had started right after Farmer Dave went on his adventure to the county jail.

So, maybe this wasn't just about me.

"Kenneth hasn't filed this yet?"

"No."

"Did he tell you what evidence he has for his claim, this totally spurious nonsense about your children?"

A hint of an expression I couldn't recognize crossed Bonita's face, but was gone too fast for me to read it, and she fingered the gold cross on the chain around her neck and finally said, "No."

"Bonita, it will be all right. I'll figure something out, right now, to stop him."

But before I could even begin to fathom what I might do, Bonita, in a wholly uncharacteristic display, released a stream of invectives, both in English and Spanish, the likes of which I had never imagined the normally calm and religious Bonita to even know, let alone say.

I was impressed by her vocabulary. And troubled by her predicament.

Bonita was my secretary, and my friend, and I needed to help her.

Meanwhile, I figured Bonita should just go home. After all, it was Friday afternoon, and sending her home early seemed the kind thing to do.

"Bonita, look, I'll think of something." For starters, I'd have to seriously consider giving Kenneth the money back, even if that meant I lost any leverage I might have. "Why don't you just go home?"

"No, I'm fine."

"Anything pressing going on here?"

"No."

"Then go home, spend some quality time with Benny."

At the mention of Benny, something like worry crossed Bonita's face and she nodded. "Okay. But first I have to do some bookkeeping stuff. By the time I finish that, Benicio will be home from school."

Idly I wondered what pressing bookkeeping she needed to do, then figured she needed to catch up on my billings, and I nodded, and retreated into my office.

An hour later, I poked my head out. "You okay?" I asked Bonita.

"I have finished my bookkeeping task, and I am going to leave now. You'll call me later?"

"Absolutely."

Bonita gathered up her purse, eyed the cardboard carton full of Girl Scout cookies, sighed, said, "If Henry comes by, don't let him eat them all," and left. I heard the back door shut after her.

Wondering what my next-best move might be, I stood there for a moment.

Then Bonita came slouching back in. Despite her earlier recomposure, she did not look good.

"You all right?" I asked despite the plain evidence to the contrary.

"Someone is double-parked, and I'm blocked in. I don't recognize the car."

Our parking lot had not been expanded since the firm doubled in size and added a second floor to the building, and clients frequently just left their cars wherever rather than hunt out something on a side street.

Bonita could wait or I could just let her take my cobalt blue, repainted, re-windowed, practically ancient Honda, and recent haven for dead rattlers. That would be the easiest, I thought, giving Bonita my car, assuming nobody had blocked it in, and I could just take Bonita's car home later.

"Here," I said, grabbing for my keys. "Take my Honda. Give me your keys, and I'll drive your car home tonight. We can trade tomorrow."

"Won't you be stuck here?"

I was always stuck here, I thought, there was no life outside this building, this law firm. But I shook my head. "By the time I leave, whoever double-parked will be gone."

After Bonita took my key and left, I marched into Kenneth's office only to find him gone. Instead of the efficient, if blond and beautiful Cristal, I found a woman I dimly recognized as someone from the word-processing pool upstairs, and she assured me, though I didn't ask or care, that she was competent to be a legal secretary.

"Where's Kenneth?"

"He had a hearing in Tampa at four. Said he wouldn't come back to the office."

"Where's Cristal?"

"Don't know."

Thus, frustrated again, I thanked her and left, and actually billed some time on some files before I snuck out early for me. At home, I made a quick call to Bonita, who, once updated that there was no update, assured me she was fine.

"Fine," I said, and asked to speak to Benny. After a wait, Benny came on the phone and did that I'm-fifteen-so-I-don't-talk-to-grown-ups thing, and I promised myself to go over and see him tomorrow and make him talk to me. Then I showered and dressed for my date with Philip, going a little conservative for a Friday night with a linen dress in pastel green and flat, forest green sandals.

Philip was punctual and brought roses and wine, and I was glad I went conservative. This man *was* from the nineteenth century.

And nineteenth-century men apparently didn't take suggestions from their women. No matter how I tried to convince Philip to take me to the Café at the Granary, the health food store in town, or the health food, vegetarian restaurant on Siesta Key, Philip insisted upon taking me to a new, fancy place on Palm Avenue, one of those places where the cool and the rich and the old who live in the condos on the bay front near Palm Avenue like to gather and show off their expensive clothes. One of those places whose slogan ought to be "High Prices, Small Servings."

And so it was that I found myself in the odd position of having nothing on the menu that I could order, other than the Zephyr Hills bottled water, though I noted that at $3.50 per bottle for what sold for about a buck at the grocery st , I wasn't sure I'd even order that.

I tried to convince myself that the salad would be fine. But I didn't know their source for raw vegetables, or how well they were washed, and I had to assume that nothing was organic.

Glancing at the other tables, I was able to tell that the bread was strictly white.

The place specialized in aged beef, and no way I was eating a dead cow, especially a dead cow that had been dead for quite a while.

When pressed, the waiter admitted the vegetable of the day was both frozen and cooked in chicken broth.

When pressed further, the waiter brought the manager, who assured me of the cleanliness standards of his fine establishment, but no, for insurance reasons, he could not let me examine the kitchen.

BS on the insurance, I thought, this man had a dirty kitchen, and I gathered my inner resources to tell Philip to pay for the wine and take me to the Café at the Granary, or home.

Philip leaned back in his chair, sipped his wine, and said, "I didn't realize you suffer from cibophobia. That explains why you are so thin."

I'm thin because I do wind sprints, keep my face out of high-fructose corn syrup, drink lots of coffee, and work out like a fiend at the YMCA, and I'm not cibophobic, whatever that is.

"I didn't realize you were such a chauvinist you couldn't take suggestions from a mere woman on a good place to eat."

"Perhaps it's not cibophobia, which, incidentally, means 'fear of food.' Maybe you have orthorexia nervosa. Do you know what that is? It's a new term. Fear of eating anything except organic foods is one of the symptoms. Health food eating carried to extremes."

"Look, short man with thick glasses, I paid good money for a diagnosis of obsessive-compulsive disorder from somebody with an M.D. and I don't need any new diagnoses from a prissy-talking attorney who can't even get a man out of jail for misdelivering a little wine."

Philip leaned back in his chair and burst out laughing.

As dates went, this one was actually going pretty well, so far.

"Just take me to the Café at the Granary, or home, please."

Philip paid the bill for the wine, slipped the waiter a big tip, and draped his arm around me as he herded me out the door.

We had a perfectly fine dinner at the Café at the Granary, a place I've eaten at many times and where I've had many the guided tour of the kitchen, and where they know how to make a vegan cheesecake that's doesn't taste at all like soggy cardboard. Using the cheesecake as demonstrative evidence, I plunged my fork in and said, "See, no fear at all."

Then Philip took me home, and coasted in the door with me. I poured us a glass of Earl's organic wine and wondered idly how many cases of wine had disappeared from Dave's rental truck before the sheriff's department returned it to Earl's vineyard. We had finished the first round when Philip took off his glasses, pulled me into his arms, and kissed me.

Umm, those lips did more than just look good.

"I was hoping we might make love now," he said, lifting himself away from me.

While I didn't verbally respond, I did pull him back to me.

About the time I was *really* getting into the kissing, the phone rang. Bearess came leaping into the room and started barking at the phone.

"Ignore it," I said.

We did, kissing some more until the answering machine came on.

"Er, ah, Lilly? This is Tired. You better call me." He left a number. He didn't sound happy.

"Dave's still out of jail, right?"

"Yes," Philip answered.

We went back to kissing.

The phone rang again, and Bearess howled at it, and jumped on the couch with Philip and me.

I shooed Bearess off, but then my answering machine squawked out: "Lilly, Jackson here. Call me. Right now." Blam.

Philip and I looked at each other, I shrugged and reached for him, and the phone rang again. Tired left another message to call him immediately.

All right. I got it. Something was up.

I called Jackson first.

Before I even said hello, Jackson thundered out, "Somebody shot the man. Shot him dead."

"Oh, my god, not Dave," I screamed.

"Dave? Who's Dave?"

"Who got shot?"

"Kenneth Mallory. Somebody shot him at his house, a couple of hours ago. I just heard. It made the ten P.M. news."

"Mierda," I said, and hung up. So much for making out with Philip. I punched in the number Tired had left.

"Tired," I said, no need for any extended hello under the circumstances. "What happened?"

"That's what I'm trying to find out. You need to come down to the sheriff's office. I need to, to, ask you a few things."

"Like what?"

"Just come on down to the sheriff's office. I'll have somebody meet you out front. No, better yet, I'll send somebody to pick you up."

"Why me?" I shouted, but he hung up.

Naturally, Philip went with me, riding politely in the backseat of an official car while I worried in the front. I mean, okay, what was I, the karmic center for murder? We were up to three bodies in the last week, and still had Saturday to go. Plus, I thought, Tired sounded as if he thought I was a suspect.

Which, as it turned out, he did.

CHAPTER 20

After all the time I had spent wishing ill winds to blow upon Kenneth Mallory's head, I actually felt guilty.

But what I also felt was uncharitable relief.

That is, until I got the gist of Tired's questions and realized he had penciled me in as the most immediate suspect in Kenneth's death.

"Hey, bud," I said, jumping up out of my plastic chair in a tacky, dank, and cramped little interview room at the sheriff's department, "I've got an alibi."

"Lilly," Philip repeated in his official, i.e., not Dean Martin, voice, "for the last time, be quiet."

Oh, yeah, Philip had been counseling me from the get-go to keep my mouth shut, and just see what we could find out from Tired.

What we had learned after a circuitous and irritating route, in which everyone in the room, including some darkly dressed man introduced as Stan Vardamon, apparently Tired's supervisor, had raised their voices two or three times, was that Kenneth Mallory had been shot six times.

Between sniping, Philip had also managed to

trick Tired into admitting that one neighbor had heard shots and called 911, while still another had seen a car speeding away from Kenneth's house.

Therein lay the rub.

The car the neighbor had seen was a bright blue Honda, and not a new model. One with unusually dark, tinted windows.

After hearing the car description, I knew what was coming. After all, Tired had had a pretty good look at my not-new-model Honda, repainted in what was technically deemed cobalt blue, which incidentally did not look all that blue on the paint-sample card when I had it repainted after Jennifer the crazed StairMaster wizard had shot it all up, but to the layman it was probably just bright blue. And for security reasons, I'd had the shot-out windows replaced with darkly tinted windows, and would have gone for bullet-proof glass until I got the quote. I mean, really, do they make that stuff out of diamonds, or what?

It laid out pretty easy: Tired thought I had driven to Kenneth's in my unfortunately distinctive Honda and plugged the man with six bullets.

"Well, it wasn't me and it wasn't my car because—"

"Lilly, shut up." Philip put a hand on my shoulder, and shoved me down in my plastic chair.

"I have an alibi," I said, and shot right back up, hovering in Tired's face. "I've been out with Philip since eight P.M. We ate dinner in a room full of people, and I—"

Uh-oh, what if Kenneth had been killed at seven-thirty?

"Will you just be quiet and sit down," Philip said. I sat down.

Then we went forty rounds, with Stan interrupting and apparently playing his version of bad cop, though Tired was wavering in his imitation of good cop, and finally, I just flat out had had enough and stood up. "If I'm not under arrest, I am going home. I trust that the deputy who brought me will take me home."

"That's probably a good idea," Philip said.

"I want to talk to Lilly alone," Tired said.

"No, that is not advisable." Philip physically edged himself between me and Tired.

"No, that's fine. I'll talk to Tired. It's all right."

"Lilly, am I your attorney or not? I am advising you, no, telling you, ordering you, not to speak with Tired without counsel present."

"Nobody tells me what to do." Oh, except for Jackson.

Proving my independence, I pranced out the door, and Tired followed me out into the hallway.

"What time did Kenneth get killed?" I asked first.

"I'll go square with you if you do with me."

"All right. I think that's a good idea." Rather, I thought it was a good idea if Tired thought I was cooperating.

"We got the 911 call, shots fired at 8:35 P.M."

I grinned in spite of myself. That would have been just about the time I was harassing the manager of the swank Palm Avenue eatery and he, the waiter, and the folks at the nearest tables would be sure to remember me.

"Alibi, absolutely," I said. "Just somebody else's Honda. Must be a thousand of them in this town."

"Where were you?"

I gave him the name of the place, a brief highlight of my exchange with the manager, and, of course, the fact that Philip would vouch for me. Tired's face visibly relaxed, and I was touched to see his obvious relief.

"I didn't think you'd shoot a person," he said, and reached out and patted my shoulder for about half a second.

"Let's go back in," I said, that is, before Philip imploded.

Okay, I was off the hot seat, but I didn't have a clue where Bonita had been. And I really doubted that there were thousands of cobalt blue Hondas in Sarasota County, not ones as old as mine, and not ones that old with dark, tinted windows.

CHAPTER 21

Philip's hand on my arm didn't feel sensual, but rather custodial, as he pushed me out the door and toward a cab.

He groused at me all the way back to my house, but he also paid the cabdriver.

Then, apparently for the first time that night, he noticed Bonita's white station wagon in my driveway. "Where *is* your automobile?" he asked, eyeing me now with suspicion instead of anger.

"Listen, do we have a client-attorney privilege here?"

"Absolutely. Now tell me, where is your automobile?"

"Bonita has it. We traded cars. Just for the night. It's a long story."

"Then perhaps you should tell it to me as we drive over to Bonita's."

Chewing my lip, I fretted over what this might mean for Bonita. Then I realized it was only a mess for Bonita if Tired found out she had my car. "So, how good an investigator is Tired?"

"Do not let that shucks and ma'am country-boy

routine deceive you. Tired is a very proficient investigator."

Oh, frigging great.

Philip opened the passenger-side door in his car for me, and I slipped in.

As we drove off, at Philip's insistence I told him how Bonita came to have my car. Then I had to answer about six different versions of questions all getting at whether the car swap was my idea, or could Bonita have arranged it?

"Look, I know Bonita. You don't. Trust me on this, she is not the kind of woman who would trick me out of my car and then use it as a getaway vehicle after she shot a man."

"What kind of woman is she?"

I mulled this over a minute, wanting to get it just right. "If Bonita's house caught fire in the middle of the night, by the time the fire truck arrived, Bonita would have all of her children safely outside and all five of them would be wearing warm clothes."

"Would she shoot a man?"

"No. Absolutely not," I said.

"Would you?"

Now why would Philip ask me that? Wasn't he my alibi?

"Would you?" he repeated.

"It depends." The most honest answer anyone can give to almost any question.

"Yes, and it often depends upon the circumstances. However, you might be surprised by how many people find themselves perfectly capable of killing someone when the right set of facts present themselves."

"Not Bonita."

But as we pulled up in her driveway with my cobalt blue car sitting there, I had to wonder for just that fraction of a second.

The door opened before I knocked and Armando stood there with Johnny Winter, an albino ferret, wrapped around his neck.

"They've been home all night. Since work," he said and clumped off.

Well, I hadn't asked, but that was nice to know, I thought, and then walked in, gesturing for Philip to follow me despite the technical absence of a formal invitation.

Though it was getting pretty late for a house with five children, all the lights were on and loud noises came from every corner. I followed the noise to the kitchen, where Benny, Henry, and Bonita were seated around a Monopoly board.

Bonita arose and said gracious things in a strange monotone.

"*¿A que te dedicas?*" Bonita asked as I introduced her to Philip, but she didn't wait for his answer.

Henry stood up and greeted me formally. But as he shook hands with Philip, his face started blotching red.

Benny would neither get up from the table nor look me in the eye.

Mierda, I thought.

"You know Kenneth Mallory got shot tonight," I said and watched them for reactions. Bonita reached for her gold cross pendant. Henry blotched a bit more, and Benny stared at the card he had just drawn.

"We heard. On TV," Bonita said. "Earlier."

As I studied her face, I heard loud squealing noises from the living room and dashed in there. The other three of Bonita's children were running around with Johnny Winter, the famous ferret.

"Hey, *Tia* Lilly," Carmen said. "Wanna pet Johnny Winter?"

No, I did not want to pet the ferret. Notwithstanding the fact that Johnny Winter the ferret had saved my life once, we hadn't become bosom buddies. He was as apt to wiz on me as on anything else, so I shook my head no toward Carmen.

"Hey, *Tia* Lilly," Javy said, and untangled his legs and got up from the floor and stood on tiptoe to kiss me on my cheek. He and Carmen at least acted perfectly normal.

Armando was sitting in a corner growling at a handheld computer-game toy thing that teenage boys seem to have glued inside their hands these days. I introduced Philip to the three kids.

"Why is Johnny here?" I asked, wondering how Newly's ferret had come to live with Bonita and her children.

"Armando wanted a dog," Javy said. "And Angela was afraid she might catch something from him and made Newly get rid of Johnny."

Okay, a ferret for a dog, close enough, I guess.

Carmen insisted she must formally introduce Johnny Winter to Philip and this apparently involved shaking paws with him, but first the ferret had to be caught, and there was a whirl of motion and run, run, giggle, giggle, and then a crash.

Hopefully that milk-glass lamp wasn't Bonita's favorite, I thought.

"Uh-oh, busted glass," Javy said, and sprang into action, chasing down the ferret amid the shards.

Leaving Javy to the task of preventing cut ferret feet, I went back to the kitchen, where Bonita, Henry, and Benny were waiting. They weren't even pretending to be busy doing anything.

"Bonita, did you go anywhere in my car tonight?" I didn't see the point of beating around the bush.

"I did not drive your car except to drive it home."

"Did you loan the car to anyone?"

"No."

"Did anyone borrow the car?"

"No."

Damn, she'd be the perfect witness. Not a word more than necessary and a perfectly pleasant, but essentially poker-faced expression.

"You didn't go to Kenneth's house? Tonight? Today? Anytime?"

"I told you I did not drive your car except to drive it home."

"You sure?"

Oh, like she might not have noticed she was driving fifteen miles down Fruitville Road to Oak

Ford, entering through ostentatious country-manor gates, and driving up to Kenneth's fake *Gone with the Wind*-type house?

A peeved expression crossed Bonita's face, which I took for her answer.

Having irritated Bonita, I looked over at Henry and Benny. They were shadowing the doorway between the kitchen and the den. Neither of them would look at me or each other. I didn't like the feeling I got in the pit of my stomach.

"Benny, why don't you and me go into your room, have a talk," I said and tried to smile.

Henry the meek, Henry the bleater, Henry the man I'd been pushing around for years stepped in front of Benny and said, "Why do you want to talk to him?"

There was no mistaking the protective stance.

"Okay, what is going on here?" I snapped. Philip made those irritating shushing noises that always make people madder. I overrode his shushing by asking again, on the off chance no one had properly processed the previous question, "Okay, what is going on?"

"Nothing," Bonita said.

"Nothing," Henry said, blotching more. "We've been home all night. Since about seven. Your car has been parked in the carport all night."

While I assessed the rehearsed quality to that and tried to catch Philip's eye, Carmen came into the kitchen. "Do you want to see my new ballerina doll?" she asked, tugging at my hand.

I held Carmen's hand, but I looked at Benny. He hung his head and wouldn't look at me.

"Philip," I said, "perhaps you should take me home. It's late."

I was exhausted. I was beyond exhausted.

I was terrified.

Terrified that Benny had done something terrible and Bonita and Henry would go to jail for perjury before they'd ever back off from their story that all of them had been together since seven with the cobalt blue Honda parked in the driveway.

CHAPTER 22

With modest modifications, Saturday is as much a workday as Wednesday at Smith, O'Leary, and Stanley. The attorneys wear jeans and the secretaries work only half days, but the law clerks drudge their regular eight hours in hopes of being noticed and promoted, and at one-thirty the top partners all disappear for their afternoon golf games with judges and rich men with influence. We baby partners, along with the associates, drone on till we can't stand it anymore.

Despite the fact that one of our own had been shot six times in what the *Sarasota Herald-Tribune* quoted the sheriff as calling "suspicious circumstances," a modest understatement, if you ask me, there we were on Saturday. And while the recently-made-dead Kenneth was definitely the topic at the coffeepot, work went on.

But Bonita didn't come in.

I punched in her home number, not to belittle her for failing to show up for work, but to inquire after her and to see if I could speak with Benny. Nobody answered.

Next I tried Philip's number to see if he was still mad over my strident refusal to return to Tired's office and turn Bonita in as the person who had custody of my Honda, the reigning cobalt blue suspect.

Philip didn't answer. I didn't like the way we'd left things. He'd claimed he couldn't be Bonita's defense attorney because there was a conflict of interest presented by his representing me, but I said I wasn't a suspect anymore, and he wanted to know if I'd ever heard of a criminal conspiracy, and I said I wasn't stupid enough to conspire with someone to kill someone else and use my car as the getaway vehicle. We sniped and snapped on Bonita's front lawn until Henry came out and offered to drive me home in the infamous Honda, and then drive Bonita's car back to her. Jumping at the chance to get Henry alone and pry information out of him, I had agreed even as Philip insisted we leave the cars where they were.

Henry and I ignored Philip, and Henry, far from capitulating to my interrogation, was a model of discretion during the ride back to my house. All I learned was what they had had for dinner—pizza.

So my Friday night had not ended up with the romantic romp I had hoped for, but my ancient blue car sat outside my office window on a fine, bright Saturday morning, and if things weren't entirely right with the world, at least my quick recovery of the suspect Honda surely reduced the chances Tired would discover Bonita had my car last night.

Okay, wrong again.

I hadn't brewed my private stash of organic, fair-trade coffee before Tired was standing in my office doorway.

"You should've told me Bonita had your car."

He sounded angry.

"Coffee?" I offered, adding, "Good morning."

"Withholding evidence is a criminal offense. Did you know that?"

"Black or with milk? Sugar?"

"Black's fine," Tired said. "No, hell, make it sweet." Pause. "Milk too."

So, okay, we had that in common and I made us both the closest thing to hot chocolate you can make with coffee and generous amounts of milk and sugar.

He sat on the couch without being invited and sipped his coffee, and then we stared at each other while I wondered if we'd known each other in a prior life, or if it was just a karmic joke that we'd become so entwined of late.

"You should have told me about Mrs. de Vasquez. Having the car," Tired said, sounding peevish. "Why didn't you tell me?"

Oh, please, like that wasn't obvious.

"How'd you find out she had my car?" I asked.

"So you admit it?"

Oops. That was sloppy of me, I thought, launching the counteroffensive. "So who made the spurious allegation that Bonita was driving my car last night?"

"Nice try," Tired said. "This would be a lot easier if we just cooperated with each other."

"Oh, yes, wouldn't it?" I gave him the full brunt of my nice, cooperative-girl smile, and then re-asked, "So who made the allegation?"

"I followed you last night. Saw where you traded cars at a house in Southgate. Got the tag off the other car, plus the address of the house. Found out Mrs. de Vasquez belonged to the house and the station wagon. Then this morning, I found out she was your secretary."

Oh. Please, please, please don't know that Benny is her son. It was bad enough that Tired knew Benny had called in the dead man in the swamp, but if he connected him with my car, Tired might become an Inspector Javert to Benny and Bonita.

"You followed me," I snapped in an offended tone, hoping to bypass any Benny/Bonita two-dead-men connection.

Ignoring my indignation, Tired asked, "Who was the man who drove her car home?"

"Her boyfriend."

"Got a name?"

"Henry Platt." Yes, I'd sell out Henry, friend and comrade that he was, to distract attention from Benny. Especially since Tired probably already knew who Henry was, or could quickly find out in any one of a dozen ways.

"What went on last night?"

"Look, Bonita was home all night, she had a . . . a dinner party. Henry was there, and all her kids.

No way she drove that car to Kenneth's. And you have to admit, a blue Honda is a very, very common car. There must be hundreds, thousands of them in Sarasota."

"The neighbor who saw it drive away, she described it pretty good. Sure sounds like your car."

"Yeah, well, why don't you just put my car in a lineup. See if she can pick it out."

"Sounds like a good idea."

"Don't be ridiculous."

Tired sipped at his coffee, sighed, and furrowed his brow. "Why'd Bonita have your car?"

"Her car was blocked in the parking lot by a client's car. So I loaned her mine."

"How were you supposed to get home?"

"We just figured by the time I left, the client's car would be gone," I said.

"So, then Bonita left early?"

"I left late. None of the attorneys leave at five." At least none who wanted a continuing future with the firm.

"Okay, you left later in Bonita's car. Did Bonita leave early? Before five?"

Uh-oh, this could get tricky. Presumably at some point Tired would ask Bonita the same thing. If we told the truth, he would ask why she left early, and if we told the truth on that, then Tired would know Kenneth was harassing Bonita with that still-unfiled lawsuit, which smelled like a motive. But if I lied and Bonita didn't tell the same lie, we'd look really suspicious. Worse still, if I refused to answer, I would look like I was hiding something. Another round of change the topic was in order.

"I bet a car lineup wouldn't even be admissible. Are you kidding? Thousands of blue Honda cars in this city, and you're just totally fixated on mine. Why do you think that is?"

"I've never seen a car that color of blue before, ma'am. That's why, and that's what the witness lady said."

"Well, all right, do a lineup then." But please, please don't ask me again why Bonita had my car until we get our stories straight.

"This afternoon. I'll set it up. You have your car at the sheriff's department, back parking lot, by, say, two P.M."

"Okay, and that's that, isn't it?" Translation: Go, now, and don't ask anything else.

"Once you tell me why Bonita had your car."

When a lie is too complicated, sometimes a very carefully edited version of the truth can be twisted to serve the same purpose. "She needed to go home early, check on one of her kids. You know she's got five children, and one of them is always getting hurt, or stranded, or sick, or something, and I don't pay much attention to the reasons, but anyway I told her to go on home. But somebody had blocked her car in, and so I gave her my car."

"How were you supposed to get home?"

"We figured the car that was blocking her's would move by the time I left, after five, and I'd drive her car, and we'd switch back this morning."

"You were gonna switch this morning? So why switch back last night?"

Mierda, I was so tired of Tired Rufus Johnson.

"It just seemed the thing to do, no reason." Yeah, that was brilliant, huh? "Look, I have work to do," I added, hoping to break up our party. "And you've got a murderer to find."

"You told me that Benicio, the boy who called in the dead man in the swamp, was your secretary's son. So that'd make him Bonita's son, right?"

Oh, God, would somebody shoot me, or at least shut me up?

"Yes." There was, of course, no way to deny what was so easy to find out.

I watched the wheels spin in Tired's head, and the muscle spasm in the back of my neck kicked me, and I wondered if I could have done any better at making things worse for Bonita if I had set out deliberately to do so.

And then, to my profound relief, Tired thanked me for the coffee and left.

Punch, punch, punch with phone numbers, desperately hoping Bonita would answer. She didn't. I called Henry. He didn't answer. What? Dead men lying around everywhere, a positive karmic convergence of malevolence, and they go off on a frolic?

My fingers hit Philip's phone number with vehemence. This time Philip answered his private office number and I blurted out, "Is a car lineup admissible in court?"

Philip fairly sputtered at the idea and more than sputtered at the fact that I had had a conversation with Tired. Yes, he was still mad, sort of, and I thought, Oh, wait till you hear all of it. So I made nice, invited him to dinner, and asked if he would escort me to the car lineup.

"Somebody needs to protect you," he said, "so I will accompany you."

Under the circumstances, those being that I needed him, I decided to overlook the nineteenth-century chauvinistic, snide, paternalistic, and just plain irritating nature of that response, though I had to sit silent a moment and then swallow twice to do so.

We made a date, and I hung up and booted up my computer for a Westlaw search, Westlaw being one of the two premier computerized legal-database services that allowed attorneys to search for the law without leaving the comfort of their office chairs.

Oddly enough, I couldn't find a thing on Westlaw about car lineups. I tried LEXIS, the competing computerized legal-research service, and found a similar lack of cases or law on point, and finally I set out to work on some of my billable files.

Calculating that if I made lunch out of a pot of coffee and an organic dried nut granola bar from a box stashed in my desk, I could bill at least three, maybe four hours, I pulled open my newest legal malpractice file. I was to defend an attorney who I rapidly concluded was an idiot for failing to correctly calculate the two-year statute of limitations on his client's case. Then I jumped up.

If Tired hadn't already gone through Kenneth's office here, he would.

Before Tired searched it, I sure wanted to go through that office a second time to make damn certain that any traces of whatever Kenneth might have had against Bonita were removed from Tired's potential discovery. I also wanted to destroy any copies of Kenneth's pleading on behalf of the bottling company against Bonita—paper and computer both. If Tired learned of any of that, he might conceive of a motive on Bonita's part to shoot Kenneth.

Practically running down the hallway, I passed a covey of law clerks who parted like the Red Sea to let me through. When I arrived in Cristal's cubbyhole, she was shredding paper in a portable shredder. Not giving a rat's ass about what she was destroying, and thinking in general that this was a good idea, I smiled and spoke and she nodded.

"Is Kenneth's office unlocked?" I asked.

"Yes, but you can't go in there."

"Why not?"

"That investigator from the sheriff's office. The chubby one. He wanted to go through there but Jackson wouldn't let him. Jackson explained all about client confidentiality and all, and insisted he had to get a warrant or Kenneth's clients and The Florida Bar would be screaming at us. So nobody is supposed to go in there until that cop guy gets back."

"How long did Tired say it would take to get a warrant?"

"Tired, yeah, that was his name. He didn't say, but it's just a matter of somebody typing up the paper and finding a judge to sign it."

"You know this how?"

"I'm a certified paralegal. I know about as much as most lawyers. More than some."

So Tired could be walking in any minute with his warrant, I thought as my heart gave a conspicuous thump-thump. I pushed toward the door.

"Hey!" Cristal spoke rather sharply for an underling and jumped up with the speed of a mad cat to physically block Kenneth's door. "You can't go in there. Tired said he didn't have the manpower to post a guard, so I assured him nobody would go in there."

"Cristal, I won't hurt anything. I just need to take care of something. Real quick."

Cristal pursed her lips and stood her ground. She wore a red blouse and was really very striking, and I thought blondes should always wear red, and then I wondered if her hair was naturally that shade of blond.

Putting aside hair comparison, I reiterated, "Cristal, I need to go through Kenneth's office. Now." I put effort into sounding like a Boss Person.

"Look, I gave my word to that officer."

"All right, so you told me to stay out," I said and pushed her aside. Cristal scrambled to regain her balance and stop me, but I was determined. We more or less tumbled into Kenneth's office together, with her grabbing at my arms to pull me back and me yelling at her to leave me alone, that I was a partner and a boss and she'd better do what I asked and to take her damned hands off me. She had a darn good grip on my left arm and was tugging at me with surprising strength.

As we spun closer to a fight, I heard rustling papers and turned toward Kenneth's desk, with Cristal still pulling on me. To my amazement, Jackson was crouched behind Kenneth's desk, ransacking his way through his dead partner's credenza. Jackson, having no doubt overheard Cristal and me jousting, thundered at me, "Leave Cristal alone. Don't you practice law anymore, or do you just push people around?"

Oh, like there's a huge difference. And why exactly was he defending Cristal when she was the one who was assaulting me?

Cristal, to her credit, sized it up quickly and disappeared out the door, back to her cubbyhole.

"What are you doing here?" I blurted out, realizing just a half second too late that I had the wrong tone for addressing Jackson, especially when he was wearing his mad-grizzly expression.

"What are you doing here?" he thundered back.

Okay, he asked loudest. "I need to find some papers that Kenneth and I were working on and I—"

"You and Kenneth never worked on anything

189

together once I pulled you away from his workers' comp crap. Now, what are you doing in here?"

"He, ah, he was going to file this suit against Bonita on behalf of that bottling company, a relief-from-judgment complaint, trying to get her wrongful-death award reversed. He might have some evidence that would support this. I wanted to find it if he does."

Jackson looked at me like I had said that Kenneth was really the Evil Witch or the Evil Snow Queen, or whatever the hell she was, and I was looking for the ruby slippers.

"Evidence of what? On what grounds?" His voice echoed against the aqua silk wallpaper of Kenneth's office.

"Just totally bogus stuff."

"Such as?"

"He was claiming Bonita deliberately lied and defrauded the court and that those kids weren't really Felipe's."

"Felipe was her husband?"

"Yes."

"Even if he could prove that, which I doubt, he wouldn't be likely to overturn the whole judgment."

"But he could make her life hell trying."

"Litigation as extortion," Jackson said, catching on right away. "So what did he really want?"

Okay, in for a dime, in for a dollar. Ignoring time-line confusions, I simplified down to the known tangible. "A sack of cash."

Jackson stared at me long enough that I started to sweat.

"You're not dealing drugs, are you?"

Oh, like that's the only way to get a paper sack full of cash. "No, I am neither a fool nor a criminal." I hoped that was true on both counts, but in any event, it drew another long stare from Jackson.

During the pause, while Jackson studied my expression and I sweated more, I blurted out, "What are you looking for?"

"His billing sheets. You know that man was billing thirty-hour days, divided up between different clients so none of them would catch the overbilling. I don't know how smart that sheriff's investigator guy is, or if he'd understand about billing fraud, but I'm not taking any chances."

"So that's what Cristal's shredding, his bills?"

Jackson barely nodded.

"We need to get into his computer," I said. "But he's got his files passworded."

"How do you know his files are password protected?"

"Look, Jackson, let's get Cristal in here to help us bust into his files and erase everything. Better yet, let's take Kenneth's computer outside and run his Hummer over it."

"You're forgetting, we're on a network, we'd have to trash every computer in the place."

"Then we erase Kenneth's files from the hard drive now and hope for the best," I said, wondering how far Tired would go with Kenneth's computer.

"Cristal, get in here," Jackson bellowed, and she came running back in.

Though I thought Cristal was hesitant about giving up Kenneth's password, which was *lepidoptera,* whatever the hell that was, she told us, and Jackson and I had Kenneth's computer on and were pulling up his files before you could look up lepidoptera in the dictionary.

Once Cristal understood we were mostly interested in erasing stuff, she was suddenly Miss Helpful, and began to explain how she could pull up all of Kenneth's files at once and show us how to erase them in one zap, instead of a file-by-file, take-all-day sort of delete.

But before she started the process, Edith, our officer-manager jackal, came barging in without knocking or without greeting Cristal or me. She waved papers at Jackson. "Kenneth never signed that personal guarantee on the firm's bank loan like he was supposed to. Every partner was obliged to sign it. That was the bank's agreement."

"Son of a bitch refused to sign until I promised him I'd back his demand for a special performance, midyear bonus," Jackson said huffily.

So this was important how, now that he was dead?

"Well, the banker I spoke with was adamant— all the partners had to sign the guarantee," Edith said.

"No problem," Cristal said, and took the papers, put them flat on the edge of Kenneth's desk, and picked up a pen. While I peered over her shoulder,

Cristal signed Kenneth's name, backdated the form to two weeks ago, and handed it to Edith.

Edith stared at the signature a moment. "That should shut the bank up," she said. And she stomped out.

As most of the secretaries could do passable forgeries of their attorney's signatures, I wasn't surprised by her talent. However, I was amazed that Edith and Jackson were willing to let Cristal sign Kenneth's name to a bank document. Bonita limits her uses of forging my name to correspondences and the occasional firm-reimbursement form.

But then Jackson said, "Let's get on with it," and we all leaned over Kenneth's computer screen.

Cristal pulled up a list of all of Kenneth's files and vacated the computer chair for Jackson, who had his finger on the key to delete the whole collection when I noticed that one of the recent files was labeled EStall.

"Whoa," I shouted, causing Cristal to flinch and Jackson to glower.

EStall could be short for Earl Stallings. And if Kenneth had something to do with the dead vintner, then I damn sure wanted to know what.

"Let me pull this one up, real quick," I said. After I made Jackson get out of Kenneth's chair, I sat down and opened the EStall file.

Despite my anticipation, there was nothing but general information on rudimentary patent law. Essentially boring and nothing that Kenneth should be messing around with, as he was not a licensed patent attorney. Certainly nothing about Earl Stallings there. To be sure I hadn't overlooked anything about Earl, I did a "find" search for every variation of Earl and Stallings and wine and vineyard I could think of while Jackson made huffy, hurry-up noises over my shoulder.

Though neither Earl nor Stallings showed up as search terms, I couldn't figure what else EStall could stand for. But nothing in the file suggested any connection between poor dead Earl, mauled by his own grape picker, and dead Kenneth, shot six times by someone driving my car or its twin.

While I pondered what else to do, Jackson reached over my shoulder, clicked the EStall file closed, then deleted every one of Kenneth's files into never-never land. Jackson was not one to be indecisive.

But I wasn't so sure that deleting all of Kenneth's files was such a great idea. Of course, Cristal would have copies of all the legitimate pleadings on her hard drive, and there were paper copies of anything we would need to continue in the finest representation of Kenneth's clients, clients who, thanks to the Cristal and Jackson covert operation, would probably never know Kenneth had been fraudulently augmenting their bills.

Cristal and Jackson, no doubt, thought we were fine, just erasing any evidence of wrongdoing.

Tampering with the evidence didn't bother us, we were trial attorneys.

Cristal wiped our fingerprints off Kenneth's computer, the credenza, the desk, the filing cabinet, and the door.

"That way," she said, and smiled one of those sweet Girl Scout Angel smiles that was wholly at odds with her Victoria's Secret body, "I can assure that cop guy that no one was in Kenneth's office today, just like he asked me, and he can't prove who erased Kenneth's computer. We'll just say Kenneth must've."

Smart for a blonde, I thought, and swallowed my misgivings. Whatever qualms I had didn't matter anyway, this was Jackson's show, and he grumped a thank-you to Cristal.

I apologized to Cristal for my earlier impudence and she assured me it was all right, saying, "I'm never surprised anymore by what you attorneys do."

Jackson escorted me back to my office, while explaining that he was personally calling all of Kenneth's clients to reassure them that the firm would continue to provide quality representation for them.

"Please send some of the noncomp files my way," I said.

Jackson nodded. Then, as if he'd already forgotten my request, he said, "Guess we don't have to give him that midyear bonus and pay off his damn Hummer after all," and turned and marched down the hallway.

★   ★   ★

Precisely at 1:45 P.M., and armed with nothing except generalized anxiety, I drove my suspect car to the sheriff's department parking lot.

Philip was already there waiting for me, standing outside by his own car. In the parking lot, blue Hondas were collected in a straight line. I had to admire Tired's efforts in rounding up four other late-model blue Hondas, one an obvious repaint job, plus a newer Honda, and even a green one.

Philip led me inside with a minimum of pleasantries on both side.

A dumpy woman in an expensive dress, and a really very sharp haircut, was standing around with Tired and that Stan man. Tired nodded at me and then he and Stan led the woman out of my sight, into an office.

When Tired came back, we shook hands, and Tired took my keys and we all went outside and watched him line up my car, third from the left, with the rest of the suspects.

Philip and I backed off to join a small circle of other curious onlookers, and the well-coiffed woman came outside.

It took her all of a minute to pick out my car.

"That's such an intense blue," she said. "You can't help but remember that. And those windows. Can't see through them."

Philip immediately began protesting the admissibility of such a lineup. As he and Tired and Stan began to argue, I realized my head really hurt and I was standing in a parking lot in the glare of the midafternoon sun with nothing but two granola bars to fuel my blood sugar. A bit dizzy, I walked off toward shade.

Philip followed, took me inside, brought me a Coke from a machine, didn't laugh at me when I had to wash the top with soap and water from the bathroom, and we sat for a bit in the relative cool of the entranceway to the sheriff's office and I gathered he was over being mad.

Neither of us gave it much thought at the time that we'd left Tired and Stan with my car and my keys perfectly unattended for a good half hour or so.

CHAPTER 23

By the time I got back to my office after the car lineup, my first priority was to find Bonita and Benny. No one answered at their house. I tried Henry's number. No answer. Finally I thought to call Benny's aunt, Gracie, who was Bonita's older sister and had once been a nun in one of those Central American counties where life was often violent and usually short. As a result, or at least this was my suspicion, Gracie was a solitary woman who spent some serious time with her wine. Despite some chilliness on her part toward me, Gracie was a rock for Bonita, the first person Bonita called upon, and hence, I knew, she was the first hit on Bonita's speed dial.

Gracie took a few minutes either to decide whether to tell me or to figure out exactly who I was. "She and the children and that pink-faced man all went to Busch Gardens. You know, that fancy zoo and theme park. Up in Tampa."

Yes, thank you, in all my years in Sarasota, a mere fifty miles south of Tampa, I'd managed never to have heard of Busch Gardens.

"Thank you. If you see Bonita, that is, when

198

you see her, tell her it is terribly important that she find me. Immediately. And not to talk to any law-enforcement officers."

"What's this about?"

"Just office stuff, don't worry."

After hanging up, I thought, Okay, Busch Gardens. Not where a family of murderers would go on a fine spring Saturday, but exactly where nice, normal people—people who don't plug other people with six bullets—would go. I felt marginally better.

Now, I needed to find Dave. Dave who was staying at Waylon's duplex. Waylon whose last name I had never once heard anybody say. I called Philip to see if he had a number or address for Waylon or Dave, but got no answer. Then I had the vaguely brilliant notion that if Dave had worked for Earl Stallings before Earl got killed, that maybe the widow had hired Dave back. I mean, she did drop the charges against him. Or maybe she would have an address for Waylon's duplex on file, as Waylon had worked there too. Or she might explain something to me that would make sense.

Instead of going home and making myself gorgeous for my late date with Philip, I jumped into my Honda, released as it was from police custody, and I drove out to Earl's vineyard.

Driving past the closed Gift and Wine Shoppe and the barn with the weird little *Star Wars* toys, I followed the dirt road.

At its end was a most peculiar house, like a large, geometrical tent, shrouded in drooping fuchsia bougainvillea, elephant-ear philodendrons, and shaggy banana trees.

I knocked on the door, and to both my relief and surprise, Farmer Dave answered.

"Great, Dave. I've been looking for you."

"Hey, sweetheart, you found me." Dave bear-hugged me and kissed me on the mouth.

I struggled free, too anxious and curious for snuggling. "We've got to talk. You need to tell me—"

Dave did the dance of the frantic and shushed me with his hands and his mouth.

Just as I got the message, I saw the paunch of Investigator Tired Rufus Johnson belly up to the door. Why was he here? And how'd he get here? I hadn't seen any big-ass, black Chevy with its collection of antennae and a state license plate that was supposed to fool people as an unmarked car.

"What are you doing here?" he asked.

A very good question. I wasn't even sure I knew.

"So what is this?" I asked. "The house, I mean. It's most unusual."

"It's a yurt," Dave said.

"What's a yurt?"

"A house like this."

Oh, well, talking with Dave and Delvon was sometimes like that.

"It's an octagonally shaped house, designed to . . . expand . . . ," Tired said. "It has something to do with . . . spirits or something."

Obviously, Tired had received an explanation that didn't quite stick.

"Come in," Tired said, in a tone redolent with the essence of an official order.

Uh-oh, I didn't like the sound of that, but to rudely refuse seemed the greater of two evils. Besides, I was curious as all hell.

As I walked in, I looked around me. The yurt looked pretty high tech to me, though inside it still felt like a really big tent. Covered in a dense, coated fabric, the yurt had a high dome with a skylight. Inside was essentially one big room, with a futon folded into a couch in one end, a smaller futon couch in front of it, and an opened futon bed in the other end of the room, Indian cotton throws and pillows scattered about, and a long, wood table in the center. On the table sat a bowl of strawberries and a carton of vanilla ice cream.

Though essentially an oddly shaped room, the inside of the yurt seemed to offer the normal equipment of a house: gas stove, a small refrigerator and a sink in a corner, and one area with a wooden screen around it, which, I suspected, might serve as a bathroom. I had noticed a pump house and a generator when I'd come up through the dense philodendron-shrouded pathway.

Dave tried to put on his social personality and said, "Lilly, I'd like to introduce you to Catherine Susan Stallings. And, Cat Sue, I'd like to introduce you to one of my best and oldest friends, Lilly Belle Cleary."

The dark-haired hippie woman stood before me. We studied each other, Cat Sue and I. Both of us, no doubt for the same reason, that being the watchful eyes of Tired, refrained from mentioning that we had met before, though not formally, the night she had dropped off a paper sack of cash at my door.

In the light of the day and the yurt, I could get a better look at her. Cat Sue was one of those middle-aged throwbacks to the sixties and she wore a long, loose, batik-printed cotton dress that looked like either a museum piece or a nightgown. So, okay, I thought, you went to Woodstock. You have to keep wearing the same dress?

Wardrobe aside, I saw that Cat Sue had been crying and that her hair was a mess of long, gray-tinged strands, some of it hanging in her eyes, and she smelled just a bit like garlic. But under all that, I could see she'd been a beauty, maybe still was when she wasn't so crumpled.

Cat Sue, a name a bit too close to catsup for my own traditional tastes, hugged Dave and burst into tears. Toward the end of her crying, she pulled herself away from Dave, and offered us all chamomile tea, and before we answered, she said her doctor had just diagnosed a heart murmur.

"Told me not to worry, not ten minutes after he said I was suffering from generalized anxiety disorder and grief over Earl, and he gave me some Xanax to calm me down. I mean, wasn't the man listening to himself? Don't worry! A heart murmur on top of Earl getting killed." She started crying again.

So spank me for not being more sympathetic, but I kept thinking she was overplaying the scene a bit. I studied Dave and Tired and saw that Dave was totally roped in, but if I read Tired's face right, he wasn't. No doubt, Tired suffered from the prevailing prejudice of homicide detectives that the first suspect in the murder of a husband is his wife. As if reading my thoughts about Cat Sue as a possible suspect, and apparently not the least disturbed about doing an interview in front of Dave and me, Tired nudged closer to Cat Sue.

"How'd you and Earl get on?" Tired asked.

Cat Sue pushed some hair out of her face and looked right at T. R. Johnson. "Why, that man was so crazy about me I had to hide my underwear from him."

Tired immediately turned beet red.

"But how'd you feel about him?" Tired persisted.

Cat Sue looked puzzled, and then as we all studied her face she seemed to be digesting the question. She frowned, then hung her head. Then she pulled away from Dave and collapsed on the futon, crashed into the pillow, and started crying again. When I looked over to Dave and saw the way he was looking at her, I thought, Oh, hell, he's in love with her.

Tired caught my eye and said, "Come on, Lilly, let's you and me step outside a minute."

Outside, we ambled through the ferns and philodendron until Tired stopped, glared at me, and said, "I've about come to the end of my rope with you people. Now, what is going on?"

Damned if I knew. "Tired, honest, I don't know. Really. I'm trying to find out myself."

"That's my job, okay, you stay out of official sheriff's department business."

I nodded, registering the fact that Tired was actually pretty mad after all.

"Now, tell me why you're here."

"To see Dave."

"Why?"

"We're old friends."

"Cut the crap. You're smack-dab in the middle of all this, and if I have to arrest you as a material witness, by damn, you're gonna tell me what you know."

Mad begets mad, and I eyed Tired with my best Hard Look and said, "Look, bud, you arrest me for anything and Philip Cohen will have me out of jail and you suspended before that ice cream melts."

"Like hell. You been hiding stuff from me from the get-go, and now you're fixing to tell me everything." Tired grabbed my arm, and held on.

"You let go of me," I said, and let my tone of voice be my threat.

Tired dropped my arm. "Sorry, ma'am," he said.

Taking that as a good moment for an exit, I pushed past him and back into the house. As soon as I was back inside the yurt, I blurted out, "Listen, Dave, you get shed of Tired and come see me. I'm going home." Close at my heels, Tired had followed me. I could hear him huffing behind me.

Neither Dave nor Cat Sue seemed to notice Tired or me. Dave had cradled one arm around Cat Sue and was taking a bottle of pills away from her with his other hand. "Kitty, you got to stop taking these tranquilizer pills. You gotta face up to it all on your own. Drugs ain't gonna help."

Tender as the scene was, and as good as Dave's advice might be, coming from a man who had spent most of his last thirty-five years stoned except during periods of incarceration, Dave's words struck me as a tad hypocritical. But I wasn't interrupting them to point this out.

Cat Sue cried and reached for the bottle as Dave tried to keep it from her. Suddenly weary beyond belief, I eased myself back out of the yurt. Tired pushed past me without saying a word. I followed him around to the back, where his car was hidden from the front by pines, ferns and philodendron, and the yurt itself.

Standing in the cleared spot near his car, Tired inhaled and exhaled with some force.

Cautiously, I walked over to him, stood and inhaled too, and smelled the rich, dark loam under our feet. I looked around me as the late-afternoon sun was shifting through the foliage, giving the philodendrons a variegated look. Earl had had himself a pretty piece of property. For no reason that was readily apparent, I felt homesick for the red hills of my own Georgia.

"Damn," Tired said. "I sure am tired of being smack in the middle of other people's messy lives."

"Me too."

Well, we'd both picked just about the perfect careers then, hadn't we? It was clear to me that Tired was over his mad, but still in over his head.

CHAPTER 24

On the way home, I drove by Bonita's, and despite the fact that neither her car nor Henry's van was in the driveway, I pounded on the door until I was satisfied that not even alien spirits were home.

Being weak from hunger, I then went straight to the Granary instead of home first to clean up. While drooling in the deli, contemplating whether I could get away with another tofu cheesecake, I also considered whether I should fix a deli meal for Philip or actually cook something.

At the moment, I wanted a date slightly less than I wanted gray, frizzy hair. But canceling seemed so not the thing to do. Deciding it was too soon to cook for him, I figured deli food would be just the ticket.

So I bought the cheesecake, sprouted-wheat bread, and a tofu potpie, which the man behind the counter assured me I couldn't tell from chicken. Sniffing and prodding, I also settled on a ripe cantaloupe, a couple of avocados, and two bags of mixed greens, which, though labeled triple washed, would definitely get another wash in my own kitchen.

For good measure, I restored both my apple and granola-bar supplies. Then, remembering the ice cream at Cat Sue's yurt, I added a few cartons of some Rice Dream, some sorbet, and some organic, low-fat, non-GMO frozen yogurt. My total bill was only slightly less than my rent for a shabby room my first semester in college.

Rushing home and calculating how long it would take me to shower and get gorgeous, I spun into my driveway at just about the same moment my new grandmom came outside and waved at me.

I waved back, but declined her invitation for tea. Once inside, I scarfed half a carton of peach sorbet, and, totally recharged by the sugar, which these days was my primary drug of choice, I put my goodies away and let Bearess out into the fenced backyard, let her back in, let her out again at her insistence, fussed at her for acting like a cat, and let her back in again, then hit the shower.

My hair was still wet and I was wearing a towel when Bearess started barking at the door. It was too soon in our putative relationship for me to greet Phillip in a towel so I peeked first and saw Dave. That reminded me I still needed to get in touch with Bonita and Benny and I let him in. Dave wolf-whistled, but I ignored him and grabbed the phone and called Bonita. She answered.

"Bonita," I said, "it's me, Lilly," as if she wouldn't know my voice. "Listen, I don't have time to explain right now, but do not, don't, do not, not, not talk to Tired Johnson at all about anything until you and I have talked in person. Okay?"

"What's going on?"

Oh, wouldn't I like to know. But Farmer Dave was snooping through my CD collection, I was dressed in a towel, my hair was frizz drying, and I had a date due in just a few minutes, so I just reiterated my instructions and said I'd call her later tonight or first thing tomorrow. And, oh, by the way, how was Benny?

"He's in his room, listening to music."

"Fine. Don't let him talk to Tired either. Promise?"

"You need to tell me what is going on."

"Yeah, that works both ways," I said, "but Dave's here now and Philip is due any minute and I've got to fix supper and get rid of Dave and smooth my hair all in about the next two minutes. So, later, all right. 'Bye." I hyperventilated and hung up.

"Hey, Belle, where's all those Willie CDs I sent you? And who's this Chris Isaac fellow? Whoa, you still got that Emmylou I mailed you for passing the bar exam."

Dave put Emmylou Harris on to play and then, as if the world wasn't doing its best to throw up on us at the moment, asked again, "Where'd you put all those Willie Nelson CDs? Lilly Belle, I 'bout sent you the whole collection."

Yes, and I had about given them to Benny when he was doing some sort of school project that ultimately involved making mobiles out of round, plastic things.

"Don't know, Dave, it's hard to keep hold of Willie. Everybody wants to borrow him."

"That's true," he said, and then Ping-Ponged to the next topic. "I'm standing in need of that sack of cash you're holding for me."

"It's not here. It's in a safe place."

"Well, put some clothes on, we need to talk."

An understatement on both counts. On the way to my bedroom, I stopped in the kitchen to put the tofu potpie in the oven to reheat.

While I was styling my hair and wondering which would make a better impression on Philip, a little makeup or a well-set table, Bearess started barking and I looked at the clock and thought, Damn, why does that man have to be punctual?

Too late for the well-set table, I left it to Dave to let Philip in and I went for the makeup, slithered into white hip-rider jeans and an iridescent green cropped T-shirt. Forgetting to put on shoes, I ran out to greet my date, resigned to Dave as a second guest for dinner.

Philip and Dave were sitting on the couch, each drinking Earl's wine while Bearess knelt at Dave's foot, slurping something from my real grandmother's good china bowl.

"Philip didn't think giving the dog wine was a good idea, but, hey, I told him, what's good for the goose, and all that. I mean, Willie gives beer to his horses."

Willie also allegedly didn't pay his taxes, but how could I criticize Dave's choice of hero when my own thought he was the reincarnation of a dead general who sucked lemons for his digestion and had piously told his underlings to "kill them all" when the Rebels trapped the Yankees at Fredericksburg.

Before I could either greet Philip or rescue my heirloom china, the doorbell rang. Bearess kept drinking.

Tired and Redfish were at the door when I opened it, and Redfish giggled, then ducked his head into Tired's neck. "I brought you this," Tired said and handed me a sack.

I peeked in. Okra?

"I was sorry I got mad at you today. There's a market in Oneco where you can usually get good okra and fishing bait. My, don't you look nice."

"Thank you. On both counts." I stood blocking the door, unsure of the next step.

"Also, you being Kenneth's law partner and all, I wanted to tell you we recovered a gun today that might be the murder weapon."

Tired stared at me so hard in the doorway of my house that I thought I might be under a microscope or something. Under his scrutiny, I figured bland, polite pleasure would be the best response. "Well, good, good for you. How long before you know for sure? I mean, if it's the murder weapon?"

"Testing itself could be done in a day or two, but it's kinda hard to say to a DFS guy that this

211

is a priority case 'cause almost all of his cases have dead bodies with them."

Figuring that was cop talk for "I don't know," I murmured what I hoped was a reassuring noise and waited. Now what? Okra and information and scrutiny all done, wasn't it time for him to leave?

"Look, Redfish and me are going to McDonald's, if you want to come along?"

Setting aside for the moment the horror that Tired thought I was the sort who would actually eat a cheap slab of dead cow on white bread, I asked, "You feed that child McDonald's?"

"He loves the French fries."

Oh, frigging great, give him cardiovascular disease before first grade.

The good-food prima donna in me kicked in and I was warming up to a serious lecture on the value of proper food when Dave came up behind me and said, "Why, Tired, hey, man. And ain't that a fine-looking baby. He sure favors you."

Tired beamed. "That your truck, out in the road?"

"Girlfriend's. On loan."

I peered out around them and saw Cat Sue's white Toyota pickup parked in the street, more or less in front of my neighbor's house, and Philip's Lexus parked in front of it on the street. What? My driveway wasn't good enough for them?

When I leaned my head back in, Dave stuck out his hand toward Tired. "No hard feelings, you hear?"

Tired took it and they shook.

"That sure is a handsome little fella," Dave said. "Can I hold 'im?"

Tired beamed again and handed Redfish across to Dave. As I watched Dave and Tired bond, I figured their fundamental country-boy personalities transcended which side of the law they made their livings on, especially where mutual admiration of a child was involved.

Redfish cooed in Dave's arms.

Oh, what the hell. I stood back and invited Tired and Redfish in, offering supper and wine.

If Philip was dismayed to discover that he would be sharing supper and me with Dave, Tired, and Redfish, he was gracious enough to hide it. He offered his hand to Tired with the proper respect and passed a fleeting compliment toward Redfish, who was busy trying to unbraid Dave's pigtails and giggling like a thirteen-year-old girl practicing her first flirt.

Great.

After I had everyone except Redfish drinking generously from poor dead Earl's wine, I escaped into the kitchen to finish preparing supper for four and a baby. What did a nine- or ten-month-old baby eat? I wondered.

The tofu potpie was warming up nicely and I was glad it was a good-sized pie as I judged Tired to be a big eater and I knew that Dave was. Thank goodness I had lots of salad, I thought, and repetitively rewashed the trice-washed (That's just what the label said, okay? How did I know it had even been washed once?) salad mix and tossed it into a bowl with some equally well-washed grape tomatoes and generous slices of avocado.

Grabbing the cantaloupe, I washed it, put it down on the counter, rewashed my hands, realized I hadn't washed off either the plunger on the liquid soap or the handle on the kitchen sink, and I washed each, then rewashed my hands, and then couldn't remember if I had washed down the counter after putting the grocery sack on it earlier, and I started the whole process over.

On my third wash of the cantaloupe, Philip, who proved to be light on his feet, asked from the kitchen doorway, "May I ask, Lilly, exactly what it is you are doing?"

"Fixing dinner."

"Why wash the cantaloupe?" Pause. "Why wash it three times?"

There is no explaining these sudden bursts of obsessive-compulsive behavior that pop out at odd times, particularly when I'm under stress, and I just smiled wearily at Philip and said, "If the skin of the cantaloupe is contaminated, when the knife cuts through it, it might carry germs into the fruit."

Philip walked up to me, took me in his arms, and said, "I apologize for laughing last night. I thought you were making a joke."

"A joke? About what?"

"Being obsessive-compulsive."

"Oh, yeah, joking about mental illness is a good way to impress a man on a first date," I said.

Philip tightened his arms around me and kissed me. A good, nice, long kiss. Not with the toe-curling sensations of the kiss from the night before, but then the night before I had not spent the day destroying evidence and chasing my secretary and her son to coordinate wordsmithed stories of why Bonita had my car the night Kenneth was shot.

Pulling out of his kiss, I washed my hands and cut the cantaloupe, cleaned out the seeds, peeled it, and put in on a platter, while Philip hovered, making the inane suggestion that he help.

"Please, go watch things in the living room," I said.

"The other gentlemen seem to be doing fine. They are discussing something tedious about sooty mold and aphids in the garden."

"Just go check on them," I snapped.

"You really are high-strung."

"Listen, short man with thick glasses, I don't need your criticism right now. I've got a sheriff's office investigator and a fifty-year-old man with pigtails and criminal proclivities drinking wine in the living room and an infant pulling on the ears of a tipsy one-hundred-pound dog. Now why wouldn't I be high-strung?" With that, Philip apologized as I shoved him out of the kitchen with repeated instructions to keep the peace in the living room. In the solitude of my own kitchen, I finished washing things to my satisfaction and began to set the table.

Though the potpie gave out too soon, and I saw

Tired poking at the tofu chunks with a puzzled look, we managed to each get enough food to quiet our nerves. We finished off everything except the fake ice cream and we drank way too much wine and Redfish showed great gusto with the tofu cheesecake, but none whatsoever toward the salad. It reoccurred to me that I didn't have a clue as to what age you could feed what to a baby, but neither did anybody else, and we all just ate and drank and acted for all the world like this was a normal party and not a gathering of lunatics.

With some trepidation, I left them all in the living room while I cleaned up the kitchen. Each man offered to help me, and to each I refused because no one cleans up a kitchen to my standards except me. Dave did tiptoe into the kitchen to kiss my neck and tell me it was a "real good supper," and by the way, "that boyfriend of yours don't know spit about baseball. And you and me, we sure got to talk, and I got to get that money back."

I put Philip's lack of expertise about sports into his plus category, ignored the comment about the money, and shooed Dave out.

Then we all sat around drinking wine and playing the wait-'em-out game to see who would end up alone with me. I was betting on Dave, but rooting for Philip, primarily on the theory that kissing would be a better nightcap than interrogating Dave about just what he was up to.

But Tired was hanging in there too, no doubt thinking that catching me in an exhausted and somewhat tipsy state might make me bubble forth with incriminating answers about the sordid events of the last week.

Bearess lifted her head and barked at the door. Nothing to do but answer it, I thought, and opened the door to my neighbor, who was wearing her Covenant Nazi expression as she poked her head in my house and looked around. Redfish was sleeping, curled in his daddy's lap, and I doubted Nazi Neighbor could see him. But her face registered a certain level of dismay at seeing Tired and Dave.

"You having some kind of AA meeting, or what?" she asked, sounding vexed.

Oh, like it was any of her business.

"A church gathering," I said. "A committee discussing the organization of a . . . research committee on the burning issue of whether the Antichrist is alive today."

"Well, of course he is. Everybody knows that. But I came to tell you that all of your . . . guests . . . they are all parked in the street, instead of in your driveway. One of the cars is blocking my driveway."

"You were planning on going out?" At what, midnight?

"That's not the point. I want that pickup moved from blocking my driveway."

Covenant Nazi took a final look at my crowd and stomped back next door.

"Gentlemen," I said, "time to go before she calls the police."

One by one, they said their thank-yous and their good nights and left. I hugged Philip and Dave both, and whispered to each to be sure to call me in the morning, but not before six. With excessive formality, I shook Tired's hand and thanked him again for the okra.

Once they were all gone, I breathed a great sigh of relief. Tired's odd confession in my doorway about the recovered gun was the only mention of the misadventures of the last few days. None of us had talked about Kenneth or Earl or that guy in the swamp. No doubt because not one of us wanted to tip his or her hand in front of the others.

After putting Bearess out in the backyard, where she promptly began barking at a wine-induced hallucination, I went inside and began frantically cleaning up. I cleaned until on the verge of my dropping, Bearess demanded reentrance and we went to bed.

Tomorrow, I thought, as I listen to muffled dog snores from under my bed, I would track Benny to the ends of the world if necessary to force from him whatever secrets he was keeping from me.

CHAPTER 25

It is entirely possible, even probable, that there is no such thing as a normal life. Nonetheless, when I awoke at 5 A.M. with a profound need to clean the already clean house and throw out stuff, I made myself roll over again and hoped to fall back to sleep because that is what I believed a normal person would do on a Sunday morning.

At six, I said the hell with it and got up. I cleaned the kitchen, the living room, and the bathroom until my next guest could eat off the floor, the wall, or the ceiling. All traces of last night's company obliterated, I made coffee and fetched in the paper and woke a grumpy Bearess and put her out.

Sunday.

Normal.

Bonita.

A logical connection. Eyeing the phone and assuring myself that it was late enough to call, I did just that, announcing in my take-no-back-talk tone that I needed to talk to her and Benny right then.

"We're on our way to Mass."

"Fine. Come by and pick me up. I'll go and we'll talk."

"You'll come in? At Mass?"

"Of course." It was Sunday and I wanted to be normal.

In barely enough time for me to slip into a conservative dress and fluff my hair, Henry, dressed just as spiffily as a *GQ* cover, rang my bell and escorted me to his van, where I crowded in with Felipe Junior and a sulky Armando. We were so crowded, Carmen had to sit in my lap.

At Mass, I never knew when to sit or stand or speak, having been raised a heathen. The only church I had much experience with was Delvon's Pentecostal church, and there one could jump, roll, shout, sing, speak in diverse languages, and plain old holler without any preordained organizational patterns and nobody thought a thing about it. But Mass was organized and I rather liked it. Delvon's church made me anxious, especially since it was Delvon who was most likely to jump up and holler in a foreign language.

After Mass, we shook hands with the priest, gathered back into the van, and Henry dropped us all at Bonita's. Naturally Bonita invited me to stay for lunch. Given that she and I had not had one moment of privacy to discuss things, and I was hungry, I agreed. There was a large, loud family discussion about what we should have for lunch. Bonita apparently runs a democratic household and the five kids outvoted us. Henry was to go and get pizza for all of us. Bonita fretted over what he might fetch for me, but I assured her that a whole-wheat crust veggie for me and Carmen, who oddly enough for a six-year-old is a total green-pepper freak, would do, fat and all. As it is a well-known scientific fact that hot tomato sauce will kill germs, pizza is a food I can eat without washing it twice. Damn that Philip anyway, thinking I was afraid of food.

Inside Bonita's house, her answering machine beeped with a collection of two messages from Tired, identifying himself as a sheriff's office investigator who needed to speak with her immediately. He left four telephone numbers—home, office, cell, and pager—all of which Bonita ignored as she erased the tape.

Time was of the essence, Tired was on the case, so I dragged Bonita into her bedroom, eyed it covertly for signs that Henry might have spent some time in it, and, finding none, launched into a manic, short-winded version of my conversations with Tired.

"So you told him," Bonita said, studying me strangely, I thought, "that you loaned me your car so that I might go home, as one of my children was ill. That's it?"

"Yes."

"Nothing about Kenneth."

"Absolutely not. Nothing about Kenneth bothering you that day."

I waited for Bonita to sigh and chastise me for the tiny bit of wordsmithing involved in this.

She nodded. "You didn't say which child?"

"No. I told Tired you had so many I couldn't remember."

"Okay."

"Okay?"

"I'll tell Tired the same thing. He's left seven messages on my machine since Friday night. Carmen has allergies. I'll tell him she was the one sick."

Whoa. Bonita was going to lie?

The telephone rang. As Bonita moved to the kitchen to answer it, I practically dashed to Benny's bedroom, knocked on the door, and tried to open it. It was locked. Okay, he was a fifteen-year-old boy. Of course it was locked.

"Go away," he said from behind the door.

"Benny, it's me, Lilly." Damn, what was that word for godmother? "Your *madrina*. Open up."

Clank. Clomp, clomp, and there he was, looking as morose as he had at Mass, but no longer dressed as nicely.

"You have to tell me what's going on. Everything. Now," I said, vaguely ashamed of the begging tone in my voice.

"Nothing's going on."

"Benny, this is me. Lilly. Come on."

"Nothing's going on." Benny shouted this. "I'm not a . . . *chismoso*." He slammed the door and I heard the sound of a click. I banged on his door and then heard him turn the music up to an unhealthy level.

Bonita came trotting down the hallway. "Don't . . . don't take offense. He's—"

"Upset?" Yes, I could see that for myself. "Bonita, what's a *chismoso*?"

"A tattletale."

Uh-oh.

Benny was protecting somebody, and the two people who popped into my mind were Bonita and Dave. Until I knew what Benny knew, it was imperative that Tired not get to him.

"Listen, Bonita, whatever you do, do not, don't, do not, not, not let Benny or Henry talk to Tired. Neither one of them can lie worth shucks, and it's pretty clear that they're hiding something, and Tired is suspicious already."

I waited for a denial or a sigh. Instead, Bonita nodded. "We are Benny's *comadres*," she said. "We must protect him."

Comadres? Literally, co-mothers, or a godmother and a mother. Bonita had never honored me with this term before and I was touched. And moved to redouble my efforts to find out the truth and protect Benny. I hoped the two were not mutually exclusive goals.

The phone rang. Nobody answered it. After the sixth ring and the beep, Tired's voice came on again.

Bonita and I listened to the message, and we both sighed.

"As soon as Henry gets back, I'll send him and Benny over to Gracie's."

This seemed reasonable and I nodded.

"What are they hiding?" I asked, hopeful somebody would tell me before I popped.

Bonita looked at me a long time before she shook her head.

When Henry came back with the pizza, I phoned Philip and asked him to come over and represent Bonita because I would bet that Tired was going to appear at the door before the boys ate the last pepperoni. We had to have that stupid conflict-of-interest argument again, but I wore Philip down and he agreed to come over.

I wondered if he charged time and a half on a weekend, like plumbers do.

As it was, Tired beat Philip by about a half hour, but Henry and Benny had made their escape before Tired got there, and before Philip arrived, Carmen charmed Tired with her detailed narrative of her version of "Snow White," which involved a Mexican princess and a toad who kissed her and something about a horse with wings.

And because Philip was very, very good at his job, all Tired learned was that Bonita and her children had spent Saturday at Busch Gardens, gone to Mass this morning with me, then gone for pizza, and that Bonita and I had traded cars on Friday afternoon so she could pick up Carmen at Gracie's because Carmen has allergies. If this was news to Carmen, she didn't let on, and I was sure Henry would coach Gracie on the same story.

And, to Tired's credit, he was unfailingly polite,

and if he knew he was being wordsmithed to, he didn't show it.

After Tired left, I went in search of Dave to have the conversation with him I hadn't had with him the night before. But for all I learned from him, as he sat on the hippie couch in the yurt with no sign of Cat Sue anywhere, I could have saved that long, slow drive through traffic on State Road 72. He insisted that he had to have "his" money back, and that he didn't know anything, hadn't personally known Mike Daniels, aka dead swamp man, didn't know Kenneth, didn't know what or if Benny was hiding anything, and his only sin was loving a married woman and stealing her husband's wine.

"So, okay, explain that wine thing, then. Why'd you steal it?"

"Ah, Lilly Belle, I just got hurt and pissed off."

Huh? I thought money was the motive. "What do you mean?"

"See, Cat Sue and me had kind of taken up with each other. Keeping company, and all. I got in deeper than I meant to, so I asked her to come away with me. You know, leave Earl. Go up to Georgia with me. Or maybe Oregon. But she turned me down, broke up with me. Gave this long, old speech about what a great man Earl was."

"So you stole Earl's wine because his wife wouldn't leave him?"

"Man, yeah. I asked myself what Willie might do, and you know, I thought of the *Red-Headed*

225

Stranger album, and just figured Willie would steal the wine and ride off into the hills."

Well, okay, there was Dave logic in that somewhere.

"Then why'd Cat Sue drop the charges after Earl was dead? Wasn't she mad at you?"

"Look, Cat Sue's . . . she's not like you. She's not good at being alone. And it's not like you think, me here with her now. We're not . . . you know, we're not . . . she's still too broke up over Earl."

Dave was telling me that he was living with a woman and doing her bidding, but without sex? My Lord, he *was* in love.

"Man, see, without Earl, she needed me," Dave said. "So when Philip explained to her that as the . . . what did he call it? Successor in interest or something to Earl's wine, you know that man talks like a lawyer, don't you? Anyway, once Philip explained to her that she stood in Earl's shoes and could drop the charges, she did just that. Cat Sue wanted me back to help her, and she needed me."

Something still didn't ring a 100 percent true here, though a 100 percent with Dave was a lot to ask. "But that night Waylon came to get the wine, Cat Sue brought him to my house."

"Yeah, see Earl got home unexpectedly, he was supposed to be in San Francisco on some wine-convention deal, but I guess he got bored or something. Anyway, I thought I had a few days, but Cat told me later that when Earl came back, he went to check on things and found the wine stolen. She figured me for it right away, and, man, she still had a soft spot for me. So, after Earl went for the sheriff, Cat Sue got Waylon and they were trying to get the wine back so they could, you know, sweet-talk Earl out of calling the police. But, like you know, that didn't work."

Dave paused, and I thought he looked wistful, perhaps like a man still struggling with unrequited love.

"So after you and Benny found that dead man in the swamp with the money, you had Benny take the cash to Cat Sue to use to get you out of jail, right?" Damn, talk about your leading question. Where was opposing counsel to object? Realizing I had just fed Dave the official Benny explanation, I waited for Dave's reaction.

When he only nodded, I pressed forward.

"Why didn't you just tell Benny to take the money to me?"

"See, 'cause I wanted Benny to . . ." Then he stopped. Dave looked at me and frowned. "Yeah. You know . . ." This time Dave paused for so long I could practically hear the wheels of deception peeling rubber in his brain. "See, I . . . Well, I reckon that would've made more sense. I mean, normally I like to ask myself what Willie would do, but, man, I didn't have time. See, things were happening so fast, I guess I just didn't think clear."

Well, that'd be a first, I thought.

As I tried to assimilate Dave's story into some Big Picture that made sense and assess just how much Dave was lying to me, he said, "You know, I sure could use that sack of money back. I've got me some expenses."

While I wasn't entirely clear that Dave's claim to the sack of cash was any greater than mine—oh, yeah, okay, he had found it in a wild-hog-and-snake-infested swamp, but I'd been hit over the head and sent to the ER in the act of losing it and had broken and entered to steal it back—I did offer a compromise. "I'll get that sack of cash back to you, but you tell me the absolute truth about the night you got arrested."

"Belle, sweetheart, I just did."

We glared at each other a bit, me accusingly so and Dave with the face of an innocent. After a few more rounds, I officially gave up and left Dave with the offer that once he told me everything, I would bring him back the sack of cash.

Still frustrated, I went to my office with the firm intention of working, but I sat and ruminated. What I finally settled into worrying about the most was Bonita. And Kenneth. And his threatened lawsuit against her. The more I worried and pondered it, the more I wanted a good look inside Kenneth's house.

Figuring Henry for another breaking-and-entering project, I phoned him at Gracie's, where he was hiding from Tired. Gracie didn't want to admit that Henry was there. But when I insisted that I already knew Henry was at her house, she put him on the line. Henry took some serious convincing, but I told him we needed to be sure there was nothing at Ken's that would hurt Bonita. That pretty much did the trick in the end. Reluctant Henry and I made a date for 2 A.M. at my house as the staging zone and I told him not to wear a suit and tie this time. Then I went home and made coffee and paced until Henry drove up, right on the dot of two.

Ever the Girl Scout of the B&E set, I handed Henry plastic kitchen gloves, put my own yellow gloves in the hip pockets of my black jeans, and we tiptoed outside, me hoping Covenant Nazi next door wasn't peeking out her windows at me.

"I'd better . . . drive, eh, use . . . take my car, van, because your car, Honda, is already . . . so—"

"Conspicuously well known in the neighborhood?" I finished up for him, as I was in a bit of a hurry.

"Yes."

"Good idea. Your green minivan will blend right into the neighborhood out there."

Thus agreed, Henry drove us out east, down Fruitville Road and toward the country estates known as Oak Ford.

Though he might have thought of it on his own, I told Henry to park on the opposite side of the street, a few houses down from Kenneth's house. We sat in the van for a minute or two, listening for dogs suddenly barking or lights flashing on.

Nothing happened. So we slipped out of his van and walked quickly, but quietly, to Kenneth's, where we saw the yellow police crime tape and all kinds of warnings not to trespass. But, as if that rule only applied to the front, we went around to the back.

Fortunately for us, the back door was neatly hidden from view on one side by a trellis with some kind of climbing vine and on the other by a decorative wall inlaid with Mexican tiles, most of which appeared to have butterfly artwork on them.

Musing that the builder certainly hadn't been home-security-oriented, I held the flashlight on the door lock for Henry, secure in the belief that the glow of the light was hidden from the neighbors by the wall and the trellis. The door itself consisted of a wooden frame painted a pale yellow, with a stained-glass insert in a butterfly design. Wearing his kitchen gloves, Henry pulled out little, shiny stick things and started tinkering with the lock.

And he tinkered.

And tinkered.

And muttered, and bleated, and danced and strutted a bit on the stage of the back patio, full of sound and fury after he jabbed his thumb with a sharp tool, and my arm was getting tired from holding the flashlight, and I snapped, "Would you hurry up."

"This is hard, difficult . . . it's a good lock, not like that one at your office."

Tinker, tinker, tinker.

My nerves were fraying. In the ultrasilence surrounding us, I could hear little tiny snapping noises inside my head as the synapses popped off

230

my nerve endings and landed not axon to dendrite as nature designed them to do, but leaping off wholly into the open space of my gray matter.

My God, I could hear the internal combustion of my own mind going nuts.

But even as I listened to my brain break down, I stood there holding the flashlight for Henry. Sweat trickled down my neck. Inside my gloves, my hands were hot and sticky.

I lowered the flashlight to rest my arm, provoking whiney noises from Henry, and in the lowered light I saw a row of potted impatiens and begonias by the decorative wall of tiled butterflies. Nice touch, I thought, Kenneth must have hired a gardener.

"Light, I need light," Henry whispered.

Help was what Henry needed. With my gloved hands, I picked up the closest clay pot of impatiens from the patio and swung it back as far as I could, then forward with some serious energy, and I knocked out the glass pane in the back door. "Works every time," I said as Henry began to make sputtering noises.

"I could have done that," Henry said, "if I'd wanted to disturb . . . wake up . . . alarm the whole neighborhood."

So how loud was that? I wondered. We both stood there, waiting for any neighborhood lights to flash on, burglar alarms or sirens to shriek, dogs to howl, guns to blast out in the night, or any other obvious or nonobvious sign that we should run like greyhounds toward the van down the street.

Seconds, maybe minutes passed. I guessed sound-proofing was one of the virtues of five-acre lots and plenty of trees and houses with air conditioners running behind shut windows.

But when not even a dog barked, we looked at each other with some amazement and not a little relief, and I stuck my hand through the hole in the glass, popped the lock and turned the door handle, and we went into the house.

Flashlights in gloved hands, we wandered to the front-entry hall, where in a moment of perverse something or other, I studied the blood splatters of Kenneth's last milliseconds among the living, and Henry made little gulping noises.

All right, I reminded myself, don't take Henry on any more B&Es. The man was not cut out for it.

On the other hand, I suddenly realized I was having fun. Not with the blood splatters, no, that was gross, but with the idea that I could plunder Kenneth's house and seek his secrets and, perhaps, unravel the various mysteries circling us like bats out of a belfry and hopefully help Bonita by finding something about Kenneth's threatened fraud suit against her.

"Let's get out of here," Henry said.

"Yeah, let's find his bedroom and start there."

"I mean, let's get out of here."

"Oh, the house. Not on your life. We came here to help Bonita. You forgetting that?"

"Then hurry."

Yeah, all right. Leaving the scene of the murder,

we prowled down the hallway of the big house until we found the master bedroom. With Henry pleading with me in a truly irritating mantra to rush, I searched the obvious places first, the chest of drawers, the closet, under the mattress, behind the picture frames (no safe), et cetera, et cetera. Kenneth's jewelry box, a large, carved wooden thing with a toy lock that Henry popped open in a second, contained a modest coin collection, a Rolex, a diamond pinkie ring tacky even for Kenneth, and six antiquey-looking rings. Women's rings. I wondered a bit at that as I admired them. One of them had a diamond, another a ruby, and one a light blue stone I couldn't place. All very nice. I slipped the rings in my pocket while Henry pretended to search through Kenneth's shoe boxes. Then I slipped the pinkie ring, the Rolex, and the box of coins into my purse, which I was lugging around for precisely this reason.

Other than pulling up the carpet, I couldn't think of anything else to do in the bedroom, and Henry was whining again that we were taking too long, so I sent him to the next bedroom, and took a gander at Kenneth's bathroom.

His prescription medications were useless to me. Typical middle-aged man with good insurance and discretionary-funds stuff—Viagra, Rogaine, and Renova.

"Lilly, Lilly, come here," Henry fairly shouted though the dark house.

I scampered down the hall to the other end of

the house where Henry was standing in front of a room that logically should have been a den or office.

Peeking in, I shouted, "Whoa," myself, and stood back, then stepped into the room through a screen door behind the wooden door that Henry had opened.

At once, I could feel the temperature change. Moist and warm. The air smelled like privet and honeysuckle in the spring. Things hummed in the corners. Henry and I shined our flashlights about the room. All about us were ferns and violets and hanging baskets and willowy plants with delicate flowers or spikes of bloom.

And butterflies.

Hundreds of them.

I eased into the room, fully amazed in a way that's hard for me to be.

Kenneth had built a butterfly garden in his den.

Henry shut the wood door. No doubt the botanist in him wanted to keep the environment right for the butterflies and ferns and violets.

Henry kept repeating, "Oh, my lord, oh, my lord."

I needed to turn on the overhead light and see this more fully. I stepped over to the one window in the room and checked it out. Plantation shutters, behind which a thick blind covered the glass pane.

Surely that would block the light from any curious neighbor. I went back to the door and switched on the overhead.

Once the room was fully illuminated, I could see rows of lights in the ceiling and various other machine-type things in the corners.

Butterflies flittered about, gracing the air with a hallucinogenic quality.

"Grow lights," Henry said, and pointed at the ceiling. "Misters and climate control and . . ."

I stopped listening to him and just looked. Once Delvon and Dave and I had gone to Pine Mountain in western Georgia because Dave wanted to consult with the head gardener at the resort about the proper blend of cow poop and lime and rock phosphate to plump up our native sand on clay, and Delvon and I had wanted to go for a long ride. At Pine Mountain, there had been a butterfly garden, a netted structure of green and light and butterflies, which had been a total wonderment to us. Delvon, Dave, and I had stood in delight inside that butterfly garden, and we'd promised to return, though we never did. But I never imagined anyone could build one inside his own house.

"This would cost a fortune," I said.

"Yes."

"Henry . . ." I didn't know what to say. Had this been the obsession that drove Kenneth to cheat and push and grab so for more and more money?

"We need to get out of here," Henry said.

We backed out the door, I turned off the light, and we made a whirlwind tour of the rest of the house.

Though I couldn't entirely shake the mood the

butterfly room had cast upon me, I focused back on the job at hand.

Two bedrooms were completely empty, and Henry and I together ransacked Kenneth's home office without finding anything of particular value or interest, but I added Kenneth's laptop to the collection of things I was going to take with me when we left.

In the hutch in the formal dining room, I found a box of antique silverware, which I figured might have been the ex-wife's. "Might as well make it look like a burglary," I quipped to Henry, and tucked the box under my arm. I couldn't carry both the laptop and the silver, so I handed the laptop to Henry and braced for protest. But Henry's expression indicated he'd entered a zone beyond comprehension of the petty, and he took the laptop like a man sleepwalking through a jungle of butterflies.

Kenneth's kitchen indicated that he didn't cook much, but drank a great deal of orange juice. The freezer had only ice, designer coffee, and a collection of frozen orange juice. The refrigerator had beer, wine, three containers of not-from-concentrate orange juice, and a plate of pellets that looked vaguely like what one might feed fish or birds or something like that.

The kitchen done, I glanced at my watch. It was getting close to five, a time when paper boys come and alarm clocks go off. But we'd found nothing concerning Bonita. Nothing helpful.

"We've got to go," Henry said for the twelve-hundredth time.

On a final spin through the den, I contemplated where else Kenneth might have hidden something about Bonita.

"Okay, stay here and get caught . . . discovered . . . eh . . . arrested. I'm leaving."

Henry started toward the front door, but I ran up to him and said, "Back door," and in concert we turned to leave the way we'd come in.

After easing out from the rear, we hid in the bushes that surrounded the house as we slipped around front and ran like scared bunnies toward his van and then drove home in an odd silence.

Back at my house, I kissed Henry on the cheek and thanked him for being a proper escort. As if he had been my companion at the theater.

"Well, I guess we've broken enough laws for one night. I'm going home now," he said, but he carried the laptop inside for me while I lugged the rest of Kenneth's loot that we had appropriated for study and to cover our tracks.

After washing off my breaking and entering in lots of hot, soapy water, I napped fitfully for an hour, and woke, startled, just seconds before the alarm went off to signal another Monday.

CHAPTER 26

The first shoe dropped about two-fifteen the next afternoon.

At precisely that time, Philip called me with the news that the autopsy report on Kenneth showed he had been shot by a .38.

Yeah, okay, just about the most common gun in America, I thought. That ought to be a big help to Tired.

"How are you such buddies with the medical examiner that you get autopsy reports?" I asked.

"I have my sources," Philip said.

Okay, the deep throat of the criminal-defense system. Of course, I had my courthouse spies too, as did most good litigators.

"But here's the particularly intriguing aspect to it," Philip added, then paused dramatically, waiting for the tension to build.

"I'm not on a jury, just tell me."

"The bullets, all six of them, were of an unusual make. An old-fashioned type of bullet."

So, what, an old-fashioned type of killer shot Kenneth? How was this helpful?

"They're 158-grain roundnoses. Not the FBI

load, which are hollow point, but the older kind. Ever heard of those?"

For a moment I couldn't breathe. I had the distinct sensation that I was choking and I put the phone down so Philip wouldn't hear me in the final death throes of asphyxiating from stress.

Of course I'd never heard of a 158-grain round-nose bullet before last Saturday when I'd found a box of them in Farmer Dave's backpack in my house, back when I was a relatively normal person with a passably pleasant life, and not the karmic center of lunatics and dead people for Sarasota County.

"Lilly? Lilly?"

I picked up the phone. I made a noise that sounded like choking to me, but must have sounded like "Please continue" to Philip.

"In the old days, when the .38 was standard police issue, 158-grain roundnoses were widely used. But those bullets didn't expand. Not only that, the roundnoses were poor performers in soft tissue and sometimes could yaw 180 degrees in living tissue. In forensic circles, those bullets became notorious for exiting the target and hitting innocent bystanders."

Oh, yuck. Please, spare me some details, I thought as I made another choking noise.

"So, that particular bullet is rarely used anymore. Given its rarity, Tired and his crew might get a break in tracking Kenneth's murderer. It's only a remote possibility though. They don't have the manpower to check every possible outlet for old bullets. Plus, now, with the Internet, the shooter could have purchased those bullets on-line."

"So, it doesn't really mean much, does it? That the bullets were, er, unusual."

"No, probably not, but it's interesting."

Oh, yeah, it was that. Interesting that the bullets that probably killed him had been in my spare guest room just days before Kenneth learned whether there is an afterlife.

For the time being, I decided to keep this information just between me, and me.

CHAPTER 27

On Tuesday, just in time to ruin my lunch, the other shoe dropped.

Officer Tired Rufus Johnson appeared, sans appointment or phone call, at my open office door with a no-nonsense look on his face. Bonita was away from her cubbyhole and out of the range to protect me from intruders without appointments.

"Did you see the story in the paper?" I asked, still innocent of the reason behind his visit. "Page two of the B section. Somebody robbed Kenneth's house."

Tired ignored this offering as a conversation topic. "I'm going to need you and Bonita to come down to the sheriff's department and let us take some elimination prints."

"Elimination prints?"

"Yes, just to rule out your and Bonita's prints from the ones we have lifted from Kenneth's house, and—"

"I know what elimination prints are," I snapped. After all, I had dated a senior homicide detective and I did watch the occasional cop TV show. "That's when you take the maid's prints to eliminate the prints of the nonsuspects from the ones of the potential killer."

"Yes. We'd like to eliminate you and Bonita from the prints we've taken at the house."

"Eliminate us, hell. You mean implicate us."

Bonita chose that unfortunate moment to reappear from the copy center with a stack of memoranda of law, and Tired greeted her and told her she needed to come down to the jail and be fingerprinted. He phrased it in a way that suggested no was not an option.

Bonita put the stack of memoranda on her desk and said, "Lilly, I believe I will call Philip."

"Yes. Do," I said.

Then I turned to a weary-faced Tired and said, "You might as well leave. We're not going anywhere with you until Philip says we must."

"Then I'll go start the paperwork for a subpoena," Tired said. "I was hoping we could do this the easy way."

After a huffy Tired left, Bonita gave Philip a cursory version of Tired's request over the phone, then put him through to me and I gave him the same story but with more words and a great deal more inflection in my voice.

Philip promised to see what he could find out. He did, as he reminded me, have his sources in the sheriff's department.

Bonita and I pretended to eat lunch, we pretended to work, we pretended we were not scared.

But all bravado aside, when Philip arrived,

Bonita hurried him into my office and shut the door.

We barely made the requisite polite words to each other before Philip got to the point.

"The sheriff's department has recovered a revolver, a handgun, from your Honda, Lilly. The day of the automobile lineup. Remember, Tired had your keys, and we left him and Stan Varnadore with your vehicle. Stan apparently took an expansive view of your having left your keys with Tired to move your Honda and he found a gun in the trunk."

"A gun? I don't have a gun," I said, rather inanely given the big picture.

"Don't worry. Either of you. Investigator Varnadore examined your Honda without a warrant and without your permission, and given that you had an expectation of privacy—remember that phrase, will you, please?—an expectation of privacy, the weapon will not be admissible into evidence."

"What gun? I don't have a gun," I repeated before my tongue stuck to the roof of my mouth.

"It's a .38. Forensics has determined that it is the murder weapon."

There was a long moment during which none of us spoke and during which I wasn't sure I inhaled or exhaled.

"My source suspects that apparently there are fingerprints on the weapon. Tired will exhaust all possible legal avenues open to him until he gets both your and Bonita's fingerprints to do a comparison."

"Did . . . do the fingerprints match Dave's?"

"I'm sure they do not or Dave would be in custody by now."

I exhaled.

"The gun has the initials JEB scratched on it, but it is not registered to anyone, or, that is, nothing showed up in the NCIC computer," Philip added.

My breathing stopped again, and that peculiar choking sensation settled in my chest and I coughed.

And in the act of coughing, I remembered the Saturday when Dave had appeared at my door, bringing with him not just stolen wine but a whole personal Pandora's box of mini-Armageddons, that I had pulled a .38 with the initials JEB from his backpack and pretended to shoot out my window. Then I'd handed the gun to Bonita.

My God, I thought, I had framed myself and my loyal secretary for the murder of my own law partner.

CHAPTER 28

With Jackson's careful tutelage, I had learned to maintain a classic poker face under even the most vexing of circumstances. And when pressed to a wall by an opposing counsel, I can smile benignly and blankly and lie straight through the crisis.

In other words, I am a good trial attorney.

Jackson saw to that before he turned me loose in a courtroom.

Notwithstanding those hard-earned skills, when I realized that Tired Johnson had in his official possession Dave's gun—a gun that had been used to kill Kenneth Mallory and that probably had both my and Bonita's fingerprints all over it—I blanched to the point that Bonita rose toward me, her sweet face a furrow of concern.

And then she said, *"Madre de Dios."*

Philip, who had been studying me, turned toward Bonita.

"I take it there is something about that gun that the two of you know, but that I do not. This might be an excellent time to share that knowledge with me."

"Attorney-client privilege," I said. "For both of us."

"Absolutely."

But I remembered that Philip had not done a retainer agreement with either of us and that no money had changed hands, so in a fit of technicality neurosis I made Philip practically take a blood oath of secrecy that transcended the mere attorney-client privilege. Plus I made him write out a hasty retainer agreement in which he verified that he legally represented both Bonita and me.

After Philip's multifaceted reassurances, I spilled my guts in a carefully edited version. I told him about Dave leaving his backpack in my house while he went out, and about the gun in his backpack, how Bonita and I had more or less played with it, and then how Dave had reclaimed the backpack, and left, with Benny in tow. But I left the story about the sacks of money, and breaking and entering, and my fears about Benny for another time. Like, you know, hopefully never, or long after some villain I didn't know was doing time for Kenneth's murder.

"I'm glad you both realize the gravity of the situation," Philip said. "Although, as I've counseled you both already, you need to be cognizant of the fact that Investigator Varnadore took that gun without either permission or a warrant, and it would therefore be inadmissible evidence because—"

Here, Philip paused and turned to me.

"Because I had an expectation of privacy in the trunk of my Honda."

"Excellent." Then Philip turned and studied Bonita, potential murder suspect and fellow conspirator to obstruct justice. Not bad for a good Catholic mother with quiet ways. Clearly my karma *was* contagious, even if my obsessiveness was not.

Then I turned back to Philip and waited for him to connect all the dots. He was quick, I'll give him that.

"Bonita, I will need to talk with Benny, today, as soon as he is out of school," Philip added.

"Yes. I will see to that."

"And he needs to understand, as do you, that as he is a minor, neither Tired nor any law-enforcement officer can talk to him without your permission. And under no circumstances will you give that permission. You understand?"

"Yes."

"And you will make Benny understand."

"Yes."

"And I will need to interview Henry, and your other children, to make sure that their stories are all the same concerning the night of Kenneth's murder, and to test the believability of the alibis."

I noted, as no doubt did Bonita, that Philip didn't say the veracity of the alibis, but the believability. Not whether they were true, but only whether someone would believe that they were true.

247

"Then I need to talk at length with Dave and Cat Sue and find out more about this Michael Andrews Daniels—"

"Who is that?" Bonita interrupted.

"The dead man in the swamp," I offered and wondered what Benny had told her, if anything, about the day he and Dave found Michael Andrews Daniels in Myakka.

"While Benny is still in school, I'm going to track down Dave and have a detailed conference with him," Philip said.

"I'll go with you."

"No. Please do not. You distract me," Philip said and rose from his chair. And then, while standing, he smiled a tight, thin-lipped smile that did not do justice to his sensuous mouth. "Now that I've convinced you of the gravity of the situation, let me reassure you."

"Oh, please." Reassurance I needed.

"First, Tired is not likely to be able to use that weapon in any legal proceedings against either of you because he did not have a proper warrant or permission."

"But, what about that . . . I forget the name of the doctrine, but it means that if the law-enforcement officer was likely to discover the evidence by other means, the courts might still admit it into evidence? Couldn't Tired use that gun against us in court under that doctrine?"

While I was wondering how Bonita knew that much about criminal law, Philip made a small noise deep in his throat, almost like an aborted laugh, and I turned to look at him.

"I am glad you asked that," he said.

In my years of observing lawyers at work I'd noted that more often than not when they say something like that, they mean the exact opposite.

But Philip seemed sincere. He launched off as if he was Professor Criminal Procedure and Bonita and I were the cute girls in the front row. "The *Nix versus Williams* case, before the United States Supreme Court. One of its law-and-order opinions." Blah, blah, blah, he explained and explained.

"It is, frankly, a possibility that the gun would be deemed admissible under a *Nix v. Williams* analysis. But do not underestimate my ability to convince a judge to exclude evidence. It is one of the things I do best. Further, I do not think we will ever get to that point, and if we do, I am confident of my ability to convince a judge that—" And he turned to me, and pointed.

"That my expectancy of privacy outweighs any other point of view."

"But do cars have the same protection against illegal search and seizure that a person's home does?" Bonita asked.

"It depends," Philip said, launching into his second criminal-procedure lecture. "The protection in the Fourth Amendment against unwarranted search and seizure is generally applicable to automobiles as well as a person's home. However, courts tend to limit that protection at times. Because a person rarely lives in an automobile, the expectancy of privacy in an auto is not as sacrosanct as with a private residence. The Fourth Amendment protection against unwarranted searches depends upon where the auto is, who is driving, who claims the protection, and where the contraband is located. Say a gun or drugs in plain view—the defendant has a problem. Or where the safety of the officer is involved, courts favor the law-enforcement officers' rights to protect themselves. But courts generally accord the trunk of a car a high degree of protection because—"

"A person has an expectation of privacy," I said, getting just a bit tired of the game.

"Yes, precisely," Philip said, standing at the door like a man on a lecture circuit missing his cue. "Now my final point is that it is highly unlikely that any of your prints survived on the gun. Criminal forensics is probably not a field either of you has had much exposure to, given the nature of your law practice."

Uh-oh, lecture three coming up.

"If both of you played with the weapon in question by simply picking it up and dry-firing it, it is not very likely, due to the nature of the surfaces and the act itself, that your particular actions, would leave latent prints of value. If the weapon had been a semiautomatic, you might well have left latent prints of value by handling the magazine if either of you pulled it out, or, since this was a revolver, Lilly might have also left latent prints of value when she opened and closed the cylinder, checking to see if the weapon was loaded. However, we know that the gun was loaded and fired, six times, *after* Lilly checked the cylinder. Since it was loaded and fired, there is a very strong likelihood that any latent prints of value on the cylinder were destroyed by handling and firing. Assuming that the person who used the gun to shoot Kenneth wore gloves, these gloves would not protect latent prints of value already there. Any movement of fingers, even with gloves, over latent prints on a pistol's trigger or magazine would destroy their value for comparisons. And, of course, if the person using the weapon had not worn gloves, but wiped down the weapon after using it, all latent prints should be destroyed."

"So, any prints on that gun are likely to be the prints of the person who killed Kenneth?" I asked, thinking my education of forensics via televised cop shows and mystery novels might be a bit short of the ideal.

"Possibly. Perhaps. Or, of the person who moved the weapon to the trunk. The important thing for our immediate concern, however, is that it is highly unlikely that those prints Tired has on that weapon are either yours, or Bonita's."

"Then why not just go and give him our prints, look like we are cooperating?" I asked Philip.

"I will not give Tired my prints," Bonita said.

The shortness of Bonita's tone of voice made me swing my head around and stare full throttle at her.

251

Philip broke the silence. "You are cognizant of the potential conflicts of interest here, are you not?"

Oh, that again. Yeah, yeah, yeah.

"Dave was my first client. I cannot continue to represent either of you if such representation is at odds, real or perceived, with protecting Dave. And if representing Lilly presents any conflict, real or perceived, with representing Bonita, then I must withdraw as Bonita's counsel."

"Unless we sign a waiver, which we will do," I said, thinking, Yeah, I read the ethics rules too, bud.

"Very well, then, you two talk it over. Now, let me go forth and find Dave." And with that, Philip finally left.

As he closed the door behind him, Bonita looked at me and asked, "You trust him?"

"With my deepest secrets," I said, and tried but failed to smile.

Of course, I didn't trust anyone, not even myself, with my deepest secrets.

The bigger question to me at the moment was whether Bonita trusted me.

"Why won't you give Tired your prints? You heard what Philip said about our prints on the gun."

"What if he is wrong?" she answered, and then stood up and left my office, closing the door behind her.

Well, damn, I thought. She didn't trust me.

Then I wondered where Bonita thought her prints might be that she didn't want Tired to find them.

Given the anxieties of the afternoon, what was left of it crept along with Bonita and me trying our best to avoid direct conversation while conducting activities that we could bill clients for, but speaking strictly for me, I mostly stared at paper and ruminated.

So it seemed perfectly in accord with the cosmic plan to toss *mierda* upon the heads of Bonita and me that day that Benny's high school counselor called Bonita to report that he had not been in school that day or the day before and that he had missed two days last week.

Playing hooky.

Not a Benicio behavior pattern.

This Bonita confided to me as I leaned over her desk, where I'd come running at the sound of a phone call that she didn't switch into my office for me, blatantly eavesdropping.

"I'm going to go look for him," she said.

Where in the whole wide world Benny might be, with the unwise energy of a fifteen-year-old boy with a Ford truck and all the riches from his sack of swamp man's money, I didn't want to contemplate. But I didn't object to Bonita leaving to search for him.

Not too much after Bonita left, I gave up pretending to practice law and headed home, tail to tail with the rest of the worker bees' cars on Shade Avenue, to the relative sanctuary of my own house.

There, I opened a bottle of poor dead Earl's wine, drank half a glass before tending to an increasingly indignant Bearess, and then collapsed in my living room, drinking the second half of the glass, and desperate for a distraction from the wheels digging ruts in my brain.

In all the chaos of the last days, I had never read the Sunday paper. Though it was Tuesday night, I thought old news, the funnies, and pithy features might calm me down and I fetched the paper from the recycling bin and spread it about me as I sat on my yoga mat on my dust-free, shinny-as-new-terrazzo floor. The scattered paper lasted precisely ten minutes before I had to gather it up and throw it out. Papers, litter, trash, people, anything on my bare floors for any length of time makes me crazy. Perhaps this can be traced back to some kind of rebellion against the utter mess and garbage of the house of my childhood.

Piles and drifts of papers, magazines, dirty clothes, dead houseplants people were foolish enough to give us, Christmas wrapping paper dating back centuries, dirt, mold dating back centuries, vermin of myriad kinds and size—the house my mother didn't keep and from which she passively evicted brother Delvon and me when I was fifteen. We'd come back from an extended school-skipping spree in Florida and found she had sold our bedroom furniture and our clothes.

Wholly unknown to social services, or anyone else, even presumably my father, who appeared to go through life without rudimentary sensory perceptions, Delvon and I just moved in with

Farmer Dave, who despite being fifteen years older, became my lover in no time at all. I had adored him since I was a puppy and he'd brought Delvon home from kiddie detention on the back of his Harley. Dave had picked Delvon up hitch-hiking since the bus didn't wait for those held after school, and the two of them had bonded on some deep level from their very first "Hey, man." In light of the depth and immediacy of the attachment between them, I had always figured Delvon and Dave had been buddies in their past lifetimes, which, given their juvenile souls, probably didn't predate the 1800s, and if their age difference mattered, I had never noticed it.

When we moved in with him, Dave had forty acres of cleared, high land in a snake-and-bug-infested corner of the county, and Delvon and I and Dave became ace farmers of skunk sativa, a hybrid marijuana with a kick-ass high. Money was never a problem; I went to school often enough, in decent clothes, and with no telltale signs of abuse, addiction, or abandonment, and nobody asked why I never answered the phone at the house of my parents.

I was gone from the grim, dark, dirty house of my childhood. I didn't look back. Delvon, Dave, and I were family. We took care of each other, and I learned to cook, to garden, to sew, and to be an ace gardener, and finally, in my senior year, seized by an ambition to be more than the common-law wife of a pot farmer, I learned to study. I discovered I was smart. When I went off to college, I began to grow up and adapt myself to the regular world, but Dave neither matured nor adapted. We stopped being lovers. But we never stopped loving each other.

And so there it was: My loyalty today to Dave was as strong as it had been twenty-one years ago. Translation: There was no way I could tell Tired that the gun and bullets used to kill Kenneth had been in Dave's possession just days before the murder.

Of course, there was no readily apparent reason for Dave to shoot Kenneth, so none of any of this made any kind of sense, but there you had it. Dave never wholly made sense. In another lifetime, that had been part of his charm.

But charm has a short shelf life when three bodies are somehow laid at the feet of the man smiling between his pigtails.

CHAPTER 29

Though I rose early, fit in a killer workout at the Y, and land-ed at my Smith, O'Leary, and Stanley office wearing a steel gray dress that screamed serious-lawyering day, my plan was busted by Bonita.

That she sat in my office and drank from my private stash of coffee was my first clue that I wasn't going to like this day any better than the day before.

"Benny has been skipping school."

"Yeah, I got that yesterday."

"The reason he has been skipping school is that he is tracking that jaguarundi. Back in Myakka, in the state park. I found him yesterday, parked way out on Clay Gully Road, where he'd just hiked back to his truck."

Before I sat down at my desk to absorb this, I poured myself a cup of coffee, opened my minifridge, and topped off the coffee with enough milk to cool it down and add a couple of hundred calories.

"Why's he so . . . obsessed with a jaguarundi?" I asked, but wondered if that was just the excuse. The excuse to go back to where he and Dave had been, to the scene where all of this had started, or that is, had started for Benny.

"He is increasingly obsessed by the wildcat and I do not know why. Benny's done this before. Even before going off with that Dave. Since, I don't know, since he wrote that paper on the jaguarundi for school. You know, the one you mailed to Dave."

Well, yeah, of course I remembered that paper. If I hadn't sent it to Dave, maybe none of this would have happened; that is, maybe it would have all happened, but without Benny, Bonita, and me being slap dab in the middle of it. I was very sorry now that I had mailed a copy to Dave, but we know what the road to hell is paved with.

"He's done this before?" I asked. "Before Dave, he's skipped school and gone to Myakka?"

"Yes, I just told you that."

"What do you think this means?"

"He is my son, but I do not always understand him. I don't know what this means."

We pondered the various feasible meanings, psychological and otherwise, of Benny's fascination with the jaguarundi, but came to no conclusion.

"Where is Benny now?" I asked.

"I believe, that is, I hope, he is at school. He promised me this morning he would not go into Myakka again. Not alone. It is dangerous out there, off the main trails, for a boy like Benny, who lets his imagination get away from him."

Jackson banged on my door and came inside at roughly the same time he knocked. He was holding a file folder by his side and I fervently hoped it wasn't another one of his unwinnable cases he was going to toss my way.

"Taking tea?" he asked, slapping the file against his thigh.

"Discussing how to handle a case," I responded. "Coffee?"

"No, thank you. You two need to get back to our cases, not being social workers. All kids worth their salt play hooky. Boys who grow up to be men, real men, go off in the woods, or the swamps, by themselves."

Uh-oh, that suggested Jackson had done a tad bit of eavesdropping.

Jackson looked at Bonita. "At his age, Benny needs to be around some men. You want, I'll take him with me next time I go hunting."

"Fishing," Bonita said. "Fishing would be better."

"Deep sea," Jackson said. "I'll set something up. Out of Boca Grande. We'll take Judge Goddard and Fred."

I thought how simple the world of a man who thinks a deep-sea fishing trip will cure a fifteen-year-old boy of his problems. Well, what did I know? Jackson had raised four sons, and as far as I knew, they were all reasonably normal, or at least stayed under the radar if they weren't.

"Lilly," he thundered, knocking me out of that thought. "That little rat-faced law clerk with the earring brought this folder to me this morning, full of stuff the clerks had worked on for Kenneth.

I found this"—Jackson slapped the file in the air as if swatting gnats—"in the pile. I thought you'd want to look at this since that EStall file on his hard drive caught your eye."

"His name is Arnold and he is a very fine young man," Bonita said.

"Who?" Jackson said as I ignored Bonita and reached for the file.

"The law clerk."

Ignoring my outstretched hand because he was staring at Bonita, Jackson made a low, growly noise, then turned toward my desk and tossed the file on its clear surface.

"You have any idea what is going on?" Jackson asked me.

"None, sir," I said.

"When you do, tell me first."

Grunt, slam, stomp. Jackson was gone, and I grabbed the file and opened it, while Bonita crowded me, looking at the paper at the same time I did. Printouts and forms and copies of *American Jurisprudence* on the how-tos of filing patents, along with some literature and case law about modifications on existing patents, but nothing specifically about Earl Stallings. The bulk of the information seemed to focus on how significant changes had to be in an existing patent before a person could obtain a new, or independent, patent.

All this did have *something* to do with a patent.

A patent and Earl. Earl and wine.

Think, think, think, I ordered myself.

What I thought of was Earl pontificating on the difficulty of making sulfite-free wine and his confident reassurance to me and the Poodle Heads the day I met him that he had a way to produce wine without mold or sulfites. Maybe he'd devised a new process. The world beats its way to a man who makes a better mousetrap—and inexpensive sulfite-free wine, maybe?

"You should take that to Officer Johnson," Bonita said.

My habit of not cooperating with T.R. was pretty well ingrained. But then I thought—Yeah, a patent. A patent doesn't lead back to Bonita, or Benny, or Dave. Or me.

Dodging traffic, and worrying, I about wore out my brain on the drive to the county jail, where Bonita had located Tired after a minimum of only three phone calls. For reasons that got lost in the Bonita-Tired phone call translation, he had to stay there for a while, but could see me if I came on out right then. While I would rather have met him somewhere other than the jail, there I was, en route with a file on patents and hopefully a small trail of potential evidence leading away from those I loved.

Parking in a visitor spot at the jail, I made my way inside and discovered that the cute girl who liked Tired and babies but had the hair from hell was again at the front desk.

"Hi, again," I said, and squinted at her hair. It

was a kind of big, layered pink do, Cindi-Lauper-does-back-up-for-Tammy-Wynette-on-drugs.

"Brock didn't do that, did he?"

It took the woman a minute or two to figure this all out. "Oh, hi. You're the lawyer who gave me that guy's card. Yeah, I remember. You were here to see Tired."

"What a coincidence, I'm here to see him again."

"Tired's coming in?"

I saw a look of anticipation on her face as she smoothed her hair and looked down at her tight pants and tugged at them, but failed to improve upon anything.

"Can you take a break, a few minutes?" I asked.

"Yeah, sure, why?"

Why indeed? Because Tired needed a girl and Redfish needed a momma.

"You wouldn't take a nine-month-old to McDonald's, would you?" I asked.

"Gawd, no. You mean for food? Naw, I wouldn't take a nine-*year*-old to a McDonald's. Except for the salads. They have good salads. Have you ever tried—"

"Okay, come on," I said. "Ladies' room." I followed her tight pants all the way to the women's room, where I had to hold my breath till I acclimated. "Sit." I pointed at a chair of questionable sanitation.

"What's your name?" Pink Head asked me.

"Lilly."

"Oh, that's pretty. I'm Susie."

262

Marveling at how quickly women can bond in a bathroom, I pulled her hair back into a wide, silver barrette I kept in my purse for my own bad-hair days, and said, "Wash your face."

Susie had a heavy hand with the foundation and blush. And she had not picked colors that appeared either in nature or that complimented her own delicate coloring. I mean, come on. Didn't she have a mirror at her house?

Damp and fresh faced a moment later, Susie looked at me entirely too trustingly for a young woman who worked in a jail and didn't know me from Adam's house cat. But I wasn't taking her to raise, just for a quick, mini-redo.

Using my portable makeup kit, fished from the bowels of my purse, I gave her the Lilly light touch, and then, knowing I'd never use any of these things again because I'd used them on her and she worked in the jail, I made them a gift.

Apparently she'd missed that class in middle school on personal hygiene and never using anyone else's lipstick or mascara. She beamed and said, "Wow, Clinique. I can't afford that, but I hear it's, like, one of the best."

"Now, go to Brock and get a decent hair color. And a decent cut."

"I tried to. You know what Brock charges? I mean, like that's half my take-home pay. My sister-in-law did this."

"Well, fire her."

I pulled out another one of Brock's cards and

wrote a note on the back, "Maybe strawberry blond, blunt, chin-length bob. Bill me." And I signed my name.

"Why are you doing this?" Susie asked, peering at and then pocketing the card.

Good question. What was I, Wonderwoman of makeovers? Or what?

As I pondered this, Susie spun around and studied herself in the mirror. "Yeah, that's better," she said. "How'd you know to do that? With the makeup and all?"

Back when I had first arrived at Smith, O'Leary, and Stanley fresh from law school with a suitcase full of jeans and the concept that Chap Stick counted as makeup, Brock had been an excellent teacher on the art of makeup and elegance in dress, and fortunately Susie's own pale complexion and blue eyes were a match for my own. So, what looked good on me wore well on her. I simplified this explanation to: "You're young, you're pretty, you don't need much paint, and nobody looks good in orange blush. And I'd peel off those fake nails. And, maybe, ditch the shoulder pads, go for cotton or linen over polyester every time, never wear plastic jewelry, and take up a sport that involves a lower body workout."

"Yeah. So, like, why are you doing this? You got, like, a mother complex?"

Hey, she wasn't that young that I could be her mother.

"Not hardly on the mother complex. But Tired's a nice man, and he and Redfish need a nice woman.

But I think his tastes run toward"—what, women who don't look like cartoon versions of country-western singers from the seventies?—"toward more low-maintenance women."

"Like good mother material?"

"Exactly."

"Yeah, okay, got it. You and Tired good friends, or just work stuff?"

"Both, I guess."

"I need to get back out there." She reached up and took off the barrette, and that pink-shag bouffant hair fluffed down around her. Ugh.

Okay, in a pinch, I can do a version of a French twist that will work unless you're going jogging. "Sit," I said. "Won't take a sec."

It took me a few minutes, mostly to fish out enough bobby pins from the bottom of my purse, but I got that French twist done, despite the manic layering in her hair. I made a gift of the barrette, which held the largest chunk of hair in place.

If you didn't notice the cheap poly shirt or the pink tone in her hair, she looked almost elegant. Very nice cheekbones and chin, I noted. Then said, "Don't forget Brock. I'll call him tonight, let him know to expect you."

"Yeah, I mean, thanks. Thank you. This is pretty weird, though, you know. I mean, really, pretty weird."

Pretty weird was good, that was a step up from the karmic convergence of malevolence that had tagged me of late.

When we got back to the front desk, Tired was waiting. He didn't look at Susie until I said, "Well, Tired, Susie here has been most helpful to me."

He looked at her, looked sideways at her again, and then said, "Hey, Susie. Helping how?"

Suddenly afraid he would think Susie had been slipping me secrets, like telling me about the gun Stan took out of my car and all that, I stammered, "Oh, girl stuff, bathroom, soda machine, you know."

Tired nodded at Susie and took my arm to herd me toward that same dirty office where he and I and Philip had met the night Dave got himself arrested because he couldn't outrun a deputy named Sprint.

"Bonita said you had something for me, ma'am," he said.

Paranoia suddenly filled me. Philip would surely counsel against my turning over potential evidence to Tired without first running it by him. Also, it seemed every time I opened my mouth around Tired, I made something worse.

But for reasons I couldn't explain, I wanted to tell him. Something about Officer Tired Rufus Johnson inspired a level of trust in me I don't usually accord members of law enforcement. Or the general public. Maybe the great fatigue in those puppy-dog eyes. Maybe the way he'd blown the gnats off Redfish's face with a steady, gentle breath, or the way he'd about ma'amed me to death. After all, this was the man who had cut the head off a rattlesnake for me.

So I blabbed. "It's possible that Kenneth was working on a patent application for Earl."

"How do you know that?"

"We found this today. It's a file with research on filing for a patent. Plus a good deal of info about modifications on an existing patent."

Tired took the file, looked at the label, and opened it. "I went through his office already," he said, the hint of an accusation in his voice.

"Yes, I know. Cristal guarded the office until you got the warrant."

"Cristal," Tired said and blushed.

Whoa, boy, I thought, you're way over your head there. Cristal didn't even date lawyers, so I doubted she would date law-enforcement types. Especially plump ones with a baby. In fact, now that I thought about it, Cristal, despite being cover-girl beautiful, didn't seem to date anyone. I started to say something to Tired to gently dissuade him from the thoughts I imagined produced his blush, but he shifted back to work mode too quickly.

"So this wasn't in his office? Or I missed it?"

"The law clerks had it in a file in the library."

Tired sighed. "You people have so much paper."

"We're lawyers." Then I basically told Tired what little I had learned from the paper EStall file, even as he studied it. And then I shared my suspicion that Earl had perhaps consulted Kenneth about the ins and outs on filing a patent application for a sulfite-free wine process.

While I watched Tired ponder the significance

of this new information, I asked him, "Okay, fair trade. Was Earl murdered or careless?" Tired hadn't been too sure one way or the other that day at the vineyard when Gandhi and I had found Earl's body.

"My money is on murdered," he said. "The autopsy showed trauma to the back of his head consistent with somebody bashing him with a heavy object. Not enough to kill him, but to knock him out. Then the grape harvester did the rest."

I physically shuddered at the image of that big machine with its metal tentacles rendering Earl asunder. "So somebody knocked him out and rigged the scene to look like an accident?"

"I think so. But there was a big rock right under his head when we found him, so if he fell on that, it could have been the source of the trauma," Tired said. "So, maybe he did fall off the harvester while working on it, hit his head on that rock, got knocked out and mauled."

But Tired sounded skeptical.

A rock? I thought. Earl's vineyard was clean. I had admired that about the place. "Tired, I had a good look around at that vineyard and I don't remember any rocks."

"No, ma'am. Me neither."

"So, somebody planted the rock?"

"A well-staged murder scene. There was some thought in it."

"Do you think Cat Sue might've had something to do with it? She seems a tad unstable," I added.

"Plus that property ought to be worth a fortune if she were to get it and sell it."

"That's the obvious. But we looked into it. That property, the vineyard, all of it is heavily mortgaged. Earl didn't have any kind of mortgage insurance to pay it off at his death either. Without Earl, the bank'll probably end up with it. Or a forced sale that'll bring her pennies on the dollar."

"Okay, so greed wasn't a motive."

"Nope, none obvious. Plus, Cat Sue's got a tight alibi. She was meeting with different potential wine buyers in and around Orlando all day, all those snooty little shopping towns around there with their high-rent liquor stores. She was trying to get some more outlets for the wine. We've checked it out and several of the wine merchants remember her."

"She would stand out," I said, thinking of the red scarf around her long hair and her floor-length billowy hippie dresses.

"Bottom line, she was three hours away about the time Earl got killed."

"Thank you for sharing," I said.

"Thank you for the file."

"Are we square now?"

"If you'll let me get your fingerprints?"

"Maybe tomorrow. Maybe. Okay?"

Tired walked me to my car, and thanked me again for telling him about the patent angle. As we stood in the parking lot, in the bright light of the afternoon, I wondered if my extreme ruckus over Tired ripping up my okra was the reason he was now with the sheriff's department instead of the city police.

"Tired, did you get into trouble with the police department over my complaint? You know, over the okra. Is that why you switched to the sheriff's office?"

"No, ma'am, not your fault. Not anybody's fault. I just didn't fit in there with all those guys from up north with master's degrees in criminal justice. I got me a B.A. out of Troy State, you know, south Alabama, and got tired of them looking down their noses at me. People at the sheriff's office are just as smart, smarter maybe, but not so stuck up."

"I can understand that," I said. For reasons not wholly clear, I felt a sudden warmth toward the man. He'd had a hard lot in life and he was carrying his load with some dignity. And with good manners.

I offered him what I could.

"You should ask Susie out. Take her to play tennis some weekend. To Ringling Art Museum, to eat at a nice place with fish and vegetables."

"Susie?"

"Yes. Susie."

"Look, the body count's pretty deep right now, and the high sheriff keeps sticking his finger in my eye," Tired said. "Little hard to think about dating."

"All the more reason," I said, and smiled my own version of a world-weary smile, and got into my car and drove off.

CHAPTER 30

That night, I awoke from my sleep when a deep, male voice spoke to me and said, "Follow the bullets."

Had the voice given me a message like "Teach the children," "Love your weird neighbor," or told me where the Holy Grail was, I might have thought the voice of God had spoken to me.

As it was, I wondered why my subconscious sounded like James Earl Jones.

And I wondered why I hadn't thought of this before. It was pretty obvious, now that my subconscious had handed it to me. I mean, yeah, okay, Philip was working on the trail of the murder weapon, but regardless of where the gun had been between Dave's backpack in my house and the trunk of my car, we all knew where the gun was *now:* in the custody of Stan the constitutionally unenlightened and Tired Rufus the beleaguered.

But that box of 158-grain roundnose bullets might still be in the custody of Kenneth's killer.

James Earl Jones seemed to suggest this.

The gun and the bullets would have traveled together, at least for a while. I knew this because

I knew, thanks to Philip and his spies in the sheriff's office, that six 158-grain roundnose bullets had plowed into Kenneth.

I thought about that box of 158-grain roundnose bullets in Dave's backpack at my house. Okay, so what happened to them after that?

Obviously Dave hadn't carried the backpack with him to the jail or there would have been quite the discussion there about the gun and the bullets. As a convicted felon, Dave wasn't supposed to be toting around guns and bullets with him. So that meant that the backpack was probably left at Waylon's duplex.

Or, and I didn't like the next thought, they had been left in Benny's truck and Benny had taken them.

If Benny had taken the backpack, and found the gun, and borrowed my car from Bonita, and . . . Or, if Bonita had found them . . . Bonita, who was quite firm in not voluntarily giving Tired her fingerprints . . . Bonita, who had a reason . . .

No, I couldn't complete these thoughts.

But I would have to ask Benny and Bonita about that box of bullets.

I looked at the clock by my bed. Four in the morning, the witching hour, the hour we wake and wonder, and the lucky take a wiz and go back to sleep, while the rest of us wrestle with our demons.

Or we get out of bed and do something.

Crawling over Bearess, on the floor, I got up, drank a glass of double-filtered water, and pondered my options, or perhaps my targets—Dave, Benny, or Philip.

Well, Philip had said to call him anytime.

After several rings, a sleepy-sounding Philip answered, not with hello, but with, "This better damn well be an emergency."

"More or less." Everything at four in the morning had the shadowy feel of an emergency.

"Lilly? Damn, don't you sleep?"

"Not so much since I stopped the Xanax and Percocet."

He muttered something I couldn't make out.

"I need to know. What about the gun and the box of bullets?"

"What about them?"

"Track them for me, can you do that? I mean, you told me that you were going to work on the trail of the gun. But what about the box of bullets? They were in Dave's backpack, and he took the backpack the night he and Benny went to Waylon's and he got arrested. Where'd it go from there?"

"What box of bullets?"

Uh-oh, I hadn't mentioned that, had I? "The box of 158-grain roundnose bullets, they were in Dave's backpack, with the gun."

"You didn't tell me about that."

"Oh." Well, excuse me, I had had a lot on my mind and was still suffering from some confused notion of protecting Dave by not broadcasting that information. Not wasting any time in chastising myself, I told Philip all I could remember about the bullets. To his credit, Philip grasped the point much quicker than I had.

"So whoever had the .38 and the box of bullets loaded the weapon with six and then had a nearly full box left," Philip said. "This person then planted the weapon in your trunk. But what would this person do with the box of bullets?"

"Yes. Exactly. If we find that box of bullets, we might find Kenneth's killer."

"The most sensible thing for the shooter to do with the box of bullets would have been to dispose of them. They might well be at the bottom of Philippe Creek."

"Maybe. But maybe not. Track the gun for me. What did Dave say about the gun? Where'd it go after he took it from my house?"

"I asked him that. Precisely that. Several times. I've been trying to track that weapon since I first learned about it."

Philip sounded fully awake now. Good, nothing an insomniac likes better that other people who can't sleep.

"And?" I asked the easiest question I could.

"Dave offered an incomplete explanation."

"What?"

"He doesn't know, or he is not fully elucidating what he does know."

"Would you cut the crap and tell me what he said?" I mean, come on, who uses words like *elucidating* at four in the morning?

"Lilly, if I ask you nicely, would you please refrain from using that word? It is not at all ladylike."

What word? Crap? Bypassing any linguistic debates, I asked, "What the hell did Dave say about the gun?"

"That he didn't know what happened to it. The backpack was apparently left at Waylon's duplex. It was gone when Dave was released from the jail and went back for it. He assumed, apparently, that Waylon had taken it with him to Lakeland. I have spoken to Waylon over the phone and he denied ever seeing the .38 and is emphatic that he did not take it. So Dave said he didn't know where the gun was. That is, until it showed up in your trunk. He has no explanation for that."

"Why are you saying apparently the backpack was left at Waylon's?"

"Because the first time I asked him, Dave said he thought he had left the backpack in Benicio's truck. But then he backed off that."

Frigging great. That left us with myriad equally worrisome options: Benny had taken the gun; Waylon had taken the gun; someone who had access to Waylon's duplex or Benny's truck had taken the gun; or we flat out didn't know.

"I'll go ask Dave myself," I said, assuming Dave was at the yurt.

"Now?"

"Yes. Shouldn't be that much traffic this time of the night."

"Lilly, it's the morning. Four in the morning. Go back to sleep."

Easy for him to say.

While I was right about the lack of traffic and Dave being at the yurt, he was less than gleeful to see me at four-thirty A.M.

"Sum'n wrong?" he asked, bleary-eyed, slack-jawed, and wild-haired.

Behind him in the doorway, Cat Sue looked at me, radiant in her long hair and her gauzy nightgown, her face somehow both alert and bewildered.

"May I please speak with Dave? Alone?" I looked directly at Cat Sue, watching her.

"Come on in." Cat Sue spoke the polite words in a slightly singsongy, but pleasant way, which Dave heard. But behind his body, she glowered at me.

As I went in, Cat Sue floated back to the futon and I grabbed Dave's arms and pulled him into the kitchen space and whispered, "I've got to know, and don't be bullshitting me, but where did your gun go after you left my house on Saturday?"

"Don't know."

"Dave, this is me. Tell me."

He rubbed his eyes, and shoved his hair, wavy from his braids, behind his ears, and he squinted as if he was outside in the bright sunlight, and then he said, "I don't know."

"Damn it, Dave. Tell me."

"Man, I tell you what, best I can recollect, I

took the backpack with me in Benny's truck. I didn't have it at the jail, so either I left it in his truck, or I carried it in to Waylon's and left it there. Same as I told Philip."

"That's the truth?"

"Lilly Belle, sweetheart, would I lie to you?"

In a heartbeat if the need was there. "Dave. This is me, Lilly. You know I'd never betray you, even if you killed Kenneth. Besides, I'm your attorney, I can't tell anyone anything you tell me. Same as with Philip. Attorney-client privilege, and all."

"Now why would I kill Kenneth? I'd never laid eyes on the man. And, you know what, I sure could use that money back."

I stared at Dave until I was sure there wasn't going to be anything else I could learn from him, and then I said good-bye, and I drove to Bonita's house, where I woke her up, but when I asked to see Benny, she told me he was asleep.

"Let me wake him up. I need to ask him something. It's important."

Bonita stood back and let me in.

Together we walked down the hallway, then knocked on Benny's door. And knocked. And knocked, and finally Bonita opened the door and we walked in.

When Bonita flipped on his light, Benny's eyes opened and shut a few times and then he looked at me and Bonita and said, *"Mierda."* And he snatched up his sheet to cover his skinny legs and plaid boxer shorts.

I waited for Bonita to correct him for cursing, but she didn't.

"Benny, what happened to Dave's backpack? The night he was arrested? He left my house with the backpack, and you in tow. When he got arrested, where was the backpack?"

Benny glowered at me and then said, "I don't know. Now get out of my bedroom."

"Benny," Bonita said, just the slightest hint of chastisement in her tone.

"*Please* get out of my bedroom."

"I will. Sorry to have disturbed you. But first, make sure. Think about it. When did you see the backpack last?"

"Don't know."

"Did Dave carry it with him into Waylon's duplex? Or leave it in your truck?"

Benny frowned and looked at Bonita, which made me look at her, and then Benny and I looked at each other.

"I don't know. Things happened fast. I don't remember."

Having awakened him, I figured I'd caught Benny without defenses or pretenses. In other words, I believed him. Thinking I was going to have to track down Waylon in Lakeland and ask him, I sighed, apologized, and then left.

It never occurred to me that the little boy I'd watched growing up, difficult as his last years had been, would lie to me.

CHAPTER 31

Wholly without any idea of what else to do, I went home and flopped down on my bed. Against incredible odds, I dozed and then woke, hot and late for work. After stumbling through my morning routine, I headed out to my humble Honda.

Bleary to my soul despite the copious amounts of morning coffee, I staggered into my ancient Honda, waiting like a noble beast of burden in my carport. My purse fell off my shoulder and thunked down beside me in the bucket seat and I grabbed it to throw it in the other seat, and when I did, I saw a rattlesnake on the floor of the passenger side of the car.

Well, damn if I'm falling for that twice, I thought, and leaned over to pick up what I blithely assumed, given my prior experience, was a dead rattler.

The snake flicked its forked tongue, hissed, and raised its head.

Uh-oh.

I froze, I held my breath, and my hand was stuck there in the air as I watched the snake.

Remembering my grandmom's admonitions to

279

never back a snake into a corner, or scare it, or piss it off, I contemplated my options as sweat began to pool on my upper lip.

It was unlikely that gallant young Tired would lope across my driveway with that peculiar cowboy gait of his and throw his knife and rescue me.

No, this time it was up to me.

Despite the fact that I had voluntarily chosen to be a trial attorney, I am not normally predisposed to encouraging physical danger. I don't rock climb, I don't ski, and I applaud bungee jumping only as a means of reducing the population and generating litigation. But, being a trial attorney, I don't fall apart under pressure.

So I thought: I have to do something. I can't remain frozen in space indefinitely, no matter how appealing that seemed to be at the moment, and I was quickly reaching the limits of my ability to hold my breath. The snake had not coiled, but as Grandmom had taught me early on, a rattler does not need to coil to strike.

The trick then was to be still until the snake calmed down and no longer perceived movement, which a snake will translate into a threat when the movement doesn't come from the soon-to-be frog dinner in front of it.

After the snake calmed down, the trick would be to hurl myself out of the car before it was riled up again and bit me.

And if I failed, I had my cell phone in my jacket pocket and could hit 911 in plenty of time not to die. I was young, relatively speaking, and healthy, and one snakebite when I was six blocks from the hospital would not kill me.

But it would be a new experience in the extremely unpleasant. And despite having chosen to be a trial attorney for a career, I do not normally invite physically unpleasant events.

So naturally I was hesitant to hurl myself toward the door lest the snake proved the faster of the two of us.

Next door, to my horror, I saw my new grand-mom come ambling out of her house, wave at me, start across her unnaturally green grass, and pause to frown at my own not-chemically-treated grass, as I'm one to let nature take its course where lawns are concerned. Then she trotted straight toward the passenger side of my car, her right hand slightly extended as if she was planning to open my passenger-side door and chat with me.

Well, okay, I wasn't going to let her pop my car door open and get bit. She might not survive it, and if she did, she was sure to sue the hell out of me. Highly motivated, I catapulted myself against my door at roughly the same time I opened it and I fell out on the driveway, screaming, "Get away," and slammed the car door. Nothing bit me.

I wondered if moves-faster-than-a-rattlesnake was something I could use in my Smith, O'Leary, and Stanley firm brochure bio.

"Get back," I shouted at Grandmom.

"Well, my goodness, you don't have to be that

rude. I just wanted to invite you over tonight for dinner."

"Watch out," I said, wheezing slightly and pulling myself up. I peered into the car. The snake was coiled. "Don't open the door. There's a rattler inside."

"Oh, my dear, I'm sure you are mistaken. You stay up too late at night, no wonder you see things."

"All right, then, don't open the door, but look inside. Just don't open the door."

Grandmom looked inside and gasped. "Now haven't I been telling you to enclose that carport? Get a garage and wild things won't crawl into your car, and you'll improve the value of your house and this whole street will look that much better."

Well, okay, she had spunk and she didn't scare easily and I had to appreciate those qualities. As I pulled out my cell phone and punched 911 for the third time this month, I wondered if there was some limit to the number of times I could call that emergency number before the county sent me a bill.

As the dispatcher sputtered to life on the other end of my line, I wondered. I had figured Kenneth for the dead fish and the dead snake. That was pretty obvious. But now that he was traveling to his next incarnation, who would want to scare me? Or hurt me?

CHAPTER 32

Sarasota is a rich city, built on a bay front that follows the curve of the land against blue water. Beyond the bay, barrier islands outlined the region with their tufts of green resort communities and sand lapped by the warm waters of the Gulf of Mexico. Sarasota has some of the finest restaurants in the entire country. It has a private service industry bar none. It has grand, high-rise condominiums full of old people who once lived up North and now reside in million-dollar rooms with panoramas of the many waterways they are too old and too urban to explore beyond the view from their balconies. It has shopping to rival any large megalopolis. It has the Ringling Art Museum, with real Rembrandts, and live theater and opera and its own ballet troupe, all of which paint the city with a veneer of sophistication. The city has pink water fountains with dolphins at downtown intersections and tile-and-brick mosaics on the streets of its restored funky old 1920s artsy neighborhoods. It has a whole subculture of people who make their fine livings servicing the retired people who move here to die.

But would you believe in all that shimmering, big-city facade, in all that teeming service industry, in all its government and its bureaucracies, Sarasota did not have a single service designed to remove live rattlesnakes from one's car.

Go figure.

The Sarasota police detective who came to my door wrote down everything I said, asked not a penny's worth of questions, wished me luck with the snake, and left.

I called the Fish and Game people, who asked a few questions, and then said that because the rattler wasn't on an endangered species list, I was on my own.

I called every one of the bird rescue groups, only to have a multitude of basically nice people explain to me in patient detail that, fundamentally, a snake was not a bird and I was on my own.

I called Jackson, who said he could come over and "shoot the damn thing," and I considered this, but didn't want to kill it now that it was no immediate threat to me—I mean, it was just a snake doing its snake thing, not the Antichrist or anything. Also, I didn't want snake guts all over the inside of my Honda, so I concluded that I was on my own.

With my grandmom neighbor, I discussed my theory that if I opened the door and waited, the snake would leave of its own accord and in its own time. Grandmom, perhaps understandably, didn't want that big rattler living in her neighborhood, and she offered a variety of wholly useless tips—like call

911—and continued to blame me for my wild lifestyle and for not enclosing my carport, and I concluded that I was on my own.

As I was standing in my own driveway, studying the yellow pages under any conceivable topic, the snake crawled up the inside of the car and flicked its forked tongue in the window.

Okay, yeah, the snake was probably as eager to leave as I was for it to go.

With sweat trickling down my neck, Bearess howling from behind my front door, my new grandmom ranting at me, and a small contingency of my stay-at-home neighbors gathering to offer utterly inane suggestions—call 911 being the lead tip despite the number of times I told everyone I *had* called 911, I thought of Tired. After all, he'd rescued me before. When I didn't catch him at his office, I called him at home. In a too-much-adrenaline-rush sort of garble, I got the basic problem across.

"Yes, ma'am. Getting that snake out could be tricky. I know an old fella from back home, operates out of east county now, out by the winery and Myakka River State Park, who I bet can help. Give me a sec to call him, then I'll come on over."

East county, that tiny corner of Sarasota County that is still wild, old Florida, with the cracker boys and the long-horned cows and the scrub and the snakes and the wild hogs and bugs and cypress swamps and back water from the Peace and the Myakka Rivers and the myriad little creeks. The real Florida. Okay, somebody from out there was far more likely to know how to get rid of a snake in a car than somebody with a master's degree in criminal justice from an urban university.

So, we'd wait. Not wanting my new grandmom to stroke on me, I hinted that now would be a good time for her to go home, but this was apparently better entertainment than her television offered her, and she hung on. Finally I took her inside, fixed her a cup of hot tea, pacified Bearess with an extra dish of dog food, and washed my hands and face and changed my blouse.

Tired arrived with Redfish in his arms, and when I stepped outside to meet him, he said right off, "This isn't an official visit, you understand. I'm just here as a . . . friend. Sheriff told me if I bring Redfish to one more official crime scene, I'm off the force."

"Where's his baby-sitter?"

"Don't know. A no-show."

"Why don't you find a good day care?"

"You know what can happen to kids at a day care, even a good one? Germs. Them kids don't ever wash their hands, and they spit on each other, and I just know Redfish would stay sick. I'm not taking any chances."

Okay, that made perfect sense to me, and a full-time nanny probably wasn't in the budget for a sheriff's department investigator.

"All right. I'll show you the snake." As I led Tired over to the rattler in the car, with my neighbors milling around waiting for the next act, my front door burst open and Grandmom came stomping toward me, then stopped.

"What a beautiful baby," she said.

As I looked at sweaty, red-faced, on-the-verge-of-a-howl Redfish, he looked past me to Grandmom and reached out his arms to her.

Grandmom opened her arms to him.

Redfish cooed as Grandmom took him in her arms, and she cooed right back. Tired and I stood back a moment, and in mutual bewilderment, we watched his son and my neighbor fall in love with each other.

After a stunned break, I made the introductions. "Dolly Gormand, my neighbor, please meet Tired Johnson and his son, Redfish."

"You, I remember you from that AA meeting," Dolly snapped at Tired.

"No, ma'am, I don't think that was any AA meeting. We were—"

But Dolly didn't care, she started taking Redfish toward her house. "I need to get him out of this sun and wash off his poor, hot little face."

We watched her go.

"She all right?" Tired asked.

"She raised three kids, and her grandchildren come and visit four or fives times a year and nobody ever had to call 911."

"I better go check her out," Tired the worrier said and took off after his son.

Tired was still inside with Dolly when just about

the most beat-up pickup I'd ever seen pulled into my driveway. Oh, like, now what?

On the sides of the truck, red lettering spelled out "Experienced Hog Hunters," with white letters below it explaining, "Catch or Kill Domestic or Wild Hogs."

A man chomping on an unlit cigar crawled out. Dressed in jeans, boots, and a plaid shirt, with a baseball cap pulled low over his face, the man walked up to me and stuck out his hand. "Percy Ponder, ma'am."

I shook his hand, which I noted was long fingered and scarred. "Lilly Cleary."

Glancing back at the truck, I waited for the other man inside to crawl out too. He didn't.

"Hear you got a problem with a snake in your car?"

"Yes. Let me show you."

Percy studied on the snake in the Honda some, and hummed, and frowned, and chewed on his cigar.

As Percy studied on the situation and I sweated, Bearess gave voice to a splendid series of howlings, almost operatic in tone, range, and quality. At the doggy chorus of dismay, the pickup-truck door opened and the other fellow got out and shouted: "Outside are the dogs and sorcerers and fornicators and murderers and idolaters, and everyone who loves and practices falsehoods."

I gave the young man my famous Hard Look, and then softened it before turning to Percy.

"Oh, don't mind him, he's just touched by the Spirit. Ate some of those cow poop mushrooms, you know the ones make you hallucinate, then he read him the Book of Revelations. Turned out not to be such a good idea, but we figure he'll come out of it sooner or later."

"How long's he been like this?"

"Year or so," Percy said in an unconcerned tone of voice.

I made a mental note to remind my brother Delvon not to eat psychedelic mushrooms and read Revelations.

Tired came out of Dolly's house next door, minus Redfish, and with a relaxed smile on his face, and I assumed some bargain of child care had been reached, and he shook hands with Percy as the Bible quoter ducked back behind Percy's pickup.

"Well, let's get her done," Percy said.

Using a long stick with a circle of wire and really thick gloves and a plastic crate with a tight lid and more nerve than most people, Percy and that young man had that snake hissing inside the plastic crate within a half hour. My neighbors began to disperse. After a shower and a change of clothes, I figured I could be at my office in time to bill at least a few hours.

But first I asked Percy what I owed him, and, surprised it wasn't more, paid him and then asked, "Where would somebody get a live snake?"

"Lotta places, maybe," Percy said. "Boyce, here"— Percy pointed at the Bible quoter—"used to belong to a church of snake handlers. They could probably tell you where to get one. And there's some fellows I know out of Wauchula that catch and sell snakes to labs and zoos and things. Plus there's just a whole mess of people in the Everglades who'd catch you a rattler for not much money at all."

Tired patted my arm. "Lilly, that's my job. You let me take care of this. I'll find out who got the snake, all right? This one and the dead one before it."

That struck me as a perfectly reasonable delegation of duties. I thanked everybody, inquired briefly after Redfish, was assured he was in good hands, and went inside and reprepared for work, then left for the office in my Honda, with all the windows down and the air-conditioning on, trying to blow out the combined scent of snake, fear, and cigar.

Once at my office, I was not the least surprised to find Bonita worried about my lateness. Before I could explain, I announced that the first order of business was for her to reschedule every single one of my hearings and client conferences for the rest of the week. I didn't care what chaos that created in my files, or what sanctions other attorneys threatened, because I was in no mood to argue out loud with people and didn't have the time to properly prepare for live performances.

As Bonita began the mass cancellation project and my snake-induced adrenaline faded, I began trying both to make up time on my unbilled, unworked cases and to distract myself from worrying. Hearings and depositions I couldn't handle this week, but paperwork I had to handle or I had to resign or die. My unread mail alone was as scary as the snake in the Honda. Thus motivated, I worked frantically on piles of paper until Jackson stormed-troopered into my office.

"Everything all right?"

"Dandy," I lied.

Jackson studied me a moment and then decided to let it pass.

"Here. Got something for you to do, since you don't seem to be litigating much anymore. Might want to try your hand at probating an estate."

What I wanted to try my hand at was being some-body else for a while, like, say, I don't know, maybe a nun in a convent somewhere in the middle of France.

But Jackson dropped a copy of a will on my desk. "Kenneth drew this up himself. There's Fred O'Leary, a board-certified estate planner not two offices down the hall from him, but no, Kenneth has to draft his own will."

I picked up the will as if it were encrusted with a virulent new strain of the SARS virus.

"He had it witnessed a couple weeks before he died. Think he had a premonition?" Jackson asked.

Or a threat, I thought, but made a hmming noise in case Jackson's question wasn't rhetorical.

"Cristal just found it this morning," Jackson said. "And get this. The personal representative named in the will is Ashton. Since he's taking the

291

cure, I'll have the probate judge appoint you the PR, as a member of the same firm and all."

"Ashton?" I blurted out, thinking, *Ashton?* Ashton, who couldn't probate Kenneth's will since he was detoxing in L.A. in a hot tub with a still-unnamed actress.

Why on earth would anybody who actually knew Ashton name him as a personal representative? Since Jennifer, his nutty beloved, had jumped off the Sunshine Skyway Bridge, the poor man could hardly zip up his own zipper, let alone handle somebody's entire estate. And, I mean, Ashton and Kenneth were not close, Ashton was not a probate attorney, and Ashton, under the best of circumstances, i.e., before Jennifer jumped and he became a drug-addled zombie, painted with a broad brush and had litigated largely from a deep reservoir of energy and seat-of-the-pants inspiration. In short, Ashton was not generally noted for being detail-oriented. And even Kenneth would know that being a PR required someone who was extraordinarily detail-oriented, as the personal representative reviews the claims against the estate and pays the legitimate bills; finds, collects, and preserves the assets prior to distribution; does an accounting for the heirs and the probate court; deals with the IRS and its irrational record-keeping requirements and indecipherable estate tax code; and ultimately pays the heirs.

Shuddering internally at the thought of handling all the endless and precise tasks in settling Kenneth's estate if I became the PR, I asked, "Cristal found this?"

"Yeah, you didn't hear me say that? How'd you think all of us missed that in his office?"

Good question. I tried to read something from Jackson's face, but he stroked his beard and studied me back as if waiting for me to crack.

I didn't have time for a staring contest with Jackson, who always won anyway, so I just asked him, "What do you think this means?"

"Beats hell out of me, doll. But you be sure to let me know when you figure it out."

Ever the Zen master of delegation, Jackson then left my office with no words of farewell.

Okay, let's give it a whirl, I thought, but first I checked to make sure the will had the standard provision for fees and expenses for the PR. Then I pulled out my time sheet, entered "Estate of Kenneth Mallory" as the client, and jotted down "conference with Jackson, ten minutes." Then I picked up the will.

Oh, and what a read it was.

Ping, ping, ping. The sound of things falling into place, yet not falling into place.

Kenneth had left his Hummer, his wardrobe, his coin collection and his Rolex to his brother, Joseph of the last-known address a lavender farm in Washington state. But the great bulk of his worldly belongings Kenneth left to his only other blood relative—to her he left his Oak Ford home, the damn teak sailboat, a heretofore wholly unknown to me small plantation in Costa Rica, a stock portfolio, and other assets including proceeds from some contract with a French company. This list of personal assets included, I noted with just a tiny pang of guilt, an antique silver set and some rings that had once belonged to the grandmother they had shared. I guessed I would have to return the silver and rings I had taken from Kenneth's house, maybe just ease them back into a general inventory at some future date.

But the will said not a word about his butterfly garden.

Beyond the mystery of what was to become of his butterfly garden, it was that other surviving relative who captured my attention.

A first cousin.

Catherine Susan Mallory Stallings.

This was definitely something both Tired and Philip should know. But before I called them with the glee of knowing something they didn't know, I wanted to find out more about Mr. Mallory's estate, with which, on a temporary basis, I was more or less entrusted.

A few phone calls later—one to Edith, our office manager, regarding the state of Kenneth's profit sharing, 401(k), and other firm goodies, and one to Kenneth's strangely chatty CPA, whose name and number Edith gave me—and I knew Kenneth wasn't as rich as he pretended to be, but he still had a few buckets of money.

After a cursory exchange of professional niceties

with his accountant, I told the CPA I was the personal representative on Kenneth's estate, assuming, as had Jackson, that switching Ashton to me would be a perfunctory act by the probate judge. After running through the basics first, I had eventually asked the CPA, "What's with this French contract?"

"Not sure. I just got a copy of it myself. Kenneth had some tax questions, you know, with a foreign corporation and all. There's a lump sum and then yearly percentages."

"Send me a copy of that, will you?"

"Soon as I get the court papers on you being the PR."

Okay, he wasn't that casual after all. "So what's with the Costa Rica property?"

"You didn't know him well, did you?" the CPA asked.

"No." I had tried not to.

"Kenneth had this master plan. He was going to retire at fifty, with a minimum of five million, to his plantation in Costa Rica. Got the Costa Rica real estate at a good price, with some slight-of-hand nonsense I can't really tell you about, CPA-client privilege and all. But you ever want some Costa Rica property, you give me a call."

"Costa Rica," I said, thinking of green volcanoes and big birds. Where Kenneth could have been the king of the butterflies.

"Good plan," the CPA said. "There, he'd be a rich man still in his prime, in a country with universal health care and excellent coffee. He was even studying Spanish and the culture."

Wow, I thought. Not a bad dream. A tropical version of my own aspiration to retire early to my north Georgia apple orchard.

"So, how was he doing on the five mil?" I asked, lulling myself between visions of butterflies and a few million in blue chips.

"Well, you know. He was going great guns until 2000. Took a bad tumble."

"Lot of tech stocks?"

"You got it. Lost about sixty-five percent of his portfolio. Then he did these panic buys—against my advice, I might add—with junk bonds, which made things worse. I mean, he was a long way from poor, but with his current income flow and his market losses, he was going to need another decade to meet his financial goals for retirement. He wasn't happy when I charted that out for him."

Okay, retirement at sixty to a Costa Rica plantation didn't have quite the same ring for him. That probably explained Kenneth's desperately grabbing at clients and billable hours and trying to force Jackson and the firm into giving him a huge midyear bonus. I took a deep breath. There might be some similarities I didn't like between Kenneth and me—a certain tenacity of focus, the plans for an early retirement, the quest for a bucolic place in which to live out peacefully the last few decades. But I didn't cheat my clients. And I didn't buy Hummers.

Kenneth could have learned something from me about conservative investments and frugal lifestyles. Too late for that. But I'd learned something from him. The modern replay of the old question: "What profits a man to gain the world and lose his soul?"

I felt unbelievably sad at the waste that Kenneth had made of his life.

"Listen," the chatty CPA said, breaking my contemplation. "Nice talking to you, but I need to run. Time's money and all. You need a CPA for yourself, give me a call."

'Bye and 'bye and there I was.

Cat Sue shimmered in as a mirage of a suspect. I sure liked her better for it than Bonita or Benny. She killed her cousin for his money. And to reclaim that nice set of silver.

But that left the mystery of her own husband, Earl, dead beneath his own farm equipment while Cat Sue was three hours away in Orlando and its neighboring cities marketing organic wine.

With so many chunks of the puzzle in front of me, I needed a sounding board, someone to verbally fit the pieces into at least part of a picture. I called Philip, who did not answer his private line. "Call me," I said to his answering machine. Then I called his secretary, who told me he was in a hearing. "Have him call me soon as he gets in," I said, and then I dialed every one of Tired's four numbers and left a trail of messages even Kenneth Mallory could have followed from the great beyond.

I peered out to Bonita's cubbyhole, but she was

among the missing. Biting back my irritation, I buzzed the front reception desk from Bonita's phone. Cristal answered.

"What are you doing at the front desk?" I asked, more snippily than Cristal deserved. It wasn't her fault Bonita had disappeared.

"Edith has me working here part-time now. Because cleaning up after Kenneth isn't a full day's work, Edith says. I mean, come on, I'm a certified paralegal. Did you know that? You need any work done, just let me know. I'd *really* like helping you and Bonita. *Really*."

Edith the office manager from the jackal school of efficiency had a highly qualified legal secretary and certified paralegal spending her mornings answering a phone? I wondered if I could convince Jackson to hire Cristal as our new office manager.

"Thanks, Cristal. I'll keep that in mind. Right now, I need you to page Bonita. Tell her to get back to her desk."

"Oh, she left the building a few minutes ago. Didn't say where to. Anything I can help with?"

"No. But thanks."

We said our good-byes, and I continued to stare for a moment at the space where Bonita was not. While standing there as if I could make her re appear by simply willing it so, I picked up the photo on her desk—the happy family, Bonita and Felipe, the last year of his life, and their five children. Carmen little more than a babe, Felipe Junior holding his daddy's hand, and Benny stretching out his neck, trying to look taller and older. And Javy and Armando, the unmatched twins, looking like they wanted to punch each other. I put the photo down, sat in Bonita's chair, and riffled through her personal filing drawer until I pulled out paperwork from her lawsuit with the bottling company. Flipping madly through paper and more paper, I finally found the company's in-house counsel's name and number and began the odyssey of calling a lawyer.

Five intervening and snippy women later, after I had given the full name and the file number of Bonita's case at least ten times, along with my own name and law firm, the company's in-house attorney finally came on the phone. I identified myself as Kenneth Mallory's law partner and got blank air for a response. "You know, the lawyer from Smith, O'Leary, and Stanley that your company hired to reopen—"

"Right. My assistant pulled up our file summary on my computer when you identified it to her."

Well, that would explain some of the wait, if not the rudeness.

"We don't have any record of a Kenneth Mallory. The Bonita Hernández de Vasquez case is a closed file. What do you want?"

"You weren't looking to reopen it?"

"No. Why?"

"I guess I made a mistake." Or had he? "You would know, wouldn't you? I mean, would someone else—"

"If we had retained outside counsel for anything, anything at all, on any case, I would know. All that goes directly through me. We had no contact with anyone from Smith, O'Leary, and Stanley, and we had no contact with a Kenneth Mallory. Do you need anything else?"

Not from you, bud. "Thank you. Good day."

So, what, Kenneth was making it all up? That was the only conclusion I could come to. Exactly why Kenneth threatened to file a lawsuit for a client who disavowed any knowledge of Kenneth or the suit remained a huge mystery.

Bewildered, I grabbed up Kenneth's will from my desk and wandered out into the hallway of my own law firm, desperate for a soul mate to help me think. I think best when I'm talking. And I talk best when there is at least one other person in the room, although in a pinch Bearess will do.

With Bonita still among the missing, tired, inarticulate, frumpy Angela won the honors to act as my personal sounding board. Having tracked her to her own office, and freed from the etiquette of polite chatter because she was long used to me, I explained the various connections.

While I was mostly hoping for that miracle of insight that often happens when I talk out something, I was also open to any ideas from Angela. She was a smart young woman, after all.

With the burden of all that random information floating in the room, Angela rubbed her belly and stared at the air in front of her nose. Then Angela pointed at the will I had brought with me and said her first word of our meeting: "Patent."

What Earl's patent had to do with Kenneth's will didn't immediately connect in my mind, but then I didn't have all those pregnancy hormones floating through my body. When Angela declined to explain further, I didn't know if she had a specific notion in mind, or a general guess was at play. Either way, I decided we should see if we could learn if Earl had a patent.

Angela, being the on-line research queen of Smith, O'Leary, and Stanley, soon had the official government website for patents—www.uspto.gov—up and humming.

"Try Earl Stallings," I said when I saw that the options included searching the patent database by name, date, topic, or number.

Angela harrumped, indicating, I guessed, her viewpoint that she probably could have thought of that herself.

Type, type, type.

Nothing under Earl Stallings.

And about four thousand things under Stallings alone as a surname.

"Try wine."

Another four thousand hits.

"Try sulfite-free wine."

A few dozen hits, but none that had any of the four thousand Stallings names attached to it.

"Try every other spelling of Stallings you can think of," I said, hovering and badgering poor

Angela at the computer. But I mean, how many ways can you spell Stallings?

At the sound of soft steps, we both turned around. Bonita stood in the doorway. "I thought I might find you here," she said to me.

Angela struggled out of her chair and she and Bonita hugged each other.

Stifling the urge to feel left out, I asked, "Where've you been?"

"Seeking the mail-room clerk to request that he hand-deliver your change-of-hearing-date notices."

"Where was he?"

"I do not know. To save time, I walked a couple of them over to the lawyers' offices myself."

Before I opened my mouth to suggest that there were better uses for her talents, Bonita said to Angela, "Try Kenneth Mallory's name."

"What?" I asked, a bit rankled I hadn't thought of that.

"For the patent search. I heard you"—Bonita looked at me—"when I was coming up, outside."

Angela the silent returned to her computer chair, sat down with evident effort, and typed in Kenneth's name.

The computer made its little hummy, whirly noises, but returned nothing.

"Okay," I said, "try Michael Andrews Daniels."

Angela gave me a puzzled look.

"He is the machinist who Dave and, ah"—here I paused to glance at Bonita—"and Benny found in Myakka. He worked some for Earl. Maybe he—"

Before I could finish my thought, Angela typed in his name, and a few variations, but found no patents registered under his name.

Dead-ended again. "Maybe we should go to my office and think this through," I said.

With Angela and her bulky inside passenger teetering along in stride, we marched back to my office, where I let Bonita make a pot of coffee while I dialed Philip's number again, only to be connected with his secretary, who informed me, snippily, I might add, that Philip was still in his hearing, he had other clients, and, as she had already previously assured me, she would have him call me.

That done, I sipped my newly brewed coffee and waited for inspiration as Angela declined coffee and Bonita stared at me. In the midst of our staring contest, Cristal buzzed into my office over the phone intercom.

"Lilly, you there? This is me, Cristal."

I punched the intercom and answered, "Hey, Cristal."

"Bonita didn't answer her phone and Edith still has me on the front desk. I'm sorry to bother you and all, but there's this guy out here, your client, the one who used to wear that yellow dress thing. Anyway, he says he really needs to see you. No appointment."

I sighed. I needed Gandhi like I needed another one of those crow's-feet curling around my eyes. "I'll be out in a second," I told Cristal.

In a day during which I wanted no more surprises,

303

Gandhi offered me another one when I saw him in the lobby. There he stood, gladioli in hand, dressed normally if not neatly, in a white shirt, pure cotton, judging from the wrinkles, and jeans. Behind his little John Lennon wire frames, his eyes were their natural hazel and his hair was a sort of stiff gray blond. His face was sort of a blotchy orange, which I took to be the fading stage of his chemical tan.

"Lilly." He beamed and thrust the flowers at me.

"Gandhi. You look"—what, almost normal?—"very nice."

"Did you hear yet from the appellate court?"

"No. Remember," I said, "I told you that it could be anywhere from two weeks to several months before the court mails me its opinion. But—"

"Yes, you told me not to be optimistic. What was it you said? That a trial judge likes to grant a summary judgment a lot more than an appellate court likes to affirm one."

"Exactly. So as I've warned you, we should expect the appellate court to reverse the summary judgment and remand your case for a trial."

Gandhi nodded.

I had the idea that wasn't why he'd come to see me and was keenly aware of Cristal's stare as well as that of some gentleman waiting in the peach leather chair that clashed splendidly with our mauve wallpaper border, but that no one else seemed to notice or care about.

"Shall we step into this conference room for a minute?" I peeked in first to be sure no one else was there, and then led Gandhi into the room beside the reception area.

"I've come to warn you that I believe you might be in some danger."

Oh, yeah, where were you with that warning earlier this morning, when it might have done me some good?

Ignoring Gandhi for a moment, I put the glads into a big vase in the center of the table and threw the dusty silk flowers that had been there into the trash.

"Don't take yourself so seriously," I said. "And stop doing readings on me. Please excuse me a minute."

On the intercom, I buzzed our mail-room clerk and asked him to please put some water in the vase in the conference room within the next ten minutes and not next week, thank you.

When I turned my attention back to Gandhi, he opened his hands, palms up, in a kind of Jesus-feeds-the-poor gesture.

"You've never trusted my talents, have you?" Gandhi sounded weary. "I might have . . . spiced up the act, but I do have unique powers."

"So, okay, tell me who killed Kenneth Mallory." I meant it as a joke.

"Aw, your law partner. Yes, I read about that. I am sorry for your loss."

Brushing aside his condolences as unnecessary, I was suddenly curious to see what Gandhi could do. "Can you tell me who killed Kenneth Mallory?"

Gandhi nodded and folded onto the floor in a yogi-meditation position and closed his eyes.

Oh, yeah, this will work.

But I waited. Maybe just a bit . . . what? Hopeful?

Above me, on the wall, the clock made little hints of noise as the hands moved, and I kept my eyes on it, timing both the mail-room clerk with his watering assignment and Gandhi. Ten minutes came and went without any water boy.

Only my vexation with the mail-room clerk kept me from total boredom as I watched Gandhi posing and breathing on the floor of the conference room. Then he opened his eyes and looked at me.

"His sister killed him."

"He doesn't have a sister." Not unless his will was wrong.

"Then a close female relative."

"Cat Sue?"

"Yes, there is something about a cat in all of this. Perhaps a wildcat?"

"Why did she kill him?"

Gandhi shrugged. "You didn't ask me that."

"Are you making this up?"

Gandhi curled up from the floor and stared at me with serious eyes. "No, I am not making this up."

"Then I have some work to do."

"One more thing. Keisha has agreed to marry me after all. I found an antique ring with rubies, just like you said. You may have powers too, to so fully have channeled her feelings."

I nodded, way past the point where I wanted to

discuss my putative psychic powers or Gandhi's love life.

"Thank you," he said.

"I'm very glad for you."

"But you have work to do," he said. "Please do be careful."

Nearly gleeful that I had a suspect who wasn't me, Bonita, Dave, or Benny, I punched in the mail-room number again and said, "If you don't put water in the vase in the conference room before I finish my next phone call, you're looking for a new job."

Then I punched in Tired's office number, which I had memorized unintentionally from the sheer act of repetition. For once, Tired actually answered.

"Gandhi Singh, my client, you know, the psychic? Anyway, he says that Cat Sue killed Kenneth. I thought you ought to know."

On the other end of the phone, Tired breathed, but didn't speak. I was borderline on feeling silly when the mail-room clerk, a teenage boy with blood connections to somebody very important, though I forgot who, came in, glared at me, and poured water at the vase and all over the conference table. And stomped out.

"Yes, ma'am. That's probable cause for a warrant," Tired said as I watched the water run off the rosewood finish and onto the rust-colored carpet.

"Look, I'm trying to be helpful. You don't need to be sarcastic. Also, Cat Sue is Kenneth's cousin."

"Yes, I know that."

"How?"

"I'm a detective, ma'am. We find out things. That's our job."

"Yeah? Did you know Cat Sue is Kenneth's primary heir in his will?"

Sound of an inhale. Pause. Tired's quickened breathing over the phone line gave rise to a bubble of satisfaction on my part. "And there's enough value in his estate to make it worth Cat Sue's time to kill him. You know, if she's into that sort of thing."

"Lilly, Lilly, ma'am, whoa."

Whoa, what? I was solving this man's case. "But Cat Sue—"

"Cat Sue has an alibi for the night Kenneth was killed. She'd spent the day in and around Orlando and some of its suburbs, shopping and stuff. Lots of fancy stores in the area."

"She went shopping?" To Orlando? I thought. Fancy stores? What, the Disney village? To assuage her grief over becoming a widow? "You got witnesses?" I asked Tired.

"I got receipts, showing her Visa charges, her signature. I got a guy in a store that remembers her—all that dark hair and the red scarf and the long dress. Made her stand out. I got a video from a jewelry store with her coming and going through the door, grainy footage, but there's no mistaking that scarf and long dress. The date and time stamped into the film."

"Why Orlando?"

"When she was trying to line up some buyers

for the wine over there, she liked the area and the shops. She was, she says, trying to get past the rough spots over Earl."

"By shopping?"

"We all deal with grief differently."

"You talked with a guy who remembers her? Described her?" I still wasn't 100 percent buying this.

"Yes, ma'am. I did. And in person."

Oh. Well, so much for Gandhi's psychic powers.

"But look, ma'am, it's dangerous for you to be messing in this. Stay out of this and that's an order."

Now I breathed for Tired over the phone.

"You hear me? Ma'am, it's for your own good. You've had two snakes in your car, and that's a pretty clear warning, you hear?"

"You take care now, Tired. Stay in touch," I said, snippily, and hung up. Tired wanted me to back off. No way. Not while a shadow of any suspicion lingered over Bonita.

On my way past Cristal the certified paralegal receptionist and back to my own office, I said, "There's a mess in there on the table. Water everywhere. Better get that mail-room clerk to clean it up."

Back in my office, Angela and Bonita were peering through a city directory for the Bradenton-Oneco area, to the north of us.

"Michael Andrews Daniels," Bonita said. "Remember the fundamentals." She pushed the open page of the directory at my face. Swamp

Man, alias Michael Andrews Daniels, was listed. Occupation, welder. His widow ran a bait-and-produce stand in Oneco, another one of those increasingly rare enclaves of Florida cracker holdouts.

"We could be at his wife's shop in half an hour," Bonita said. "I am not sure how this man might fit into things, but there are the . . . strange coincidences of timing, place, and his connection to Earl."

Place—yes, I hadn't really thought about that before, but Mad's body was found near the winery, in a section of wild Myakka that backed up to Earl's property. Mad did work for Earl. And he did die the Saturday all of this seemed to have started.

Given the possible continuum from Mad to Earl to Kenneth, I thought, Oh, what the hell, why not? Dodging big trucks and slow cars full of old people in the fresh air of a fine spring day to question the widow of a man who died in a swamp with $30,000 in cash would probably do us as much good as anything else.

Angela declined the invitation to go on a potential wild-goose chase in the next county, but Bonita and I piled into my Honda and headed up U.S. 301 toward Oneco.

Once past the knot of traffic where the Tamiami Trail and 301 merge in a teeth-grinding melee, I inhaled. "Look, Bonita, I called the in-house attorney for the bottling company. They were never planning to sue you for fraud. That guy, their in-house counsel, had never even heard of Kenneth." I waited.

Bonita sighed and rubbed her gold cross.

"Kenneth was making that up, I think. Or at least he had never contacted the company."

Bonita continued to sit mutely.

"Maybe Kenneth had some kind of evidence and was going to contact the company later?" I poised my statement as a question, hoping to elicit a helpful and enlightening response from Bonita.

When no words came, I glanced over at Bonita, though taking one's eyes off the road on U.S. 301 is a life-defying act. Bonita stared out the window, and rather pointedly avoided looking at me.

"You knew this?" I asked.

"Yes. I called a secretary I know with the company." As she spoke, Bonita turned her face to me, and I flicked my eyes back and forth between her and the traffic.

"A woman I worked with a long time ago," Bonita continued. "We were friendly, so she checked around for me. My lawsuit files were in storage. The computer summary didn't show any recent activity on the case, and there was no record of any contact with Kenneth."

I studied on this for a moment. "When did you find this out?"

"The Monday after he was killed."

"So, you were maybe planning on telling me this when?"

"You've been very busy."

This time I was the one making the long sigh. "You want to tell me what Kenneth was up to?"

Bonita didn't speak. Out of the corner of my eye I saw her turn back to the window. She would either tell me what she knew or she wouldn't. Like most lawyers, I fancied myself persuasive in the utmost, but I also knew from experience that nothing I might say could make Bonita change her mind.

We passed the rest of the trip in silence, but arrived in Oneco in record time. As we walked into the produce store, a display of cactus crowded the entrance.

Bonita stopped and studied the cactus. "I haven't had any fresh *nopales* in a bit," she said.

"May I help y'all?" A woman with stooped shoulders and thick glasses and a big head of hair that almost balanced out her hips smiled at us.

"Are you, by chance, Mrs. Daniels?" I asked.

"Yep."

While I struggled for a segue into asking if her recently-made-late husband had anything to do with two other dead bodies and possibly a patent, Bonita began to gingerly pick out some of the cactus.

"You want, ma'am, I got me a boy who'll trim those prickles right off for you. But once they're peeled, you need to fix 'em real soon."

"Yes, that would be nice," Bonita said, and handed her sack to the big-haired, big-hipped Mrs. Daniels. "Having the spines cut off would be easier."

"Yoo-hoo, Jose," the big-hipped widow called out, and a squat young man, looking more Indian than Spanish, came out of the back and took the sack. He didn't make eye contact with any of us.

I thought Jose looked a bit like Armando and started to say so, but then remembered reading in one of the books Bonita had given me about Mexico that the so-called highborn Mexicans, the Criollos, those of Spanish descent, often do not like being confused with the native Mexicans, that is the meso-American Indians. Though Bonita had never displayed any signs of ethnic or other snobbery, I bit back my comment anyway. Then I stared at Bonita. Nothing Indian about her. Tall, willowy, chocolate-colored eyes, chocolate-colored hair, cream-colored complexion, the very picture of a Spanish woman of class. College educated in California, she had only the trace of an accent. Her children, though looking more Mexican than she, sounded like the average children of the U.S.A.

As I pondered how well they had all acclimated, Bonita spoke to the young man. *"Que le vaya bien."*

Jose nodded and ducked away. Bonita then introduced us to Mrs. Daniels.

"Attorneys, huh? Don't know as I need an attorney," she said.

Jose brought the sack of de-thorned cactus back and handed it to me. "I'll get these," I said, and moved toward the check-out line where a man with bug eyes and a weak chin was working his jaw in a way that put me in mind of a pop-eyed goldfish.

"I can afford my own *cacto,* thank you," Bonita said, and reached for the sack.

"Let me treat, okay?"

While I held on tightly to the sack as Bonita tugged at it, Goldfish Face guy rang up something for a man in front of us and then turned to me. "While you gals make up your mind who's gonna get that, I gotta get this guy some worms, you hear?"

"I'll ring those up for you," Mrs. Daniels said, and stepped in behind the cash register.

"Could we talk to you a moment? About your late husband?" I asked, molding my face into the shape of a nice person who felt a good deal of sympathy. "We are very sorry about your loss."

"You knew Mad?"

"No, we didn't have that pleasure. But we, that is, I, knew one of his employers," I said. "Earl Stallings."

"Now wasn't that a shame, him getting kilt like that, and on his own tractor."

"Yes, ma'am, a real shame," I said, not bothering to point out that technically it was his grape picker that ate him, not his tractor. "And that's part of what we'd like to discuss with you, Mrs. Daniels."

"Call me Mary Angel," she said.

"Oh, what a pretty name," Bonita said.

"Yes'um, I like it."

Goldfish man came back and I asked Mary Angel, "Could we go somewhere private and just chat a minute?"

"I done already talked with the sheriff's office man. One with that cute little baby, but he ought not to be toting that child around like that."

314

No, he shouldn't. But I passed on discussing Tired's problems as a single dad and said, "If we could just go over things again, just the three of us."

"What's y'all's interest in this?"

"Earl was our client," I said, and silently dared Bonita to tsk-tsk me.

"Well, what's Earl got to do with me?"

"That's what we'd like to find out."

"Well, I could use me an iced-tea break. You two want some?"

"Yes, please," Bonita said.

Me, I wasn't sure, glancing around the produce stand for signs of high hygiene standards and finding none.

We followed Mary Angel back to a hot, tiny office that brought out several of my phobias at once when I saw the clutter, the dust, and the bottles of bug spray.

From a tiny refrigerator, Mary Angel brought out a pitcher of tea that looked like syrup and poured three glasses. I knew I'd never be able to actually drink it, but the glass felt cool in my hands.

"Awright," Mary Angel said. "Ask me what you want to."

I did.

Apparently tea and sugar were this woman's version of alcohol, and her words soon poured out like someone on her third vodka and with a story to tell.

Michael Andrews Daniels, aka Mad, had indeed

worked for Earl. They were working up models of a new kind of grape picker because the standard models still had a lot of problems. "That picker thing Earl had wouldn't even back up, or was it turn around?" she queried, as if Bonita and I would have a clue. "And tore up them grape plants something terrible."

"Did Mad and Earl invent a new kind of harvester?" I asked, beginning to figure out that if a patent were at the heart of this mess, it probably wasn't for sulfite-free wine.

"Oh, no. Mad jes' did what he was told to do. Earl was the inventor, but Mad did plenty welding and such," Mary Angel explained. "I got no patience with men playing with models, so I didn't pay much attention to Mad when he'd explain what they were doing."

"And you explained this to Officer Johnson? You know, the officer with the infant?"

"That's right, and to some other guy named Stan. I liked that deputy with the baby, he was nice to me."

"Did Mad ever go to a lawyer?"

"What'd he need a lawyer for?" Mary Angel asked. "He was nothing but a welder and a machinist and a man went out to the swamp and had the bad luck to step on a rattler. Why y'all trying to make such a fuss over bad luck's beyond me."

Maybe she didn't know that someone had chased Mad's car into a ditch before Mad abandoned the car and ran into the swamp?

"Did he ever mention a Kenneth Mallory?" Bonita asked.

"That does seem to ring a bell somehow," Mary Angel agreed.

But despite further questioning, Mary Angel couldn't place why Kenneth's name sounded familiar.

"Didn't like that tea much, did you?" Mary Angel asked, looking at me with the sound of finishing up in her voice.

"Diabetic," I said. "Sorry."

"Well, you should've said, I had me some bottled water in there."

Suddenly thirsty, I waited for the offer. But when it didn't arrive, I figured I could buy a bottle on the way out and we made our thank-yous and left Mary Angel's office.

On the drive back, we ran the new information around a bit but arrived at no firm conclusions beyond the obvious need to pursue the potential Mad-Kenneth link further.

Once at Smith, O'Leary, and Stanley, I left Bonita and tracked Cristal back to her desk outside Kenneth's office. "Finished at the front for the day?" I asked, showing modest personal concern for her before I pestered her to give me all of Kenneth's appointment books for the last year. Then I boldly strode into the law library like someone with billable materials and dumped the appointment books on the first hapless law clerk who looked up.

"What's your name?" I asked, but didn't bother to listen.

"Look, this is important and I promise you a promotion to associate if you find the name M. A. Daniels, or Mike, or Michael Daniels anywhere in these appointment books."

"That's all?"

"That's all."

"Can do." The boy beamed with the belief that he'd be an associate within a week, not knowing I didn't have that authority. Young man wants to be a lawyer, he needs to learn early on not to be so gullible, I thought, feeling no guilt at all as I left the library.

As I walked back to my office, Edith's voice came over our intercom. Sounding more wrath-of-God than office manager, she said, "Paging Jackson. We need you up front. There's a sheriff's deputy with a warrant to search the whole building."

I understood instantly that this was Edith's warning, giving each of us a modest head start, and I imagined that the sound of shredders and flushing toilets would rise up around me in seconds. Rather sanctimoniously, I concluded that there was nothing I needed to shred or flush and sauntered back to my office amid the scurry of attorneys toward their own hidden stashes of whatever.

Then I happened to remember I had stuffed Kenneth's laptop in my back credenza. After stealing it out of his house, I had opened it at home to find his hard drive completely blank.

Given the glossy initials "KUM"—like I'd put that on my laptop—Kenneth had had embossed on the case, I had concluded that the laptop was all for show. Not wanting it to collect dust in my house, I had brought it back to the law firm to slide into Kenneth's office at the first chance. But every time I tried to do just that, Cristal was guarding the golden gates and I didn't want her knowing I had Kenneth's laptop because that invited speculation as to exactly how I had gotten it, and as a general principle I thought it best not to let my new hobby—breaking and entering—become the fodder of office gossip. So Kenneth's laptop had been sitting in my credenza until Edith's warning made me remember I had stolen merchandise in my office. Highly motivated, I practically knocked down the rat-faced law clerk with the earring as I sprinted for that credenza.

Dashing past Bonita, I rushed into my office. Flustered as I was, I heard the sound of Bonita's chair sliding back as she rose to follow me in. Panic drew her like honey.

I ripped open my credenza door. The laptop was gone.

And a cardboard box of 158-grain roundnose bullets with the letters "JEB" scribbled on the side sat neatly in the space that Kenneth's purloined computer had recently occupied.

"Shit," I screamed, not even bothering with the more poetic sounding *mierda* that Benny had taught me so I wouldn't sound crude.

Crude was the least of my worries.

"The laptop. Kenneth's laptop, where is it? Who's been in my office?"

Bonita shook her head. "I haven't touched it since you put it there. And to my knowledge, no one but you and I have been in your office."

No time for further cross-examination. I snatched up the bullets, but not before Bonita had a good look too. Throwing my gray jacket over the box, I bolted out the back door and aimed straight for my ancient Honda. Once inside my car, I sped away, darting briefly the wrong way down the one-way Morrill Street behind our office building and out into the relative safety of the traffic and confusion on the Tamiami Trail.

I made it home in record time and sprinted for the cool, clean sanctuary of my own house.

But once inside, I realized keeping those bullets in *my* house was not a good idea. Being freaky about paper in my personal space, a definite problem for a lawyer, I didn't have any gift-wrapping paper inside. So I ran outside to my newspaper recycling bin, pulled out the Sunday funnies, and trotted back inside where I wrapped up the box of bullets in the funnies, drew a bow on it with a red Magic Marker, jogged next door, and rang Grandmom's bell. She answered in a flounce and a hurry, Redfish gurgling happily in her arms.

"Can I hide this present at your house? Just until the birthday party?" I smiled so forcibly my jaw made cracking noises.

"Well, hello there," Grandmom said.

"Hello there," I backed up and said.

"Of course you may," Grandmom said. "Please come in." Then she eyed the present. "Don't you even know how to wrap a gift?"

Her consistent disappointment in me made me think it was kind of like having a real mother. My own mother didn't pay enough attention to me to be disappointed.

"It's for an environmentalist. You know how they hate to waste paper. Trees and stuff, you know."

"Well, if you change your mind, I have a good collection of wrapping paper. I'll show you how to do it up really nice."

Grandmom's constructive criticism aside, the cool rooms of her house opened to me like a safe inner sanctum, and I listened for a half hour to her theories of child rearing while playing with Redfish and declining offers of food.

But my mind raced with the questions of who had put the bullets in my credenza and why Tired Rufus Johnson was armed with a search warrant for the Smith, O'Leary, and Stanley law firm.

Okay, I was officially paranoid now.

That night, Philip rang my doorbell as I was trying to cajole Bearess into eating some stir-fried okra.

"You left several messages," he said. "I hope you do not object to this impromptu visit."

"Come on in." I led him to the kitchen, where he and Bearess took remarkably the same attitude toward the okra, so I poured Philip some of Earl's wine, split my salad with him, poured Bearess some dog food, and sat down to eat my okra.

While Philip was giving me a rundown of his day, I waited for the most dramatic moment to tell him about my day's events. If there was a competition going here, I knew I'd win with the box of 158-grain roundnoses. But then the doorbell rang again.

Philip hovered protectively as I opened the door to the junior law clerk. "How'd you get my address?" I demanded.

"Er, the, eh, Edith gave it to me. I told her you said this was important."

Not as important as having a chat tomorrow with Ms. Too-Free-with-Her-Information about never giving out my phone number or address to anyone, ever, no matter what. Okay, maybe she could give it out to Lenny Kravitz. But office-manager jackal or not, Edith needed to be reminded of my privacy rights.

But back on track, I asked, "Did you find Mike Daniels in Kenneth's appointment book?"

"Eh, um, no."

"Stop stuttering. Then why are you here?"

"I, er . . . um, found that . . ."

I noticed that the young man was sweating profusely. Okay, he couldn't talk without an *um* every breath, he didn't respect privacy, and he sweated too much. Unless his father was a Supreme Court justice, this boy's future was not bright.

"What?" I snapped.

He flushed and sweated and ummed. Finally Philip introduced himself and asked the clerk if he would like to come in and share a glass of wine.

The boy stepped inside. "I, um, didn't find Daniels's name."

"Yeah, I got that."

"But, um, I did find, um, that two pages were torn out of his, um, appointment book."

"What dates?"

He told me with a maximum of five more ums, and left, never having partaken of the proffered wine.

"You scared that young man," Philip said. "Did you know that?"

"Don't be silly."

"You should be nicer to people."

"Yeah, and not say *crap*, got it, short man."

"You should be nicer to me," he said. "And I'm not short, you are just exceptionally tall."

I looked at Philip until I saw that I was making him nervous. As I studied him, I tried to separate my need for his professional services from any personal desires I might have for him. When I'd first met him, I had been so smitten I couldn't form sentences. But now, well, now I wasn't so sure.

Leaning into Philip, I kissed him, thinking physical contact might answer that question in a way staring at him had not.

It was a good kiss, Philip was right there, and right into it. His hands stayed the hands of a gentleman, but his body pressed against me in a decidedly roguish manner.

"I am hoping we might make love now," he said, taking a break from the kiss.

"I was hoping we might go back to Smith, O'Leary, and Stanley and see if we can find any time sheets in Cristal's stuff that would explain where Kenneth was on those two days he tore out of his appointment book. Plus, there's some stuff I need to tell you about."

Philip sighed. "I'll drive," he said.

On the ride over, I brought Philip up to date with my day's discoveries. We played endlessly with the question of who could have the bullets *and* access to my office. The only people who could have the bullets were Benny if he'd kept the gun and bullets, Bonita if she'd taken them from Benny, Waylon if he'd ended up with the backpack with the gun and bullets, Dave if he'd recovered them from Benny or Waylon. Of that list, only Bonita had access to my office.

But Bonita had looked as surprised as I was when we'd discovered the bullets in place of the laptop.

Besides, Bonita would never, not in a million years, plant those bullets in my credenza.

I said this to Philip over and over, applying the trial-attorney rule that a statement repeated frequently enough takes on the tone of truth.

"Are you sure?" Philip the doubter asked. "Wouldn't she do it to protect Benny?"

"No," I said. But I wasn't sure. In a tight corner,

if Bonita had to choose between me and Benny, then obviously Benny would win. And I wouldn't blame Bonita in the least for that. But Bonita was too smart to get herself into that kind of trap.

Wasn't she?

After we talked Bonita-and-bullets scenarios to death, we arrived at no particular conclusions about who was killing whom, or why. But at the office, after grumping around in Cristal's files, we discovered modest pay dirt. In Kenneth's travel-reimbursement folder, we found copies of forms showing that Kenneth had filed mileage-reimbursement requests for a round-trip to Oneco for client conferences on both of the dates he had torn from his appointment book. The form was blank where a client's name should have been.

But, hey, since Mad lived in Oneco, it was too much to be a coincidence.

Before we left Cristal's files, I did a free-association snoop and cruised through her personal files—Visa bills and such. For a legal secretary, she had pretty expensive tastes, especially in clothes. She had her receipts in perfect chronological order—Saks at Southgate, St. Armand's Key, Winter Park, another Winter Park, Saks, St. Armand's, et cetera, et cetera, all true shopping Meccas for the rich. This made me think she had a rich man out there somewhere. The gossip from the Sisterhood of the Secretaries had never caught Cristal dating anyone. Hmm, a rich man, especially a rich, married man, would

325

explain her secretiveness. When I started pursuing copies of her health-insurance claims, Philip suggested I was being a bit rude. So I quit.

On the way home, Philip made concerned noises about what to do with the wrapped box of bullets. Weighing the alternatives, I opted for leaving the box exactly where it was.

Bullets aside, back at my house an ardent Philip made me promise to forget everything except him, assuring me we'd work on the case tomorrow. We drank Earl's wine and we made out a bit self-consciously on the couch. But all the time my mind whirled around the possibility that Mad's death had set in play a chain of events apparently destined to end with me being framed for Kenneth's murder.

Eventually Philip accepted that tonight wasn't going to be his night for making love and left.

I finished the bottle of wine, did sit-ups and push-ups, glared at the clock, and wondered if I could make myself wait until a decent time in the morning to track Kenneth's mileage-reimbursement request back to Mad.

Wine and weariness aside, I had about convinced myself to drive to Oneco when Bearess raised her big head and growled at the door.

When I peeked through the peephole, I saw Tired, holding Redfish.

"I was picking him up from your neighbor lady," Tired said. "She's a really fine woman, you know. She speaks highly of you. I know it's late, ma'am, but I saw your lights on and wanted to see how you were doing. Rough morning and all."

"Come in," I said. "I'm fine."

Tired lumbered in, weighed down with Redfish.

"Find anything with the warrant? At the law firm today?"

"No, ma'am. Nothing but a bunch of nervous lawyers with piles of paper."

"What were you looking for?" I didn't really expect an answer.

"Had a tip from one of Kenneth's clients that he was heavy into cocaine. I sort of pushed that to a law-and-order-type judge for a warrant to check out the whole firm."

My word, I thought, how well my plan of defaming Kenneth as a cokehead seemed to be working now that it didn't matter in the least.

"Follow me," I said, "and I'll pour us some wine."

"Sounds fine, ma'am, but first I got a question for you."

"Shoot," I said, and then chastised myself for a bad word choice.

"That Jackson fella. He got any reason to kill Kenneth?"

"Jackson? No. Jackson's not a killer." But I paused at that. Jackson the Vietnam veteran, Jackson the reincarnated Stonewall, Jackson the severely pissed off at Kenneth. Jackson caught over a barrel by Kenneth's demands for a huge bribe to not take his clients and leave the firm. But I said, "Not his own law partner."

"But he sure didn't like Kenneth much, did he?"

"No. Nobody liked Kenneth much. But Jackson wouldn't bring all the complications down on the law firm that murdering a major partner causes. He's had to work triple time to reassure Kenneth's clients not to leave the firm." What I really thought was that if Jackson had killed Kenneth, he wouldn't need six bullets. One through the heart would have done it.

"But you agree Jackson pretty much despised Kenneth?"

"Yes. We all pretty much despised Kenneth."

"Why's that?"

With Tired trailing me, I went into my kitchen and pulled down a wineglass for him and a new one for me. And I pondered whether I had the energy to explain Kenneth to Tired.

When we sat back down in my living room, I took a sip of wine and said, "I'll give you an example. My first year at the law firm, Kenneth made me do a completely spurious appellate brief in a workers' compensation case where the claimant was in really bad shape. A fireman. The man had no family. Filing the appeal, even as ridiculous as Kenneth's argument was, stopped the payment of the fireman's comp benefits. Under the statute, as long as the employer contests the comp and there's any kind of court proceedings pending, the comp payments are put on hold."

"Doesn't seem right," Tired said.

"No. It isn't. It invites litigation for the purpose

of delay. Which is what Kenneth was doing. While Kenneth and I dragged out the appeal, the man lost his home because he couldn't work and he couldn't get his comp checks. He ended up living in his car. Then he died, no workers' comp meant no health care, no income. Because he had no dependants, his comp claim died with him. Kenneth withdrew the appeal. He'd done what he set out to do—he'd delayed payment of the fireman's justly due compensation until the man had died, taking his claim with him. That saved the company a bundle and it's shoveled cases to Kenneth ever since."

"You did that? You helped Kenneth do that?"

"I was too young and too green not to do what I was told. If I'd refused writing that brief, Kenneth would have fired me." Yeah, okay, I know *now* that's no excuse. One of the reasons I never let men tell me what to do, that is, except Jackson, is the residual remorse I felt over the fireman I helped Kenneth kill by a perfectly legal use of the Florida Workers' Compensation statutes.

"Tired," I said, wanting to redeem myself in his eyes, "I didn't fully understand and I didn't know how to refuse Kenneth, and I . . . I carry that guilt, all right? But when you were just starting out, there must've been something you did because a superior told you to do it."

Long pause. Tired drank his wine, not sipping but almost gulping. I studied his face and saw that his eyes were guarded and sad. Yeah, Tired had done something bad too, back when he was a green recruit.

Then Redfish reached down and yanked Bearess's ears and the dog jumped up in Tired's lap and licked Redfish, who giggled fit to choke, while Bearess wagged her tail so hard the whole couch shook. Tired and I relaxed, laughing at how well our children were playing with each other.

Moments later, I thought how weird the world really was. If anybody had suggested to me the day that Officer T. R. Johnson had ripped up my okra plants that the same Officer T.R. and I would coast into a wary friendship, I would have laughed hard enough to spit.

But there he was, sitting on my couch in my living room, getting tipsy on poor dead Earl's wine, with a gurgling baby in his lap and a diaper bag on the floor and a wiggling dog pushing her head between us.

While I studied on how all this had come to be, Tired said, "Shame, really. Earl, he made a good wine and seemed a decent man."

"Yes," I said, and leaned out of reach of Redfish, who was aiming at my hair.

"My daddy used to make wine, over in Fort Lonesome, he got him enough wild scuppernongs, that is, he made us kids pick 'em enough, to make a few gallons of wine."

Scuppernongs. I nodded, and thought of the wild vines of bronze grapes back home. Earl had

330

cultivated a darker cousin and called them muscadines, but at the root center they were the same southern natives.

"That wine would flat knock you on your butt, I tell you what. When folks would ask my daddy what he did to give his wine such a kick, he'd tell 'em that he added a cup of wildcat pee, wildcats being about as common out in the scrub near Fort Lonesome as damn Yankees on the Tamiami Trail. Said he put wildcat pee in the wine to give it bite." Tired giggled.

Wildcat wine? Well, okay. That made me think of my grandmom, my real one, and how she made this concoction she called peach wine, with which she was prone to liberally dose Dan and Delvon and me at the first sign of a sniffle, a tummy ache, or when we made too much noise during *As the World Turns*. Once on a sleep-over visit, my normally sober father had drunk a couple of glasses and got flat drunk. The next day, as he gathered up my brothers and me to take us back to the cluttered gloom of our own house, he had asked his mother-in-law what she used to make her wine so strong. She'd told him with a perfectly straight face that she added mule urine to give the wine kick.

Thinking of my grandmom and her mule-peach tall tale, I laughed until tears ran down my face. When I recovered, I apologized to Tired.

"No, ma'am, don't say you're sorry. You're supposed to laugh at that story. I told it to some folks in Sarasota at the PD, and they looked at me like I was some sorry redneck who don't wear shoes or use toilet paper."

Tired's mistake, I thought, was that he told that wildcat-wine story to carpetbaggers, people from the great urban North, who came to plunder Florida for its jobs, its developmental riches, or its natural resources, and who didn't understand the natives like Tired.

"Well, Tired, you ought to know by now that crackers have a different kind of humor than all those city people from up North." I knew he would know I didn't mean offense by using the term *cracker*, not when I was just one speech-and-diction coach up from being an obvious Georgia version myself.

"Yes, ma'am."

I looked at Tired's face, young but aging in the sun of his native state and the stress of looking at dead bodies and trying to raise a child on his own, and my heart softened.

"You know Bonita didn't have anything to do with this, don't you? Cobalt blue car or not."

"Yes, ma'am. It's just that the high sheriff, he keeps poking his finger in my eye and telling me to arrest somebody. Kenneth was a big shot. The press is gonna eat the sheriff up if we don't get somebody quick."

"You've got to look past Bonita, then. You don't have a motive for her anyway, do you?" I wanted to test the waters on that as I wondered if Tired had heard any hint that Kenneth had been threatening Bonita.

"No, ma'am, no motive. I'll give you that. But motive doesn't always count for a lot. Not when you got good, tangible evidence."

"Like prints on a murder weapon?"

"What?"

"Prints on the gun, you know. That's why you wanted my prints and Bonita's?"

"No, ma'am, you're gonna have to fuss at your spies. You got some bad information."

No prints on Dave's gun? And here I'd nearly beaten myself up over the fear that I had accidentally framed myself and Bonita for murdering Kenneth.

"Then what . . . why'd you want our prints?"

"Fingerprint on the doorbell. Just as nice and pretty a latent print as you've ever seen. Thought it might be worth looking at yours and Bonita's. Don't match Dave's."

"Well, it's not going to match mine or Bonita's either. You can just quit barking up that tree."

"Bad as I don't want to, I gotta do more than take your word for it."

"Yeah, but, Tired, come on. You know me now, and you're getting some feel for Bonita. We're not stupid. We're not going to ring a man's doorbell, shoot him, and then run off in a distinctive car. Okay? We'd drive a rented car, some common-place American sedan, wear gloves, go late in the night, and—" Suddenly I thought this might not be the tack to take.

"Yes, ma'am. I'll give you that it doesn't make good sense. But whoever shot Kenneth, shot him in a panic. Six shots. Four of them pretty wild, one hardly hit him at all. But two got the job done. So that tells me whoever shot him was scared, and scared people don't think good."

"Scared lawyers think good, though. It's our finest trait, nothing like a little flight-or-fight juice to rev up our brains. And that goes for Bonita too. You don't raise five children and be a legal secretary without the ability to function well under pressure."

Tired sighed. "I don't think it's either of you, truth told. Don't you tell anybody I said that."

Tired looked so woeful, I leaned over and pecked his cheek with a little kiss and damn if Redfish the opportunist didn't snatch a handful of my hair and yank it for all he was worth.

But long after Tired and Redfish left, I thought about that perfect print on the doorbell.

And I thought about how adamant Bonita had been that day I'd suggested we voluntarily give Tired our prints.

Then I wondered how long before Tired got Bonita's prints from immigration.

CHAPTER 33

My hair was still damp the next morning when I hurried out the door, pointing my ancient little cobalt blue car toward Old U.S. 301 and a trip to the address Kenneth had listed on his reimbursement form.

Traffic being minor at dawn, I was there in no time. The address was a large warehouse-type building with a sign out front that read: "Mike Daniels's Welding."

Not surprised by the sign, I parked my Honda modestly out of view on the side of the warehouse and got out for a good look. Temptingly, the front entryway was a jalousie-style door, a design popular in the Florida ranch houses of the fifties and sixties, along with terrazzo floors and an orange tree in the backyard. Notoriously easy to break into, these jalousie doors were a configuration of narrow panes of overlapping glass, styled from a safer time when homes were not the common target of anyone who needed a spare buck.

I stuck my fingers between the panes of glass on the door and pried them open, then ripped through the screen with a metal nail file from my purse, reached in and turned the doorknob, and entered Mad's office.

It crossed my mind that this was my third breaking and entering in the last two weeks, and I hoped I hadn't made some sort of subconscious decision to revert to my days of traveling left of the strictly legal. Being Dave's marijuana gardener in my adolescence was one thing, something forgivable and without hard prison time for a first timer. But three B&Es, that was something I needed to think about. Was there a twelve-step program for burglary, I wondered, a B&E Anonymous that met in the library on Thursday nights?

But I pushed that from my mind to worry about later. Now I needed to see what I could find.

What I found were guy things. Tools. Piles of paper and piles of guy things.

Finally, under a greasy drop cloth I found a filing cabinet. I rummaged through the records, mostly receipts, bills, and primitive contracts for welding jobs, but found nothing about Earl or Kenneth. Then I checked under the cabinet and found an envelope taped to the bottom of a drawer. I tore into this, but it turned out to be nothing but some crude pornography. Apparently Mad had a thing for women with big butts. I hoped that meant he and Mary Angel had been happy together in that department, as her bottom certainly qualified. I tossed the stuff aside and started crawling under what passed for a desk, looking for more taped envelopes.

While I was on my hands and knees, rear toward the door, someone banged into the warehouse and I hit my shoulder jerking myself up and around as quick as I could.

There wasn't any lie that was going to cover this, so I hoped for luck or speed as I finished crawling out from under the desk to face Mary Angel standing over me with a very big handgun.

"What in the Sam Hill are you doing in Mad's office?" she asked.

"If you'll just put that gun down, I'll tell you."

"Lester called me, said somebody in a bright blue car was snooping around in here."

Well, good for Lester. "Lilly Cleary," I said. "You might remember me, from yesterday, at the market. Earl's lawyer."

"I remember you."

While her tone didn't suggest fond memories, she did put the gun down. "What are you looking for?"

Okay, to the point. I could respect that. "Something that would explain to me why Kenneth Mallory had this address on his mileage-reimbursement sheet for two days in January."

Mary Angel walked toward me, her gun hanging at her side, until she saw the pornography. She picked it up and threw it in a garbage can. "I told him not to bring that trash in the house. But a man's office, well, that's a man's office."

I nodded.

"Mad wasn't a bad man."

"No, ma'am, I haven't seen any evidence of wrongdoing on his part," I said. "But I think he might have been sort of murdered."

"Murdered? Man stepped on a snake."

"Anybody tell you his car was chased off the road, into a ditch, on Clay Gully Road?"

Mary Angel looked like she was trying to remember something, or maybe just make up her mind. "Yep. Deputy with the little boy told me it looked like somebody was chasing him, and he might've lost control or something."

"Did anybody tell you Mad had a suitcase full of cash with him when he ran into the swamp?"

Eyes to eyes, Mary Angel took my measure. After a considerable moment, she asked, "Where's the money?"

Her tone of voice told me a hard-core business deal was at hand and I need not bother with charm or bullshit. "I've got half of it. The boy who found Mad and called the police has the rest."

"I don't want to smear Mad's good name in this community. But truth is, I need that money." Mary Angel paused, apparently weighing the pros and cons, then spoke, signaling her decision. "You'll get me that money back, won't you?"

"As soon as you tell me what you know."

"How do I know I can trust you?" Mary Angel's practical side was, no doubt, honed from years of retail sales.

"I don't bring you the money, you report me to Tired for breaking and entering."

"Tired ain't got no jurisdiction in Oneco. I'll report you to our own sheriff."

"All right. Deal—the money for the truth."

"Mad's not used to doing bad, that's why this went wrong."

"What happened?"

"Some lawyer fella from Sarasota, probably that Kenneth Mallory, I could describe him, but I never got no name from him."

"What did he look like?"

"Forty-something, regular build, salt 'n' pepper hair, glasses, wore a damned pink shirt, nice enough looking 'cepting he was real . . . ordinary, I guess, had butterflies on his tie."

"Yeah, that'd be Kenneth."

"Well then, it was Kenneth came out here, looking Mad up and all, asking him about stealing the engineering plans to Earl's grape picker and offering to pay him for them. Best I could tell from what I overheard and what Mad told me, the lawyer fella was some kind of kin of Earl's and Earl had bragged to him that he was fixing to have a new, improved grape harvester that'd be worth a lot of money."

"You mean the harvester that Earl got killed with?"

"No, not that one. But like that one, only better. I mean, he and Mad had what Mad called a prototype, only a couple of little 'uns. Like models, you know. Earl was so proud of those models he'd showed them to that lawyer kin of his. That's how he knew about Mad having the specs and all."

"That would be those models in Earl's barn. Looked like *Star Wars* toys, only bigger than kids' toys?"

"I reckon. I never saw 'em. Earl started from the grape picker he had and kept tinkering on it 'cause it mashed up the grapes something terrible. He'd made a bunch of changes to it and was planning on getting him a patent someday."

"So, Mad stole Earl's plans and sold them to Kenneth?"

"Yep. But you remember, Kenneth put him up to it."

Hardly a case for entrapment, I thought, and then pondered this new information. "But—"

"Near as I can figure it, Earl never knew diddly-squat about the stolen plans. Least Mad didn't think he knew. But the more Mad thought about it, the more afraid he got of going to jail. I told you, Mad wasn't any good at bad ways. Got where he couldn't sleep he was so scared of what'd happen to him in a prison. He weren't no big man, you hear? So Mad up and run off."

"You think Kenneth chased Mad as he was fleeing? Why?"

Mary Angel ducked her head. And didn't answer.

"You might as well tell the rest of it." I made my voice sympathetic.

After a hard stare at the floor, Mary Angel sighed and looked up. "I don't know what good it'll do anybody, but I'll tell it. Mad figured since he had to leave town that the lawyer fella hadn't paid him enough. So he was going by his house and get him to give him some more money. Next thing I heard was a state trooper knocking at my door, saying Mad was dead."

I nodded. In a slack sort of way, some of this was making sense. Kenneth learned about the potential value of Earl's designs, hired Mad to steal the plans, and then when Mad tried to blackmail him something had happened at Kenneth's house that led to the car chase down Clay Gully Road. That had to be how it had gone down.

But after Mad crashed his car and ran into the Myakka wilderness, why didn't Kenneth follow him into the swamp and finish the deal?

I thought about Kenneth, prissy, well-dressed Kenneth in his pink shirt, his macho Hummer, and his butterfly garden. Money hungry, and crazy, and mean. But not brave enough to run into a swamp full of snakes and wild hogs and alligators and swarms of poisonous bugs and plants.

No, you'd need a man like Farmer Dave to run into a dangerous wilderness and drag back a man with a suitcase full of cash.

With a clarity that felt like bad mayonnaise in the gut, I realized that Dave finding Mad and the money wasn't just Dave's karma. No, Dave must have gone looking for him.

I had to go. I promised Mary Angel to bring her the money as soon as I cleared up a few things, and I started to leave.

Then I asked, really nicely, if I could borrow her gun.

"You know how to handle this? It's a Glock."

"Yes. I grew up in rural Georgia and I can handle a gun." Dave and my grandmother had seen to that.

"Awright. I'll sell it to you then."

"Take Visa?"

"Cash." She named what I'd guessed was a fair price.

I gave her what cash I had on me and promised the rest. Mary Angel took me at my word that I'd make good on the difference.

CHAPTER 34

A wiser person might have called Tired and waited.

But a wiser person wouldn't have left home at fifteen, weeded a marijuana patch for a living, fallen in love with Farmer Dave, and maintained a loyal connection to him long after having fallen out of love with him. Being a trial lawyer didn't necessarily mean I had overall good sense.

And if I called Tired with this new information, it might deepen the hole Dave had been digging for himself.

I wanted to think in a way driving the interstate didn't allow, so I went the back way, down Verna Road, and passed through the quaint cracker town of Old Myakka, finally hit State Road 72, and headed toward the winery.

The burning questions in my mind as I spun closer to the vineyard were why exactly had Dave gone after Mad, what exactly was Dave supposed to do with him when he caught him, and did this mean Dave had something to do with Kenneth's murder? What Mary Angel had told me suggested that Kenneth might have hired Dave to bring Mad back, and probably not to congratulate Mad on a wise career move. But despite the speed of my imagination and my high level of adrenaline, I didn't really have a refined plan. Maybe all I wanted was one final stab at making Dave tell me what he knew. Or to give him a chance for a good head start if he was in too deep.

With the rapid heartbeat of unrelieved anxiety, I turned down the dirt road to the winery with every intention of confronting Dave. But as I passed the Gift and Wine Shoppe, I saw the barn with its red-brick-bordered garden of gardenias and hibiscus and I wondered if the grape harvester that had killed Earl was inside.

Against my will, my mind flashed out a full-colored panoramic of the day Gandhi and I had found Earl under the grape harvester.

The grape picker. Big and ugly. A metal monster with long, sharp arms.

But with a white iris painted on its side. Something like a fleur-de-lis. That was French, wasn't it? The king's flower, or something.

A French symbol.

Ping, ping, ping—the dots connected with enough force to give off heat and energy. Kenneth's assets included a new contract with a French company.

Maybe Earl hadn't perfected enough changes to the original grape harvester for a patent in his own name, but no doubt the original maker of the machine would pay a lot for designs that would vastly improve its product. Kenneth would have seen this as an obvious shortcut to money.

With that shortcut in mind, it might have seemed easy to a greedy man planning on leaving the country anyway to sell Earl's plans to the original French manufacturer.

I had to take a look at that harvester. After making sure Cat Sue's white pickup wasn't anywhere around, I spun my Honda behind the barn and got out. The barn door was not locked and I pushed through it, and in the well-lit interior I spotted the grape harvester off in a corner.

In the second it took me to get to it, I also had my cell phone yanked out of my purse. Sure enough, there was the fleur-de-lis. And beside the painted flower, a metal tag affixed to the machine read "Fleur-de-Lis Harvester International."

I punched the Smith, O'Leary, and Stanley button on my cell and wished for the hundredth time that there was a way to bypass the front desk and reach Bonita directly. Cristal answered and I asked for Bonita without greeting her.

After a pause that made me grind my teeth, Cristal said, "Lilly?"

"Yeah. Edith has you on the front desk again, huh?"

"You know Bonita's worried about you? Where are you?"

"I'm fine. Just put me through to her. Right now. It's important."

"Okay. Sure thing. Anything else?"

"Hurry," I said.

Fortunately for the sake of my teeth the next voice I heard was Bonita's. "Where are you? You are late," she said, not bothering to disguise the chiding tone.

"I'm at the Stallings vineyard. In the barn. Do something real quick for me. Go to the patent website and see if a Fleur-de-Lis Harvester company has a new patent for a grape harvester."

"What is going on, please?"

"Bonita, just do it. Call me right back."

While waiting, I paced, I hummed, I ground my teeth until my jaw made audible popping noises, and then finally my cell rang.

"Yes. That company was granted a modification on its old patent. This happened a week before Mr. Daniels was deceased from the snakebite."

"Call Tired and tell him that. I've got to find Dave." I hung up with Bonita calling my name and I jammed my cell phone in my purse, on top of the Glock.

So wily old Kenneth had hired Mad to steal the engineering designs and he had sold them to the Fleur-de-Lis company, which had no doubt used them to extend the life and value of its original patent. Surely that was the French contract—the one Kenneth's CPA said provided a lump sum plus a percentage of the profits. Kenneth's final financing of his Costa Rica retirement.

That strongly suggested Kenneth had staged

Earl's fake accident to cover up his theft and sale of Earl's plans.

So who killed Kenneth?

As much as I didn't want to admit it, that left Bonita or Benny or even the meek Henry as suspects, each motivated to head off Kenneth's threatened lawsuit against Bonita.

Or Dave.

Dave might have killed Kenneth for Cat Sue, the heiress with both a motive and an alibi. I didn't want to believe it. Dave had never been a violent man, but I remembered how he had looked at Cat Sue that day at the yurt while Tired and I had watched. A man that much in love might do just about anything.

I suddenly understood that it would be in my best interest to leave this barn.

But as I turned quickly away from the harvester, the door opened. Like a genie in a big bottle, Cat Sue floated into the barn, all willowy in a white gauzy long skirt.

"Oh, hi, you again. You do pop up," she said, sounding friendly and maybe just a tad stoned.

"Is Dave here?" I asked.

"You looking for Dave in the barn?"

"Yes."

"Oh, well, I don't think he's in here."

"Where is he?"

"So who exactly are you?" Cat Sue asked. "I mean, that you're always dropping in?"

"Dave and I go way back," I said. "And I'm

347

Dave's lawyer. Didn't Philip explain that I was his co-counsel?"

"That means you're bound by that attorney-client privilege thing, right?"

Technically I was not Cat Sue's attorney, though I was willing to fudge that line to her. "Exactly," I said and smiled the particular smile of a lawyer telling a whopper. "You and Dave both. Total privilege, anything you want to tell me."

"Far out," she said. "So you're just . . . Dave's lawyer and an old friend?"

"Yes," I repeated, nodding as if I wasn't plainly trespassing in a barn in the middle of a murder zone. "Where's Dave?"

"Moving out of Waylon's. Shame about Waylon, dying and all."

"Waylon's dead?" I asked, panicked at the thought of another murder.

"Not that Waylon. The other one."

"The other one?"

"The singer. You know . . . the singer."

Oh, yeah, the dead singer Waylon.

"He's got my truck."

"Waylon?"

"No. Dave."

"So," I said, thinking, Yeah, definitely a tad stoned.

"So," Cat said.

Looking for a segue from so and soing, I said, "Cat Sue, I'm really sorry about Earl. He was a nice man. I could tell that from the time I met him."

Cat's eyes puddled up a little. "Yes. He was a nice man. And smart."

So why did you take up with Dave? I wanted to ask. But didn't. Sexual attraction had no rules. Maybe weird attracted weird. Cat and Dave both dressed like 1969. Plus Earl had that ambition about him that suggested more time in the barn with his grape-harvester models than in the house with Cat Sue, while Dave had all the free time of the barely employed to lavish upon her.

"Do you know who killed Earl?" I asked.

Cat's eyes puddled some more. "Do you?"

"Maybe. At any rate, I have some news," I said, thinking I'd try the buddy-buddy approach, especially since I had that Glock right there in my purse. "Do you want to go up to the gift shop and talk about it? I wouldn't mind a bottle of water."

"Sure. Yeah," Cat Sue said, but didn't move. "So, what's your news?" Yards of that long skirt were billowing around her when I saw with a precursor of alarm that she stood between me and the only door out of the barn. I walked toward her and the exit, but she stood her ground.

Not without concern, I inhaled and said, "Earl had figured out ways to significantly improve that harvester, hadn't he?" I pointed over my shoulder toward the big machine and watched her eyes flit toward it and then back to me.

"Excuse me, please," Cat Sue said. "But I do have an alibi for Earl."

"I know that. Tired told me. Nobody thinks you killed Earl."

"I got an alibi for when Kenneth was shot too," she added. "I was in Orlando and Winter Park. Check with Tired, you'll see."

"Yeah, shopping, I know."

As I moved a step closer to the barn door, something not unlike an electric shock went through my entire body.

Orlando. And its nearby suburb Winter Park, the shopping mecca.

Uh-oh.

Cristal had a Visa receipt from Winter Park. Now that I thought about it, people from Sarasota didn't routinely shop in Winter Park, not when the riches of St. Armand's Circle beckoned, close at hand. Try as I might, I couldn't visualize the date on Cristal's receipt, and realized I probably had not noticed it the night I'd found the receipt while looking for Kenneth's travel forms. But Cristal had been out of the office the day Kenneth was killed, I remembered that.

My mouth dried up but my hands began to sweat. Cristal definitely had a key to the Smith, O'Leary, and Stanley office building and, what with the banker's hours Bonita and I had suddenly been keeping, it wouldn't have been hard at all to sneak in the 158 roundnoses and steal the laptop from my credenza.

Cristal of more or less the same height and weight as Cat Sue, Cristal in a dark wig and a red scarf and a hippie dress, armed with Cat Sue's credit card and a talent for forgery, could have easily created that Winter Park shopping alibi.

And Cristal surely would have been introduced at some point to Cat Sue as her boss's only local family.

Cristal with the secret private life, Cristal who didn't date lawyers. Cristal who didn't date—men.

Oh, *mierda*. Cristal the temporary receptionist who could have easily listened to my conversation with Bonita. The one in which I said I was in the barn at the Stallings vineyard.

Cat Sue shifted into an open stance, her feet well grounded, with the solid look of someone not planning on backing out of the way of the only exit.

"I'm really thirsty. And hot. Could we go to the gift shop?" I hoped I didn't sound whiney or afraid.

"Can do," she said, but took no step toward leaving the barn. "But first, explain that attorney-client thing again. I might need some legal help."

"Sure. What do you need?"

"Oh, you know. Stuff."

"Well, then, let's do it formally. I'll draft up a retainer agreement for you when I get back to the office. We can talk fees later." I put my right hand on the clasp of my purse, which was slung over my left shoulder, and took a couple of steps toward the door Cat Sue was blocking. "In fact, I'll drive you back to my office right now and we can get those papers signed."

"Maybe not just yet," Cat Sue said.

In what I hoped was as speedy a move as when I jumped out of my car faster than a rattlesnake, I jerked open my purse. I had my hand on the Glock, but the gun was jammed under my cell phone and hairbrush and I couldn't get it out quite as quickly as I'd figured.

As I struggled with the damn gun, Cat Sue swung her whole body toward me, knocking me sideways. While I tottered under the impact, she grabbed the strap of my purse and yanked so hard she pulled me down on the dirt floor of the barn. Then she sat on me, reached for my purse before I could make my arms work, and pulled out the Glock.

So, okay, spank me, I blew that. But quick-drawing guns from purses wasn't a skill I had needed much in my litigation practice.

Cat Sue and I stared at each other. We breathed hard.

"Damn," she said. "I thought this was over."

"You're my client now," I said. "You don't need that gun."

"I gotta think a minute."

Okay, let me help Cat Sue think, I thought. "Way I got it figured is Kenneth was the bad guy all the way through this."

"What?" Cat looked puzzled.

"You know, I could breathe better if you didn't sit on my stomach."

Obligingly, Cat Sue slid down to my thighs. I could inhale easier, but she still had me firmly anchored. Though my hands were free, the Glock I had so recently purchased to no good avail kept me from flailing my arms in any attempt to dislodge her.

No, I was going to have to talk my way out of this one. "Like I said, Kenneth was the bad guy. First he paid Mad to steal Earl's harvester designs. Then he sold them to that Fleur-de-Lis company in his own name and cut you and Earl out of the profit loop. Then Kenneth chased Mad off the road. I'm not sure why, to kill him, or get the money back, or something. But then he was too prissy to go in the swamp after Mad, so he asked you to send somebody after Mad. Right?"

"Kenneth," she repeated. "Yeah."

"So tell me."

"It's a long story."

"I don't think I'm going anywhere right now."

Cat was a bit bleary-eyed, I noted, but she held the gun like a pro. "Earl had worked for years, I mean, years, figuring out the bugs on that grape picker. He went to Kenneth for advice on whether he could get a patent for improving something that already was, and Kenneth said only if Earl made some totally major changes. So Earl figured he needed to make a few more modifications. He was working on getting a wider picking tunnel, and simulating hand harvesting in the vertical trellis."

Yeah, whatever on the mechanics. "So, Kenneth *was* the bad guy," I repeated for effect.

Dreamily, as if she hadn't heard me, Cat Sue said, "Earl figured he'd get that patent in a couple of years and we'd be rich."

"So you're the victim, not the bad guy, and can let me up. You can explain all this to me in my office."

Ignoring my last plea, Cat Sue said, "Earl had this real important wine conference in San Francisco. Everybody who was anybody in the American wine scene was there. We had to start marketing our wine nationally or we didn't have a chance to stay afloat until Earl started making money off his patent."

As interesting as all this was, my legs were cramping under Cat Sue's weight. "Could you just get off me? My legs are going to sleep."

"Oh, I hate that. That tingling feeling is so awful." But Cat Sue didn't get up. Rather, she said, "But, see, everybody was so mean to Earl in San Francisco. They made total fun of his wine and said Florida couldn't ever produce a wine that would sell outside of Dixie. 'Cracker wine' was what one fella called it and laughed about muscadines as wine grapes. Earl got his feelings hurt so bad he just left, caught an early flight home."

I tried to sort of kick my legs around to get the blood flowing, but for a thin woman, Cat Sue weighed a lot when all of her was across my thighs.

"You wanta hear this or not?" she asked as I wiggled ineffectively under her.

"By all means. It's fascinating."

"See, when Earl got home that Saturday, first thing he did was go check on things. And right off, he found that the wine in storage had been stolen, so he runs off to track down the sheriff about his stolen wine and leaves me here by myself."

"At least sit on my ankles," I said. "You're really hurting me."

"Oh, sorry." Cat Sue slid down a few more inches.

"Thank you, that's better. Now, please continue," I said.

"While Earl's off chasing his stolen wine, Kenneth comes up all in a dither. He told me his yardman had just stolen a whole bunch of money from his house and Kenneth had chased him to just up the road from here. But the guy wrecked his car on a curve and ran into the swamp, with the money. See, Kenneth wanted me to send a couple of my Mexicans into the swamp and bring back the man and what Kenneth said was his money. He was way too scared of getting dirty or a tick bite to go after him himself."

"But you sent Dave instead?"

"See, Dave needed the money. Kenneth said he'd pay the Mexicans a ten percent finders' fee."

Yeah, Dave would go into a swamp for three thousand, I thought, especially since subsequent events suggested he intended to keep all of the money. But Dave's risk-versus-benefit analytical defects aside, I had to get out of here before Cristal came. Hopefully it was just a matter of sweet-talking Cat Sue into getting off me. But first I had to know if Dave was part of anything worse than planning to steal the whole sum total of the money. "Did Dave know what was going on at that point?"

"No, Dave didn't know anything bad. I didn't even know the man was Mad. It was, like I said, just me figuring Dave needed the finders' fee 'cause him and me had just broken up. You know, between Earl and Cri . . . er, carrying the gift shop, I just didn't have time for a boyfriend and all, and he was leaving town."

"You didn't know that he'd stolen Earl's wine?"

"Not right then, no. I was just trying to get Dave some traveling money. That's all. I always did like Dave. If I'd known he'd taken care of that by stealing Earl's wine, I wouldn't've bothered asking him to go after Mad."

Okay, a bit dizzy, I thought. What with Mad running and Farmer Dave stealing and Earl coming home early, I could see how everything had gone to hell in a hurry.

"So, neither you nor Dave did anything wrong. All you did was ask a friend to recover some money Kenneth said his yardman had stolen from him."

Cat nodded vigorously and I had the feeling I was making up her defense for her. "That's right," she said.

Taking all this in, I realized that the Saturday Dave came to my house, he was looking for a sack of cash in a swamp, not a jaguarundi. But why would he take Benny with him to pretend to track a wildcat?

Then I remembered that first he had wanted me to go with him, no doubt for safety. Growing up like we had, roaming the red hills of south Georgia, we knew to take a buddy when traipsing off trail in the woods and swamps of the great south. What happened to Mad had proved this lesson. So when I couldn't go with Dave, he had taken Benny to watch his back and yell for help if something happened.

Mierda. Dave was in town long enough to fall in love and commit a few felonies but didn't come calling until he needed me to wade out in a swamp to fight wild hogs and snakes over a sack of money. That made me mad enough I had to swallow hard a few times.

Then I forced myself to refocus. "Kenneth killed Earl, didn't he?"

"Yes," Cat Sue said. "Son of a bitch even bragged about it to me. Said he didn't have any choice because Mad turning up dead was eventually going to get Earl figuring things out."

"You mean Earl didn't know what was going on?"

"No, why would he? He was trying to get his stolen wine back and still figuring on another year or two before he'd've perfected his grape-picker plans good enough to get a patent."

So, okay, there's Earl, just churning away and working on the perfect mechanical grape harvester while Mad and Kenneth totally decompress. No doubt Mad's panic mode triggered the same in Kenneth, especially given the aborted blackmail attempt. With Mad so conveniently out of the way, it was easy to imagine Kenneth driving up Tuesday morning to visit Earl, knocking him over the head, and staging the accident scene. After all, Earl wouldn't have a clue that Kenneth was any threat.

"So, how'd you find out about Kenneth selling Earl's plans?"

"Cristal figured it out. She's real smart, you know? A certified paralegal and all. After Earl was killed, she got to thinking things through after I told her no way Earl gets himself killed accidentally on that thing. Cristal remembered this contract with a French company that Kenneth had been real secretive about. So she hunted out that contract and brought it to me and we put two and two together."

And came up with a plan to kill Kenneth right back, I thought.

It had to be Cat Sue—with a wigged Cristal flaunting Cat's credit card a three-hour drive from the murder scene, perfecting an alibi. I'll be damned, Gandhi was right.

On the remote chance I could convince Cat Sue I was a total idiot and believed either that she did not kill Kenneth the evil lawyer, or that I believed she had done so in self-defense, or that I was bound by attorney-client privilege, I kept my own counsel about the Cristal and Cat Sue conspiracy to commit murder.

"So," I said, trying to pull my face and voice

into that of the complacent believer, "while you were in Winter Park, somebody killed Kenneth."

"Yes. You did." Cat Sue beamed at me. "That's why you had the gun in your car trunk and the bullets in your office."

Okay, to tell or not to tell about the gun being inadmissible and the bullets being wrapped in the Sunday funnies next door at Grandmom's house on Tulip. Hmm, hmm, hmm—wisely I opted not to tell and went for another dodge. "Whoever killed him, it would be self-defense. I mean, Tired told me Kenneth had a gun and got off a shot."

"Self-defense," Cat Sue said, apparently mulling this over.

Yeah, right, I thought, self-defense with six shots and a preconceived alibi. That would be a very enthusiastic self-defense. I wiggled my legs forcefully under the increasing burden of Cat Sue's body on top of me.

"You know I got nothing against you or anything." As she said that, Cat Sue scooted up until she was sitting on my stomach again. "But framing you doesn't look like it's going to work out, what with Bonita taking your car and all. So I'm gonna have to do something else with you."

"But you don't need to. I'm your attorney. You just hired me. I can't report any of this or The Florida Bar's ethics commission will have my license."

"Really?"

"Really."

Cat Sue appeared to be studying on this. Before I could think of what else to say, I heard the sound of a vehicle pulling up outside the barn. Oh, please, please, please, cosmic forces, God of Delvon, blue gods, wood spirits and guardian angels for attorneys everywhere who won't butt out when told to do so, please let that be the posse. Even just Tired. Even just Dave.

Of course, it was Cristal.

I mean, why not? I'd practically told her where I was and what I was doing.

"Cristal called me earlier, said you were inside the barn snooping," Cat Sue said as I struggled to look at Cristal prancing into the barn. "She told me that I should hold you here."

Obviously Cristal had listened to my call to Bonita. Naturally she was also armed.

As I contemplated my limited future, Cristal walked over to Cat Sue and stroked her face. "You all right, baby?"

"Yes," Cat Sue said. And finally she rolled off me and stood up.

"I told you that live rattler wouldn't scare her off. You don't know this woman," Cristal said to Cat Sue, as if I weren't even there. "She's doggedly persistent."

Hmm, "doggedly persistent." I rather liked that, but stopped myself short of thanking Cristal as I pushed myself up into a sitting position. "So the dead snake and the fish, that was Kenneth?" Oh, yeah, like that mattered now.

"That was Kenneth. That's where Cat got the idea for the live snake," Cristal said.

Not to be sidetracked, Cat Sue said to Cristal, "She says there's this attorney-client privilege and she can't rat on us, but I don't trust her. Maybe we can, I don't know, shoot her, put her in a wine barrel, haul it out—"

"Wait a minute," Cristal said. "Let me think."

"Look, killing Kenneth was self-defense," I said, putting that dogged persistence into a persuasive mode. "Philip Cohen is an excellent criminal-defense attorney and I know he and I can get either one of you off. But if you kill me, that's first degree. Florida still has the death penalty, you know? Even for shooting your own lawyer."

"Self-defense?" Cat Sue said. "Yeah. Kenneth pulled his gun on me. I knew he had to kill me to cover up his killing Earl and stealing his designs."

"Then it's perfect self-defense. Philip and I can get you out of this, absolutely." Tentatively I stood up, testing my legs and the attitudes of the two women holding guns on me. "We'll call Philip out here, he'll coach you on what to say, and then we'll explain it to Tired. It will be all right."

"Self-defense." Cat Sue said it dreamily.

And for a moment I even believed it myself.

Until Cristal laughed. "Premeditated self-defense. Sure, Philip could make that work."

"What?" Cat Sue asked Cristal.

"The fake alibi. You don't set up an alibi and

then kill somebody in self-defense," Cristal the certified paralegal explained to Cat Sue.

"Damn Kenneth, getting us all into this," Cat Sue said. "Kenneth always looking down his nose at Earl and me, lording it over me he's the great white lawyer. Greediest man I knew. Kenneth took all of our grandmother's things when she died. I didn't get anything and you wouldn't believe the silver she had."

Yeah, actually, I would believe the silver.

"But the worst of it," Cat Sue said, "was Kenneth killing Earl with that grape picker. Kenneth said what's wrong with me, didn't I get the irony of killing him with his own damn grape harvester? Kenneth probably planned to kill Earl and me all along, but was stalling for the best time. Mad's getting killed kinda changed things."

"Those modifications on the harvester, were they really worth plotting a double first-degree murder?" I asked, recoiling at the depth of Kenneth's greed. Out of the corner of my eye, I gazed at Cristal, who alternately watched me and Cat Sue.

"Yes. A grape harvester that wouldn't bruise the grapes, why that'd be like the cotton gin. It would reduce labor costs significantly. With a sixteen-inch bucket conveyor, a good harvester like the one Earl was perfecting could handle twenty tons per acre. Big market for such a machine in California and Michigan, as well as France, Chile, and Israel." Cat Sue suddenly had an earnest-businesswoman tone for someone so recently camped on my stomach.

But I didn't care so much about profit margins as I cared now about keeping Cat Sue and Cristal talking, because as long as they were explaining things to me they weren't stuffing me in a wine barrel. "What exactly happened at Kenneth's?" I asked in my best cross-examination mode.

"Kenneth answered the door with his gun out and admitted he killed Earl so he wouldn't get in trouble for stealing Earl's plans and chasing Mad to his death. Then, like, after that, the man had balls enough to offer to pay me off, give me half. Like I would trust him, kin or not. Like I'd let Kenneth get away with killing Earl. See, Earl was a good man and he didn't deserve to die and I was tired of Kenneth doing shit and getting away with it, and I knew it was just a matter of time before he'd kill me too, so I pulled out Dave's gun and I shot him."

"But Tired said Kenneth fired a round too," I said.

"Yeah, but that man couldn't shoot straight. Even close up. The kick on the gun threw him off. Lucky for me that gave me time to shoot him."

"So, he fired first. It *was* self-defense."

"Yeah," Cat Sue said and nodded again.

"I already told you, nobody will believe it because we set up the alibi first," Cristal said, sounding just a tad put out.

Okay, so the self-defense bluff was pretty much

over. "Why didn't you just turn Kenneth in to the sheriff instead of killing him?" I asked, seeing no further need to wordsmith as only physical action and karmic intervention were going to save me now, but even at death's door I was terribly curious.

"Money," Cristal said. "I destroyed all copies of a will Kenneth drew up himself. Do you know, he left everything to the National Butterfly Association?"

Kenneth had left his fortune to bugs with wings?

Then it hit me: Cristal the certified paralegal, Cristal the forger. I was probating her will, not Kenneth's.

"I did a good job on that will," she said, not shy in her own praise. "I prepared and signed it, leaving nearly everything to Cat Sue. Forged a couple of witnesses' signatures. With a token in the will for Kenneth's brother. I mean, the brother wasn't close at all, so I didn't think he'd contest anything. Also I heard from Ashton he was coming back soon, so I figured he'd be the perfect PR. I mean, he certainly wouldn't get a handwriting expert to examine it. Then Cat and I would have all of Kenneth's estate, plus the Fleur-de-Lis contract to pay off the debts on Earl's place."

Okay, money would do it. I wondered idly if Kenneth's greed had been contagious and Cristal had caught it like the first winter flu through an office. Or, is greed just the human condition?

Cat Sue turned to Cristal, saying, "Attorney-client or not, I say she's gonna rat us out for sure.

I can't go to jail. Cristal, sweetie, you just know I wouldn't do good in a prison. Not with my heart murmur."

"Damn. We need to think," Cristal said. But then she added, "Come on, Lilly, let's go to the winery."

"You take good care of her," Cat said as Cristal pointed her gun at me.

I walked out in front of her. Okay, what *would* Willie do?

Stomp, stomp, stomp. Whoa, what was my hurry? I stopped walking and turned around to face Cristal, planning a last-ditch appeal. But as I stared at Cristal's tense face, Bonita materialized from behind a giant hibiscus by the barn.

As sweat poured down my face, Bonita, the good Catholic mother, picked up a brick from the hibiscus-garden border and threw it at Cristal, hitting her solidly in the back of her shoulder and spinning her around. Cristal stumbled to the ground, stunned, but her hand still held her gun.

Grabbing for the gun was too big a gamble, especially with an armed Cat Sue just inside the barn. I dashed at Bonita, grabbed her arm and screamed, "Run," as if that wasn't the obvious option.

CHAPTER 35

We ran.

And we ran, and we ran, taking the ground in front of us in giant leaps. Down the path between the rows of grapes, we galloped. More intent on protective cover than pavement, I steered us toward the wooded fringe of the vineyard rather than down the dirt road to the highway. With the armed and deadly girlfriends presumably coming after us, I didn't want the clear target of our backs out in an open space. No, I wanted dense trees and foliage.

So we ran, and ran, deeper into the woods, following no path, but spinning our way through the underbrush into the live oaks and cypress woods, thick with moss-hung trees and grounded with a spongy, wet floor, green with lichen and ferns, and we ran deep enough that we began to pass from the trees into the scrubs and thickets of a Florida hammock. We were nearing the edge of Myakka River State Park, where the Myakka River would soon make a swamp of the hammock. We were gasping for air. I put out my hand and stopped

Bonita, there in one of the last great expanses of true Florida wilderness.

We needed to breathe. We needed to see where we were. We needed to listen for sounds of a gang of girl killers following us. I looked around. Standing as still as I could while catching my breath, I listened, but didn't hear any thrashing in the bushes or other sounds of anyone chasing us.

Before us lay the palmetto scrubs where rattlers and boars and the myriad forms of wildlife that were capable of harming a person lived their lives, but also where the scrub jays, white-tailed deer, and gopher tortoises went placidly about their gentle lives. Perhaps a panther or a jaguarundi might still prowl, wholly unaware of the monster housing developments working their way toward their meager habitat, guaranteeing their eventual extinction.

Florida wilderness is nothing if it isn't the ultimate example of the yin and yang.

But I was too scared to be philosophical. I wanted to keep running until I was safe in the protective custody of a sheriff's deputy. First, though, I gasped out what I had been wondering as we ran. "How did you know?"

Her face flushed, Bonita peered over her shoulder. Apparently satisfied that no crazed killers were immediately behind us, she said, "Cristal presented me with a bottle of Earl's wine for a Christmas present last year. Since I do not drink, I gave it to Gracie, but then I remembered that and thought about it—Earl's wine is not sold anyplace yet except at his winery."

"So you figured Cristal and Cat Sue and Earl knew each other?"

"Yes. But I was not sure how any of that mattered until you ran out of the office that day with those old bullets."

"Like we talked about, it had to be somebody who could have gotten the bullets from Dave's backpack but who also had access to my office. But how'd you—"

"The laptop."

"Kenneth's laptop?"

"Yes. You see, while Cristal was working the front desk this morning, I happened to find occasion to search her office."

"She wouldn't leave the laptop in her office?"

"No, she put it back in Kenneth's office."

Oh, what better place to hide something other than where it belonged. Kenneth's laptop in Kenneth's office. Especially after Jackson and Officer Tired Johnson and I had already searched it. Talk about your "Purloined Letter" concept.

"So, okay, when you found the laptop, you figured Cristal was part of the puzzle," I said. "And then when I called you from the barn, you put it together."

"Not immediately. I was standing at my desk calling Officer Johnson when I saw through the window that Cristal was running to her car. So I hung up and followed her. She got away from me in the traffic, but I believed I knew where she was going. It made sense to me that she had listened in on our conversation and had gone to do you harm."

If I hadn't been so hot and breathless, I would have hugged Bonita.

Looking about her, Bonita pointed to a greenish log with lidded eyes on the bank of a branch of tea-colored water. "That's an alligator, isn't it?"

"Yes, but you aren't a small wading bird or a toy poodle, so it won't hurt you unless—"

"We should leave this place," Bonita said. "Now."

Yes, we should, I thought. As we started walking, swarms of flying, biting bugs fogged us as we moved deeper into the cypress swamp.

Though we were walking fast enough that chatter was hard, I had to ask. "Who was Benny protecting? I mean, that night at your house, when he said he wasn't a tattletale?"

"It is complex."

"Hey, I'm a lawyer. We love complexities."

"He probably meant he was protecting me. But he also might have meant Dave. Maybe even Cat Sue, because he'd promised."

"How so?" I asked, and swatted a devil's walking stick out of my way with the back of my hand, but still drew blood from the thorns.

"I think we should not go deeper into this swamp," Bonita said, and picked her feet through some muck and rubbed a spiderweb off her face.

"What? You want to go back?" But as I turned

around to look at what going back meant, I realized I didn't know. I mean, okay, a swamp looks pretty much the same in any direction, especially when you're running. The ooze and underbrush had closed behind us, leaving no appreciable trail marking our passage.

"So," I said, "the bad news is, we're lost. But the good news is, Cat Sue and Cristal probably can't find us."

Bonita sighed, rubbed her cross, and started walking toward a modest high spot in the expanding dankness. "The night the deputies arrested Dave and Waylon, Dave told Benny to take his backpack to Cat Sue. Apparently there were sirens as the law went out to Waylon's, so Dave had time to arrange things. Not much time. But enough. Dave also gave Benny a suitcase full of money."

So despite my telling Benny not to tell his mother about the money, he obviously had.

"Dave told Benny he could keep half the money for all his . . . trouble. But Benny said Dave was clear that he wanted Cat Sue to have the backpack," Bonita said. "Benny had promised Dave not to tell anyone."

"How'd he know where to go?"

"Benny's finding the yurt was easy. They were already near it and he needed only to drive east on State Road 72 until he saw the winery sign."

So Benny had taken Cat not only the money, but Dave's gun and his 158-grain roundnose bullets. "And?"

"Cat Sue was at the yurt, and Benny told her about the dead man and what Dave had said. He said she was very agitated. But she let him in and let him take what appeared to be about half of the money."

Bonita stopped, tilted her head as if she were hearing the sounds of pursuit, and stood still.

I looked around and listened. Still no sounds of the crazed girlfriends.

"What happened then?" I asked, and flicked a tick off my arm.

"As Benny was trying to leave, Kenneth was driving up the road in his Hummer. Kenneth blocked the road and wouldn't back it up. So Benny got out of his truck and asked to pass. They recognized each other and Kenneth demanded that Benny explain himself, so Benny told him he was just out driving around on a Saturday night and had tried to buy some wine for a party. Then Kenneth threatened Benny that if he told anybody, he, Kenneth, was there at the winery, he would hurt me."

Poor Benny, I thought, though I gave him plus points for the quick, inventive lie.

And then I realized that Kenneth, bent as he was on a killing spree so he could retire to Costa Rica financed by Earl's harvester designs, could well have killed Benny. I wondered if Bonita had thought of this. Maybe killing children was too much even for Kenneth.

"Benny and I, in trying to understand, did not

believe that Kenneth at that time yet knew the welder was dead in the swamp, but we do not know."

Something suddenly crashed behind us and Bonita and I both yelped and jogged a few steps and then turned. A large, wild hog stood behind us. A boar with gray tusks protruding from its long snout, looking for all the world like something out of a Tarzan movie. Or hell. Two more hogs crashed out of the scrubs and milled around the first one.

Oh, frigging great. Where was Percy Ponder the wild-hog hunter when we needed him? As Bonita and I began a hasty backing up while watching the feral hogs, they crashed on through the wet underbrush and went their way.

"Let us, please, concentrate on getting out of here," Bonita said.

"Maybe we should follow the boar," I said. "You know, the wild hogs and deer make trails and if we find one, the walking will be easier, plus the trail might cross a real road somewhere."

"I am not following those pigs," she said.

While I contemplated pointing out that I was closer to a rural survivalist expert than she was, Bonita turned back to the direction she had already chosen and marched forward. So, okay, she was the one with all the saints, I thought, and followed, still trying to get my mind around what had happened the night Benny took Dave's gun to Cat Sue at the yurt. I mean, if we were going to die in the outreaches of Myakka State Park, at least I wanted to understand the events that conspired to drop me in this wet jungle full of things that could hurt me.

"So, that thing with the lawsuit," I said, connecting a few more dots, "that was Kenneth threatening you to guarantee that Benny didn't tell Tired about seeing him that night at Cat Sue's?"

"Yes."

I could only guess why Kenneth had gone back out to Cat Sue's that night; he must have been looking for word about Mad. Possibly he was planning to kill Mad if Dave had dragged him back alive. Maybe Cat Sue told Kenneth I had Mad's cash, or maybe he followed Cat Sue when she brought the money to me and had waited for me so he could knock me over the head and steal it back. Talk about not knowing when to leave bad enough alone!

We might never really know precisely what had gone down, but if Bonita and I got out of this quagmire of gators and pigs alive, and Dave didn't go to jail, then I'd settle for a murky big picture.

And speaking of murky, there was still that question of why Kenneth's threat had scared Bonita. "So, okay, what was that nonsense about some of your children not being Felipe's?"

Bonita walked in silence for a long time. I had about given up on an answer when she said, "My sister, Gracie, was a nun in El Salvador. She smuggled children out."

I let the implications of that splatter against me like a face full of raw eggs.

"Wow," I said, stunned back to my adolescent vocabulary. That's why Armando looked more like an Indian and not at all like Javy, his so-called twin. And Benny? Benny, who at least looked like Javy. That is, in a general, wiry, dark-haired-boy sort of way. "What about Benny?"

"Benny, Javy, and Armando are all El Salvadorians. Armando was rescued half starved from a destroyed native village. Javy and Benny were children of what the government considered a dangerous radical. If they had stayed there, they would probably have died with their father."

"But how?"

"Gracie was part of a mission, a group of rescue people, and they all knew skilled men who could create birth certificates. Gracie's people smuggled the three of them into Mexico while Felipe and I lived there, but we could not adopt the children because they were illegal babies. So we hired the men to make us the forged papers and planned to move so the neighbors would not talk and create trouble. What Gracie's men prepared was good enough to get us all in this country when the orange-juice factory wanted Felipe as one of its engineers. Of course no one challenged any of us at that point because the American company wanted us to come."

"Carmen and Felipe," I said, remembering the vastly pregnant Bonita lumbering around.

"Yes, after we were here in this country, they were born, after Gracie had been expelled from

El Salvador, and we were all living here, thinking we were safe."

"Benny knows this?"

"Now he does."

He was just a kid. But I thought Benny had taken all this pretty well. Then I remembered Benny dodging me, Benny skipping school, Benny locking himself in his bedroom, Benny shutting his mom out, and Benny hiding behind his Walkman's noise. Tough little kid that he was, he'd done some hard adjusting after finding out his life was based upon a nun's act of mercy and some forged papers.

But the burden on Benny was not as hard as the one on his mother. Obviously Bonita had been afraid that if Kenneth messed around with his lawsuit, the immigration people would deport her children back to El Salvador.

Frankly, I didn't know if they could have been deported or not. I would hope not. But I'd read some scary stories in the papers over the years about our government deporting worthy people, even children, over minor technicalities and with what appeared to be capricious whim. So I could see where Bonita would be afraid to risk it. I wondered if this was why Bonita had never become a naturalized American citizen. Maybe she didn't want immigration taking a second look at the papers on her children.

"Do Armando and Javy know?"

"No. I will tell them when they are sixteen."

Bonita stopped walking for a moment, so I did

too, which had the immediate effect of causing a black mist of gnats to glom on to us. All of this information was almost too much to absorb.

"We must never speak of this again, you and I," Bonita said. "Or to anyone."

"Yes, yes, I understand. But how did Kenneth know?"

"I am not sure he really did. My belief is that he thought that I had the first children out of wedlock, or had been unfaithful, so that Felipe was not their father. Otherwise, I believe he would have threatened me with immigration, not with a lawsuit. One time I caught him studying that photo of us on my desk. Another time, he asked me why Benicio wasn't named after Felipe. Our Hispanic tradition calls for naming the firstborn son after the father, not the third son."

Well, okay, after all, that day I had studied the same photograph, I'd wondered myself why Armando looked so different from the rest of them.

"We must not speak again—"

"Yeah, I know. But you aren't done yet. That night Kenneth was killed. My car. What happened?"

Bonita sighed and pushed a three-leaf vine out of the way, while I shuddered at the thought of the poison-ivy itch to come. Then she said, "Our office computer security is very . . . loose. The afternoon you loaned me your car, I broke into the book-keeping files on the hard drive. We have all heard rumors of Kenneth's billing excesses."

"Yes. The thirty-hour days."

"I found documented evidence of his fraudulent billing. That night, Benny drove your car to Kenneth's house with me so that we might convince him to leave us alone. Like a trade, I would not show the bills to his clients and Benny would not ever tell anyone about seeing him that night. But Kenneth had to promise to leave us alone."

Good for Bonita, I thought. If those thirty-hour-a-day bills had come to light, Kenneth would have lost his clients, been investigated by the ethics division of The Florida Bar, and possibly been prosecuted by the state attorney's office.

"Only," Bonita said, "Kenneth was . . . the door was unlocked. He was already dead. I had pressed the doorbell, but when no one answered, Benny pushed open the door and saw him first. He took hold of me and we ran off."

Mierda, but Benny had been through a lot. My own childhood suddenly looked ideal. At least there had been no murdered bodies in it.

"So it *was* you in my car the neighbor saw? You and Benny?"

"It was wrong. We should not have run. But we were afraid. Afraid no one would believe us, or that even if they did, an investigation might come back to those forged papers."

"And Henry, later that night, at your house? You called Henry in for the alibi," I said, asking and answering my own question.

"Yes."

"Why didn't you call me? I'd've alibied you."

"Yes. I thought of that. But you might have lost your law license if it ever came out. And Henry, Henry was so eager to . . . prove himself. It made him feel very masculine to help us."

Wow. Even under the pressure of finding a dead man and the fear of immigration, Bonita had been considerate. But at what cost? I wondered. "Are you all right?" I asked her.

She nodded. "We will find our way out of this *pantano* and not speak of any of this again."

We both had a lot to think about. But first we had to get to safety. We were lost in the wet, buggy, scary world of a wild Florida cypress swamp. I realized this was a new variation of the dragon and the whirlpool. Lost in snake heaven, with deepening swamp in front and with a gun-toting hippie killer and her forger-schemer girlfriend possibly behind us.

As we stood there, lost in the thicket and contemplating our limited options, Bonita said, "Lilly." Her voice was soft and very sad. "It is our cat."

Following the line of Bonita's hand as she pointed, I stared into the marbled shadows in the underbrush. Like letting my eyes adjust to darkness, it took me a moment to make out the transplanted South American cat. First I saw a dappled, coppery shape in the shade of the deep scrub, then I registered its movement, then I focused on the jaguarundi.

When I finally saw it, I could not look away from the wildcat. Sleek, low to the ground, definitely feline, and with a very long tail and big panther eyes, the animal stood there in front of us, not more than twenty feet away.

"He'll help us," Bonita said.

Yeah, right, like we were in a Disney movie.

As the gnats thickened, I waited for the cat to run off. But it didn't.

"Gandhi told Benny that Felipe's spirit lives in a jaguarundi, here in Myakka."

"That's why Benny did that paper and kept trying to find the jaguarundi, isn't it? Skipping school and all?"

"He's waiting for us to follow him," Bonita said, her eyes wistful as she stared at the cat and ignored my question.

So, okay, it wasn't any weirder than anything else that day. Without speaking further, we walked toward the wildcat, which turned and prowled through the scrub, slow and easy, while we followed it.

We walked as quietly as we could, lagging behind the jaguarundi and occasionally losing sight of it. But every time we lost the cat, Bonita seemed to know what track to take until we saw it again. Once the jaguarundi growled at us when we got too close, and we had to back off. But finally, with the faint trace of a cat barely in our vision, we came to a gutted, muddy road. Ghostlike, the jaguarundi disappeared back into the swamp: a long, low wildcat, then a shadow, then poof!, nothing.

Exhausted and hot and itchy from the descending mosquitoes feasting on us, Bonita and I followed the dirt road to a bigger road and finally to a park-ranger station in the state park.

After the initial babble of officiousness, the ranger was Johnny Helpful and shoved a phone toward me and I called Tired at the sheriff's office. Tired was out, some woman said. "Okay, let me speak to Stan." I didn't like Stan, but at least he already knew who I was.

"Stan's out too," she said.

"Who's in that I could speak with about the person who shot Kenneth Mallory, the lawyer."

"Just a minute, please."

Muzak assaulted me along with my rising itch and irritation, and I was about to hang up when a man came on the line and introduced himself as chief deputy so and so. I explained who I was, but suddenly mindful of the fact that I might actually have created an attorney-client privilege with Cat Sue, I edited my summary of events at the Stallings barn and winery.

After telling Mr. Chief Deputy that activities which invited official scrutiny had occurred at the vineyard today, I asked that he relay this information to Tired.

"Don't go back to that Stallings place," he said. "I'll send a deputy to pick you up. Stay put, you hear?"

Yeah, I heard. But there is just something about a male voice issuing a direct order that has, like, this totally negative impact on me. Plus, Bonita and I needed to find Benny and tell him this madness would soon be over. After Bonita and I washed our hands and faces and slurped some ice-cold bottled water, I sweet-talked the ranger into taking us back to the barn.

By the time we got there, the place was alive with sheriff's deputies and I spotted Tired's black Chevy. Good, the posse had arrived in time.

Tired trotted over to me and hugged me while the other deputies stared. After he and Bonita shook hands, I turned to watch two deputies pushing down Cat Sue's and Cristal's heads as they loaded them into a patrol car.

"Got them just about a mile away, running through the woods. Crashed through, leaving a clear trail."

"Probably trying to chase Bonita and me," I said.

"We've got lots to talk about," Tired said. "First, though, ma'am, I figured that was your purse in the barn. Your cell phone was ringing, so I finally had to answer it."

I looked at Tired with both fatigue and curiosity.

"Dave saw all the cop cars and sirens when he was coming back here. I reckon he got scared, left, and went up to a store and called you," Tired said. "First I had to tell him a hundred times you were fine, that you were at a ranger station in the park. Then I told him he wasn't wanted for anything as far as I knew but that he needed to come in for questions. But he said no, he figured he'd pass on that, that Cat Sue had broke his heart, but he wasn't going to testify against her. Said something about a red-headed stranger that I didn't get."

"It's a Willie Nelson song about this man who missed his little, lost darling and wandered around, living in the hills with her horse."

Tired nodded. "Anyway, ma'am, Dave said to tell you he'd catch up with you later, somewhere down the road."

Damn, I thought, I never did get him back that sack of the dead man's money.

EPILOGUE

As vexing as being Lilly Cleary can be, I wouldn't want to trade places with Philip Cohen.

Philip had hired himself on to defend Cat Sue against first-degree murder charges in the shooting death of Kenneth Mallory, the murderous and greedy lawyer with the butterfly obsession.

And having hired on to defend Cat Sue, nothing would do but that he had to defend Cristal against charges of conspiracy to murder Kenneth and forgery in making Kenneth's fake will. While technically Cat and Cristal could have been charged with the attempted murder of me, at Philip's urging I had convinced the state attorney's office to settle for criminal-mischief charges, a charge that might cost them a fine if it didn't get dropped altogether by the time of their trial.

In contrast to poor Philip, all I had to do, at least in the foreseeable future, was defend my client, one Gandhi Singh, against charges of malpractice brought by the rich woman from Longboat Key who claimed to have been kidnapped by space aliens.

383

Yeah, the appellate court kicked back Gandhi's summary judgment with a tersely worded legal opinion that roughly translated into: Let a jury figure it out.

After Angela and I had researched to death about a dozen legal theories for Gandhi's defense, I had decided to go with the obvious—just pick a straight-laced, conservative jury, which is about the only kind of jury you can get in Sarasota anyway—and paint the Rich Nut Lady Plaintiff as crazier than Gandhi.

I mean, how hard could that be?

So here we all were, back in the litigation lottery world of tort law, stuffed into Judge Goddard's courtroom, waiting for him to finish chewing out the plaintiff's attorney for a witness-list snafu and then Angela was going to cross-examine one of Rich Nut Lady's expert witnesses, the one who was hired to testify that the plaintiff might actually have been kidnapped by Martians.

While preparing for trial, I had figured Angela could handle that cross-examination, though I had written and rewritten the exact questions for her to ask the ET expert, made her practice her body language and facial expressions a hundred different ways and times, and then reconciled myself to the idea that she would cross the guy any way she wanted to.

After all, Angela was all grown up. She'd been a lawyer for three years. And a mother for a few months. A fine baby girl, born with a minimum of fuss, right on time, and with a head full of mahogany hair, Newly's chocolate-colored eyes, and Angela's pert, little nose and rosebud mouth. Already we could tell that Ada Mae Harper Moneta, named after her maternal great-grandmothers, would stop traffic all of her life.

From our counsel table, I watched Judge Goddard, then nervously poked Angela to tell her to get ready. The judge seemed about done fussing at the plaintiff's attorney. Angela nodded back at me, turned to look at Newly in the bench behind us, holding on to Ada Mae and smiling as if he was the only man in the entire universe to ever father a child. As everybody smiled at everybody, Angela held out a finger to Ada Mae, who grabbed it and squealed in little-girl joy. Glancing at the jury, I noted the positive effect of this and leaned back into my counsel chair, trying to keep my generalized anxiety at bay. Gandhi patted my arm. "It will be all right," he said.

It would be. Angela, once delivered of her child, had returned in no time at all to lawyer loquaciousness. Brock had fixed her hair back to a glorious auburn. I had trained her well. And she had innate talent. Time to her let go and cross the witness, I thought, and forced myself to stop fidgeting and folded my hands in my lap.

And then, while Angela introduced herself to the witness and reeled him in with some trust-me-I'm-the-nice-girl-next-door questions, I turned back for a moment to smile at Philip, who had come to the courtroom to cheer for me.

Philip, though he should be, was not disturbed over his case of the two girlfriend criminals, Cat Sue and Cristal, who were still in jail, waiting for Philip's magic to find them a way out. He was confident he could twist the law into a defense that would get them out of prison with some of their lives left to live. According to Philip, beating Cat Sue's first-degree murder and Cristal's conspiracy to commit murder charges was as simple as keeping out the fake alibi, the only thing that established a premeditated aspect to Kenneth's shooting death on Cat's part or pulled Cristal into his shooting.

Even as I prepared to defend Gandhi against malpractice, Philip pruned the case law to support his motion to suppress any evidence of Cristal in a dark wig in Winter Park creating a false trail of Cat Sue shopping a full three hours away from Kenneth at his end. If Philip pulled this off, it would be at the expense of Tired Rufus Johnson, who had been hot on the trail of the two girlfriend offenders after all.

For all my vanity that Bonita and I had solved Tired's case for him, he had figured it out a step or two ahead of us. Turned out the reason Tired wasn't in the office when I called him from the Myakka ranger's station was because he was already on his way to the vineyard with arrest warrants. What had started Tired on this path was his trip to Smith, O'Leary, and Stanley, armed with a search warrant looking for evidence of Kenneth's cocaine use on the remote possibility that this had some bearing on his murder. While Tired found no cocaine-related evidence, he had discovered and taken some of Cristal's Winter Park Visa receipts. He hadn't told Cristal because he didn't want to spook anyone. The Winter Park Visa receipts Tired snuck out of Cristal's files were on her own credit card, but they were dated the same Tuesday that Cat Sue had been in Orlando and Winter Park selling wine, the same day that Earl had been killed. In Tired's mind, that connected Cat Sue and Cristal, and once he'd made that link, he dug out enough of the story in bits and pieces. As the persistent Tired had learned, Cat Sue and Cristal had been keeping company on the sly, and a woman matching Cat Sue's description had hired a man from Chokoloskee, a renegade town at the southern edge of the Everglades, to put a live rattlesnake in my car. And the day before Tired got his warrants, a handwriting expert the sheriff's office had great confidence in had declared Kenneth's signature on the will a forgery.

But those receipts that Tired had taken out of Cristal's personal files had started it. And therein lay the centerpiece of Philip's motion to suppress. Tired did not have probable cause for the search warrant—all he'd had was an anonymous tipster and a constitutionally unschooled judge. And if the receipts were illegally obtained without a proper warrant, then all the rest of the evidence that was based on those receipts was as inadmissible as the receipts.

It could be that easy.

Or not.

The faked will didn't look good, Philip admitted, though he hoped it could be explained as a desperate afterthought; that is, after a purely self-defense and panicked shooting of Kenneth by the hysterical-with-grief widow of the man Kenneth had already killed, the spunky widow tried to save her endangered vineyard with the help of a certified paralegal who had a remarkable ability to forge her boss's signature. At most, Philip feared, the forged will would look too opportunistic and might convince a jury to step over self-defense and into second degree for Cat. And, of course, there was little escape on the forgery charge against Cristal, but the Florida criminal-justice system didn't execute forgers, and barely imprisoned them, as that was merely a white-collar crime.

So, yeah, the faked will was a problem for Philip's girlfriend clients. And for me. The probate-court judge figured that since he had already appointed me as the personal representative of Kenneth's faked will, I might as well stay on to probate his estate after that will was cast out. Hence, as Kenneth's PR, a result that no doubt has him spitting fire in hell, I was still digging around in the aftermath of Kenneth's poorly lived life.

Thanks to Cristal's search-and-destroy mission, no one ever found a real will. Without a written will, Kenneth's worldly goods would pass according to the intestate statutes. Much to his surprise,

Joseph the lavender farmer from Washington found himself sole heir to Kenneth's estate. When Joseph had materialized out of the great Northwest, Henry set in on him about the butterfly garden, so that the first official act of Joseph the heir was to arrange for Sarasota Jungle Gardens to take it over.

Then Joseph called up the Hummer dealership and told them he wasn't paying another dime on what Kenneth owed on the damn thing and that they should come take it away.

While Philip and I applauded his acts, Joseph endeared himself further by liquidating enough of Kenneth's estate, with my official approval, to pay off a balloon mortgage on Earl's vineyard, and with everyone's blessings, he moved in. Other mortgages hovered, but didn't press, and with Cat Sue offering advice from her jail cell, Joseph set out to become an organic vintner. And he was paying for Cat Sue's and Cristal's defense. Maybe he hadn't seen Cat since high school, but she was family. And if she was family, he explained to me, then so was Cristal.

Given Joseph's example, I returned the silver and the rings and other things I had taken from Kenneth's house the night Henry and I broke in searching for evidence, and in a fit of contrition reduced my legal fees to the estate by half.

Nobody ever told Tired about Kenneth threatening Bonita or the sack of cash Mad had with him, so Tired never knew. In fact, there was a lot Tired never knew, as I honored my pledge to Cat

Sue and our hastily created attorney-client privilege and I kept my mouth shut. True to my word, I took my half of Mad's money that Henry was safeguarding to Mary Angel, who had the good grace not to pester me about the other half. Benny donated his part to the Nature Conservancy and asked that it be earmarked to buy habitat for the Florida panther.

Benny was more convinced than ever that Felipe's spirit lived in the jaguarundi at Myakka after Bonita and I told him we had followed it to our safety. He kept going back into the wilds of the park looking for the cat. In a truly weird cross-cultural male-bonding experiment, Jackson, Gandhi, and Henry started going with him—Jackson as the alpha-male tracker-woodsman, Gandhi as the spiritual guide, and Henry as the aspiring stepfather. Not surprisingly, with the four of them thrashing about, they've never seen the reclusive cat. But Benny keeps them going out there as regular as the first Saturday of the month comes around.

With his wildcat obsession unabated, though at least accompanied now, Benny remains under the watchful eye of Bonita. Tuned to Benny's emotional health, Bonita and I had gone back to work, trying to make up for lost time and billing and we never again spoke of what she had told me in the swamp. After all, I was good at keeping secrets. But I wasn't the only one. Truth is, none of us ever told Tired about the collective obstructions of justice that Dave, Bonita, Benny, and I had all engaged in with our misguided notions of protecting those we loved.

While we were all protecting our secrets, Gandhi had married Keisha two weeks before his trial. An ardently attentive Philip and I had sat with Tired Rufus Johnson and Susie at the wedding, with Grandmom Dolly from Tulip Street holding Redfish and eyeing Susie like a future granddaughter-in-law who wasn't quite good enough.

And now, here we all were, in a courtroom on an autumn day, watching Angela make her debut as Angela, Woman Trial Attorney. After three years of hearings, depositions, and all the pretrial posing and paperwork of lawsuits, she was primed for the real action.

But even as I watched Angela twist the plaintiff's expert around her finger without using a single question I had written for her, somewhere out on the road, a fifty-year-old man with pigtails and a Georgia accent was trying to travel off his broken heart.